BYRON

A RUNAWAY STAR

A Biographical Novel

Gretta Curran Browne

SP/
Seanelle Publications Inc.

© Copyright Gretta Curran Browne 2016

The right of Gretta Curran Browne to be identified as the Author of the Work has been asserted by her in accordance with the Copyright, Designs and Patents Act 1988

First published in 2016 by GCB Publications

All rights reserved by the Author. No part of this publication may be reproduced, stored in a retrieval system, or transmitted in any form, or by any means, without the prior written consent of the Author and the Publisher, nor to be circulated in any form, binding, or cover than that which it is published and without a similar condition being imposed on the subsequent purchaser.

ISBN: 978-1-912598-27-4

Typeset in Georgia 10/18

Cover Design: The Cover Collection
Cover image by permission of Mr Alain Delon

www.grettacurranbrowne.com

The Boy ... The Man ... The Legend

PROLOGUE

Annabella

'Opinions are made to be changed, else how is the truth to be got at?'

BYRON

Chapter One
~ ~ ~

In the summer of 1814, any person from the South who had previously travelled up North knew that the *Northeast* of England appeared to be an empty place. Empty of most things, except a small number of towns and a small number of people.

And while travelling along the roads one saw from the window of a carriage ... a village here and there; the odd inn that still burned candles – not even *oil*-lamps; and occasionally one saw a coal mine.

Apart from that it was a desolate place of barren hills and moors – and wind – always plenty of gusty winds around your head, especially in the little seaport town of Seaham in Durham, a place ruled by the Milbankes who lived at Seaham Hall.

Although, in fact, there were very few people in Seaham for the Milbankes to rule. Those few men who were not employed down the local coal mine, were employed as staff at Seaham Hall, as were their wives and daughters. The pay was not good, but it gave them a livelihood, and in these desperate times any sort of living was a blessing to be thankful for.

Sir Ralph Milbanke was the brother of the once-beautiful Lady Melbourne, now one of the most respected ladies of the *haute monde* in London, due not only to her marriage to Lord Melbourne, but also to her five-year affair with the Prince of Wales, which had endowed her with enormous prestige and deference amongst the ranks of the *monde*.

Occasionally, visitors from London society who dropped in to Seaham Hall on their way further up North, soon realised that the Milbankes were not exactly significant people, but the country cousins of significant people – very decidedly their country cousins: well-bred, but displaying a rather narrow provincialism in their ways, dress, and manner.

In the library of Seaham Hall, Sir Ralph Milbanke was making his daughter, Annabella, read and comment upon the latest paper he had written for *The Scientific News* about the new Society he had formed. He had also named himself as its President.

Annabella endeavoured to give the paper her strict attention –

Society for Preventing Accidents in Coal Mines.
President: Sir Ralph Milbanke

This Society, constituted as above, and having for its object, the prevention of those sudden and disastrous Explosions in Coal Mines ...

Annabella read on and on, occasionally making a pencil note in the margin, which caused her father to smile with pride. Annabella was *such* a clever girl. She took after him in all that, of course. A good brain. The rest of her she got from Judith.

He glanced through the window and saw his wife meandering about the grounds as always with her metal-diviner – still convinced that there might be a tin or copper mine under the Seaham land.

All a ridiculous waste of time really; but as Judith kept reminding him – if there was some substance below ground that could be mined – "then think of the money it could bring to us, dear, the *money!*"

Oh, yes, he always agreed – one must always think of the *money* – which was truly the only source and soul of life. How the devil could one get by without it?

And that was a question that had been keeping him from his sleep of late, leading to all sorts of aches and pains and even stiffness in his legs. "How the devil could one get by without money?"

"There, Dad, all done," said Annabella, relieved to finally be able to get away from her father and run up to the privacy of her bedroom. She had a private letter she anxiously wanted to write; a letter she wanted to send out in time to catch the evening post.

At her desk, Annabella sat in her chair, and took up her pen to write to Lord Byron.

As your friend, I will bear with your faults, and my patience with them is more than you will exhaust. Therefore I shall not be repelled from you by the irritable feelings of self-dissatisfaction which I imagine you sometimes disguise under an appearance of laughter. Once or twice I have fancied that I have detected in your face a laughter "false to the heart". Do you not sometimes laugh when you feel sad, because you are too proud to accept of sympathy?

Remember that regard to any parts of your character, which I misconceive, your simple & serious assertion to the contrary is sufficient to convince me.

May I know your sentiments concerning Religion? Do not suppose I have a fancy to convert you – first, I do not believe you need conversion – secondly, I do not believe it in my power to convert you...

She paused, feeling somewhat dejected. Things had not worked out in the calculated way she had thought they would.

She had rejected Lord Byron's proposal two years ago partly for the purpose of making him more keen on her, more intrigued; and hopefully leading to him eventually falling truly in love with her. After all, had her dear father not often philosophised that – *"A man always wants most, that which he cannot have."*

Yet, over time, the very opposite had materialised; leaving her a little hurt and bewildered by Lord Byron's seeming lack of interest.

Even more humiliating was the time – when she had sat reading Byron's tale of *The Giaour* and had been so *certain* that she could read between the lines of his poetry, concluding that his lament over the *'loss of his true love'* was a reference to herself – but she had soon realised her mistake, when her letters to him in London often went unanswered for weeks; and then a reply containing a mere few polite lines.

Now it was *she* who was doing all the chasing and making all the advances to him – all the *proposals,* including an invitation up to Seaham Hall – an invitation to which he had not yet answered

She put down her pen and dropped her head into her hands, closing her eyes, feeling desperate, truly desperate. She was now twenty-two-years old and life was passing her by; and two years of it had already been wasted on an experiment that had failed miserably – what a *fool* she had been to reject Lord Byron's proposal, what a silly fool!

The tables had been turned on her, and now she did not know how to get them to stand up right again and put her back in control. All men needed to be controlled, and a perfect example of that necessity she saw before her eyes on a daily basis in her own home. Her dear father would be a hopeless *softie* with people without her mother's firm control.

She continued writing the letter, ensuring that every word was the *correct* word, conveying exactly what she was endeavouring to say. Lord Byron was so fluent himself with language, she would hate for him to think that she was not up to his standard. In many other things she was far *above* his standards – his affair with Lady Caroline Lamb was an example of his sinful and frivolous ways – but hopefully that could all be dealt with in the future.

Some time later, when she had written another lengthy page and the letter was finished, instead of calling a servant Annabella decided to post the letter herself. She was a great believer in secrecy, and she had no wish for any of the servants to know to whom she was writing.

Of course, her parents had given their consent to her correspondence with Lord Byron, and her former governess, Mrs Clermont, also knew; but as for the rest of the household, – it was none of their gossiping business.

~~~

When Annabella left the house with her hat on, Lady Milbanke watched her daughter walking over the grounds towards the side gate, her head held high like a beautiful young princess, causing Lady Milbanke to smile with satisfaction. All that training as a young girl, teaching her to carry herself like a lady ... walking up and down with books on her head ... had paid off well with Annabella. Was there ever a more glorious girl?

Yet there was a worry.

Returning to the house and the library, Lady Milbanke looked keenly at her husband while removing her rubber gardening-gloves. "She looks rather despondent of late ... do you know why?"

Sir Ralph glanced up from his paper. "I have no idea." A moment later he looked again at his wife. "*Who* looks rather despondent of late?"

"Annabella."

"Oh, Annabella ... does she?"

"I hope it's not anything to do with Lord Byron," said Lady Milbanke. "I don't know him and she keeps her letters so secret that I cannot even make a guess as to whether her despondency is due to him. If so, I would not be surprised. Your sister may think him wonderful, but I do *not* like the audacious tone his poetry. Still, all that nonsense aside, the man is *rich*, Ralph, a man of wealth."

Sir Ralph frowned thoughtfully: "Yes, he must be collecting a lot of money for his poetry now, and he has his own estate of Newstead Abbey ... that must be worth a decent fortune."

"And he is a *Lord*, dear, a Baron, so any woman he marries would immediately inherit the title of *Lady,* and as a Baron's wife she would immediately inherit her own coronet to wear on her head. Is that not what our dear Annabella *deserves* – a wealthy husband who will put a coronet on her head?"

"Indeed." Immediately Ralph sat up more forcefully. "Then whatever is wrong with her, *you* must make it right, Judith. You are both females, my dear, so it would be easier for you than for me."

"Quite," said Lady Milbanke tersely, and left the room to go upstairs and change for dinner.

Later, at dinner, while Annabella sat silently chewing her food, both parents watched her anxiously. In their eyes she was pure perfection in every way, and they had brought Annabella up to know that – how perfect she was – which accounted for Annabella's rather cold and dismissive attitude to less perfect beings. She was the daughter of Sir Ralph and Lady Milbanke and she made sure everyone in Seaham remained aware of that.

And unfortunately for them, Sir Ralph and Lady Milbanke were unable to see their daughter in the same way as all others saw her – a cold and priggish girl, small in stature, and with very ordinary looks – "*More as like any young woman you would see on any common or road,*" some of the locals were known to say.

But then both parents could be forgiven for adoring their daughter in such an unusual way. They had been in their forties, married for fifteen years and childless, before the miracle of a child had surprised and delighted them both.

A *miracle* of a child – a *beautiful* and *perfect* girl – and so Annabella had remained to them ever since. As the years passed and she began to grow up, they could see no fault whatsoever in their beloved daughter; and over time, Annabella, likewise, could rarely detect any fault in herself either.

"*Vain*," said the locals. "*Vain and spoiled and stands on her high pedestal looking down at the rest of us.*"

The one and *only* error that Annabella believed she had ever made, was rejecting Lord Byron.

Despite her attraction to his handsome looks and rather beautiful blue eyes, she had thought him flighty and immoral and not sufficiently religious. She considered him to be a very *bad* young man – a roué and a rake and a libertine – his affair with her cousin-in-law Lady Caroline Lamb had proved that.

And that was the *only* reason he had proposed to her in the first place, she was sure of it – to free himself from the clutches of love-mad Caroline.

Why else? Herself and Lord Byron had barely known each other at that time, and she was clever enough to know that it had all been the scheme of her very clever aunt, Lady Melbourne – endeavouring to make a convenience of *her*, Annabella – by persuading Lord Byron to propose to her, in order to get Caroline away from him and back into the arms of her husband, who was also Lady Melbourne's son, William Lamb.

And what a delightful pleasure it had been to see the sheer *shock* on Lady Melbourne's face when she had not accepted the offer, and turned down the most eligible bachelor in England!

Annabella's prestige in London had immediately soared at the news, followed by two other proposals of marriage, which she had also immediately declined – the first because the man had no wealth – and the second because the man had no brains. How could a highly intelligent woman such as herself, live with a man with no brain in his head? It was a deficit not to be endured, no more than the deficit of a man with no wealth.

Yet her prestige had also quickly declined, and once again few people paid any attention to her, leaving her sitting by the wall at balls and parties as usual, which had truly bewildered her.

"It's only because they know you are an heiress," Caroline Lamb had taunted cruelly. "It was your *money* they wanted to marry, not you!"

Annabella had smiled at that, but like the good Christian that she was, she had forgiven Caroline's jealousy.

And what of Lord Byron? After her refusal he had not ignored her and left her sitting by a wall – no, he had immediately taken himself off to Cheltenham where he had stayed for some time – all due, her aunt had said, to her rejection of him, leaving him broken-hearted.

Now she suspected that was a lie, but she did not know it for certain.

And then, through her friend Miss Milner in London, she had learned of reports about Lord Byron's incredible kindness and generosity to those in dire straits or financial need. Any penniless writer or destitute widow never sought his help without a financial reply.

Annabella had then began to wonder if Lord Byron really was a very *bad* young man after all? It was a question that had filled her thoughts at night when she lay on her pillow thinking about him ... finally deciding him to be "a very *good* bad young man."

~~~

In London, that very *good* bad young man was on his way to a party at a house in Grosvenor Square. It was not the sort of party that members of the *beau monde* such as the Hollands or Jerseys or even the French novelist Madame de Staël would attend, for it was a party hosted solely for young men who enjoyed fun and flirting and playing at the game of love. No intellectual discussions allowed.

Most of the young women were high-class courtesans and entry was by invitation only.

As he entered the large drawing-room where a small three-piece orchestra was softly playing music by the French windows, a footman holding a tray offered him a glass of champagne.

He lifted a glass, looked around the room and saw the friend who had invited him here tonight, Beau Brummell. Yet before he could take a step someone in the corridor behind him touched his arm.

He turned to see an exquisite little beauty smiling at him and he smiled too.

"Fleur!"

"Mr Brummell, he gave you my message?"

"No, he merely sent a note inviting me to come tonight."

Byron was still smiling because Fleur had always been his *favourite* courtesan. Like her name, she looked like a delicate flower and she herself was delicacy itself in every way. Her eyes were blue, and her complexion, like her hair, was very fair, and yet her face was saved from paleness by a sweet and pleasing blush in her cheeks.

"I wanted to see you," she said, "I have been crying to see you, because in two days I must go back to Holland. My father insists."

"You are leaving London?" He placed his glass back on the tray and moved her down to a dimly-lit part of the hallway where they could speak more privately, but as soon as they paused in a corner and before she could say another word he put his lips on hers in a kiss so melting and fiery she responded into a softness of hot desire and could refuse him nothing.

They spent the night in her bedroom in languor and pleasure and by the dawn, when he was preparing to leave her to return to his own bed and sleep, she was very sad as she asked him, "Will you come to Holland to see me? Our house is very large and beautiful with many rooms. And if you come, and if you won't be my husband, you can still be my lover ... my only lover, for now I love only you."

He smiled, and to her he seemed like a pitying angel as he answered her truthfully. "Outside this house we will always be friends, my love, but only friends."

"So, if only a friend, you will come to see me in Utrecht? You will think it a pretty city, and the canals are more beautiful than Venice."

"Than Venice? Then, yes, I may go, because during these past few weeks I have been feeling a strong urging passion to go travelling again."

Chapter Two

~ ~ ~

The following day, in the company of her maid, Ann Rood, Annabella travelled in the family carriage to the town of Sunderland, six miles away.

She spoke not a word to her maid in the carriage, because her mind, as always, was engrossed in habitual thoughts. She felt a little shame at what she was going to do today, but in view of the rumours that she had heard, the temptation was irresistible.

In Sunderland, she left Rood waiting in the carriage while she went inside the bookshop, expecting to see Mr Gasgoigne, the portly owner, behind the counter.

Instead, she saw a young man standing by the window, looking out to the street, so he must have seen her step down from the carriage.

Yet he made no movement to turn and look at her, holding his pose; his hand high on the window-frame as he gazed out with a moody expression on his face.

Annabella caught her breath for a moment, for his head was covered in a mop of rich dark hair, and cut a little too long in the front and at the back in order to give him a Byronic appearance. The shirt under his coat also had the large open Byronic collar above the black Byronic cravat, loose and elegant.

Yet when he slowly turned to look at her, there was no doubt about his face ... it had none of the beauty of Byron's face, and his eyes were small and beady and brown, not large and bright and blue.

Annabella half-sneered with derision. She knew it was the fashion in London for young men to try and look like Byron, dress like Byron, act like Byron, but she had not known that such nonsense was being carried on up here in the North-East.

Finally, he slowly turned and gave her a pretentious sleepy-eyed look.

"Miss Milbanke from Seaham Hall," she said, "I have come to collect a book I ordered."

"Miss Milbanke?" He showed no recognition of the name. "Then perhaps it is under here." He bent to look at the shelf below the counter. "There is only one order under here ... now let's see ..."

The book was still in its wrapping from the publisher, but a name had been written on the front by Mr Gasgoigne. "Ah, yes, Miss Milbanke ..."

His hand elegantly pushed back the fall of dark hair on his brow. "As it is wrapped, I'm afraid I don't know the price."

"Tell Mr Gasgoigne to send the bill to Seaham Hall. And may I ask where he is today?"

"Oh, he's just stepped out for an hour. I am merely holding the fort for him."

"Are you his new assistant?"

"Goodness, no! I am his nephew. I normally reside in Cambridge, at King's College."

"And I suspect you are a poet?"

"Yes, a poet." He gazed at her with a slight smile of surprise. "How did you know?"

"Oh, I suppose it is because you remind me so very much of the poet ... William Worsdworth," she said, and walked out of the shop.

"Rood," she said, seating herself down inside the carriage, "is not Mr Wordsworth rather ugly?"

"I've no idea, Miss."

"I'm sure he is. I saw a sketch of him once ... or was that Mr Coleridge? Well, I believe both are as ugly as each other, so that alone will leave that affected young fake in the doldrums for at least a week.

~ ~ ~

Safely back in her bedroom, Annabella turned the key in

the lock, and then turned the handle to make sure the door was firmly locked. Heaven forfend that her mother or governess should walk in and discover the type of book she was about to read – a romantic novel!

She pulled at the wrapping paper, still fearful, knowing that if any of her circle of acquaintances found out the type of book she had bought, she would be intellectually ridiculed for lowering her mind to such a level.

For years there had been uproar in the Northeast and everywhere else about these new *Circulating Libraries* that were opening up everywhere, providing cheap and trashy books for everyone to read. She would not be seen dead near a Circulating Library, which was why she had privately ordered and *bought* her book, with instructions to Mr Gasgoigne that it remained wrapped.

One had to be very careful about these things, for such was the alarm about this new danger to society, even the Bishop of London had recently published an article in *The Times* about the dangers of young women reading romantic novels, insisting such novels led to desire and depravity – which had made her mother almost faint at the prospect of Annabella ever reading one. *Desire* was a foolish and sinful notion for the lower classes, and not for young ladies who would go on to be wives and mothers and the upholders of morals in society.

Nevertheless, Annabella could not resist, and settled down to secretly read her copy of *Pride and Prejudice*.

Throughout the afternoon, when knocks came on the door, she insisted that she was feeling unwell and needed to be left alone to sleep; and then once back on her bed continued reading on and on ... the silly Bennet family getting on her nerves with all their nonsense, but it was Elizabeth Bennet and Mr Darcy whom she found of most interest, simply because while down in London, she had overheard two young ladies talking about Mr Darcy, and the fact that in the book he had amazingly proposed not once to Miss Bennet, but *twice*.

Was it so? Could it be? It would take a very brave man indeed to do such a thing having once been rejected.

But, yes, at the end, Mr Darcy *did* propose again to Miss Bennet, leaving Annabella to lie back and cogitate on it all. Was it simply because Mr Darcy knew that Miss Bennet had been angry with him, the first time she had refused him? Or was it because this was just a silly and fictional romantic novel?

~~~

During the days that followed Annabella took her usual walk along the cliffs, pausing every so often to gaze down at the waves breaking upon the rocks.

Having grown up in such a bleak and desolate place as Seaham, she had absorbed into herself much of its bleak and silent climate. She was not a talker, but a thinker, and she spent much of her time thinking ... *'It is my nature to feel long and deeply and secretly'* she had confessed in her last letter to Lord Byron, but would he understand the *message* behind those words? And if he did, how would he respond?

He did not respond; a week passed, ten days, and still no reply.

Stricken day after day with ever-increasing disappointment, Annabella sought relief and refuge from her thoughts in one of her regular bouts of hypochondria and took to her bed, complaining of all kinds of aches and pains and sensations of nausea, convincing herself and everyone else that she was very ill.

Lady Milbanke, and Annabella's governess, Mrs Clermont, rushed to her bedside.

"What is it, dearest?" Lady Milbanke's face was pale with anxiety.

"Come on now, pet," urged Mrs Clermont, lifting

Annabella's cold hand and chaffing it warm. "Tell C where you feel poorly?"

When Annabella did not answer, her eyes shut, Lady Milbanke stared at Mrs Clermont. "What's the matter with her?" she demanded. "Should we send for the doctor?"

"Nay, I think it's just one of her occasional attacks of the vapours," replied the governess, and scurried for the smelling salts.

Lady Milbanke gazed down on her daughter's pale face. "My poor child," she said, gently stroking the brown hair on Annabella's head. "She is so fragile, so sensitive, the slightest thing disturbs her constitution."

"It's a little rest she needs now," said Mrs Clermont, "so you go on down, my lady, and leave her to me."

Reluctantly, Lady Milbanke quietly left the room as Mrs Clermont moved over to the dresser where she placed a flannel in a bowl of water, wrung it out, and then scurried over to the bed to place it across Annabella's brow.

Mrs Clermont, a woman of forty-two, was small and thin in face and body, yet she had the large watchful eyes of an eagle.

Upon her mother's death, at the age of eleven, Mary Clermont had been taken in by Lady Milbanke as a scullery maid. By the time she was twenty years old she had risen in the ranks to become Lady Milbanke's personal attendant. And later, when Annabella had come out of the nursery at the age of seven, Mary Clermont had risen to the highest rank of all, as Miss Annabella's governess.

It was then that she was given the courtesy title of "Mrs Clermont" even though she was unmarried. This change in her status caused no inconvenience to Lady Milbanke or Annabella, for they had always referred to her simply as 'C'.

She was a domineering and suspicious woman who constantly inspired fear and loathing in the rest of the staff; many of whom believed that her rapid rise in the ranks was due to her being a regular mischief-maker against others; always watching, always cunning, and always reporting to Lady Milbanke.

And now that Lady Milbanke had gone, Mrs Clermont pulled up a chair to sit down, leaning over the bed to gently pat the flannel on Annabella's brow.

"We're alone now, pet," she said softly, "so are you going to tell me what has you feeling so unwell?"

Annabella's eyes stayed shut, her lips set in an inflexible line.

"Come on now, pet, tell me what's going on in that busy head of yours? I won't tell your mother. No. It will be our little secret."

Annabella's eyes slowly opened, a small smile on her lips. "You like secrets, don't you, C?"

"Only when they are needed."

Annabella pulled the flannel from her brow. "So you tell me a secret for a change, and I promise I won't tell. Have you ever been in love with a man?"

Mrs Clermont tried to smile, but her face had turned pale. "I know all about love," she said quietly, "real love, true love, but not for any man. And now I will tell you why."

Annabella was so surprised, she let herself sink slowly back onto her pillows, her eyes never leaving C's face as she listened.

"I came into service in this house when I was no more than eleven years old," Mrs Clermont began with a tinge of sadness. "And it has been my fate through life to suffer under the constant effort of repressed feelings, not in themselves wrong, no, but too strong for the circumstances in which I have been placed ... It is no pleasant thing to have no one to love or be loved by... "

Her eyes turned to Annabella.

"So it was upon *you,* and you alone, in the days of your infancy and childhood that I could lavish fondness and indulge my affection. And I loved you with all the intensity that comes from undivided affection. I have loved you from the day you were born, and I still *do*, and ever shall, and it is not even in *your* power to prevent it."

Annabella stirred uncomfortably on her pillows, thinking C to be somewhat pitiful and pathetic when she spoke in this way, although she had always enjoyed Clermont's devotion.

"And that is why I advise you, Miss Annabella, in your own interests, to break off all correspondence with the poet Byron. He may be a lord, but he has spoken out publicly against the King and the Prince Regent in the most scandalous way. He is not such a man as is fit for a virtuous young lady as you. And I would also say –"

"No more!" Annabella's eyes flashed. "How dare you interfere in my private concerns? I have allowed you to go so far, but no farther shall you go."

Mrs Clermont crumbled meekly under her idol's rage, supplicating her with sincere apologies and terrified of being deposed from Miss Annabella's favour, not after all the years it had taken her to achieve every inch gained. The Milbankes were a hard family to please, and Miss Annabella the hardest of all.

But if the girl was to fall in love with a man and marry, where would that leave her? She would be left alone and friendless and defunct, without any proper position in the household ... not unless Lady Milbanke was prepared to keep her on as a companion and confidante? In the past, as her personal maid, they had shared many secrets together.

"Go, Clermont, go!"

"Aye, pet, aye, I'll go. I know I've upset you but *you* know that I always only have my girl's best interests at heart."

Annabella was sure that was true, and relented slightly when Clermont said meekly, "Will I bring you some tea?"

"Oh, very well, but make sure it's as hot as can be, not

lukewarm like this morning."

"Aye," agreed Mrs Clermont smiling, knowing she was halfway on the path to being forgiven, "As hot as hot can be. You just rest there now, pet, and I'll be back up in a few minutes with the tea tray."

~~~

After a few days of Mrs Clermont's constant and devoted care, Annabella grew tired of lying in bed all day because it kept her from her sleep at night.

She returned to her daily walks of long and deep thoughts. Would Lord Byron accept her father's invitation and visit Seaham? How wonderful if he did come ... and yet it was strange that he had not yet replied to the invitation.

Later that afternoon she anxiously wrote to him again:

My dear Friend,

In only one case should I willingly relinquish the pleasure of your correspondence – if it were to become disagreeable to you. I shall now try to make better use of it than late, since I infer from your silence that my dream of seeing you is to end.

I continue well, with prudence, but any approach towards the ways of the fashionable world of London, causes a return of complaints which originated there. Without a good reason, a fashionable London life must always be slavery to me, although I endured it patiently and cheerfully because my Mother was made unhappy by my repugnance to scenes and places where she deemed it advantageous for me to appear.

I entered those places and met with those people with a caricatured opinion of their follies and vices, and looked upon them with coldness and indifference. Madame de Staël's manners were to my taste disgusting, and I did not seek to know her. After leaving London last year in disgust, I spent months of seclusion in salutary reflection, and returned with a little more charity. I had become sensible that it was a sinful pride in mortals to be offended at what God has to behold every day, and suffers.

This then became my task – to perceive the loveliness of the human character through all the incumbent shades of error. After each time I met you last year in London, I was vexed by the idea of having been cold towards you. It would have remained a source of regret had not the means of removing so false an impression (did you receive it?) been in my power. I was so anxious then and since to make my real feelings known to you.

I do not study much. My constitution requires many hours of sleep, and besides I do not enjoy the acquisition of knowledge for its own sake. Books of poetry and philosophy are the only ones I wish to read. I have read your 'Lara' – Shakespeare alone possessed the same power as you have shown in diving into the great deep of the human heart.

Yours sincerely
A. I. Milbanke.

Chapter Three

~ ~ ~

A week later, still no reply – and Annabella's secret hopes were dashed yet again.

Or was it all due to some fault in the post? The mail was notoriously incompetent and letters were always going astray, and that's why most people scribbled their letters in rough before writing them out again neatly in a fair copy – how else were people to remember what they had said to this person or that person in a letter on any given day? Especially as most literate people spent half their lives writing letters to friends and acquaintances. It was the only method of regular communication with people you did not actually live with.

Perhaps Lord Byron had not even received the letter inviting him to visit Seaham? After all, any gentleman with any decency would have the courtesy to reply to such an invitation. It would cause him great discredit if he did not. And Lord Byron was a gentleman who had always been very polite and courteous, even in his letters of reply to her.

After some thorough inquiries at the Seaham post-house, she wrote to Lord Byron again.

My dear Friend,

Pray write to me – for I have been rendered uneasy by your long silence, and you cannot wish to make me so. Though my Conjectures as to the cause, which have much anxiously occupied my thoughts, have been various – they have never assumed any motive on your part but the best.

Of mine I am not equally confident. I have perhaps

been too careless in forms of expression, having expressed & omitted so injudiciously that it might be impossible to understand my meaning. Or my meaning itself may have been faulty.

Lest there should be any failure in the delivery of my letters, to you – I have written thrice since I had the pleasure of hearing from you – for being prepossessed (too strongly perhaps) with the idea of a better mode of communication between us.

I wish to see you in the near future, and am happy to think I shall not wish in vain.

ever your friend
A. I. Milbanke.

Returning from one of her walks on the cliffs, she entered the house looking somewhat pale and windblown, to be met by a grim-faced Mrs Clermont.

"This letter has just come for you," she said "And no postal charges to pay, so it must be from His Nibs."

Annabella hated that crude expression, often used by Northerners when speaking of someone in a superior position.

"His *lordship*," Annabella corrected, pink-cheeked with delight as she took the letter and hurried up to the privacy of her bedroom to read it. Would he say something more *personal* this time? Something that would give her an indication of how he felt about her now?

"My dear Friend", she read, and then was filled with relief to learn that he had been out of town and away from London in Hastings, where he had taken his sister and her four children for a holiday of sea air ... "*Had I been in London your letter would have been answered immediately.*"

Oh, the joy! She made herself more comfortable in the armchair by the window, snuggling down to enjoy every word, only to be somewhat disappointed to see that he had mainly responded to her questions in two of her earlier letters to him ...

You ask me some questions, and as they are about myself, you must pardon the egotism into which my answers must betray me.

You don't like my "restless" doctrines – I should be very sorry if you did – but I can't stagnate. If I must sail let it be on the ocean no matter how stormy – anything but a dull cruise on a level lake without ever losing sight of the same insipid shores by which it is surrounded.

You say I never attempt to justify myself. You are right. At times I can't and occasionally I won't defend myself by explanations; life is not worth living on such terms

I now come to a subject of your enquiry, which you have perceived I have always hitherto avoided "Religion".

My opinions are quite undecided. I may say so sincerely. I believe doubtless in God. If I do not at present place implicit faith on tradition of any human creed, I hope it is not from a want of reverence for the Creator, but the created.

But the moral of Christianity is perfectly beautiful, and the very sublime of virtue – yet even there we find some of its finer precepts in earlier axioms of the Greeks – particularly, "do unto others as you would they do unto you."

Pray how old are you? It is a question one may ask safely for some years to come. I begin to count my own years – I am six and twenty in summers – six hundred in heart – and in head and pursuits about six.

Yours most sincerely
BYRON

P.S. – I wrote my last letter to you so hurriedly being on the eve of leaving London – that I omitted to mention (with my best thanks and respect to Sir R) that I regret it will not be in my power to proceed to Seaham during the present year.

Her breath caught in her throat, and for a moment she thought she was going to choke with disappointment at the sheer *casualness* of his last paragraph.

So despite the invitation he would *not* be coming to Seaham?

A feeling of sickness began to rise in her, but most of all she felt anger – anger at her own stupidity for allowing herself to show her feelings when usually her emotions were kept under a strict and cold constraint. She had been too open with him, using language that was not usual in a mere friendship, allowing him to respond so offhandedly to the invitation which should have been regarded as a great honour to him, instead of something that could be taken or declined with ease.

And did this not prove the correctness of her father's wise and guiding philosophy that – *A man always wants most, that which he cannot have.*

Well, she would soon let Lord Byron know that he was mistaken in his view of her – letting him know that she had been friendly with him merely through kindness and nothing else, and any mistaken wish for anything *more* than friendship, on his part, was hopeless.

She had rejected him once, and now she would reject

him again with pleasure. Why she had ever thought she liked him in the first place she did not know. All men were truly beneath her contempt.

But now she would not be able to put those snobbish London females in their place after all – she had been so looking forward to enjoying their jealousy when she wrote to a few of them to say that their idol, Lord Byron, had travelled all the way up to Seaham just to see *her*.

Her rage propelled her out of the armchair and over to her desk where she sat down and wrote a reply to him. When it was completed with a flourish of her signature, she put on her hat and cloak and was soon marching determinedly across the grounds on her way to get the letter into the last post – down to that city of *evil*, London.

As she stepped through the side gate and began to walk down the lane, she was stopped in her tracks by a dog barking at her. "Stop that!" she said angrily. "Stop that and get out of my way!"

But the dog kept on barking, his tail wagging as if wanting to play.

In frustration she rushed to the side of the lane and furiously picked up a broken branch from a tree and held it towards the dog warningly ... and seeing the warning in her staring eyes, the dog immediately stopped barking, slowly backing away from her, before turning and running down the lane as fast as his four legs would take him.

PART ONE

Saint Peter sat by the celestial gate,
His keys were rusty, and the lock was dull,
So little trouble had he been given of late,
Not that the place was by any means full.

The angels were all singing out of tune,
And hoarse with having little else to do,
Excepting to wind up the sun and moon,
Or curb a runaway young star or two.

'Vision of Judgement' – Byron

Chapter Four

~ ~ ~

Returning to London, after spending a month with his father and family in Whitton Park, the first person John Cam Hobhouse called upon, was his best friend, Lord Byron.

"Did you have a good time away, Byron? Did you see Scrope Davies in Harrogate?"

Byron looked at him archly. "That would have been difficult, Hobby, even with my perfect eyesight, since I was two hundred and fifty miles away from Harrogate, in Hastings."

"Hastings? I thought you said Harrogate?"

"Well, I didn't."

"So, what news?"

"About what?"

"Anything at all. Pray be more civil, Byron. I have just spent a month with my herd of young siblings who have now taken up their new garden game of screaming at full pitch at anything and everything."

Byron looked at him. "Poor Hobby, how on earth did you cope with such torture?"

"Badly."

Hobhouse moved over to Byron's desk and resumed his habit of sifting through the post. "Any more letters from that Harriette Wilson?"

Byron stood thoughtful for some moments. "Actually, Hobby, there *are* some letters which you could read and possibly help me to understand ..." He sorted through his papers and took out some letters.

"Now sit down, Hobby, sit down and read carefully, and tell me if you can understand what the devil I wrote to upset the lady."

Hobby did as he was bid, always eager to know what

was going on, or *had* been going on, in his absence.

The letter to Byron was from a young foreign lady living in England named Henriette D'Ussiéres, full of compliments to him, and making some strange allusion to throwing herself into the Serpentine river if he did not reply to this her tenth letter to him.

"Could I really see you? Oh God, what a temptation! I believed you lived in a house, but the man who brought back my Harp-lute said he heard you lived in the Albany. What is the Albany? If I go, suppose I should meet some of your servants, what would they say? If I were known, I would be lost. Even those persuaded of my innocence would condemn me ..."

And so it went on, and all so ridiculous in Hobhouse's opinion. Byron received hundreds of letters like this and to answer them all would keep him busy from morning to night. Yet he made no comment as he picked up Byron's letter of reply to the lady and began reading it ... deciding that Byron must have been in a bad mood when he penned it...

" – and the next thing to recollect is that "no man is a hero to his Valet" so I am a hero to no person whatsoever, so pray do not treat me with such outrageous respect and awe – which makes me feel as if I was in a strait waistcoat – but you shall be a heroine if you prefer it, and I am

Yr very humble Servt
BYRON

P.S: You say – what would "my servants think?" 1stly, they seldom think at all – 2ndly, they are generally out of the way – especially when most wanted – 3rdly, I do not know you – and I humbly imagine that my servants are no wiser than their master."

Hobby looked up. "Not much wrong with that. She was pushing herself onto you, and you pushed her back. Although why you even *bother* replying to someone who threatens you with throwing herself into the Serpentine is beyond me."

"Oh, no, wait – I have given you the *wrong* letters. No, here, *this* one –" Byron looked at it to make sure – "from Miss A. I. Milbanke ... she regularly writes me long prosing and moralizing letters and expects equally long replies by return of post."

Hobby read the letter from Miss Milbanke asking Byron to *"Pray write to me ... I have written thrice since I last had the pleasure of hearing from you ..."*

He looked at Byron. "I don't see what you need to understand? This letter is no different in sentiment than the one from Miss D'Ussiéres and so many others."

"And here is the copy of my reply," said Byron. "Now what I have I said so wrong in that letter to offend her?"

Again Hobhouse read through the letter, although why Byron felt obliged to answer so many questions put to him by someone he barely knew, was beyond Hobby's comprehension.

"You were foolish to get involved in any question about religion," he said. "I don't know Miss Milbanke, but from what I have heard of her, she is extremely religious and a stickler for virtue."

Byron pondered, and then looked at Hobby. "That must be the reason then. She does not approve of what she perceives as my complacency about adhering to any religion. Although I was not expecting her response to be so antagonistic towards me."

"Antagonistic?"

Byron handed Annabella's last letter to Hobhouse "She was the one who first wrote to me expressing her wish that we should be friends, but this sudden and swift change of mind and mood has me bewildered."

Hobhouse held up the letter to read it ...

Before a certain stage is reached, our affections are, I believe, under our command, at least I have had some cause to think so, and I hoped yours were checked in time.

The determination that mine towards you shall remain at that stage, is founded, if you care at all to know why, on a simple yet well-considered reason – which is presented by a comparative view of your character and my own – that they are ill adapted to each other.

Not, believe me, that I depreciate your capacity for the domestic virtues. Nevertheless you do not appear to be the person whom I ought to select as my guide, my support, my example on earth, with a view still to the after-life and immortality.

"How very odd," said Hobhouse, and could not help thinking that Miss Milbanke herself must be as *odd* as her letter.

"I suppose I will have to reply to her, in one way or another," Byron said, "though Lord knows what I will say."

"Say nothing," Hobhouse advised. "After such a letter, why should you answer her at all?"

"Because she is Lady Melbourne's *niece*. I would prefer to suffer any discomfort than upset my dear friend Lady Melbourne."

Hobhouse threw Miss Milbanke's letter down onto the desk, firmly of the opinion that Byron should have no further contact with her.

"What say you to my suggestion that we go to the Cocoa Tree Club? I hear there is a very good songstress appearing there tonight."

"A very good songstress?" Byron could not resist. "Why not? Shall we collect Scrope on the way?"

"He's probably already there with Beau Brummell,

both busily shaking the dice and gambling all against the House."

~~~

Some hours later, inside the Cocoa Tree Club, Byron spoke to Hobhouse of his keen desire to go travelling again.

"What?" Hobby was surprised. "Where?"

"Greece, I suppose."

"Why Greece, when you have already been there and seen it? And what about your life here – and your poetry?"

"If I am a poet," Byron said, "it was Greece that made me one."

"Don't be ridiculous. You were a published poet before we went to Greece, so how have you come to that conclusion?"

"It was in Greece and the Morea that I wrote Childe Harold's Pilgrimage. If I go back, Hobby, will you come with me?"

Hobhouse shrugged. "I would consider it, of course. But are we not rather old now to be gadding adventurously over Europe?"

Byron stared: "Too old – at twenty-six?"

"I'm older than you," Hobby reminded him. "I am now twenty-*eight*."

"Even so, you are hardly in your dotage."

"Then, well, yes, I will *consider* it."

Hobhouse then spent the next few days doing just that, considering what his life here in England would be like without Byron – *dull* and dismal with few laughs or fun in it – and for how long would this sojourn overseas last? No more than a year or so, so why not?

And upon their return, even if they stayed away for a year or so, upon their return he would still under thirty – the *earliest* age when a man should start thinking seriously about his life – finding a wife and settling down and all that – so, yes, Byron was right, there was still plenty of time to go adventuring in the meantime.

Chapter Five

~ ~ ~

Hobhouse had made an appointment to see his Bank Manager to arrange the funding for his trip abroad, and he was now flushed with excitement at the prospect of going travelling again; until Scrope Davies very curiously said to him – "So what do you think of Byron going abroad again?"

"I think it's a jolly good idea."

"But why to a flat and cold place like Holland? And going with *Ward* of all people?"

"What? Holland? Ward? What are you talking about? It's *Greece* that Byron is going to, and his travelling companion, like the last time, will be *me*."

"No, Hobby, I think you must be wrong there." Scrope said. "When I bumped into John Ward yesterday he was full of enthusiasm, telling me that he and Byron were going to Holland and were booked on a ship leaving London in a fortnight. It seems they intend to travel on from there to Athens."

"But *Ward* – Ward is years older than Byron, so what would they have in common?"

"He's no more than seven or eight years older, Hobby, and I would say that he and Byron have absolutely nothing in common. I admit, it surprised me too."

Hobhouse was outraged. "Is this not a typical example of what I have always said to you about Byron. He is as *unreliable* as a woman, as fickle as the wind, and all his promises are as uncertain as tomorrow's sun."

Scrope could not help smiling a little. "And I imagine there are one or two women here in London who would agree with you on that, Hobby."

"But do you agree?"

"No, as a matter of fact, I don't agree." Scrope replied. "Byron is Byron, and when he wants to go somewhere he goes. He is not one for waiting around for someone else to finally make up their mind. You should know that by now, Hobby."

"Why and how should I know that?"

"From the *last* time. He was all set to go off to Greece on his own, bags packed, everything arranged, until you showed up at the last minute to join him."

That was true; Hobhouse could not deny it. "Still, he is older now, and so should be less impetuous."

"Byron does everything on impulse. Even his poetry is written on impulse. That's why he can write it so fast."

"Nevertheless, Scrope, this is really bad play. Byron arranging to go off to Holland with Ward only a few days after asking *me* to go with him to Greece."

Scrope Davies shrugged. "He who hesitates ... misses the boat ... isn't that what they say, Hobby?"

"Not quite," Hobhouse replied tersely. "But in any event you are missing the point, Scrope. Our mutual friend Lord Byron, despite reaching the age of twenty six, still retains a streak of gullibility, and so in going abroad he needs to be protected. Would you not agree?"

"Protected? From what?"

"From himself, and men like John Ward who heap all sorts of praise on him, and then slyly *cheat* him."

Scrope Davies, for the life of him, had not a clue as to what Hobby was talking about.

"I've not the damnedest idea what your complaint is, Hobby. Byron does not seem in any way gullible to me, and John Ward is a man of the highest rank. And don't forget, when Ward's uncle dies he will inherit a fortune and become the Earl of Dudley."

"What bally difference will that make? A title won't make Ward a better man. I remember in the first few weeks of our travels in Portugal, when Byron and I met John Ward in Lisbon, Ward kept telling everyone how Lord Byron was a most charming fellow, and consequently, with Ward being English and so friendly, it never even occurred to Byron to question the price when Ward *grossly* overcharged him for three English saddles."

Scrope frowned. "Did *you* not question the price?"

"How could I? We had been riding for five days further on from Lisbon when Byron told me how much he had paid. But there, you see now, Scrope, you *see* how Byron is not as clever as he thinks himself to be? I could give you at least *ten* examples of how he has judged things in the *wrong* way entirely."

"I have not the time." Scrope half-smiled. "And I don't believe you, so give me just *one* example?"

"Well, for instance, right there in Lisbon when Byron made the first of his European swimming feats. He swam right across the Tagus from the south bank to the north bank in what I timed to be just under two hours. A marvellous demonstration of his strength and skill as a swimmer."

"So, what's wrong with that?"

"Did he tell you about the Tagus? No, he just bragged about being the only man on earth to have succeeded in swimming across the *Hellespont* in Greece, from Europe to Asia, a journey he completed in only one hour and ten minutes."

Scrope was losing his patience. "I'll be damned if I know what the devil of a point you are making. He *is* the only man to have succeeded in swimming across the Hellespont. There were a number of Greek witnesses, as well a sergeant of the British army and others who watched him do it."

"Yes, but my point is that on the day, the swim across the *Tagus* with its high winds and counter-current was a far more *dangerous* exploit than even the Hellespont. Yet Byron judges the Greek swim as the greatest achievement of all."

"Because it was in *Greece* – the romantic land of gods and heroes – and everyone knows the Hellespont is dangerous on every day of the year, not just one. Hobby, why must you always be so damned *correct* about everything?"

Hobhouse stared. "Because it's far more useful and satisfactory than always being *incorrect* about everything. And I was simply making a point about Byron's many errors of judgement."

"Such as arranging to go abroad with the cheating John Ward, instead of good old honest you?"

"Exactly."

Scrope Davies had to laugh, thinking that Hobby was taking his fame as "*Byron's best friend*" far too seriously these days, and a lot more seriously than Byron did.

~~~

Byron took his friendship with John Cam Hobhouse very seriously. Hobhouse was not only his best friend, but a true friend, in fair weather or foul, and no matter how much Hobby had annoyingly nagged him at various times, Byron knew that Hobby always had his best interests at heart.

And now he had come to depend upon Hobby's good sense and advice to steer him away from taking a step wrong, which he often felt inclined to do, such as now ...

Standing inside the open door of his drawing-room, and wearing the cutest bonnet, was Miss Henriette D'Ussiéres, the young lady who had written to him with threats of drowning herself in the Serpentine.

She was pretty enough, but entirely devoid of false shame or the maidenly modesty with which young ladies generally cloak their artifice – and how on earth had she managed to get past Fletcher into his drawing-room?

"Your servant, the man who opened the door, he looks to me such a *good* man," she said. "But out there, in Piccadilly, while I was searching for the Albany and looking like a lost lamb – a man, half-gentleman, half-beggar followed me – gave me two gentle knocks on my arm, and said he would take care of me. Was that not terrifying?"

She rushed around admiring everything in the room, the bookcase, – "Oh, I have always believed in the doctrines of Jean-Jacques Rousseau!" And then rushed on to "The sacred writing desk!" running her fingers over it – "Oh, such beautiful sofas" ... and then she stood to stare at a crucifix on the wall ... "How strange, when they say you are an atheist?"

"It is from a monastery in Athens," Byron said, and was about to say more but she gabbled on:

"How I envy your cleaning maid! If I was your maid I would be so attentive to all your commands! Neither careless nor too fussy. Just the sort of fire you would like – no cracking of doors – I should always come on tiptoe – your books and papers in the same place every day – I would sometimes peep in and see you dreaming your angelic verses – over there by the window. And I would – "

"Miss D'Ussiéres!"

She heard the irritation in his voice and looked at him, dismayed. "You are displeased? Heavens! – what have I done? My admiration is passionate but I am very inoffensive. I have done wrong? Lord Byron is offended? How can I make amends?"

He endeavoured to be polite to her, although her intrusion was audacious. He asked her some questions about herself.

"You are French, Miss D'Ussiéres?"

"*Suisse.*"

"Oh, from Switzerland, a *Suissess*. I do beg your pardon."

"No, I must beg yours! You are so kind, uncommonly kind, and a hundred times more handsome than – Oh, conceive my joy! To know I am now so much more than a complete stranger to you. I have loved you long, and now I have seen you love you more. And this is no romantic vision, no, I have never read a romantic novel, but I –"

"My lord..." said Fletcher, coming into the room, "I must remind you of your appointment with Lord Holland in ten minutes." He looked at Miss D'Ussiéres. "His lordship's carriage is waiting."

She stared at Byron with dismay. "I must leave now?"

Byron nodded. "Thank you for calling, and I wish you a speedy journey back to Switzerland."

"But I am not going go back to Switzerland, not for months."

Fletcher was gently taking her arm to escort her out. "As I told you, Miss, this building is for gentlemen only, and it would cause quite a scandal for a young lady to be seen visiting an unmarried gentleman in his rooms, quite a scandal."

Fletcher had come in on time with the usual excuse, and Byron turned to his desk, tired of it all, *damned* tired of it all. For a long time now he had known that he was a man who attracted women, but that did not necessarily mean he was attracted to every one of them in return. A few, yes, he had loved, and one he had adored, but females like Miss D'ussiérres and others and especially Caroline Lamb who haunted him and pushed their way uninvited into his private residence, repelled him.

He sat down at his desk and picked up the thorny letter from Miss Annabella Milbanke to which he had not yet sent his reply. He read through her letter once again, informing him that she thought his character ill-suited to hers, and then he wrote her a short and curt note, laced with his rapid dashes –

Dear Miss Milbanke – Very well – now we can talk of something else! Though I do not think an intimacy which does not extend beyond a few letters and still fewer interviews in the course of a year, could be particularly injurious to either party.

Yet, if I rightly recollect – you told me that some remarks had been made upon the subject of our correspondence – then it is perhaps as well that even that should end.

This is a point upon which only yourself can best determine – and on which I have nothing to do but acquiesce.

Pray make my best respects to Sir Ralph and Lady Milbanke, and accept them for yourself.

very sincerely,
BYRON

He blotted the page, enclosed it in a cover and then stood to pull the bell-rope for Fletcher, who came in smiling. "She's gone, and I told her it would be very unwise to return, but I don't think she listens to anyone but herself."

Byron handed him the letter. "Make sure this goes on the three o'clock."

Fletcher took the letter and peered curiously at the name on it. "Miss A. Milbanke ... you get a lot of letters from her these days."

"Fletcher?"

"Yes, my lord."

"Scram."

PART TWO

The Hebrew Melodies

~

"Lord Byron's manner was free, natural, and graceful; his expression of face truly beautiful, which commanded attention from all around him. He also possessed that reserve and modesty which always accompanies real talent."

Isaac Nathan

Chapter Six

~~~

Isaac Nathan was born in England, the son of a Polish refugee who had fled Poland due to the persecution of the Jews during the invasion by Russia.

His father, Menehem Nathan, was not persecuted at all in England, but this freedom was not as glorious as he had expected upon his arrival, when he discovered that all Jews were secretly regarded as social *outcasts*, and sometimes not so secretly either. The Law, for example, allowed them far fewer rights than those allowed to even the Catholics.

For himself, Menehem did not care. To be left in peace was good enough; but for his first-born son, Isaac, he worked hard to provide him with the best that England could offer. He also taught his son to be proud of his Polish and Jewish heritage.

Growing up, Isaac's one true love was music, studying first at Cambridge, and then with the London Maestro, Domenico Corri, to learn and perfect his skill at composition.

Now, in 1814, to the joy of his aging father, Isaac was composing a collection of Hebrew melodies, and still could not quite believe that after only one interview, in which he had brazenly asked England's highest poet, Lord Byron, to write a series of Jewish-themed poems to go with the music – that incredibly kind and charming young man had instantly agreed, admitting he had always felt a great sympathy for the Jews, and believed their race and religion should not be a bar against them in the professions.

"But he is not a *Jew*," Isaac's colleague John Braham protested, "so how would he know what it was *like* to be a persecuted Jew in Jerusalem in those ancient times?

He is a Gentile, so how could he know how to *write* about that?"

Isaac had then showed Braham the two Hebrew poems that Lord Byron had already written before he had ever met Isaac, handing over the copies which had been given to him by Douglas Kinnaird.

"Now tell me, do you think any Jew could write a Jewish poem better than that?"

Braham had read the first poem –' *By The Rivers Of Babylon We Sat Down and Wept'*

"It is based, as you see, on the story of the Jews being driven out of Jerusalem into exile by the soldiers of the Roman, Titus," Isaac said. "As a boy, Lord Byron told me, he was often engrossed in the stories of the Old Testament in his Bible, and he says that he was *always* on the side of the Jews.

With a great deal of doubt, Braham had sat down to read the first poem.

<u>By The Rivers Of Babylon We Sat Down And Wept</u>

We sat down and wept by the waters
of Babel, and thought of the day
When our foe, in the hue of his slaughters
Made Salem's high places his prey ...

Braham had read on to the end, Isaac remembered, and then had silently lifted the second poem, *"The Destruction of Jerusalem by Titus"*, finally coming to the end and looking up at Isaac with tears in his eyes.

"Are you *sure* he is not a Jew?"

"He says he denies nothing, but doubts everything, so he does not know *what* to believe."

"And yet he writes like this about the people of Israel and the God of Moses?"

John Braham was even more impressed when he finally met Lord Byron whom, like Isaac, he found not to be stiff and snobbish as one would expect from an aristocrat, but polite and reserved, although sometimes he displayed a propensity for unexpected wit and humour.

Now, in a large room in the basement of the Drury Lane Theatre, in the company of Nathan's small orchestra, Lord Byron was standing by the pianoforte listening to the ancient Hebrew music as John Braham's beautiful voice sang about King David and his love of the harp, for which Byron had written the poem, *The Harp The Monarch Minstrel Swept.*

Isaac Nathan suddenly lowered his baton and made a sound of displeasure, turning to Byron.

"I want to stay very true to the ancient Hebrew chants and preserve the airs. But to do that, in this last verse I need four more lines to complete the music to the end. Could I ask you, Lord Byron, to help out the melody with four extra lines to take me there?"

Leaning against the pianoforte, Byron looked down at the music sheet and read at the last line of the lyrics he had written about King David's harp upon his death – *"Its sound aspired to Heaven and there abode."*

"Nathan, I have already sent you up to Heaven. It would be difficult to go any further."

Nathan's attention was called by one of the orchestra asking a question. Nathan politely and deliberately explained his answer, and then he turned back to his Lordship who told him – "Here, Nathan, I have brought you back down again."

Startled, and unable to comprehend how he had done it so quickly – in pencil – Nathan took the paper which Byron handed to him, containing a further four lines which completed the melody ...

It's sound aspired to Heaven and there abode.
Since then – though heard on earth no more –
Devotion and her daughter Love

*Still bid the bursting spirit soar
To sounds that seem as from above.*

Byron not only loved music, but also understood it, and he was happy enough to stay throughout the afternoon and long into the evening with Isaac Nathan and his musicians ready to help out wherever he could, changing a line here, shortening a line there, until Nathan had it all arranged to his complete satisfaction.

Then, seeing that his Lordship was about to take his leave, Nathan exchanged a smile with John Braham and gave a nod to the orchestra.

"Lord Byron, pray stay a few minutes longer. I wish you to hear a new piece I have composed for one of your non-Jewish poems."

"Oh? Which one?"

Nathan raised his baton to the orchestra, leaving Byron to listen to his most personally heartbreaking love poem, being sung by John Braham.

*She walks in beauty, like the night
Of cloudless climes and starry skies;
And all that's best of dark and bright,
Meet in her aspect and her eyes ...*

Glancing at him, Nathan had expected Byron to be delighted with the surprise of hearing one of his secular pieces of poetry sung to music, but there was an expression of sadness on his face as he listened, and Nathan became convinced that there must be someone from *real life* connected to the feelings that the lines expressed.

Nathan lost himself in the music and the words, knowing that in this piece, Lord Byron was representing the various shades of perfection in female beauty, by comparing the serene placidity and harmony of facial features to various objects in nature.

As the final gentle strains of the music came to an end, Nathan turned to look at the poet ... and the poet looked back at him with a half-smile, giving Nathan a nod of appreciation before raising his hand in a brief salute and leaving the room.

"So do you think he liked it?" John Braham asked Nathan. "I don't think so."

"*Dziewczyna romans myśle,*" Nathan sighed. "I think the soft melody reminded him of the girl in the song ... perhaps even more than the words."

Chapter Seven

~ ~ ~

The following morning, Byron was at his desk, communing many of his rambling thoughts to his private journal. He had slept no more than a few hours the night before, and then not refreshingly, and so his thoughts were jumbled and disorganized.

The sun was beaming brightly outside his window, but he was sitting at his desk in a cloud of intellectual darkness, unable to write a word of poetry.

Got up this morning and tore two leaves out of this journal – I don't know why.

I am bored beyond my usual tense of that yawning verb, but I am too lazy to shoot myself – and it would annoy Augusta, and perhaps even ––

S called yesterday and said I was turning into a solitary hobgoblin, yet I think I prefer to be alone. The more I see of men, the less I like them. If I could say the same about women too, all would be well.

So why can't I? I am now six and twenty, and my passions have had more than enough to cool them, and yet – and yet – always a YET and a BUT – "Excellent well, you are a fishmonger –get thee to a nunnery".

He paused, and sighed; his elbow on the desk, face resting on his left hand, and then continued writing:

Who would be a poet? My publisher John Murray told me he had a letter from his brother in Edinburgh who says to him, "You are lucky in having such a POET" – something as if one was a pack-horse that belonged to him.

It reminded me of Mrs Packwood who replied to some inquiry – "Laws, sir, no – we keeps a poet!"

Fletcher knocked and walked in full of excitement. "My lord, you'll not believe it when I tell you what I've just been told!"

"Fletcher, could you pray explain to me *why* the valets of other gentlemen only come when they are called, yet you barge in here whenever you wish? If you keep doing it I shall dismiss you and find someone less excitable and more considerate."

Fletcher, who had heard that threat too many times before, burst out with his news – "They are all talking about you in America, my lord, in *America!*"

"Indeed? And you overheard them all talking, did you? All the way over there in America?"

"No, my lord, I was told it by Lord Bury's valet. He said he had overheard his master talking about a letter he got from a man in New York in America, and the man said he was coming to England next year for the sole reason of hoping Lord Bury would get him an introduction to Lord Byron, because every gentleman from New York to Ohio was reading Lord Byron."

"And the name of the man in America? Did the valet overhear that?"

"Yes, my Lord. His name is Mr Washington."

Byron sighed his irritation. "Fletcher, this is all the usual title-tattle and made-up gossip of you valets, always trying to impress or outdo one another. There is only *one* man in America named Washington, and he is now dead.*"*

"No, my lord, he's alive and that was surely his name," Fletcher protested. "Wait now, I have it writ down."

He commenced to hurriedly take some papers out of his coat pocket, bits of shopping lists and other scraps, until he finally found the piece he was looking for and stared at it ... "Mr Washington Urving. ...."

He handed the scrap of paper to Byron. "Least, we *think* that's how it's spelt."

Byron looked at the name, knowing he would now remember it, if and when needed.

"Well, if he comes all the way to London from America and Lord Bury asks, I shall certainly agree to an introduction; but now will you ask Mrs Mule to pray make me some tea?"

When Fletcher had gone, Byron sat musing, feeling quite pleased with himself. If true, it seemed he had done *something* right in his life so far, and told his journal about it:

These are the first tidings that have ever sounded like "Fame" to my ears – to be read on the banks of the Ohio!

To be popular in a rising and far country has a kind of "posthumous feel", and very different from the ephemeral "éclat" and fête-ing, buzzing and party-ing compliments of the well-dressed multitude here.

~~~

Later that afternoon, Hobhouse stood in Byron's drawing-room staring dubiously at him, not quite sure whether to believe him.

"So you did *not* ask Ward to go with you abroad?"

"No, he asked me."

"Yet you agreed."

"I did not. Ward and I merely *talked* about it – seeing all the canals in Holland – but then I used your usual evasion method, and said I would consider it."

"And did you actually consider going abroad with that odious little creature?"

"Come now, Hobby, he is not odious. Ward may be occasionally mean-minded, ill-natured, and an absolute bore, but not odious."

"Beau Brummell detests him."

"Oh, why so?"

"Because he is *odious* – and that is Brummell's word for him, not mine."

"Oh well, Byron shrugged and sat back on the sofa, "it is all irrelevant now, because Ward's uncle died a few nights ago, so I doubt he will be going anywhere in the near future. Not with that huge inheritance of his to collect."

Hobhouse hesitated. "So ... is our journey to Greece still on?"

Byron sat for some moments thinking about it. "I believe I would prefer Italy."

"Why?"

"Well, as Scrope said yesterday, we have already traversed all over Greece, so why not somewhere new this time? And as I am now fluent in Italian, that would be a great help to both of us."

"It would, and I've always wanted to see Italy, especially Rome," Hobby agreed eagerly. "So when do we go?"

Byron smiled, and gave back to Hobby a taste of his own medicine. "I will *consider* it."

"Very well, but pray don't take too long ," said Hobby, standing up to leave. "It's very unsettling for me, y'know, to think I am going abroad, and then to be told I am not going; and now it seems I am still going, but have no idea when."

He turned back to Byron. "Are you still coming to the opera tonight? I have reserved a box for us."

Byron frowned. "Why? I have a regular year's subscription to my own box."

"At Covent Garden you do. Tonight we are going to Sadler's Wells."

"Oh, *are* we?" replied Byron in a mimic of Hobby's top-drawer voice. "To see what, pray?"

"Grimaldi in *Don Juan*. Scrope and I will collect you in a cab at seven."

~

Moving back to his desk, Byron saw a letter lying there, pushed to the side, which had arrived earlier this morning ... a letter from Miss Milbanke, but he had not opened it.

Firstly, because it had surprised him, when in his last letter to her he had suggested their correspondence should end, and so he was not expecting to hear from her again; but mainly because her letters were usually so *long*.

Amazed, he saw that the letter was quite short in comparison to her previous tomes, so perhaps it contained her own frosty *adieu* to him?

But no, her opening paragraph was full of concern, due to her hearing from Lady Melbourne that he appeared to be in very low spirits of late, and in writing now, her only wish was to be a caring friend to him.

He sat back, wondering why Lady Melbourne should have thought he was in low spirits? In her company he was always talkative and pleasant.

Still, now he understood why Miss Milbanke was writing to him in a friendly way again – she was concerned about his "low spirits" and no doubt she believed they were due to her last thorny letter to him.

He read on...

I shall wait with patience for as little or as much of your regard as you may be able to give. My esteem for you is confirmed by our recent correspondence, and I shall always be gratified by any proof of your remembrance.

Act then towards me as best accords with the state of your mind – there is no reason for constraint on our correspondence, which is sanctioned by my father and mother. I do not feel the slightest uneasiness respecting my letters.

Write therefore, if you think me deserving of so much confidence, whenever it is possible that you may find relief in the disclosure of your feelings, or of any events past or present, to one who promises you in return truth and kindness.

I said the comfort would be mine, for the idea – is it a vain dream – of alleviating the bitterness of your despondency if only by the wish to do so, would give me real comfort. It is my happiness to feel that in some degree I live for others.

For the purposes of consoling and calming the mind, I feel the friendship of women is often better adapted than that of men. There are some whose wish to serve you might be nearer, or be of more avail than mine, but you must not look for them in the circles where I have met you.

*Yours affectionately,
A. I. Milbanke.*

He sat back, surprised. What a kind woman. He had misjudged her. No man could remain unaffected by such an unselfish letter. And because she was so considerate, he must quickly bring her worries on his behalf to an end, by writing back to her immediately and convincing her that he was in the very *height* of spirits.

My dear Friend,

I look upon myself as a very facetious person, and nobody laughs more, and though your friend Joanna

Baillie says that "laughter is the child of misery" I do not believe her (unless in a hysteric), tho' I think –

Fletcher came in to ask him if he was still going to the opera?

Byron looked at him vaguely, and then remembered, "Yes, but now I am going with Mr Hobhouse. Although when he calls, do *not* tell him I already had tickets for Sadler's Wells tonight. In fact –"

He lifted a fresh sheet of vellum and wrote a quick note to Gentleman John Jackson, his boxing master.

Dear Jack – Grimaldi sent me some tickets for the Wells

A loud knock on the apartment door sent Fletcher scurrying.

Byron finished his hasty message, found the opera tickets in a drawer and enclosed them with the note in a cover.

Fletcher returned holding up yet another letter. "That porter is a decent fellow to keep bringing your letters over here and saving my legs."

Byron took the letter and placed the note and tickets in Fletcher's hand. "I want you to deliver this to John Jackson immediately. If you take a cab you will be there and back in no time. Tell him the tickets are for tonight's performance."

"Righty-ho, my lord. You know I love jaunting in the hackney cabs."

Byron looked at him warningly. "Only to John Jackson's and straight back. Not all around Leicester Square and up to Barnet and everywhere else. I am merely a poet, not a millionaire."

He opened the letter in his hand and read it quickly, a smile moving on his face ... the short letter was from his friend and fellow-poet, Thomas Moore, informing him that Bessy had given birth to a beautiful girl child, whom they had been pleased to name Olivia Byron Moore.

"Is it good news, my lord?"

Byron looked up from the letter. "Are you not gone yet?"

"No, but I'm going. Is it good news?"

"Yes. Thomas Moore's wife has safely birthed a girl child."

"Ah, that's nice. A daughter will look after him in his old age. I have always liked Mr Moore."

"So have I. And his wife Bessy is very likable too." Byron smiled again, his eyes widening in surprise. "By Mahomet! I think I am beginning to like *everyone* today! Even you, Fletcher."

"Thank you, my lord."

"Now go!"

Chapter Eight

~~~

Most people in London loved the theatre and the opera, and tonight Sadler's Wells Theatre was packed for the opening night of *Don Juan*.

The box, which Hobhouse had reserved, was on the right-hand side, almost above the stage. Directly opposite, on the other side of the stage, Byron could see Lady Melbourne in her own box, and smiled and raised his hand to her. In response she excitedly fluttered her fan back to him.

The box above Lady Melbourne's had been reserved by Beau Brummell, but that notable gentleman had not yet arrived.

Another reason why Londoners loved the theatres was because they were ideal places to *meet* up again with old friends and catch up on all their news.

Byron's eyes moved from one box to another and saw that Lady Melbourne had now moved into Lady Westmoreland's box to sit down and gossip, whilst Lord Westmoreland had removed himself to go off for a chat with Madame de Staël who was wearing a Turkish turban of bright yellow fringed with silver.

And so it went on – everyone visiting the boxes of others and no one in their own seats, and would not be, not until the five-minute announcement.

His eyes returned thoughtfully to Madame de Staël and her Turkish yellow turban ... the *Eastern* fashion was all the rage now in London, yet throughout all the months he had spent travelling around Turkey, he had never once seen a Turkish *woman* wearing a turban, and he was sure that no one else had either ... Lord oh Lord, such were the English misconceptions of the East.

"Why is the Wells always so *cold?*" said Beau

Brummell, entering the box in a fur greatcoat, causing the three friends to stare at him.

"You do know that we are still in summer," said Byron, his eyes moving over Brummell's magnificent fur coat.

"Summer! You do not mistake this for summer do you? A little more of your summer will just finish me!" replied Brummell, pulling up his fur collar.

"If you are feeling under the weather, then why did you come out ?" said Hobhouse in his practical way.

"Because it is a *Benefit Night* to raise money for charity," said Brummell. "And tonight's performance better be a damned sight warmer than this theatre – at five guineas a seat and fifteen guineas a box it should be red hot!"

The five-minute announcement came. "There it goes, so I'm off."

"Shall we be seeing you later in the supper room?" asked Scrope Davies.

Brummell shrugged. "Only If I am not found frozen to death in this ice-box afterwards. And I do hope it is not only *cold* food they are serving tonight."

Byron could not help smiling, knowing that now Brummell had made his appearance in such a fine style, every young gent in the theatre would be seeking a similar fur coat to wear in the autumn, even if the weather was mild.

Minutes later Brummell appeared in his box, surrounded by a coterie of friends; and now the audience in the stalls turned their binoculars away from the box occupied by the beautiful Lord Byron, to focus on George Brummell.

If nothing else, George Brummell truly did deserve the nickname of "Beau" for he was a very handsome man. Tall in his height, and his hair was very fair. His face and its expressions were also agreeable to gaze on. His person, too, when he took off his coat, was indeed rather good; and who could find fault with the taste of his clothes, when so many young gentlemen, for years, had made it a rule to copy the cut of Brummell's coat, the shape of his hat, or the tie of his neckcloth; for all were in the very best of style. A wonderful designer of male clothes, and a true leader of fashion, yes indeed.

At the one-minute call, when the theatre's footmen began dimming the lamps, the audience in the stalls sat back in an elevated mood of enjoyment, for the personal presence of two of London's *magnificos* at tonight's performance would give them enough gossip to pass on to their friends for weeks.

And so to *Don Juan* ... played by Joseph Grimaldi himself, which surprised Byron, who thought he was surely too old for the role. He had anticipated that Grimaldi's seventeen-year-old son would play the young *Juan,* but no, Grimaldi Junior was scampering around in the role of Scaramouche.

Less than an hour later, Hobhouse could not restrain himself, leaning over to Byron and whispering scathingly, "And they say the Wells theatre committee are paying Joe Grimaldi the handsome wage of six pounds a week for this!"

Byron shook his head, sadly disappointed. He had long been an admirer of Grimaldi, who had become famous playing the role of the Clown in all the *Harlequinades,* and here he was again – playing the role of Don Juan as a *clown* – instead of an excited and sexually-awakened young man who was in the throes of learning to adore women.

"There's no real humour in it, just farce," he whispered back, "slapstick and farce and silly pantomime."

The production was so bad, the audience in the stalls were getting close to booing Grimaldi off the stage when the performance, mercifully, came to an end.

On leaving the box and heading for the Round Room, the first person to hail Byron was his boxing coach, John Jackson.

They shook hands warmly and Byron asked, "You did not mind my sending you the tickets, Jack?"

"Mind? Mercy me, no! I have never in my life paid five guineas for a seat in a theatre, and now, after tonight, I know I never will. My head is aching from all that wild screaming."

Byron smiled bleakly. "Poor Grimaldi, he has raised some good money for charity tonight, but his reputation will now suffer for it ... although young Don Juan has been hammered in his prime and left for dead."

Jackson nodded. "Once the critics get their reviews out tomorrow, who would want to come and see him? He was not funny and naughty as I expected, but downright annoying."

And that seemed to be the general opinion in the Round Room, where supper was being served to those who had reserved a seat.

Beau Brummell, minus his fur coat, was, as usual, surrounded by admirers. It was the fashion to court his society, and many did, for any gent who seemed to be in his favour immediately found his own status had shot up in everyone's estimation, because everyone knew that Brummell did not easily suffer fools.

Brummell had great wit, but he could also be cold and satirical, and that was the mood he appeared to be in now, breaking free from the group around him and walking over to Byron with a scornful look on his face.

"Is it true what I hear," he asked, "that you were actually mad enough to consider going abroad with Ward?"

Byron shrugged. "Ward has his faults but no one is perfect."

"Well, no matter, but do *not* allow him to come near you tonight, Byron, because tonight the man is simply odorous beyond bearing."

"There, you see?" said Hobhouse to Byron. "I told you that Brummell also finds Ward odious."

Brummell turned his eyes to Hobhouse. "Tonight I

said *odorous*, not odious. Tonight the man stinks to high heaven."

Brummell made a gesture with a slight nod of his head, causing Byron and Hobhouse to turn and look down to the far end of the large round table where John Ward was sitting eating supper amongst friends, laughing and telling jokes with a mouth full of chicken.

"I say!" exclaimed Hobhouse, "It's hardly fitting for him to be out socialising and laughing like that so soon after his uncle's death. And why is he not wearing a black armband?"

As if sensing their eyes on him, John Ward suddenly looked round and, seeing Lord Byron, he let out a hail, jumped to his feet, and then started a hurried walk down the room, still holding a leg of chicken.

"What a dainty little thing he is," observed Brummell, smiling wickedly. "Harriette Wilson once told me that she threatened to stuff him away in one of her bonnet-boxes if he did not behave himself and leave her alone."

Byron was smiling, well aware of that particular young lady's manner of straight talking, yet felt bound to add, "Ward may be deficient in physical stature, but I am the last person entitled to point a finger in that direction."

George Brummell looked sideways at Byron with his discerning eyes and saw what he had always seen – an extremely handsome young man, taller than the average, slender yet masculine, so –"Why not you, pray?"

"Because of this," said Byron, pointing to his right foot.

"Oh, balderdash!" exclaimed Brummell." Surely you know that we all have great *respect* for that limp of yours. And you carry it so well! It renders you *distingué*. So much so, in fact, that I have noticed some of our dandies actually imitating your limp, solely to add to their attempt to achieve the *Byronic* look."

Byron had to laugh at such absurd flattery.

"And talking about *looks*, that reminds me," said Brummell. "Today I went to view three pictures of you painted by Phillips, and damn me if I could see any resemblance to you in any of them."

"That's exactly what I said," Hobhouse cut in. "They look as much like Byron as I do, which is not at all."

"Heighho," Byron shrugged, his smile quickly vanishing as John Ward approached and he got a whiff of what Brummell had been inferring – backing off slightly as Ward said, "Byron, dear fellow, what did *you* think of tonight's debacle?"

Byron merely stared, for Ward, unlike his usual self, was wafting in the very essence of the worst perfume that even a whore might wear. In fact, everything about him had changed. His shirt was as starched as stiff cardboard and white as snow. His waistcoat – such colourful embroidery! And then a wave of glittering *diamonds* on his fingers! But none of it was as overpowering as the perfume – something both he and Brummell detested to smell on any man.

"Ward," he said with some disbelief "you have turned into a veritable *peacock!* Why so?"

"Oh well, you know, with my uncle ... but then one must let these things pass and buck up, so I treated myself to a new wardrobe and a night out at the theatre."

"And your perfume?" asked Brummell. "What is it? I know it, for I have smelled that essence on others. Would it be a splash of *eau-de-large inheritance*?"

Scrope Davies saved Ward from having to answer, coming in from the theatre to tell Byron that Lady Melbourne wished him to visit her in her box.

"Is she still here?"

"Oh, yes, all the boxes are still full with everyone gossiping. I've just had a long talk with John Jackson and he ... my God, what *is* that smell?"

"A lady calls – so if you will excuse me gentlemen?" Byron made a hasty departure, leaving John Ward to the mercy of Beau Brummell and John Hobhouse.

But Ward was having none of it. Hobhouse he did not fear, but Brummell's sarcastic wit terrified him; and he too made a hasty retreat, back to his seat at the far end of the round table, still holding his leg of cold chicken.

"Is Ward still the Member of Parliament for Downton?" asked Scrope.

Hobhouse was shocked at Scrope's lack of knowledge about Parliamentary matters. "No, John William Ward ceased to be the representative for Downton years ago. He only held the seat for one year, and then he represented Petersfield for another year, before moving on to Wareham for five years, and now he is the Tory MP for Chester."

Beau Brummell slowly turned his head and looked curiously at Hobhouse. "Is your head always filled with such lists of facts and figures?"

"Indeed," Hobhouse replied very seriously. "*Exact* facts and figures are of the utmost importance in the world of law and politics, y'know?"

Brummell gave a sigh and moved on, strolling back to the noise of his own circle while Hobhouse stood staring after him.

"Did you see that, Scrope? The way Brummell answered me by just ... walking away."

Scrope Davies, a long-standing close friend and familiar with the ways of Brummell, smiled with amusement. "He does that quite often when he loses interest. What is he like, eh?"

Hobhouse shrugged. "I don't know what he is like, unless it be his father or his mother. One of them *must* be responsible."

~~~

Lady Melbourne's box, like all the opera boxes at Sadler's Wells Theatre, was a spacious bulge of red velvet containing five gilt-edged seats; three at the front and two behind.

She greeted him with her usual warm smile when he entered.

"Lord Byron, I am *so* happy to see you out and about again. Now, I've sent Penniston off to amuse himself elsewhere so that I may enjoy one of our private little tête-à-têtes together."

Byron as always bowed politely, and then sat down beside her. He had great affection for Lady Melbourne, and also respected her worldly wisdom.

"Now, have you given any further consideration to my suggestion of taking a wife?"

"A wife?" He smiled at her in the usual way when she said something ridiculous, although he decided to play along and humour her.

"You may be right. Perhaps having my own wife would be my salvation, because I'm sure the wives of my acquaintances have done me little good."

"So," she said smiling, "you are determined to be flippant with me?"

"How else can I respond to such a question?"

"By telling me about Caroline," said Lady Melbourne. "I'm told she has been seen a number of times at your apartment at Albany."

"Not at my request." The mere mention of Lady Caroline Lamb annoyed him. "She is *your* daughter-in-law, living in your house and married to your son, and yet she still continues to haunt and plague *me*. Cannot either of you restrain her?"

"More to the point, Lord Byron – cannot *you* keep her out?"

"Keep her out? It is impossible! She comes at all times, and at any time, and the moment the door is opened in she walks. She is not rational, so what can I do? I can't throw her out of the window, but I will *not* receive her."

"So what happens when she walks in?"

"I leave it to Fletcher to get rid of her, by telling her I

am not at home, or away somewhere in the country, or up at Newstead, anything at all he can say or lie to her, and so far he has been successful in eventually getting her to leave – but she is driving me to the top of my bent!"

"She is whispering to her cronies that she is certain that you and she will be eloping abroad together very soon, to one of your Greek islands."

"And they *believe* her?"

"Knowing what a liar she is, *I* certainly don't believe her," said Lady Melbourne, "but I can't answer for others. And my fear is not only for you, but the damage all this whispering might do to my son's parliamentary career."

Byron could see the real worry on Lady Melbourne's face. "I can tell you now, on my honour," he said, "that I would rather spend the rest of my existence with the dead in purgatory than one minute more in the company of Caroline Lamb. And you may tell her so."

Lady Melbourne smiled. "I shall, and with great pleasure. I shall also tell William, although he seems to care very little about it all ..." She shrugged. "He might have forgiven her if she had attempted to be more *discreet* about her attachment to you, but all this passion and *delirium* in her head about herself and you going abroad to live happily ever after."

Lady Melbourne fanned herself briskly as if it was all getting too much to bear.

Byron sighed. "There has been so much confusion and ill-humour about my going abroad, I don't think I will attempt it now ... unless I go alone ... or with my friend Hobhouse."

"You make a very odd couple, you two." Lady Melbourne mused. "You are so ... well, *you* ... and Mr Hobhouse is so very stable and *correct* about everything. I'm sure you would find life a lot more relaxing if you were to marry a pleasing and pleasant girl like my niece, Annabella."

Byron smiled. "Annabella is the most prudish and *correct* person I know."

Lady Melbourne found it hard to disagree, still unable to forget her niece's absurd response two years ago when Annabella had handed her a paper, listing all the virtues she required in a man, if he was to qualify to be her husband. Until then Lady Melbourne had not realised that her niece from Seaham possessed so much vanity about herself, so much *egotism*.

She had fumed for days, finally telling her niece angrily –– "*It is almost impossible, while you remain up on those stilts on which you are mounted, that you should ever find a person worthy enough to be your husband.*"

And that priggish young madam had answered, "You must allow that I am not on stilts, only *on tiptoe*."

Still, all that was past, and the situation in Seaham was becoming precarious, so a suitable husband had to be found for Annabella soon, very soon; and yet the only possibility that Lady Melbourne liked, and would dearly *love* to have in her family, was Lord Byron.

"But you really don't *know* Annabella, do you?" she said. And then queried, "Or do you have another young lady in mind?"

"As a wife? No, I have no one at all. So what do you suggest I do about it – advertise?"

She laughed and slapped his arm with her fan. "Do not tease me with your silliness."

"Very well." He stood to take his leave. "Will I see you at Earl Grey's on Saturday?"

"Yes, but in the meantime, you *will* do your best to keep Caroline out of Albany, won't you?"

"I will and I do." Byron frowned, still puzzled. "What I can't understand though, is how she even gets to my front door in the first place? The porter has been warned to not allow her to pass, and *he* insists that after his first refusal to her, she has never returned ... so how does she get in to the building?"

PART THREE

Lady Caroline Lamb

~

"Never loved so before?" Then I pray never to be loved so again."

Byron to Lady Melbourne.

Chapter Nine

~~~

John Murray often worriedly wondered if he was being rather disloyal to Lord Byron by allowing Lady Caroline Lamb to visit him at his publishing premises so regularly.

Yet what else could he do – when she bombarded him with visits and presents and book orders? Oh, yes, she never came now without an *order* for some book or other in her hand.

Today she arrived in his office carrying a small spaniel in her arms.

"My dear Mr Murray, would you like one of these – a Marlborough spaniel? They are very rare. In all England, only the Duke of York and I have them."

"Thank you, Lady Caroline, but no ... my wife, I'm afraid, has an aversion to dogs of all breeds."

"An aversion? Silly woman. Does she not know that a dog can be a woman's best friend?"

She sat down on the chair by his desk and set the spaniel at her feet, speaking orders to the dog in her low caressing voice ... a voice that could disarm most men ... but not John Murray.

Yet he could not help feeling sorry for her, being so insane as she was about Byron, causing her now to be reduced almost an outcast from high society due to her ridiculous shenanigans at balls and soirees, and all for the sole purpose of getting Byron's attention.

The dog pacified at her feet, she whipped off her hat and shook out her short blonde curls, smiling at him curiously as she asked, "So how is the Childe?"

Murray sighed. He had made it clear to her, *very* clear, that as Lord Byron's publisher he had a duty of discretion not to discuss his author with her in any personal way, and she had vowed most sincerely *never* to mention Byron's name to him again – choosing instead to refer to him always by the name of one the heroes in his books.

"The Childe?" he asked.

She nodded. "Childe Harold. Is he well?"

John Murray paused, wondering how to answer without causing offence; and, as always, very aware of the difference in their rank. He was, after all, a mere businessman, but she was a niece of the Duchess of Devonshire, a granddaughter of Earl Spencer, and the Prince Regent was her Godfather.

Seeing his hesitation she asked eagerly, "May I send you a basket of roses to cheer up this dull masculine office of yours?"

"Lady Caroline, there really is no need to offer me any gifts."

"But you are always so *kind* to me. I know not how to thank you."

"There is no need, truly, no need."

"Would you like me to get you an invitation to see the inside of the Prince Regent's house? Or the Elgin Marbles? I want to reward you for keeping my secrets, so you only have to *command* me and they shall be yours."

"Lady Caroline ..."

"Mr Murray." Her voice became agitated. "Surely you understand, sir, that upon this earth I know of nothing more *disagreeable* than having to labour under continual obligations."

John Murray sat up in his chair. "Lady Caroline, you are under no obligations to me."

"Yes, I am, and I shall be even more obliged now if you will agree to tell me something about *Lara.*"

"Lara? Well I sold six thousand copies of it on the first day of sale."

She smiled. "And was Lara pleased with you for doing so on his behalf?"

And so it went on, a conversational-game about *Lara* and *the Childe,* the *Giaour* and the *Corsair* and both understanding they were all code-names for Byron.

Her face took on a tragic expression and she closed her eyes, speaking in a half-whisper. "I will never forget those moments of perfect happiness with him. There is nothing in heaven or on earth like him ..."

John Murray sat silent, as always, allowing her to talk. What else could he do?

"I *pray* not to be blamed," she said softly. "Yet how many more angry looks from Lady Melbourne? How many more frowns from others will be my fate? And perhaps from *him* ... his blue eyes will glare ... " She shrugged. "But I cannot be any worse off than I am *now* – as someone said when they were manacled in the pillory."

"Lady Caroline, you are married, he is not ... it is not right."

Again she shrugged. "What is the meaning of right and wrong? All is but appearance. Those that look innocent can be guilty. What is guilt? If I cannot sleep in my bed, why should I lie down? There are balls and assemblies, operas and plays, and who dances more gaily than I do? Who *dare* say I am not good? Who dare say I am guilty of anything? *Love* is not a crime."

John Murray managed to distract her by showing her a new edition of a book by Lady Morgan, *The Wild Irish Girl."*

"Have you read it?"

"Yes! And I have met her too, Lady Morgan – when I was in Ireland. Oh, she is such a darling, and I have promised her the full use of my carriage whenever she decides to come to London."

"That was kind of you."

Caroline smiled playfully. "Oh, the dear Lady Morgan, I loved her! She kept referring in admiration to how tall I am, which as you can see, I am not very tall – a mere five foot three inches, but as Lady Morgan is only four foot high herself, she seemed to think I was truly *statuesque.*"

"Is she really – Lady Morgan? No more than four foot high?"

"I suspect her father might have been leprechaun," Caroline said.

They talked for a while longer about Caroline's love of Ireland and the family estate over there, until the spaniel became cranky and she lifted him up in readiness to leave.

At the office door, when the spaniel was pacified, she turned and looked at John Murray for a long silent moment, her mood sad again. "God bless Lara, and send him much joy."

John Murray nodded.

"And even though he now thinks of me as some Cosimo di Medici... " she went on in her low voice, "the fact that I *did* love him is too certain ... and that I *cannot*, and shall not change is the fault of my nature ... for God be my witness, Mr Murray, I tried very hard for it this year. I tried hard to forget Byron, but ...."

Her words fell into an abyss of silence, until John Murray put a hand on her arm and escorted her down the stairs, past the waiting-room on the ground floor where he knew she sometimes hid herself in the hope of seeing Byron arriving or leaving; and again he could only feel tremendous sympathy for her. Her infatuation seemed to be of a type that was beyond any cure.

Such an impossibly sad situation for a woman who saw no happy future for herself now, and yet her age was only twenty-nine.

~~~

Later that night Caroline sat alone on the window-seat of her bedroom, staring out at the darkening night. The trees in the garden below were now no more than ghostly shadows in the long and dull silence.

The room behind her was warm with the soft lights of

oil lamps covered in warm shades of blue and pink French porcelain and a small log fire burned peacefully in the yellow marble fireplace, yet she was unaware of the lights and warmth behind her, feeling only the coldness of her life and the desolation of her emotions.

Few people understood love, *real* love ... and neither had she ... no, not even when she had married William Lamb ... not until she had met Byron. Oh, the *grief* she had felt when he had started to avoid her – although some said she had brought it all upon herself with her behaviour, sending her servant to him with as many as twenty letters every day and then pursuing him everywhere and anywhere she could find him ...

And *some* even accused her of being a selfish bully, of hounding and persecuting him; but that was because they just did not understand what she had experienced and what she had lost – the love and the laughter and the *fun*. Until then she had no memory of such enjoyment of life, it was beyond her comprehension and beyond any comparison.

Now what had she to live for? Nothing but a dreary life with a dull husband and a mother-in-law who hated her.

And now that loathsome mother-in-law was talking constantly in her drawing-room of her wish for Lord Byron to marry, and always looking towards her, Caroline, as she said scathingly – *"If nothing else, it would free him from the persistent and ridiculous badgering of so many silly women in our society. Have they no shame?"*

She suddenly heard the sound of someone sobbing and looked around, towards the door, expecting to see her maid ... until she realised it was herself that was sobbing, mourning for the life she could have had, but now had lost, never to be happy again.

She needed a friend to talk to, somebody sympathetic, somebody who *understood* her, but everybody hated her now – except one – John Murray

... dear Mr Murray, always so kind and calm with her, a man with a good heart ... but it was too late at night to be calling on him, his wife might object ... but she could still *talk* to him.

Wiping at her eyes, she left the window-seat and moved over to her escritoire, opening a drawer and taking out sheets of vellum, and then with her pen began speaking to John Murray as if she was sitting in the same room as him.

She wrote as if in a fever, as if talking directly to a beloved and trusted confidante, telling him of the terrible pain she had felt at Lady Melbourne's words, because she feared those words may come true, and if so, she would be unable to bear it.

> *... I think I will live to see the day when some beautiful and innocent Lady Byron shall drive to your door & I picture to myself how you will receive her. How every remark of hers you will admire. And how bright and cheerful she will appear to you compared to me – And I really do believe that when that day comes – I shall buy a pistol at Mantons & stand before the Giaour & his legal wife & shoot myself.*

When the letter was finished and sealed, she pulled the rope continually for her maid, until the girl appeared.

"Get one of the servants to deliver this letter to number fifty, Albermarle Street, immediately."

Returning to the servants' hall, the maid found that most of the under-servants had retired to their beds, and no wonder – most were up at the crack of dawn to begin their daily duties of lighting fires in the kitchen and Morning Room and Drawing-Room, and heating pails of water for her ladyship's bath – so to send one of them out at this hour was unfair.

Instead, she gave the letter to one of the lads still up, and instructed him, "Deliver this first thing in the morning. I'm sure Mr Murray is asleep himself now, so her ladyship won't know it didn't go tonight – not if we don't tell her."

Chapter Ten

~~~

The following morning, John Murray was not only very disturbed by Lady Caroline's letter, but also puzzled by Lady Melbourne's statement that Byron should now marry. Where on earth did Lady Melbourne get such an idea?

He did not like it, not at all. Experience had taught him that married men rarely wrote their poetry or prose with the same *passion* as the unmarried ones. And none wrote more passionately than Byron.

The more he thought about it, the more he concluded that the very suggestion of it was ridiculous, quite ridiculous, because of all the single young men he knew in London, the one he would wager to be the *least* interested in marriage, was Lord Byron.

~~~

A few streets away in Byron's drawing-room in Albany, marriage was the main subject of conversation, and what Byron was being told, utterly perplexed him.

Francis Hodgson, his Cambridge friend, whom so recently in Hastings, had been talking happily of his prospects of marriage to the young lady he loved, Susanna Tayler ... was now almost in tears because his marriage proposal had been rejected.

"But *why?* You led me to believe that she was as eager for the match as you were, so why has Miss Tayler now rejected you?"

Hodgson sighed. "You misunderstand me. Miss Tayler did not reject me, her mother did. Susanna is just as miserable about it as I am."

"So why did the mother reject you? You are a respectable man, an Eton and Cambridge Scholar, a devout Christian who has now taken Holy Orders to enter the Church as a Reverend, so what more could the mother require in a son-in-law?"

"Money."

Byron stared. "*Money?* Is she so mercenary?"

"No, not exactly..." Hodgson looked away, deeply embarrassed by it all; yet the truth must now be told. "Do you remember in Hastings, when I told you that my dear father had died the month before, and I was about to inherit from him?"

"Yes."

"Well, I did inherit – all his debts – amounting to the huge sum of one thousand pounds. Nothing more, apart from a few old books and pieces of his furniture. He was a Rector too, so of course he had no property to leave, his house being part of his living, and I knew that would be passed on to the next Rector."

"Could *you* not take up the position as the next Rector to follow your father into the house?" Byron asked. "You are fully qualified and sworn and Holy-Ordered and all that."

"No, the living was immediately given to another candidate within days of my father's death. And how could I take up a position in Humber when I am still a Fellow and tutor at King's College in Cambridge."

Hodgson's voice became croaky, as if just talking about all this deeply pained him.

"So now ... now Mrs Tayler has said she cannot allow her daughter to marry a man who is debt-ridden with no hope of paying the debts off – and how am I to find that amount of money on my pay as a tutor or a cleric – I have no hope at all."

Byron looked at Francis Hodgson and felt a deep compassion for him. He was such a good fellow in every way, and such a good friend ... maybe the good did not inherit the earth after all?

When he voiced this, Francis Hodgson smiled bitterly. "It is the *meek* who are supposed to inherit the earth, but they never do, unless their meekness makes them sly, and they eventually get their hands on an inheritance some other way."

Hodgson shrugged irritably. "Something has gone terribly wrong with the human race since the days of Christ. Since then the *meek* are respected, and the *weak* are to be pitied, and that is often not right but plain wrong. Too often I have seen it – how the *weak* usually exhaust and eventually destroy the *strong*. They allow the strong the delusion of thinking they are the most powerful while they use their weakness to get everything they secretly want, including their own rigid will!"

Byron had not a clue as to what or whom Hodgson was talking about, and surely not Miss Tayler's mother?

"No, of course not," Hodgson replied. "Well, actually, *yes,* in a way ... she is a gentle and sweet woman, but she is now also a widow with no husband to lean on, so she leans on Susanna who *is* quite strong, but even she is now worn out with all these objections. I used to think Mrs Tayler was a weak woman, but now she is displaying a surprising strength in having her will obeyed."

"All these objections? I thought you said her *only* objection was your debts."

The embarrassment was back on Hodgson's face, not sure how to explain it, or even to dare say it ... He had such a friendship for Byron, and was so very, very fond of him, but this could destroy their years of friendship in a snap.

"No ... " he said hesitantly, "she has more than one objection to me. She has *two* objections. It's quite ludicrous really ... but she has made it very plain that she does not believe I could ever be the *best* suitor for her virtuous daughter ... due to ... well, this is very difficult for me to say ... due to my friendship with you."

Again Byron stared. "Me?"

"Yes, you, my dear friend – or as she calls you – 'the *scandalous* Lord Byron'."

Byron almost laughed, and started to rise from his chair, then reseated himself, looking at Hodgson with an expression of wonder. "Where did she get that impression of me? She has never met, nor seen, and so does not even know me."

"No." Hodgson shook his head in weary agreement, "but, like half the population of this country, she has heard all the scandal of your relationship with Lady Caroline Lamb, a married woman. It was in all the newspapers, you know? How Lady Caroline tried to kill herself with a knife in your presence."

"In my presence? I was not even in the same part of the house! I knew nothing about it until Lady Westmoreland told me."

"*I* believe that is the truth, but who else will believe it if the newspapers say differently."

"All London knows the truth," Byron countered. "Half of them were there and can attest to my innocence in that outrageous pantomime of hers."

"All London perhaps." Hodgson looked at him gravely. "But London is not *Oxford.*"

"Oxford?"

"Where the Tayler family live."

"Do you mean to say ... *all* of Oxford is against me?"

"No, only the mothers, and I would not say they are *against* you, nothing so personal, but they do severely disapprove, not only of you, but also your poetry, especially in *Childe Harold* where you appear to approve of the enjoyment of *vice.*"

Byron did not speak for several moments, deciding not to say openly what he wished to say.

"And the worst of it is," Hodgson went on in a distressed tone, "it is not even Susanna's mother who so truly disapproves of you, but her uncle, the Dean of Christ Church."

Byron was startled. "Christ Church in Oxford?"

"Yes."

"Because of Lady Caroline Lamb?"

"No, no." Hodgson shook his head. "The Dean never wastes his time reading the rubbish in the social pages. And I doubt Mrs Tayler would ever mention such gossip to him. She is far too reserved a lady in her manner to mention such things to her brother. And apart from that, even the Dean knows it is the fashion for young men to have amours and live what he good-humouredly calls – *'a fast* life.'

"So *what* then? If you know the reason for the Dean's objection to your friendship with me, then pray tell me?"

"Because of your views, Byron, your *views*. They don't go down well in the Tory shires. It is your extreme and outspoken radical opinions on politics and religion and the present government that have given you such a bad reputation in the shires. It's not what you do, but what you say and write and publish that in the minds of some, damn you beyond all redemption – especially your condemnation of King George and the Prince Regent."

"So, it is forgivable to be a libertine," Byron said ironically, "but damnable to be a lover of liberty?"

Hodgson nodded. "Of course, the Dean has *no idea* that, politically, I too am a Whig."

"Which is where you and I differ then," Byron replied, "because I no longer consider myself to be either a Whig or a Tory – politically both are almost as bad as each other; and that's why I now choose to refer to myself as a *Democrat."*

"Oh good God, no!" Hodgson almost jumped with fright. "Pray *don't,* Byron, not in public."

Byron stood up from his seat and went to the window, staring out for some long moments, before turning back to Hodgson. "So even if you had no debts, your friendship with me would still disqualify you?"

"Yes, but Byron ... please ... they do not know you as I do. You must understand, they are not *worldly* like you. They have never travelled outside England. The Dean is not a man of the world, he is an academic who lives in books. His world and that of Mrs Tayler is one of cultured politeness and Oxford customs and restraint of behaviour and speech at all times."

"In other words – stagnant and dull."

"Perhaps – but Susanna is not like them. She has read all your poetry and thinks it is glorious."

"So does the Princess of Wales, and has said so publicly – did that not sway the mother or the Dean?"

"Oh," Hodgson shrugged, "they are both true devotees of the Prince Regent. To them, Princess Caroline is a bad-mannered German who has made the Prince's life a misery."

Byron did not speak for several moments, rendering Hodgson utterly miserable now. To lose Susanna was heartbreaking, but to lose his friend also?

Byron sat down at his desk, taking out papers and other documents, lifting his pen and beginning to write in his rapid way.

Hodgson stared at him ... surely he was not writing poetry now? Byron always culminated his emotions into poetry when he was unhappy or distressed.

"They do not know you," Hodgson said quietly. "They would like you if they did."

"And perhaps not, and be it so. I have no intention of sucking in my mouth meekly to make people approve of me."

He tore off a strip of paper, blotted it, and held it out towards Hodgson. "But at least allow me to help you with this."

"What?" Hodgson rose and walked to the desk, taking the paper and almost staggering backwards when he saw it was a cheque to his name for the sum of one thousand pounds.

"Oh no, my dear fellow, no, *no,* I could not accept this! How could I? Why would I?"

"Because you know it is rude to refuse a gift." Byron lifted a cloth to clean the nib of his pen. "I always meant to give it to you, as a wedding present, and there it is, a little early perhaps, but this way it might be of more benefit to you and your adored."

"A wedding present ..." Hodgson was on the verge of astonished tears, because now a marriage to his beloved Susanna *might* be possible.

"If I take it now, I will find a way to pay you back."

"By saying a pious prayer for me occasionally," Byron smiled. "Take it, and inform Oxford you have ceased your association with the scandalous Lord Byron. Now off you go – I have an epic to write before midnight."

Francis Hodgson had no intentions of going anywhere yet. This was all wrong. This was abominably *unjust*. Byron was more than just a friend. At times, in his attitude and actions, Byron had often behaved more like a *brother* – as he was doing now – handing over not a penny more nor a penny less than the huge amount of money he knew his friend so desperately *needed*.

Hodgson put a hand to his eyes, wondering what *Jesus* would do in a situation like this? Would he act like a Judas and take the money and then go away and allow the name of his friend to be besmirched and dishonoured?

No, in the Bible, Jesus had quite a lot of angry words to say about those who judged and condemned others – *"Let him who is without sin be the first to throw a stone! ... You hypocrite, first take the log out of your own eye ... Beware of practicing your own righteousness before others ..."*

Not that Hodgson had ever allowed his friend's name to be besmirched. He had, very firmly, told both Mrs Tayler and the Dean that Lord Byron was not only an aristocrat, but a fine and decent young man with a good heart, and he regarded his friendship with his lordship to be an honour ... but they had not been swayed.

Hodgson leaned across the desk to see if Byron had actually started writing his epic, and saw that he was merely doodling circles, waiting for him to leave.

"Byron ... this money will only solve one of their objections, but I have had an idea ."

Byron glanced up. "I have heard some of your not-very-good ideas in the past. So what is this one, pray?"

"You. I value our friendship, and I cannot disown it, not now nor ever. And I also know Susanna would not want me to ... so could you possibly consider helping me further by coming to Oxford to plead my case with Mrs Tayler and the Dean?"

Byron stared. "What good would that serve? And if I was to arrive in Oxford in person to plead your case, would it not make the situation worse?"

"No, because I am quite *certain* that once they meet you in person, they will see that you are not as scandalous as they have judged."

Byron smiled. "To judge or not to judge, *that* should be the question, although I don't give a damn about the answer either way."

Hodgson stood looking at him with an expression of gentle agony and misery. "Would you, pray, not even consider it?"

Byron did, for several long moments, then came to a decision. "I have arranged to meet my sister Augusta and her children at Newstead on Sunday. So if I am to go to Oxford and then get back to London before heading off to Newstead, we would have to leave today."

"Today? You mean you *will?*"

Byron stood and pulled the rope for Fletcher. "I can't help you with the mother, mind, but in my own defence I can certainly take on the Dean of Christ Church."

Hodgson struggled to collect his wits, his excitement changing to caution. "But, Byron, for *my* sake, pray do not mention to either Mrs Tayler or the Dean your extraordinary admiration for Napoleon."

"As if I would – to anyone in a conservative stronghold such as *Oxford*."

"And also – pray do *not* mention your admiration for the late George Washington either – not after we have just come out of yet another war with the Americans. The Dean would be outraged."

Byron turned up his eyes in exasperation, but was prevented from answering by the arrival of Fletcher in a very agitated state. "My lord, I *must* speak to you ... privately."

"Not now, Fletcher. Mr Hodgson and I are about to leave for a journey to Oxford. We will lodge overnight at an inn, so pray pack my wash things and a change of clothes in my travel bag as quickly as you can."

"But, my lord, what I have to say to you is very important."

"Then *say* it."

Even more flustered, Fletcher glanced at Hodgson, and then stared at his lordship. "It's Miss D'ussierres, my lord."

"Who?"

"Miss D'ussierres, the young lady from Switzerland. She gabbled her way past me again and now she's waiting to see you. I told her you had male company but she won't go, so desperate is she to see you."

Byron could not believe it. "And where is she now, Fletcher?"

"Hiding in the mop and broom cupboard, my lord."

"The mop and broom cupboard – where is that?"

"Off the kitchen, my lord. She insisted on hiding in there because she does not want your visitor to see her waiting for you. I've begged her to leave before Mrs Mule comes back from the shops, but she won't go."

"Then we must persuade her," Byron said. "You quickly see to my packing, and I will see to Miss D'ussierres. You will excuse me, Hodgson?"

Hodgson was speechless. *A female hiding in the broom cupboard!*

In the kitchen, Byron opened a door and discovered it led into a food pantry. He closed it, and opened the door next to it, and found Miss D'ussierres in her bonnet, sitting on a stool surrounded by brooms and mops.

"Well, this is pretty behaviour I must say."

For a moment she seemed shocked to see him standing there, and then jumped up and flung herself at him in delight. "Oh, but not as pretty as *you*, milord!"

He held her at arm's length. "Miss D'ussierres, does your mother know you are not at school today?"

"School?" Her big eyes stared at him. "My finishing school was finished one year ago. I am a finished *woman* now."

"Miss D'ussierres, may I show you something? Something that is very precious and personal to me?"

She returned his smile with gratified excitement and nodded. "Come along then," he said, taking her hand.

She could not help giggling as they walked hand in hand through the kitchen. "I dream of this. I am so excited to know what you wish to show me."

"I want to show you *this*," he said, leading her into the hall towards the front door. "This door is very precious to me, because it protects my personal privacy, you see? And the only people who are welcome to enter through this door, are those who come at my personal invitation. I don't like intruders. So I would be obliged if you would kindly now leave, Miss D'ussierres, and pray do not intrude yourself into my private home again."

Her face turned scarlet.

He opened the door. "Also, I am about to leave for Oxford in order to discuss a marriage to a young lady."

The colour left her face as swiftly as it had come, leaving her pale and staring and wordless.

"Off you go," he told her, and she abruptly hurried through the door, which he then closed.

Some hours later the door was opened to John Hobhouse, who was welcomed in the usual casual way by Fletcher.

"Lord Byron is not at home, Mr Hobhouse."

"Not at home? But we had an arrangement for this evening. So where is he?"

"He went dashing off in a great hurry to Oxford earlier today, but he hopes to be back by tomorrow night."

"Oxford? Why the deuce has he gone to Oxford?"

Fletcher shrugged. "I dunno, but he went with Mr Hodgson."

Hobhouse fumed. "He should at least have had the courtesy to send me round a note."

"He should, sir."

"Well, when he gets back, Fletcher, will you be sure to tell him that I need to know about *Italy* soon, one way or another, I *need* to know."

Chapter Eleven

~ ~ ~

Lady Caroline Lamb had not slept, tossing and turning throughout the night, occasionally lying wide awake and staring into the darkness while her mind plotted and planned.

She knew this present unhappy state of affairs was no fault of Byron's. He had been turned against her by Lady Melbourne. He had been warned to have nothing to do with her by Lady Melbourne, because all Lady Melbourne cared about was her precious son, William Lamb, and his important career as a politician.

How many times had she severely warned her, Caroline, not to disgrace William – and she had probably given the same severe warning to Byron also – because like her son, Lady Melbourne also believed that one day William Lamb could become the Prime Minister of Great Britain.

A hint of sun peeking through a chink in the heavy drapes suddenly caught her eye, causing her to turn and stare at the thin sliver of yellow light which instantly lifted her spirits and brightened her mood. The morning had arrived at last, thank goodness, and a new day was waiting!

With an impatient bound she sprang out of bed and headed to her dressing-room, carefully selecting her clothes from within a muslin cover hanging at the very back of one of her large wardrobes. These were her "special clothes" and she had worn them quite often of late. Of course her plan might not work, he might persist in his refusal to reconcile with her, but even one hour of exultant *hope* was preferable to a long day of certain misery.

From the bottom of the wardrobe she took out a

medium-sized brown cardboard box, empty and light. which she tucked under her arm and then walked to the door, ready to go, and whispering to herself Byron's favourite motto —"*Carpe diem!"* — Seize the day.

She opened the door, and peered down the corridor. No one was about; she heard no sound, no voice, not even that of a servant.

She moved stealthily down to the back-end of the corridor, and then crept down the carpeted stairs that led to the back door and out to the garden. From there she ran quickly and nimbly out onto the path that led around Melbourne House and out onto the main road in Whitehall.

It took her no more than twenty minutes to reach the Albany building in Piccadilly, walking quickly past the front entrance and the porter, and on around to the back entrance in Vigo Street, where she stood to wait and watch from behind a tree.

Her careful scrutiny in the past had taught her a lot about Fletcher's habits and routine; and now she waited and watched for Fletcher to come out of the servant's entrance to take Byron's dog for his regular morning walk, which usually lasted for no more than half an hour. She also knew that he always left the servants' door of the apartment unlocked, for his own easy access when he and Leander returned.

An hour later she was still waiting. Why was he so late today?

Another hour passed and still no sign of the damned fellow. Surely Leander must be barking his complaints by now. Why was Lord Byron not rousting Fletcher out of his bed to give the dog his walk?

Some minutes later she saw Fletcher come out into the courtyard and she quickly stepped back, pulling her hat further down over her brow and pretending to be looking at the label on the empty cardboard box ... until, finally, she saw that Fletcher and the dog had passed the porter on the back gate and both were now heading up

Vigo Street.

She slipped into the courtyard and approached the porter's window with head down, holding the cardboard box, her voice low and deep: "Delivery for Lord Byron in A2."

The sleepy-eyed porter waved her on, as she knew he would, as he had done a number of times before. She was dressed as a delivery boy, her coat and breeches cheap and drab, and being so petite and slim, it was easy for her to disguise herself as a boy of sixteen or so.

She descended the steps to the left of the back door and minutes later she was inside the long subterranean corridor which ran the length of the building, and which only the servants knew. Here, there were kitchens and laundry rooms which she quickly passed, until her eyes caught sight of Mrs Mule in one of the laundry rooms, busily gossiping with another servant.

Caroline smiled; so her path was clear. She quickly climbed the steps up to the ground floor, and slipped in to the apartment of A2 through the servants' door.

All was silent, all was peaceful ... was her beloved Byron still asleep?

Passing though his chambers she reached his bedroom and quietly opened the door, slipping inside, only to see that the room was empty and his bed had not been slept in.

She stood stock still, wanting to cry: all her plans and efforts had been in vain.

So where was he? She knew he often stayed out with his friends at the clubs until three or four in the morning, but not until this hour – not unless he was asleep in some other woman's bed?

The very thought infuriated her. Why could those silly women not leave him alone? So many of the young ladies in London society pursued Byron without any discretion at all, and now she was tired of warning them all that he was "mad, bad and dangerous to know!"

Some of the religious young women were shocked

and declared they would pray for him, yet she knew that others, who were not religious, prayed for him in another way.

She moved into his drawing-room, a large and bright pleasant room with a very high ceiling and a wide bow window. A long table stood in front of the fireplace, covered in books. She moved past the sofas and towards the books, wondering what he was reading these days? They had not had a happy and engrossing conversation about books for such a long time.

To the side of the fireplace stood a large screen covered with prints of famous boxers on one side and famous actors on the other. None of this interested her. She moved over to his desk by the window and began to look through the papers still lying on its surface ... a page of pencilled circles, and underneath it, a half-written letter in ink to Lady Melbourne.

She read through the opening pleasantries, furious that he should be corresponding with Lady Melbourne at all – and *behind her back* too! Both of them – corresponding privately and secretly with each other.

She continued reading his letter ...

I have got myself a new physician. It is very odd; he is a staid, grave man, and puts so many questions to me about my MIND, and the state of it, that I begin to think he half suspects my senses.

He asked me how I felt, "when anything weighed upon my mind?" and I answered him by a question, why he should suppose that anything did?

I was laughing and sitting quietly in my chair the whole time of his visit, and yet he thinks me horribly restless, and talks about my having lived "excessively, and out of all compass" at some time or other, which has no more to do with the malady he has to deal with than I have with the Wisdom of Solomon.

Tomorrow I am invited to the Berrys: on Wednesday to the Jerseys; on Friday I am asked to a Lady Charleville's, whom I don't know, and where I shan't go. We shall meet, I hope, at one these places.

Caroline dropped the letter as if it was filth ... *We shall meet, I hope ...*

Yet to herself, his most faithful love, all he seemed to hope for was to avoid.

Enraged with jealousy, she sat down on Byron's chair and used his pen and ink to write him a scolding note:

How extraordinary! My mother-in-law actually in the place I held – her letters instead of mine – her heart instead of mine – but do you believe that she or any other can feel for you what I felt? You will never love or will be loved by another – of that I am certain because no one can love as well & devotedly & entirely as I could – and did – and this one day you will know.

Yrs, Medora.

Chapter Twelve

~~~

In Oxford, sitting relaxed in his chair in the book-filled study, Byron listened, with deliberate patience, to all the objections that Charles Hall, the Dean of Christchurch, made against the poem of *Childe Harold's Pilgrimage.*

"Harold is not immoral," Byron said. "He is just not *enslaved* by morals."

"And therefore one must presume the same of Harold's author," said the Dean.

"And would you presume the same about Milton, sir?"

"Milton?"

"Yes, in *Paradise Lost,* Milton gives most of his attention to the Devil, and at times he even appears to feel some sympathy for him, so would you say Milton could be judged as a secret sympathiser of Satan?"

The Dean, after his first incredulous shock at such a question, laid the palms of his hands on his desk, and then spent two engrossing hours with Lord Byron in scholarly debate as each dissected many parts of *Paradise Lost* and gave their personal views on it.

The Dean began to realise that he was talking to a young man of great intellect and study, as well as a touch of Adonis about his looks, but the most impressive facet of all was his amazing memory.

The Dean listened with entranced astonishment as Lord Byron was able to discuss verse after verse of *Paradise Lost* without having to look down at the pages of the book at all; and his understanding and repetition of the Latin parts of the text were faultless.

"So," Byron continued, "if it is right to judge the character of a writer based on the content of his work, should we also judge God on the basis of *His* work?"

The Dean blinked. "What do you mean?"

"According to Milton in *Paradise Lost*, the authority of God derives from His being the "author" of all creation. Yet we do not judge God on the continual bad deeds of humans. That would surely be unfair?"

"Indeed it would."

"As unfair as judging Mr Hodgson on *my* faults and follies?"

"I suppose," replied the Dean, now seriously thinking about it, "that I *have* been rather unfair to Mr Hodgson. He is, after all, a King's Scholar who has taken Holy Orders to enter the Church and is now, I believe, hoping to be given a Chaplaincy..."

"I consider my friendship with him to be a great honour," Byron added sincerely. "He is seven years older than myself, and consequently he has been my mentor since my younger days at Cambridge, and hopefully he will continue to be so."

In the drawing-room of the Dean's house, Mrs Tayler sat in her favourite chair by the fireplace, wearing a black gown and a cap of white lace over her greying hair, while Hodgson and Susanna sat apprehensively in the same room, still waiting for the verdict.

The fact that Mr Hodgson no longer had any financial liabilities to obstruct the proposed marriage had removed all objections from Mrs Tayler.

"Of course, being Susanna's uncle, the ultimate decision must be the Dean's," she said to Hodgson. "But as for Lord Byron ... well, I must confess, during my own interview with him ... he smiled the *heart* out of me."

She lifted her white handkerchief to her face to hide her embarrassment at such a confession, and followed it with a girlish giggle, which caused Hodgson and Susanna to exchange a hopeful smile.

"But then," added Mrs Tayler, "I'm sure any sensible lady in Oxford, faced personally with Lord Byron's respectability and *rank,* as well as the irresistible charms of his manner and appearance, would also judge that the Lamb woman must have flung herself at him like a common trollop."

~~~

A short time later, after Lord Byron had politely declined an invitation to stay with the family for dinner, insisting he had to get back to London, the Dean and Mrs Tayler stood beside Hodgson and Susanna as all four came out to wave him off in his carriage.

It had been agreed that Hodgson should stay for a few days longer with the family, all objections to him erased – especially the main objection, being the huge sum of his debts, which now did not exist, due to the munificence of his friend and benefactor, Lord Byron.

When the day itself was finally over, in the bedroom allotted to him in the Dean's house, Francis Hodgson was still feeling very relieved and emotional at the turn-around of it all. He passionately loved Susanna, and now, at last, she was going to be his wife.

Too excited to sleep, he wrote a letter to his uncle, Reverend Francis Coke, informing him of his altered financial situation, and of this singular example of true friendship.

My noble-hearted friend Lord Byron, after many offers of a similar kind, which I felt bound to refuse, has irresistibly in my present circumstances (as I will soon explain to you) volunteered to pay all my debts, and within a few pounds it is done! Oh, if you knew (but YOU do know) the exaltation of heart, aye, and head too, I feel at being free from these depressing embarrassments, you would, as I do, bless my dearest friend and brother, Byron.

At his insistence, we went together in Lord Byron's

carriage to Hammersley's Bank in Pall Mall, where the money was transferred from one account to the other. He said he "always intended to do it'" and seems only to have waited for the opportunity when the gift would be of greatest service.

I did then, in good conscience, offer to give him a bond or a promissory note bearing interest, which Byron resolutely refused, with such words as these: "What is the use of you giving me a bond? I shall only destroy it'.

After which, he immediately accompanied me to Oxford to plead my cause with the family of Miss Tayler. Now where are the hearts of those who can undervalue, who can depreciate this man?

Chapter Thirteen

~~~

The building of Albany was deadly silent when Byron entered the hallway. Every resident had gone to his bed hours before.

Instead of putting up at an inn, he had travelled on through half the night, and now only Leander stirred to greet him when he entered the apartment.

A letter lay on the hall platter. He took it with him into the drawing-room, sitting down on the sofa to quickly read it while Leander settled down again at his feet.

It was another letter from Miss Annabella Milbanke, prim and sensible as always, asking for his opinion on a selection of modern history books she might read?

Modern history books? His tiredness overcame him, and he threw that letter down, rising from the sofa to go to bed and sleep; all else could be dealt with tomorrow.

~~~

He had slept till noon, and had just finished washing and dressing when Fletcher entered his dressing room wearing a face of exaggerated alarm.

"My lord, Mr Hobhouse is here to see you, and he looks enraged!"

Byron looked at Fletcher. "Enraged? Why so? Did you tell him I was leaving for Newstead today?"

"No, my lord, I told him nothing, because he ordered me to hurry you up to come out to him."

Byron shrugged. "Have you everything packed for our journey?"

"I have, my lord."

"Then make me some tea and we will leave as soon as I am done with Mr Hobhouse."

Hobhouse was standing by the window when Byron entered. "Well, Hobby? Fletcher tells me you are *enraged* about something?"

Hobhouse raised his brows. "I am not enraged, but I *am* annoyed."

"Why?"

Hobhouse hesitated. "Oh, well, this is all extremely unpleasant for me, y'know ... but I thought you should be informed. To be forewarned is to be forearmed, as they say."

Byron took the teacup and saucer from Fletcher and sipped his tea. "Forearmed? Is someone preparing to call me out in a duel?"

"Nothing so simple. I took coffee with Samuel Rogers this morning, and it seems that while you were off in Oxford, he attended a party at Lady Westmoreland's last night, where a certain person whispered to him that *you* have been indulging in a secret affair with Lady Melbourne."

Byron almost spluttered his tea. "Lady *Melbourne?* She is old enough to be my mother!"

"Or even your *grandmother*," Hobby replied, "since you are still in your twenties and she is in her sixties."

Byron put down his tea. "Did Rogers say *who* the certain person was?"

"No, but he told me that he thought it was all nonsense and warned that person about the silliness of spreading such ridiculous scandal. He told me to say nothing to you, but I thought you *should* be told, if only to warn you to be *less* friendly with Lady Melbourne when you meet her at social engagements in future."

Byron stood thoughtful. "I can think of only one person who would be demented enough to spread such vindictive gossip."

He put down his tea and moved towards his desk. "I had better send a note to Lady Melbourne warning her also. Although it would be wrong to say that it *is* Caroline, without certain proof. Did Rogers give you even a hint?"

"No, once he had mentioned it, he moved on to other things."

Byron was staring down at a letter lying on top of the papers on his desk, his eyes furious. "God damn! – how the devil did she get in here – *how?"*

He lifted the letter and handed it to Hobhouse and then leaned across the desk to pull the bell rope for Fletcher, while Hobhouse read the letter in disbelief –

How extraordinary! My mother-in-law actually in the place I held – her letters instead of mine – her heart instead of mine –

"Fletcher, have you been at my desk while I was away?"

"No, my lord. I never go near your desk. I know not to."

"Then pray explain how Lady Caroline Lamb was able to get into this apartment and write a letter at my desk?"

"What?" Fletcher stood at the door, his eyes agog. "She couldn't have, my lord. I was here all the time and I saw neither hat nor hair of her, I swear! On my oath!"

Byron's temper was rising. "Then explain *how* she was able to write a letter at *my* desk!"

"Maybe ... maybe ..." Fletcher was wringing his hands in confusion ... "Maybe it's a letter you opened last night and don't remember opening it."

"No! She used *my* pen!" He held up the pen. "Or else *you* did."

"Me? Use your pen? You know I can only be doing with pencils, my lord."

Hobhouse interrupted: "What makes you think it was *your* pen that was used to write the letter?"

"Because she did not clean the nib! I *always* clean the nib before I set the pen down. And the ink used in the letter is *my* ink – Japanese ink – its colour is like no other."

He threw the pen into the waste-paper basket. "I shall

not write a note to Lady Melbourne, I will go and talk to her in person before we head off to Newstead. Is Mrs Mule coming in today, Fletcher?"

"No, my lord, she knows we will be away for a week or two."

"Then let's get this place locked up securely, every room. We will deal with the porters on the gates as soon as we return."

Hobhouse stepped forward. "Byron —"

"I cannot delay any longer, Hobby. I *must* see Lady Melbourne before I leave London, and I don't want my sister and nieces to arrive at Newstead before I do."

He looked at Hobhouse. "Unless you would like to come to Newstead with us, Hobby? You are welcome to do so."

Hobhouse hesitated for a moment, and then shrugged. "Thank you, no. I am not prepared, nothing packed. No, the journey *I* am interested in Byron, is *Italy*, are we going, or are we not?"

Byron had not given Italy a thought, yet now he wished he was leaving for Italy *today*, anywhere away from Caroline Lamb and her insidious mischief.

"I can't let Augusta down, Hobby, but we will discuss Italy as soon as I get back, shall we?"

"Can I have your word on that?"

"You can have my promise."

~~~

Lady Melbourne was not at all distressed; in fact she was highly flattered that anyone in their right senses might believe such a rumour — that Lord Byron, whom London society still paid an unprecedented homage, amounting almost to idolatry, should, at twenty-six, be having a secret affair with a woman of sixty-two.

It was really quite absurd. Yet she was smiling to herself while her back was turned to Byron in order to speak to the butler. "Dutton, please see about some tea and perhaps a pastry for Lord Byron."

"Yes, my lady."

"Nothing for me," Byron said quickly. "My time is too short."

Lady Melbourne waved Dutton away and turned a stony face to Lord Byron, sitting down in her chair and pretending to be shocked, utterly shocked.

"Only Caroline," she said, "could conceive such a notion and spread such a scandalous rumour."

"You will speak to her, and put an end to it?"

"Indeed I will!" Lady Melbourne had no intention of putting an end to it. It had been a very long time since she had been an object of envy among her lady friends of a certain age, and this rumour would have most of them spitting *green* blood with jealousy.

Byron said irritably: "I am at a loss to know what more I can do about her, that I have not already done. She may hunt me down – it is in the power of any mad or bad woman to do so by an man – but snare me she shall not."

"Of course not," agreed lady Melbourne.

"Yet how am I to bar myself from her? She has no shame. She has been an adder in my path since I returned to this country. She has crossed me everywhere. She has watched and *guessed* and been an absolute curse to me. Now she is sneaking into my home and spreading false rumours about affairs, and now I can take no more."

Lady Melbourne sighed deeply. "I understand. I know the torment she has put you through. As to her latest rumour, I shall ask Lord Melbourne to speak to her also. He will be very cross that such an imputation should be made against his wife." She quickly gave Byron a sweet smile of assurance. "He will know of course that it is all ridiculously untrue."

Byron nodded, embarrassed that he had been forced to even mention it to her.

"But then most rumours are outrageous," said Lady Melbourne, a tilt to her head as she eyed him. "Have you heard the latest one from Madame de Staël? Now that really is a shocker."

"About whom?"

"About you, I regret to say. It seems that the last time Madame de Staël observed you and Mrs Leigh at a party together, she thought you were both rather too affectionate in your behaviour for that of a brother and sister."

Byron stared. "I love Augusta with all my heart, because she *is* my sister."

He sat back, stunned at this new allegation. "I see brothers and sisters being affectionate to each other all the time. Why should Augusta and I be any different? And Madame de Staël..." he frowned, "what put that into her head?"

Lady Melbourne folded her hands neatly on her lap. "Well, she is French, and she whispered it only to me, by way of protecting you with a word of warning about some of the things you say in public."

"Such as?"

"On the night in question, she says there was a discussion on the subject of *incest*, and instead of showing disapproval, you laughingly implied that in your first draft of *Bride of Abydos* the two lovers were brother and sister, and not cousins as they were in the published edition. And then later, when Madame saw you and Mrs Leigh so affectionate together, she drew her own French conclusions."

Byron was beside himself with exasperation, jumping up from his chair. "I will not tolerate any smears against Augusta. They may say what they will of me, but *not* my dear sister. You *know* Augusta! You know how *shy* and insecure she is at these social events, and why I always stay beside her if I can."

"I do know," Lady Melbourne agreed, her face expressing sympathy and compassion. "But what I wonder now, and what I fear, is what will the *next* rumour be?"

"Who cares?" He shrugged his annoyance. "And you should advise Madame de Staël to find something better to do with her eyes than spending an evening *squinting* at two people from a distance."

Lady Melbourne gave no indication that she would say anything to Madame de Staël. She leaned back in her chair and sighed again, her face grave. "I can only say that at times I am wrung with pity for you. And yet, all these rumours, all this gossip, and all the infringements on your privacy ... all would immediately come to an end if you were to take my advice and marry, but only to the *right* person."

Byron looked at her archly. "Whom you believe to be your niece, Miss Milbanke?"

"I do," said Lady Melbourne, giving him one of her kindest smiles. "If you were my son, I could choose no other young lady more suitable for you. Would you not at least *consider* it?"

Byron did, for all of three seconds, before replying apologetically. "I honestly don't think I could cope with all her metaphysical discussions."

"Oh, that's because she is also shy!" Lady Melbourne laughed. "Like your sister, Annabella is also very shy. Everyone is much bolder when writing letters, and she probably writes on those subjects thinking they would interest you. In reality Bell is one of the *quietest* girls I know. And her conversation is usually quite normal."

"I must go," he said, turning to leave. "I have delayed too long as it is. You will speak to Caroline?"

"I will speak to her, very sharply, this very night. You can rely on that."

"Thank you."

"Oh –" she suddenly raised up her hand to halt him – "before you go, Lord Byron ... Mrs Damer was asking me most excitedly this morning, if I knew whether you intended to respond to her invitation and be present at her dinner party next week?"

"A thousand excuses to Mrs Damer with whom I beg

not to dine."

He gave her a quick smile, and then disappeared out to the hall.

When he had gone Lady Melbourne rose from her chair and went to the window, standing just behind the drapes as she watched him climb into his carriage. She was so very fond of him, and as much as she sympathised with him, she now dreaded the fact that she would have to confront Caroline on his behalf, yet *again*.

It was pointless, truly a waste of time, because Caroline always responded to her in the same way. She always meekly admitted she was wrong, and made promises to be good in future, and then beg for forgiveness for acting so foolishly.

And so Caroline did again, later that evening, admitting to Lady Melbourne that her latest foolishness was because she dreaded the thought of Byron marrying someone else, or his leaving the country.

"For him to go, and for me not to be able to see him... it would be death!"

Lady Melbourne could hardly contain herself. To think this woman was her son's *wife*.

"It is my opinion, Caroline, that if you persist in your present behaviour – you will drive him to marry. And if not to marry – to drive him out of England."

Caroline's face turned very grave for a long moment. "No," she quivered, "I would not wish to drive him to do either of those things ... but *you* might, always saying he *should* marry – and to that hideous niece of yours."

"You think everyone is hideous except yourself," snapped Lady Melbourne. "Caroline, I have warned you, and now I will not listen to another word from you."

She walked across the room, leaving Caroline sitting at her escritoire. Opening the bedroom door, Lady Melbourne paused to coldly look back at her daughter-in-law.

"And Caroline, pray stop spreading your scurrilous lies about me, or there will be severe consequences for you, I promise. And pray never bring up Lord Byron's name again, not in this house, and not in my presence."

Caroline flicked her hand dismissively. "I never bring up his name, for I act by his name as the Israelites did by that of their God, I name him not."

At the end of her patience, Lady Melbourne swiftly left the room fearing she might scream. Caroline was a deceitful little liar who knew how to get away with her lies in front of William and others because she always managed to insert enough truth in them to be believed.

It was true that Caroline never did voice Lord Byron's name these days, because now, when questioning others about him, the silly strumpet always referred to him as *"the Childe"* or *"the Giaour"* or *"Lara,"* as if those fictional characters were all one and the same person as Lord Byron himself.

In her bedroom, Caroline had already started writing a note to John Murray –

When you see the beautiful Corsair again, for God's sake do not name me to him. Do not say I write to you. He tells everything to Lady Melbourne.

Chapter Fourteen

~~~

At Newstead, as the days passed, Augusta was beset with worry about her brother. He was moody and sensitive, and had become absolutely outraged when a letter had arrived that morning from his attorney, John Hanson, complaining about the payment of one thousand pounds transferred from his account to Francis Hodgson.

"Hanson says this is yet just *another* example of my 'typical overgenerous lifestyle'," he told her, "and begs me to see to my own debts, instead of relieving the debts of others."

Augusta had felt her face redden, due to all the help he had given to her and George with their debts. "What about the mines at Rochdale?" she had asked. "Surely Hanson knows there is a fortune yet to come to you from them – at least sixty thousand pounds – an absolute fortune."

"No, it will not be that much, not now, because Hanson knows that a small fortune has already been spent over the years in court fees and legal fees – *his* legal fees – Yet now he is scrutinising every pound I spend."

Augusta's suggestion of finding a new lawyer had reduced Byron to silence ... finally explaining that he would find it impossible to leave Hanson.

"He was very kind to me as a boy, taking care of all my needs like a stand-in father. So I could not dispense with him now. Not now that he's older and slower and becoming more like my cranky *grand*father with all his complaints. No, if I was to dispense with him now it would be a cruel return for all he has done for me in the past."

He left her then, in ill-humour, and went out to the garden to play with the children and the dogs. Watching him from the window, she saw him laughing, and heard the three girls screeching in merriment while the dogs barked excitedly.

During this visit to Newstead, the only time she had known Byron to laugh was when he was playing with the children and the dogs, keeping them occupied and entertained most of the days in order to give her a rest, or so he said.

In truth, she suspected the real reason was that he loved being in the company of the children who made no *serious* demands of him, except to have fun and play. His physical energy was tireless, yet in the evenings, after the children had gone to bed, he seemed laconic and depressed.

He had told her about Caroline Lamb finding a way into his private residence, as had some Swiss girl who had pushed her way in. And Miss Eliza Francis and others who were always at his door. She knew he was tired of it all, and now craved only peace and stability in his life; but all her urgings for him to find a suitable young lady to marry, who would give him that peace and stability, had been rebuffed.

So she was very surprised when he said to her at dinner that evening – "According to his last letter, Tom Moore and his wife Bessy also think I should settle down and marry. And being the good friends that they are, they have even *selected* their perfect choice for me, Lady Adelaide Forbes."

Augusta almost choked on her mouthful of food and grabbed up a napkin. She had selected her own choice for him – Lady Charlotte Levenson-Gower.

"And do you find their suggestion attractive?"

He shrugged. "Lady Adelaide and I have met frequently at parties, but our association has never progressed beyond the everyday flirtation of everyday people. As soon as we left the premises, I'm sure she forgot me as quickly as I forgot her."

He paused. "There is *one* girl I have often thought would make me a happy companion ... Miss Bessy Rawdon. She and I always have great fun flirting with each other, and we get on very well in our conversations, because she also has been to Greece."

Augusta sighed, not wishing to hear any more about Byron's beloved Greece.

"Do you think Lady Melbourne would approve of Miss Rawdon?"

"No. I mentioned her once, and Lady Melbourne dismissed her out of hand, which was rather unfair, because Bessy is quite lovable."

"As a friend, yes. I also found her likable, but I suppose ..." Augusta paused, knowing the very strong influence Lady Melbourne had on her brother, "I suppose her ladyship has very high standards."

"I don't know about that. All I know is that she believes there is only one person in this world suitable for me, and that is her niece, Miss Milbanke."

"Her niece?" Augusta frowned thoughtfully. "I don't believe I have ever met her niece, so I can't give my opinion one way or another."

"Well, she writes very prim and pious letters to me quite regularly. And you *have* met her, last year, when she was in London with Lady Melbourne."

"Have I?" Augusta blinked. "I'm sure I don't recall. When *exactly* did I meet her last year?"

"At Lady Davey's musical evening. The night of the flute-player. Don't you remember? I left you in the trusted care of Lady Melbourne, and her niece was standing right beside her."

"Oh, the *heiress*. Oh, well, if you were to marry her all your financial problems would be solved. Personally though, I prefer my friend, Lady Charlotte Levenson-Gower."

"Oh yes, *your* friend ..." Byron suddenly smiled. "I forgot to tell you. Last week, at Lady Jersey's, your friend and I got fairly checkmated together in a corner, where we talked for a very good half hour, but it was only by persuading her that I was in a greater fright than herself, that she finally got over her shyness with me."

Augusta's face was beaming. "So now, what do you think of her?"

"I think her very pretty and pleasing and I only heard her say one disagreeable thing all night, and that was her mother and herself and the whole family would be leaving town soon to go up to Scotland."

Augusta nodded. "Yes, the family have a house in Scotland. Probably going up for the shooting season. Oh, Byron, pray let me write to her and tell her of your interest."

He moved his head in a gesture of negation. "No."

Augusta sighed. "Byron, on your next birthday you will be twenty-seven, the perfect age for it, so *why* are you so against marriage?"

After a long reflective silence, Byron said quietly, "I have no heart to spare, not for love, and I wish for none in return. I have only ever loved one."

Augusta understood and replied in the same quiet tone, "Byron, if you are referring to Mary Chaworth, that is gone and was never to be. Especially now that the poor girl has had a breakdown and been declared mad."

Byron gave her one of his sulky looks. "I think we are all mad, especially everyone in that madhouse called London, and perhaps none moreso than me. So it's unfair to point the finger at poor sick Mary."

He left her then, clearly in bad humour again, and Augusta felt sorry that she had sounded so unkind. It was not her nature to speak or think unkindly of anyone; but she could see no happy future for her brother in his present state.

~

Byron headed up to his own private sitting-room to read

and answer the letters that had been forwarded on to him from London and delivered earlier that afternoon ... *How fast those damned mail coaches fly!*

An hour or so later he took himself outside to the grounds of the Abbey to breathe in the air.

The twilight had passed and now as he looked up at the sky, the white stars burned in the silence.

He stood gazing upwards until the stars took on a dreamlike radiance, a mystic gleam from somewhere far beyond all knowledge, and he found himself wondering once again what was up there? Beyond the starlight?

The *moon* and the *evening star* ... so often stared at by humans, and yet all stars received their light from the sun. Yet humans could no more stare at the sun than they could stare at God ... not without going blind ... so no wonder the ancients of past times believed that the sun *was* God.

He gazed up for a long time at the brightest star in the dark sky.

Sun of the sleepless! Melancholy star!
Whose tearful beam glows tremulously far...

He suddenly felt alone and lonely, his gaze roaming over the still waters of the lake.

The air, which was fresh and sweet as it always was at Newstead, suddenly took on a pungent smell and he turned towards it ... smiling as he saw old Joe Murray coming towards him, holding a lantern and smoking his pipe.

"So, my lord, stargazing again?"

Byron shrugged. "Yes, stargazing, but my mood is in the *clouds.*"

"Of course I knew you would be out here. That's how I came now to find you?"

"Why so, Joe?"

"Well, with your sister being here and all, I didn't like to interrupt you with reports on the household while you've been away."

"Which are?"

"Oh, there's none. All's been well," Joe puffed on his pipe, "but I like to report to you anyway."

Byron smiled and suggested, "Shall we walk and talk?"

"Aye, oh aye, if that's what you wish" Joe replied with an eager air, "if that's what you wish, my lord."

For the next hour the two of them, with immense pleasure in each others company, talked and walked by the light of the stars and the lantern, the clear night air regularly clouded above their heads with puffs of smoke from Joe's pipe.

"Have you ever smoked a pipe, my lord," Joe suddenly asked. "It can be very soothing at times."

Byron nodded. "I have, yes, when I was in Greece, just to try it, but it was not a pipe like that one. It was a glass pipe."

"A *glass* pipe?" Joe was flabbergasted. "A pipe made of *glass*? I wouldn't think that could last very long before cracking."

"It's called a *hookah* pipe, and it has a glass bowl at the bottom which contains hot water to moisten the tobacco, and when you inhale through the pipe it gives you a dense and flavourful smoke."

"Moisten the tobacco?" Joe made a face. "I don't like the sound of that.! Moistened tobacco? What did it taste like? Did it taste anything like our own tobacco?"

Byron didn't know, because the hookah pipe he had smoked had contained mainly sweet water and heady opium – but he couldn't tell Joe that.

He held back a smile as he said, "I wouldn't recommend it, Joe, not for you. Stick to your dry English pouch."

"Aye, and my *wooden* pipe too," Joe declared. "Damp tobacco in a glass pipe? Why, I've never heard of such a daft thing in all my life."

Chapter Fifteen

~ ~ ~

The following afternoon, wandering alone in the garden by the South-East wing of the house, Byron found his mother's lost wedding ring.

He knew it was hers as soon as he saw it, lying on the dark earth by a rosebush. The gold was subdued by years of rain and frost in the winters, yet it still glowed unobtrusively in the soft light.

He was so surprised by the find; he took the ring indoors to show to his sister.

"My mother was very distressed when she lost this ring, because it was the only thing she had left from my father," he told Augusta. "Crying her eyes out, and making the servants search every shelf and corner of her rooms for it, day after day, but no joy. And yet today – there it was! It must have slipped off her hand when she was tending to her roses ... maybe when she was pulling off her gardening gloves the ring came off, and then dropped near the bush without her being aware of it."

The ring entranced Augusta, because Byron's father was her father too. "May I hold it?"

He handed her the ring and she stood for some moments staring at it "It's amazing how well, despite the elements, it has still kept its bright colour."

He nodded. "According to my mother the ring is pure French gold of twenty-four carats, so it doesn't rust or tarnish easily. That's what she kept bawling to the servants when it was lost – 'Pure gold, twenty-four carats, find it'!"

"And now *you* have found it, all these years later ..." Augusta looked at him with a strange expression on her face. "Do you think it's an omen? Or some sort of sign or message from her?"

Byron looked at his sister. Normally he would have dismissed such a suggestion as ludicrous, but ever since his mother had begged him not to go abroad - due to a premonition that if he went she would never see him alive again – and she never did; he no longer dismissed omens or portents of any kind.

"My mother was only forty-four at the time, and in fairly good health" he said, "so she could not have been expecting to die herself before I returned. Yet that's what happened, the day before I returned to Newstead she died of a stroke, and her premonition of never seeing me alive again proved true."

Augusta nodded silently. She was very superstitious about these things, a great believer in premonitions and signs. "What is it that Shakespeare said ... 'There are more things in heaven and earth '..."

"than are dreamed of in our philosophy..." Byron continued . "It's from *Hamlet* ."

"So," Augusta said quietly, "maybe it *is* a sign, a message to you from your mama."

Byron frowned. "Saying what?"

Augusta rolled her eyes. "*Byron,* only last evening I was advising you to settle down and marry! And *now* – now today you have mysteriously found your mother's *wedding* ring. I would say that is surely a sign that she is trying to advise you also."

He looked at her sideways. "My mother is dead, lying in a coffin down in the vault of Hucknall Church, so she is beyond advising me about anything."

"Exactly," Augusta nodded. "Her body is beyond helping you, but not her *spirit,* not her *soul,* which Jesus told us is *above* and *beyond* the ravages of death."

Byron tried to laugh, but his superstition and his childhood years of being cudgelled by the Calvinistic religion came back to disturb him.

"And what about the ghost of the monk that you insist you regularly see here at Newstead?" Augusta asked.

"I *do* see him, truly, but no one will believe me. It's only my wing of the house he haunts, because those were *his* chambers when he was the Friar of Newstead Abbey."

"And he does not frighten you?"

"No, he's very benign, a man of God, as they say. He just drifts in and drifts out quite peacefully. I have never been frightened of him, not even when I first saw him as a boy of ten."

Augusta was not in any way shocked, because she truly believed that she, too, had seen ghosts now and again, during her younger years living at Castle Howard up in Yorkshire.

"You know how grand and magnificent Castle Howard is? Even the *servants* look so very pristine and grand. And yet, when I lived there, sitting at my bedroom window at dusk – that blue time just before twilight – I often saw different people walking across the lawns, but they were not grand at all, they were dressed like *peasants*. I didn't know who they were, and when I asked, I was told I must have imagined it, because *no* peasants were allowed anywhere within the thirteen hundred acres of the estate, let alone walk across the front lawns."

"Perhaps it was your imagination, forming images?"

"No, because *why* would I imagine peasants? Why not kings and queens or knights? I had lived with my grandmother, Lady Holderness, until then, and I don't believe I had ever seen anyone *below* the aristocracy at that time – apart from servants, but even servants are always dressed in uniform, not raggedy old clothes."

Byron smiled cynically.. "Some would say we are both mad."

Augusta nodded. "I think Lord Carlisle often thought I was mad, and sometimes I thought I must be too. Until one day, reading through some old documents on the history of Castle Howard in the library, I learned that between the years of 1701 to 1706 a local village full of peasants had been lost in the building and landscaping of the estate – *and* lost from the *east end* of the garden front, which is where my bedroom window overlooked."

Byron did not like the way this conversation was moving. Superstition did come to him often, but now he was beginning to feel even more disturbed, especially when Augusta silently handed back to him the lost wedding ring. For some reason, the ring reminded him more of his father than his mother, because his father had bought it – for an heiress, and not for one heiress, but for two – Augusta's mother, and then later it was passed on to his own mother.

"Do you not think it strange," he said suddenly, "that for all his laughter and high-jinks and marrying two women ... when our father died, he was only thirty-five."

"So young," said Augusta sadly. "It was all the gambling that killed him."

"No, it was the suicide."

Augusta was silent. He looked up from the ring in his hand and saw the white spectral mask of her face, in shock.

"You did not know?"

Augusta could barely move her lips. "I was told ... he had died of pneumonia ... due to staying out every night in winter ... gambling." She drew in a deep breath. "So how ... how did he do it?"

"He drank poison."

"And how do *you* know it?"

"My mother told me. She showed me the letter from France. No one had spared her from the truth, so she did not spare me."

Augusta suddenly sat down, overcome with the unbearable weight of her shock and sadness. She had always loved the cherished memory of her father, and being five years older than her half-brother, she had known him much better and for longer than Byron ever had.

"He must have felt so alone, and so *unhappy*," she said, and dropped her face into her hands and began to cry.

Byron could not speak. He could only look at his sister with compassion and love, while wishing he had not been so forthright. But he had not known that she did not know. He had always assumed she knew, as he did; but her grandmother must have kept the truth from her. Or maybe Lady Holderness had not known the truth herself. His mother never communicated with that family, and he had often heard her telling strangers that John Byron had died from tuberculosis.

And now poor Augusta's loving heart and certitude of mind about her beloved father had been crushed by his thoughtless words. Her shock, he knew, was too sudden and too devastating to be helped by any more words now from him.

Instead, he went to find the housekeeper, Nanny Smith, telling her that Mrs Leigh had received some upsetting news, so would she make some tea and go and comfort her. "You women are much better in these situations than men."

And Nanny Smith, in her kind-hearted way, readily agreed, ordering a maid to make the tea, and then rushing down the hall to give her help where it was most needed.

He then glanced at the clock. It was only twenty minutes past two.

He wandered down to the water's edge, stepped inside the rowing boat, and rowed out far to the centre of Newstead's Great Lake, where he laid down the oars inside the boat, and then lay back himself on the head-cushion and let the boat drift where it may, his eyes fixed on the sky as he did a lot of thinking, mostly about his father.

Only now, at the age of twenty-six, did he realise that thirty-five *was* a very young age for a man to die.

And Augusta was right. His father must have felt very

lonely and unhappy to end his own life. He must have felt there was nothing left to live for. Suicides always felt there was nothing left to live for ... not one person, and not one tomorrow, not when all their hopes were gone to dust.

Watching the sky, Byron felt tears in his eyes, and realised that, for the first time in his life, he was weeping for his father. Augusta had made him see John Byron in a totally different light, not as a dashing and handsome rake, but a lonely, lonely man.

Chapter Sixteen

~~~

Dinner was always served at six at Newstead Abbey, in the blue dining room, on the ground floor; yet Byron did not arrive to join Augusta in the dining room, which puzzled Joe Murray as he waited ready to serve. His lordship, he knew, was not a man for hungrily tucking into food, and he sometimes missed dinner altogether; but never when he had a guest in residence.

Augusta sat at the table wearing a cream silk frock and a smile on her face as she looked at the butler, determined to be cheerful when her brother arrived. She had recovered from her shock, and now only felt very sorry that Byron had not been spared such terrible news when still a boy. Now her only concern was to remove any burden of guilt he might feel about upsetting her.

As the time dragged on and Mrs Leigh waited, Joe Murray kept glancing at the clock. He knew his lordship often spent the afternoon and evening in work and solitude and was apt to not notice the time passing.

"Perhaps I should go up and remind him of the time," Joe said to Augusta. "I know he would not wish to keep you waiting, not if he was reminded of the hour it is."

Augusta nodded, and Joe made his way upstairs, but his lordship's private rooms were empty.

"By, this is a puzzle," Joe said to himself, walking over to his lordship's bedroom window which overlooked the front lake ... and then he saw the rowing boat ... empty ... drifting far out on the waters of the lake.

Joe scrambled his way down the stairs, alarming Augusta who heard his rushing footsteps passing the open door. Her hand went to her throat, and a moment later she was up on her feet, also rushing out of the room to see what was going on.

She caught up with Joe at the water's edge, and both stared at the drifting boat.

"Oh *dear God* ..." Augusta cried, but Joe had collected his senses and calmed her.

"Calm down now, there's nowt to fear. His lordship has done this many times before."

Augusta's head was shaking nervously. "Done what?"

"Fallen asleep in the boat."

Joe cupped his hands around his mouth and gave a loud call over the lake – "*Lorrrrrd Byyyyronnnnn.*"

A moment later a dog's head popped up above the top of the boat and Leander barked back and kept on barking ... until Byron slowly sat up in the boat and looked towards them ... and then raised his hand in a wave.

Joe could not hide his annoyance.

"He used to do the same with Boatswain, right back to when he was only a lad – take the dog out with him in the boat and the two of them would sleep for hours. It's the water, you see, when he lets the boat drift like that, the gentle motion of the water lulls them to sleep."

He cocked an eye at Augusta. "Mind, I couldn't do it, leave off the oars, can't swim, you see, but his lordship is a great swimmer."

Augusta, still in a state of shaking nerves, was staring at Byron rowing the boat back. She felt as distressed now as she had felt earlier. The shock and dread in those moments of fearing she had lost her beloved brother had felt like an eternity.

Tears of relief were running down her face when Byron stepped back onto the land and Joe busied himself pulling the boat ashore.

"Oh Byron, you scared the heart out of me!" she said. "How am I going to keep on coping with you and your careless ways?"

Laughing, he hugged her. "Just keep on loving me, dear sister, as I will always love you."

"Where's Fletcher?" Joe suddenly asked. "I've seen neither hair nor hide of him all day."

"Gone into Nottingham to see his relatives," Byron replied. "So don't scold him when he returns, Joe. He's entitled to some time off."

"Which is something I *never* get," Joe answered crabbily. "Not a day nor an hour during all my years here at Newstead."

"And if you ever allowed yourself a day off, Joe, what would you do with it?"

"Well, I'd ..." Joe paused to think about it, and shrugged. "I'd not laze around, that's for sure, so I suppose I'd have to find something to do."

Byron grinned at the old man, and looked at Augusta. "Have you had dinner?"

"No, I was waiting for you."

"Then let's go and *eat*. The sweet air on the lake has awakened me with an intense appetite."

~~~

That evening, as they sat drinking wine by the fire in the library, Augusta again brought up the subject of Byron settling down in England and marrying.

Byron turned up his eyes and quoted Voltaire – "Oh '*woe* to him or her who says all they *could* say on any one subject'."

"It would relieve you of all your debts," Augusta reasoned, "if you were to marry an heiress."

"Unlike my father, I could never marry for money."

"No, but money aside, just think of it, Byron, settling down in peace and stability. No more Lady Caroline Lamb persecuting you, or strange women sneaking into your apartment. And here at Newstead – instead of just having your dogs to play with, you would have children, your *own children* ... sons and daughters. There is no greater joy in life, no greater achievement, than bringing up your own family."

After a silence, a very long silence, Byron finally answered, "If I *was* to marry, and share my home and life with someone, what I would want is a companion – a friend – not a sentimentalist."

Augusta's blue eyes stared at him. "Do you mean ... you are considering it?"

Byron was surprised that he was, and wondered if he had consumed too much wine, or was he simply just *pretending* to consider it to please Augusta after the awful hurt he had inflicted on her today.

He smiled and said flippantly, "It might be nice, now I think of it, being married and waking up on a Sunday morning and going down to breakfast and kissing my wife's *maid."*

Augusta frowned. "Byron do be serious. All that would have to stop if you married."

Byron smiled. "All what?"

"All that flitting from one woman to another and none of it serious."

Byron looked at her. "Some of it *was* serious."

"And now?"

"And now perhaps I should forget all about romance and do as you say and look forward to settling down with a companionable wife and a crowd of children."

Augusta nodded. "I think you would suffer less of your dark moods if you were settled and married. Oh, Byron, *pray* let me write on your behalf to Lady Charlotte Levenson-Gower? You found her very pretty and pleasing, didn't you? So would she not make you an ideal companion in marriage?"

"She might, and if she were to be my wife she also might do as she pleased – leaving me to do the same."

Augusta jumped to her feet excitedly. "I'll write to her *now,* this very night, and get it posted in the morning."

Byron turned to see her already sitting at the desk. "Why the rush?"

"Because she will soon be going up to Scotland with her family, and it will allow her to think about it while she is up there – although I don't believe she will *need* much time to think about it. All I will say, as *your* sister and *her* friend, that when you both spent time together last week, you thought her very pretty and pleasing and liked her very much. She will know what my letter means, but it will not *commit* you to anything."

"Oh well, if there's no risk ..." Byron turned back to the fire, musing. "I don't really care much about beauty, nor about fortune. But I should like ... let me see ... loveliness, gentleness, cleanliness, and *my own* first born ... Was ever a man more *moderate* in his wishes?"

Later, in his bedroom, not feeling at all sleepy due to his slumber in the boat, Byron wrote a letter to Lady Melbourne, full of amusement at Augusta's attempts to find him a prospective wife.

'She wishes me to marry, and is sure if I do not, I will only step from one scrape into another – particularly if I go abroad.'

~ ~ ~

The morning post brought a letter to Newstead that infuriated Byron.

"Now she is writing to me here at Newstead," he said "Is there no escape from that woman?"

He handed the letter across the table to Augusta who read the letter from Lady Caroline Lamb with eyes blinking – especially when she came to the part about herself –

Tell your sister to try & not dislike me. I am very unworthy of her, I know it & feel it, but as I may not love you nor see you, let her not judge me harshly – let her not pass me by as Lady Gertrude Sloane does, & Lady Rancliffe. Tell her I feel my faults – but try &

make her forgive me, if you can, for I love that Augusta with my heart, because she is your sister, and dear to you.

Augusta lifted her eyes and stared in astonishment at her brother. "Whenever I have found myself in the same room as Lady Caroline, she has always glared at me with a *devil* in her eyes."

"And in her heart too!"

It was all too much, a situation, that Byron was finding harder and harder to bear – the constant pursuit and invasions into his life and privacy by Caroline Lamb. There was no let-up from it, no rest or peace.

He wrote in complaint to Lady Melbourne, again entreating her to use her wisdom and authority to try to make Caroline see sense and correct her behaviour, if only to regain her own dignity; ending his letter with an insightful warning –

"But remember, Lady Caroline is a lady who knows how to play a deceitful part."

Chapter Seventeen

~~~

Lady Melbourne's letter of reply about Caroline was alarming.

She is like a barrel of gunpowder at the moment, and the slightest provocation will make her explode into all kinds of mischief against you. Your only refuge from her persecution is to be married, and to someone who knows and is not fooled by all her deceits, such as my niece Annabella.

Sitting next to him at the table, Augusta was reading her own letter, a hand to her lips in disappointment as she read the reply from her friend, Lady Charlotte Levenson-Gower.

"It seems," she said to Byron, "that your interest in Lady Charlotte has taken her very much by surprise. And now she is in a terrible muddle about it all, poor thing. However. she feels duty-bound to send her apologies, because ... " Augusta read the last paragraph again ... "after a number of consultations between the two families, she has accepted a marriage proposal from Henry Charles Howard, a son of the Earl of Surrey."

"Then Henry Charles Howard is a very lucky man," Byron replied, handing his own letter to Augusta to read.

"Although Lady Melbourne is wrong," he said, "because I do have another refuge from the persecution of Lady Caroline Lamb, and that is to go abroad."

He laughed at his sister's gasp of horror. "It would not be for *ever*, just a year or so. Then, when I come back –*then* I may be more ready and willing to settle down."

Augusta's mind was racing to find an alternative, and

found it in Lady Melbourne's letter.

"She will be very upset, Lady Melbourne, especially after all the help and guidance she has given to you in the past."

"Why so?" Byron looked at her in puzzlement. "I have neither said nor done anything to offend her."

Augusta cleared her throat. "Well, you know how gossip flies in London, so I do hope she never hears about the letter declaring your interest in Lady Charlotte Levenson-Gower, *disregarding* her niece completely."

Byron frowned. "First of all, it was *you* who wrote the letter to Lady Charlotte. And I have not disregarded her niece completely. Miss Milbanke and I exchange friendly correspondence quite regularly, and she is no more interested in marriage than I am."

"How do you know that?"

"Because I foolishly proposed to her two years ago, and she mercifully rejected me."

"At the start of your fame? She sounds very wise. If you are so certain she will reject you again, perhaps you should allow me to write to her anyway, if only to please Lady Melbourne, and also to stop all her further efforts to persuade you."

Byron shrugged. "You may write, but she will certainly refuse. She is full of virtue and religion and believes I am one of the lost. Her main interest is in *reforming* me. Miss Milbanke once told me in a letter, by way of rebuke, that the most beautiful words in the human vocabulary, are not those expressed in poetry, but in prayer."

Augusta stared at her brother – a devout Christian herself, or at least she tried to be – Miss Milbanke sounded very appealing to her now, especially as Lady Charlotte was no longer a possibility. A good Christian wife was just what Byron needed to give him peace and stability.

Old Joe Murray entered the room and stood waiting

respectfully until Byron turned to look at him. "There is a matter about which I must speak to you at once, my lord."

"About?"

"About the household bills, my lord. Mrs Smith wishes to make some purchases in Nottingham which I think are unnecessary, so I told her you should be the one to decide yea or nay"

"I don't see why you can't sort these things out between yourselves."

Joe's chin lifted imperiously. "It seems we can't."

"Or you *won't*," Byron accused, rising from the table

Augusta sighed as he left the room with old Joe, knowing that Byron always gave in to the wishes of Nanny Smith over Joe, and that would put the old man into an aggrieved sulk for the rest of the day.

~~~

Later, in the library, Augusta showed Byron the letter she had written to Miss Milbanke on his behalf.

Byron caught his breath in shock as he read it. "No, no, this is too *definite*. All you are really wanting to know is if her interest in me goes beyond that of the religious evangelist."

Augusta was baffled, believing she had written a very pretty letter to Miss Milbanke, but made no protest when Byron took the pen from her hand saying – "In any event, she has always insisted upon our correspondence being *confidential*, so I doubt she would appreciate receiving a letter from my sister."

He moved over to the desk. "And she *knows* my handwriting, so I must write the letter myself – if only to prove to you and to Lady Melbourne, that Miss Milbanke has no interest whatsoever in me as a suitor. And when that proof comes, you can have no more objections to my going abroad.

He sat down at the desk opposite Augusta and commenced to write the letter in his usual honest and rapid way –

Dear Miss Milbanke,

There is something I wish to say – and as I may not see you for some time – perhaps for a long time – I will endeavour to say it at once. A few weeks ago, you asked me a question – which I answered. I have now one to ask you – which if improper – I need not add that your declining to reply to it will be sufficient reproof.

The question is this – Are the "objections" to which you alluded – insuperable? – or is there any line or change of conduct which could remove them? – I am well aware that all such changes are more easy in theory than in practice – but at the same time there are few things which I would not attempt to obtain your good opinion – at all events I would like to know – still I neither wish you to promise or pledge yourself to anything – but merely to learn of a "possibility" which would not leave you the less a free agent.

"There –" He handed the letter to Augusta, who took it and read it, deciding that as insubstantial as it was, it was still a step in the right direction.

She waited patiently while he wrote the fair copy and then told him, "Now seal it, and I will get it posted for you."

~~~

Augusta did not see much of her brother for the rest of the day, unable even to join him for dinner, due to baby Libby being so very cranky with her nanny, wanting no one but her mama; and at five months old, Augusta was still breastfeeding her.

By the time Augusta finally left the nursery to retire to her own bed, she was feeling tired and cranky herself, and would have felt even more so, if she had been aware of yet another letter which her brother was writing at the desk in his bedroom.

My dear Hobhouse,

I have thoughts of going direct and soon to Italy, and if so – will you still come with me? – I want your answer first – your advice afterwards – and your company always: – I am pretty well in funds, having better than £4000 on deposit at Hoares – a note from Murray for £700 – and the Newstead Michaelmas rents will give me from £1000 to £1500 – if not £1800.

Altogether I should have about £5000 tangible – which I am not at all disposed to spend at home, because you and I know, Hobby, that a mere shilling abroad will buy the same as a full pound buys here.

Now I would wish to set aside £3000 for the tour – do you think that amount would allow me to see all Italy in a gentlemanly way? – with as few servants and luggage as we can help.

If we set off, it should be soon – the earlier the better. Now don't engage yourself – but take up your map.

ever dear H.
Yrs – B.

He gave the letter to Fletcher to take over to the hut for collection in the morning. "Do it tonight, Fletcher, and when you come back I will tell you about it, because it involves you."

"Me?" Fletcher was agog with curiosity. "Would that be summit good or bad, my lord?"

"I think you might be pleased, but I shan't tell you

until you get back from the hut."

Now that his decision had been made and the letter to Hobhouse had been written, Byron could feel his excitement increasing. He was always happy amongst the children of the sun; and Italy contained not only song and sunshine, but cities such as *Rome* and *Florence* and great works of art ... and Italian women were said to be some of the most beautiful in the world.

He made his way down the stairs to find Joe Murray, while quietly humming a few bars of Mozart's *Don Giovanni*. He had always loved opera, and no people sang opera better than the Italians.

Fletcher was panting like a blown horse when he returned from the hut – eager to hear what good thing was going to happen that might please him.

He found his lordship in the library with Joe Murray. "It's done, my lord, the letter – so will you tell me now?"

Byron looked at him. "Tell you what?"

"What you said you'd tell me when I got back from the hut."

"How would you like to go abroad again,?"

"Abroad?" Fletcher's eyes popped with surprised delight. "Back to Greece?"

"Well, maybe – but first a tour of Italy."

Joe Murray didn't like the sound of this at all. "And how long would you be gone this time, my lord?"

"A year or so. Why the frown?"

"Oh ..." Joe shrugged, "It's just that I *am* getting older by the year, so I need to know these things, in case I don't see you again."

Byron laughed, because Joe, in his mid-seventies, was stronger and healthier than many men who were thirty years younger.

"I'll wager you will outlive us all, Joe."

Chapter Eighteen

~~~

A grey drizzle covered the earth the next morning.

Unable to venture outdoors to play, Augusta's three little daughters sought out Uncle Byron who allowed them the run of the house – up and down the long corridors with the dogs chasing after them.

With the baby still whining and cranky in her cradle, Augusta pleaded with them to quieten down, which subdued the girls sulkily – until Byron decided to take his three little nieces off to the library – sat them down in front of the fire, accompanied by the sprawling dogs, and began to tell them stories about his life in London.

"One night a few weeks ago," he told them, "I went up to the Exeter Exchange on the Strand to see the animals in the new indoor zoo. Poor animals in their cages, but they seemed happy enough to talk to me."

Georgiana's eye widened. "Did the animals *talk?*"

"In their own way, yes, just like the dogs talk to us with their barks and growls."

The children looked around at the lazing dogs and seemed to understand, nodding their heads in agreement.

Leander, sitting by his lordship's knee, pricked up his ears and rolled an affectionate eye at him.

"In fact," Byron said, "the animals never *stopped* talking and calling across to one another with their comments. And oh – the *converzatione* – but the tiger talked too much."

"What did he say?"

Byron described the tiger – "prowling around as if he owned the place, growling and snarling like King George, constantly complaining and boring everyone. The most beautiful animal of all was the *panther*."

The girls' questions all came at once and Byron enjoyed the fun of answering them.

"Some of the animals were *very* strange. One was called a hippopotamus ..." he described the look and size of the hippo ... "and I must say, to me, he looked very much like Lord Liverpool in the face. In fact, all of the animals reminded me of someone human. There was an *Ursine Sloth* who had the very voice and manner of my valet, Mr Fletcher."

A few weeks previously, Byron had indeed gone up to the Exchange to view the animals, and everything he said to the girls was true.

"One of the star attractions was an Indian elephant, who was eleven foot tall, and named *Chunee*. The elephant took my money and gave it back to me again – took off my hat – opened a door – trunked a whip – and behaved so well that I wished he was my butler."

Augusta could hear the children's laughter as she approached the library, pausing in her steps to stand and listen ... she could hear Georgiana's voice raised in a question followed by excited questions from the younger two ... all sounded engrossed and fully occupied, which induced in her a feeling of sheer relief.

As tired as she felt, and unable to resist taking this opportunity, she quietly turned and made her way back down the corridor towards her own room, where she kicked off her shoes and lay down on her bed to grab a short rest.

"A few minutes sleep is all I need," she muttered as her eyes closed, "just a few quiet minutes is all ..."

Chapter Nineteen

~~~

The next morning, when he awoke, Byron could see that the long summer had finally reached its end. Rain and wind were lashing his window and there was a sharp chill in the air of his room.

He lay in his bed, listening to the wind, and thinking dreamily of the glorious sun-soaked islands of Greece. In his mind he saw again the lush green olive groves, abundant flowers, and the sun-soaked yellow beaches. How many times had he lazily swam through Greece's warm blue waters?

Yes, he decided, most certainly, after their tour of Italy and before returning to England, he would insist to Hobhouse that they cross over from Italy into Greece and spend a few months there once again.

But first – back to London. The city was always warmer in autumn than the climate out here in the country.

Augusta was busily overseeing the packing of the children's clothes when Byron later found her. "Are you returning home today also?"

Augusta nodded. "If only because the children are less excitable and easier to manage when they are settled at home. We have all had a lovely holiday away from the same old routine at Newmarket, but now the children need to get back to that routine and their own beds."

"We will lunch together first, before we go our separate ways," he said "When do you return to your role as Lady-in-Waiting at St James Palace?"

Augusta shrugged. "Whenever they send for me. It is only a temporary position. "

"But you always enjoy it?"

"I do," Augusta agreed, "because I like the company of the other ladies ..." She gave him a bleak smile. "At times, it can get very boring down there in Newmarket."

Byron grinned. "Especially with a husband who talks about nothing but *horses* all the time."

She slapped his arm in sisterly reproof, and he left her to go in search of Joe Murray to discuss his own departure.

Later that morning, during their early lunch, Joe Murray entered the dining room holding a platter with a letter on it. "This is for you, my lord ... young Rushton has just brought it over from the hut."

Byron took the letter and looked with surprise at the sender's name written on the back ... *Miss A. I. Milbanke*. He opened it quickly and read the contents, his face turning quite pale as he did so.

My dear Lord Byron,

I am almost too agitated to write – but you will understand. It would be absurd to suppress anything now. I have long pledged to myself to make your happiness my first object in life. If I can make you happy, I have no other consideration. I shall trust to you for all I shall look up to – all I can love. This is a moment of joy which I have too much despaired of ever experiencing – I dared not believe it possible ...

His face now looked so pale that Augusta feared he was about to faint. "Byron – what is it?"

"Miss Milbanke ... she usually takes at least a week to reply because she writes reams ... so I did not expect her to answer by *return of post* – and in such a way."

Augusta was confused. "So what does she say?"

"That she is very happy to *accept* my proposal of marriage."

"What?"

He gloomily handed the letter across the table to

Augusta saying, "It never rains but it pours."

Chapter Twenty

~~~

Returning to his apartment in Albany, Byron discovered that *'Miss A. I. Milbanke'* had not only replied to him by return of post – but had sent her acceptance in *duplicate;* one letter to Newstead and another to his address in London.

"She's making sure he can't say he didn't get her letter," Fletcher complained to Mrs Mule.

Fletcher did not like this it at all, because now their adventure overseas was uncertain. And whoever she was, this Miss Milbanke seemed *determined* not to let his lordship escape to anywhere.

"I don't know what I think," Byron told the horrified Hobhouse when he called in the following day. "All I did was make a tentative inquiry as to her present disposition towards me. No 'proposal of marriage' was actually made to her, and yet she seems to have read it as such."

Hobhouse was not in the mood to be agreeable. "You must have said *something* that implied it was a marriage proposal."

"No, no!" Byron was certain. "I clearly remember what I wrote in the letter and those *exact* words have been running through my mind all the way throughout the journey back from Newstead – *'I neither wish you to promise or pledge yourself to anything – but merely to learn of a possibility, which would not leave you the less a free agent'.*"

Hobhouse had long been too familiar with the extent of Byron's incredible memory to now doubt it on something so important, and which he had written only a few days ago.

"So what are you going to do?"

"I don't know. I have not seen her for almost a year,

since she was last in London. And that's all I did do then, *see* her across various rooms."

"Is our tour of Italy on or off?"

"I don't know *what* is on or off. Can you not understand the predicament I am in, Hobby? If I write back to her saying she has misunderstood, and I pull out and reject her now, she will think I am doing it as an act of revenge for her own rejection of me two years ago."

He put a hand to his brow as if he was suffering from a thumping headache. "I've done nothing else but think it through all the way back from Newstead, and that *is* what she will believe, I know it."

Hobby's exasperation was rising. "So why did you write to her in that way in the first place? Why make a *tentative inquiry* at all?"

"Mainly to appease Augusta. But I did *not* expect such a response – in fact, quite the opposite. Until her letter I had not even a *suspicion* that she had any romantic feelings towards me."

"And yet I did warn you!" Hobby snapped. "Anyone who has read her letters, as I have, could see that she was dropping hints to you on every page. But I suppose ..." Hobby's tone turned sarcastic, "I *suppose* because so many women drop more brazen hints to you all the time, hers was not something you particularly noticed."

Byron gave him one of his slow underlooks, then turned and walked across the room towards his dressing-room. "I need to take something for my headache."

Hobhouse sat down on one of the sofas, furious and fuming. He had been a rigid protector of Byron for so long, but how could he protect him from *himself* and his unreasoning impulsiveness?

Mainly to appease Augusta? How damned ridiculous!

And yet ... and yet if those were the actual words written by Byron, and he did not doubt that they were, then Miss Milbanke had absolutely *no right* to take those words as more than a tentative inquiry – and absolutely *no right* to rush back her acceptance of a marriage proposal that had not in fact been made.

Slowly ... slowly ... Hobhouse began to wonder if Miss Milbanke was in fact a very *clever* young woman.

~~~

In Seaham, Miss Milbanke was already writing to all her acquaintances, bragging about her proposal from Lord Byron, telling them all – *"The attachment has been progressing for two years, and I now admit it with feelings of happiness that promise to be as durable as they are deep."*

She knew this would lead them all to believe that Lord Byron had been secretly pursuing her during that time; and her inherent vanity overcame her completely when she wrote to Miss Milner, one of her regular correspondents who had mentioned a number of times in her letters about the constant rumours of Lord Byron's look of moodiness and despondency when out in public.

Annabella now informed Miss Milner – *"For his despondency, I fear I am but all too responsible for the last two years."*

Upon receiving Annabella's letter, Miss Milner was rather surprised; for now there was a new rumour going around London that Lord Byron had recently declared his interest in Lady Charlotte Levenson-Gower – and that only a few weeks ago too – but Lady Charlotte had been forced to inform him that she had already accepted a proposal from Henry Charles Howard.

Still, it would be tactless to mention that to Miss Milbanke now, and certainly not a charitable or Christian thing to do. Nor would it be wise to mention to Miss Milbanke that Lord Byron had only appeared to be gloomy and despondent during the past few *months*.

No, that would not be charitable or Christian at all.

Yet, Lord preserve us, if Miss Milbanke thought that anyone in London would believe that Lord Byron had been pining after *her* for the past two years. And if she did think people would believe it, then the poor girl had to be a slight delusional ... But that's what living in the lonely backwoods up North often did to people, and who could blame them. The North was a desolate place. At least it was when she had last ventured up there.

~ ~ ~

In her Whitehall drawing-room, Lady Melbourne was reading a letter from her sister-in-law up in Seaham, Lady Milbanke.

Sir Ralph, she informed Lady Melbourne, had now written to Lord Byron giving his consent to the marriage, but as to Annabella's choice, well, what could one do when a girl was so in love, and so determined in her fixation on only one man? And from the beginning –

"I have always known that Lord Byron was the only Man who ever interested her."

Lady Melbourne lowered her eye-glass and turned a furious face to her husband.

"Then why could Annabella not be honest and open and *say* that from the beginning? Why all the nonsense about him not being religious enough or virtuous enough and all that superior silliness of hers?"

Lord Melbourne lifted his eyes from his newspaper and shook his head. He had never liked Annabella, and now he thought Byron must be a fool.

"It's a pity really," he said, "because there was a time, in the House of Lords, when I thought he was rather a clever young fellow."

~ ~ ~

John Hobhouse told Scrope Davies who had told Beau Brummell who now called in on Byron with an exaggerated air of disbelief.

"*You* – to marry? And to Miss Milbanke – and yet you have always declared yourself to be an atheist!"

Byron looked at Brummell. "I have never declared myself to be an atheist, but in any event, what has that got to do with it?"

"Miss Milbanke – are you really daring to tread on such *sacred* ground? They say she is so virtuous that she once confessed that she has never indulged in a *hot* bath in her life, the water always and only ice cold."

Naturally, as a gentleman, Byron was about to speak in Annabella's defence, until he saw the jesting smile on Brummell's face.

"Seriously though," Brummell said, "I have come to wish you the best. Although ..." he added, taking a seat and relaxing, "if you think you may have been too rash, you *are* entitled to change your mind. I have done so myself in the same situation."

Surprised, Byron stared. "You have been engaged to marry?"

"Oh, many times." Brummell smiled. "Whenever I have been smitten with any young lady, I have always made her an offer of marriage before even attempting a kiss – merely out of common courtesy."

Within minutes, as usual, Byron found his mood lightening as he lost himself in Brummell's humorous tales.

"No names, but there was one young lady that I very *seriously* proposed to, and when she accepted I was over the moon ..." Brummell sighed and took out his snuff box ... "I had every intention of standing at the altar with her, until the young lady in question unwittingly presented me with a situation that I knew would make it simply *impossible* for me to marry her."

"Which was?"

"She regularly ate cabbage. I mean, really, there *are*

135

limits."

Byron smiled, knowing Brummell too well to know that all this jesting was just his way of telling his friend that no marriage proposal was written in stone.

"And yet *my* perceived proposal is now written in the morning newspaper for all the world to see..."

Byron showed Brummell *The Morning Chronicle* in which Sir Ralph and Lady Milbanke had been pleased to announce – *The Betrothal of their Daughter, Anne Isabella, to The Right Honourable George Gordon Lord Byron of Rochdale."*

Chapter Twenty-One

~~~

Checkmated!

Byron began to view the entire situation as a *fait accompli;* something that could not now be changed – especially when he received a happy letter from Augusta, who had obviously seen the announcement in the newspaper.

My dearest B + As usual I have but a short allowance of time, but a few lines I know will be better than none – at least I find them so. I want to know dearest B + your plans – when you come + when you go – when the Cake is to be cut – when the Bells are to ring – by the bye my visitors of yesterday are acquainted with Miss Milbanke & they did praise her to the skies – they say her health has been hurt by Studying – I have not a moment more my dearest + except to say ever thine – Augusta.

Later that day he also received a letter from Lady Caroline Lamb, and was almost too frightened to open it. What evil would she be threatening him with now? What new method for his destruction?

To his relief, her letter was quite brief and contained no threats.

You are to be married I am told; I hear it from all sides. You are safe – the means you have taken to frighten me from your door are not in vain.
Farewell for ever oh for ever – I will not see nor write nor think of you again."

Caroline was devastated. In an immediate attempt to save face as well as her pride, she called on John Murray and pretended to be pleased.

"I trust in God that Byron will be happy," she said brightly. "He has chosen one who is good and amiable and who deserves well of him."

John Murray was astounded. "Byron is to be married?"

"You don't know? Everyone else does."

"This is the devil of all news! I shall have no new poem this winter then?"

"I wrote to him," Caroline said, "telling him I shall never write nor think of him again. He is the *worst* of all human beings, because I did hope he would write back giving me some sign that he still cared for me – but no – he sent me back a note written in a style that I assure you quite *froze* me. Although it was superlatively kind and condescending."

She looked at John Murray sullenly. "How has he disposed of all the other unfortunates I wonder? I speak of them by the dozens, you see?"

"Lady Caroline I *am* sorry," said Murray, feeling more sorry for himself and his publishing business.

"Oh," she shrugged, "do not feel sorry for *me!* Feel sorry for the Corsair, because I don't believe he will ever be able to pull happily with a woman who goes to church as often as clock-mice, understands statistics, and has such a bad figure."

"And I doubt that any his female readers will be pleased at this news..."

Caroline could see that John Murray was more worried about his own concerns, which depressed her even more.

So much so, that as soon as she had left Albermarle Street she called in to see her cousin, Lady Harriet Granville, the daughter of her late aunt Georgianna.

Caroline knew she would receive solace from her cousin, because the Devonshires had always hated the Melbournes.

Lady Harriet – known to relatives and close friends as *'Harryo'* – welcomed her warmly and made no pretence of her astonishment about it all.

"So Miss Milbanke's marriage to Lord Byron is declared, and now all the Melbourne family are full of it. How wonderful of that sensible and cautious prig of a girl to dare take on such a heap of poems and rivals."

"Did you see it in the newspaper?" Caroline asked.

"No, I was obliged to call on Lady Melbourne at home, where she *insisted* upon reading to me part of a letter from her niece, because '*Annabella wants her happiness made known'.*"

"And the part she read – what did Annabella say?"

"Oh, praising him with rapture and saying she can never sufficiently rejoice at being the happy object of his *choice*. All very braggish."

"I could tolerate it, even accept it," said Caroline, "if it was anyone but *her*. I thought she did not like him, not a bit, and yet now I learn she has slyly been writing to him in secret for a long time and Lady Melbourne *knew* she was writing to him."

Harryo narrowed her eyes suspiciously. "I do believe this is all the work of Lady Melbourne. You know how *devious* she can be under all that sugar and silk."

Caroline did not doubt it, although she did voice her suspicion that Annabella was equally as devious.

"Oh my dear *dear* Caroline," said Harryo with kind sympathy. "Let us have some good strong wine, for I do believe you are going to need it. Those horrible Melbournes are now going to rub your face in all their rejoicing."

~~~

John Hobhouse could not believe Byron's apathy and fatalism about it all.

"I can't very well go to Italy now," Byron said.

"So even though you don't know her, you intend to marry her?"

"I know her better than most men in London society

who marry their wives. One pleasing look, one choice, and two strangers get married. At least Miss Milbanke and I have got to know each other fairly well through our correspondence."

"So, a courtship conducted through the post," Hobhouse scoffed, "followed by a marriage without any romance?"

"Oh, romance," Byron shrugged, "that's usually over in a week; or so they say. I've seen enough bad marriages to know that very few love-matches live up to their expectations – including the marriage of my own parents."

There was a brief irritated silence, while both waited for the other to speak.

"I have given it great thought," Byron said, "And I do believe that marriages go on best when they are based on friendship and companionship."

"Is she beautiful?"

"No, but I like her looks ... from what I can remember of them. She is pretty enough, but not so beautiful as to attract too many rivals."

"Like Lady Frances Webster?"

"Yes ..." Byron frowned, "like her. Nor do I think Miss Milbanke will get up to silly games with every man who enters her home."

Hobhouse was at a loss as to what to say next. He was not a romantic man himself, but he knew that Byron was *very* romantic in his thinking.

"As I recall," he said, "Miss Milbanke did mention the word *love* in her acceptance letter."

"She means *affection*," Byron replied. "How could it be more at this stage? And friendship often does lead to great affection, although some will insist on calling it love."

Hobhouse flushed slightly, looking away from his friend and close companion about whom he had admitted to Scrope Davies only a few weeks earlier, that he had come to "love him more and more every day."

"Yes, well, I trust *our* friendship has some affection in it now, after all this time. Or do you disagree with that also?"

Byron gave him a quick rueful smile. "Hobby you are my *best* friend, and always will be, I hope? When this happens ... will you be my groomsman?"

If this happens, thought Hobhouse, because he also knew how changeable Byron could be.

"If you are there, I'll be there," Hobhouse replied diplomatically. "Of course I will."

~~~

Caroline Lamb was also beginning to have doubts that Byron would actually go through with the marriage, or maybe it was just all the wine she and Harryo had drunk that was cheering her into optimism.

By the time she got back to Melbourne House and the privacy of her bedroom, she was so wobbly on her feet she poured out a brandy to steady her, which made her giggle as soon as she had downed it.

She poured herself another one – holding up the glass as if in a toast and declaring to her reflection in the long mirror – "So that hideous Milbanke female, that tight-lipped sly-eyed sanctimonious prude who is now looking forward to becoming *Lady Byron,* has told the Corsair that she too spends some of her time writing poetry, did she? Well, by golly, so do I!"

She staggered over to her escritoire, knocked back her brandy, and sat down to write a poem, and when it was finished, she considered it so marvellous she sealed it in a cover and then rang for Dotty, her maid.

When the maid entered the room Caroline put her finger to her lips and made a "shush" sound to let Dotty know she was sharing a secret. "I want you to slip out straight away and deliver this straight away to the *Morning Herald."*

"Straight away, Lady Caroline?

"Yes, because I want it published in tomorrow morning's edition. It's a ..." Caroline tried to think up something... "It's a *party* I am planning in honour of Lady Melbourne and I want everyone to come to it."

Dotty smiled. "I'll take it straight away, my lady."

"To the *Herald* remember – not the *Morning Chronicle*. I hate that rag and will *never* read it again."

"Very good, my lady."

"Oh, and Dotty ..." The girl turned at the door. "Do not ever mention this delivery to anyone else in the household, and especially not to Lady Melbourne."

"No, my lady."

"Because, I must confess, I am beginning to *not trust* you, Dotty. And if word of this ever gets out to anyone in this house, you will be dismissed and out on the street quicker than you can say Lord Almighty."

The girl's face reddened. "If it's about the letter to Mr Murray, my lady, then I –"

"Oh stop dawdling, Dotty, and go. If you keep my secret I may start trusting you again."

Dotty turned and left the room as fast as her legs would take her, ready to sprint all the way to the offices of the *Herald*.

Caroline poured another brandy and started to giggle again. "Oh to be a fly on the wall and see the Corsair's face when he reads *that*. And if he thinks Annabella wrote it – as most will – he will be furious with her for such public smugness.

The following day, the *Morning Herald* published a poem written by a female who gave her name only as "Miss M-(LB)-K" and many did believe that it had been written by Miss Milbanke.

To Childe Harold

Pray! Let a jealous rival strive in vain
To draw him, sated, back to lawless joys.
For firmly are our youthful hearts betrothed,

And our congenial souls fast bound in one!
Now since a spark of his poetic fire
Hath caught my glowing soul, I will become
Love's proxy for his Ninth prolific Muse,
And yield to him every ninth revolving Moon
A sweet Childe Harold to delight his Sire!

Byron had stopped reading the morning papers, because they always gave him bad news. If he was not written about in one as the "*villain*" of the day, he was praised in another as an "idol" of the day.. All slush or gush and he had stopped reading all of them, so the poem passed him by without notice.

~~~

In Mayfield Cottage in Derbyshire, Thomas Moore received a letter from Byron, which more than surprised him.

My dear Moore – I am to be married, that is, I have been accepted! Miss Milbanke is the lady, and I have now received her father's instruction to proceed there.

She is said to be an heiress, but of that I really know nothing certainly, and shall not enquire. But I do know that she has talents and excellent qualities.

I certainly did not dream she was attached to me, which it seems she has been for some time. I also thought her of a very cold disposition, in which I was also mistaken – it is a long story, and so I won't trouble you with it.

As to her virtues etc., etc., you will hear enough about them from others (for she is a held up as a kind of "good example" in the north). It is as well that one of us is of such fame, since there is a sad deficit in that way upon my part.

Tommy showed the letter to Bessy, who was excitedly delighted to know that their dear Byron was affianced to such a *good* woman.

PART FOUR

Miss Milbanke

~~~

Miss Milbanke may have been deceived in the expectations she formed in uniting herself with Lord Byron, but she was not deceived by Lord Byron, she was deceived by herself. A little less passion and a little more reflection would have convinced her of the propriety of accepting Lord Byron's proposal of a delay.

John Cam Hobhouse

Chapter Twenty-Two

~~~

In Seaham, Annabella's main concern now was about her parents, who were becoming increasingly fractious about the delay of Lord Byron's arrival at Seaham to officially agree the marriage settlement.

"He was expected within in a week, in accordance with tradition, but now *two* weeks have passed," complained Lady Milbanke, considering the delay to be no less than a slight on her prize of a girl.

"Even the servants are beginning to wonder when the famous fiancée is going to appear?"

Sir Ralph's mind was engrossed in more practical matters. "Newstead Abbey ..." he said, lingering on the name. "Do you think I should have a word with my agent and ask him to find out what precisely it is worth ... building, land, income from tenants and all that?"

"Why bother? His lawyer will have all those precise details for us. That is if we ever get to *meet* his lawyer!"

~~~

John Hanson had in fact gone down to Devon, and the reason why had deeply saddened Byron.

Earlier that year he had been a groomsman at the wedding of Hanson's youngest daughter, Mary Ann, to Lord Portsmouth. He had known Mary Ann from when they were both children, having spent his weekends living with the Hansons while he attended Dr Glennie's school in London.

At Mary Ann's wedding, he had seen nothing wrong or untoward in Lord Portsmouth, other than a man in love. But now, it seemed, he had been declared a lunatic, and apparently he had always been a lunatic. And Lord Portsmouth's brother and former heir,

Newton Fellowes, now had him locked away in his own home in Devon, insisting that Mary Ann had always known that his brother was mad, accusing her of marrying him solely to get herself a title, and her hands on Lord Portsmouth's money.

It was a shocking accusation. As if any decent and well-brought-up young lady would do such a thing. And especially not one as sweet and honest as Mary Ann Hanson.

Fletcher appeared in the room in a state of great agitation, and looked – to Byron's eyes – as much like a lunatic as Lord Portsmouth ever could.

"What is it now, Fletcher?"

"Is it today we are going up north, my lord?"

"No."

"But I have everything packed because yesterday you said we would be going to today."

"Yes, but I have a number of things still to do, and there is no urgent hurry. Besides, Mr Hobhouse is coming to see me today on a very important matter."

"So shall I send Mrs Mule to get in some more milk?"

Byron stared at him blankly. "How the devil should I know?"

~~~

Hobhouse arrived at three of the clock, as reliable as always.

They had been talking for some time and reaching no conclusion. Hobhouse knew that Byron was not in any way precipitate or even eager to hasten the marriage to Miss Milbanke.

Now Hobby was at a loss for what to say next. Byron had got himself into this situation, and only he could get himself out of it.

After a long silence, Byron said, "Hobby, my main concern is that I feel utter repugnance at the thought of marrying *anyone* while my finances are in such a state."

"And yet it is well known around town that Miss Milbanke is an heiress to a fortune," Hobby reminded him.

"Maybe so, but that's not the point. A man should be able to show the security of possessing a sufficient income for his wife and himself on the day of the marriage."

Hobhouse shrugged. "Well, this will teach you not to be handing out your money to anyone who needs it. You really are a fool in that respect, Byron."

Byron looked at him thoughtfully. "I could resort to simple honesty," he said. "I could tell Sir Ralph Milbanke the truth about my financial affairs and make an offer of waiting a year or so. That would give Miss Milbanke and her family the opportunity of delaying, or even breaking off the engagement."

Hobhouse agreed. "That is an *excellent* idea. It will at least give some proper time for all parties to reconsider the situation more carefully."

And Hobhouse believed that *more time* was what was truly needed now. This was the strangest marriage arrangement he had ever heard of. Two people who barely knew each other, and had not seen each other for more than a year, so there could not be any real *love* on either side. How could there be?

Although he knew that Byron was quite capable of falling in love with a girl within minutes of meeting her, he doubted that Miss Milbanke was so casually romantic in her dealings with the opposite sex. In all her superior sermonising in her letters to Byron, she displayed herself as a young lady of the highest purity and virtue, but also one who was rather vain about herself.

So, therefore it had to be ... that her main desire was not only to possess the *name* of being Lady Byron, but also the *fame* of it. Did not he himself also preen himself occasionally on his own small fame around town of being "Byron's best friend".

Yet that was very different to marriage. Friendships could be broken off in an instant, but not a union that was ruled irrevocable by State and Church ...

Of course, some people *did* get divorced, but very rarely, and those who did were no longer considered as being fit for good society. So, yes, Byron's suggestion of offering a delay was the very *best* solution of all.

"Especially as you did not actually *propose* marriage to her in the first place, nor even mention the word marriage. Or did you?"

"No, and to prove I did not ... " Byron went to his letter-case and took out a letter. "Here is the original scribbled page of the letter that was written at Newstead and then sent to her in fair copy – the exact words."

Hobhouse read through the scribbled page and had to agree. "It's an intriguing letter for a young lady to receive, yet nothing more than a guarded inquiry as to her feelings towards you ... there is nothing here to indicate a definite proposal."

"So shall I offer a delay of a year or two – due to my finances?"

"Yes, and when her father learns of your poverty, he will no doubt send you packing as a cad and a fortune hunter."

Hobhouse had to grin at his own use of the words about Byron's *poverty* – a man who possessed great assets in his estate and land and also from the proceeds of his successful poetry.

"I should go up there soon, though," Hobhouse advised. "Otherwise John Hanson will be up there before you, signing your life away."

"No he damn well won't!" Byron replied. "Hanson finally lost the right to do that when I reached the age of twenty-one."

Chapter Twenty-Three

~ ~ ~

The next morning Byron prepared to leave London and travel up to Seaham, ushering his dog inside the carriage while Fletcher climbed up top to sit on the bench next to the driver.

It was going be a long and boring journey and so Byron brought along with him a number of books that he had not yet had the time to read.

By the time the carriage reached the Great North Road and Barnet he was engrossed in his reading, while Leander amused himself at the window, standing up on his hind legs and staring out at the passing landscape.

To Fletcher, as the days passed, the journey seemed endless. He knew Lord Byron had sent a letter from London to Miss Milbanke informing her of the day he would arrive in Seaham. but due to his lordship's leisurely reading and unhurried delays at the various inns on the way, they were already days late.

A lateness which infuriated Lady Milbanke, and exasperated Sir Ralph who was more impatient to meet the lawyer than the future son-in-law.

And if neither of them arrived – or if Lord Byron had turned back – Sir Ralph decided, then legal action for a *Breach of Promise* case would immediately be started against his lordship.

Lady Milbanke had reached the end of her patience. "It is now the first of *November* and still no sign of him. It's insufferable to treat our dear girl in this casual way."

"Shush, dear, or Annabella may hear you."

"And now all this waiting is just one long persecution for us all," said Lady Milbanke. "Really, it's too bad!"

"But he is rich, my dear, he is *rich*, remember that. Money makes one forgive all."

"And yet I have not quite forgiven *you* for making us

almost bankrupt and in desperate need of a *wealthy* husband for Annabella," retorted Lady Milbanke. "Not *quite* forgiven you, Ralph."

"Now, my dear, you know how that kind of talk discommodes me."

"But what else are we to do?" Lady Milbanke went on. "She had two full seasons in London without a suitable offer. And to send her down for a *third* season would be extremely embarrassing for us all. And what would be the point – when it's Lord Byron she wants, and Lord Byron she is determined to have."

"I'm still waiting for my agent to get me a private valuation on Newstead Abbey," said Sir Ralph. "The sale of that could save us."

"I need a drink," said Lady Milbanke. "This waiting is driving me mad."

Sir Ralph rose from his chair. "I'll pour for us both. A stiff brandy, my dear, that will calm your nerves."

Only Annabella, sitting up in her room, remained calm, and even boasted of it in her diary:

He has been expected for the two preceding days. My Mother is impatient and dissatisfied at the delay. I remain calm with that perfect self-possession which has not suffered any interruption since the time that I accepted the offer of marriage.

The following evening, Annabella was again sitting in her room reading when she heard the carriage outside. Instantly she was on her feet, putting out the candles while deliberating in her mind what should be done and how?

She rushed to discuss his welcome with her parents, resolving that she would meet him first, alone. They agreed, and so it was arranged.

He was in the drawing-room, standing by the side of the chimney-piece when she entered.

He did not move towards her as she approached him, but when she extended her hand to him, he took it and kissed it briefly, in the way of most London gallants.

There was a long silence. He broke it. "It is a long time since we have met," he said.

Annabella could hardly speak, her reply inarticulate as that strange spell that was Byron's own began to silently disrupt her calm and perfect self-possession.

"I must not lose him now," she thought, *"I must not and will not."*

~ ~ ~

In his bedroom that night Byron wrote nervously to Hobhouse, confessing that *"the character of wooer in this regular way does not sit easy upon me."*

He now felt so nervous about the situation, that upon saying goodnight to Miss Milbanke, he had awkwardly shaken her hand in the manner of a polite stranger.

He had always felt uncomfortable with strangers, and Miss Milbanke had not made it any easier for him, sitting in prim silence with eyes downcast and pink-cheeked, while her parents made the usual polite conversation.

And Miss Milbanke herself, he realised, was also a stranger, for having not seen each other for more than a year, and then only to exchange a sentence or two when they had met at parties, now made it difficult for him to know how to open up a conversation with her.

Her demure silence throughout was strange, and had surprised him, for although other women wrote to him full of flattery, this was a girl who had written *sermons* to him in her long letters.

He went to bed feeling miserable, glad to have the company of Leander who climbed up onto the bed beside him, snuggling into him above the bedclothes as if he too felt the strangeness of this isolated place.

So strange, in fact, with the winds from the sea

howling outside, Byron had left one candle burning in the bedroom. He had always felt uneasy sleeping in the dark on the first night in a strange house.

"No ghostly Newstead monk here though," he said to Leander.

Hearing him speak, the dog lifted his head, and nuzzled closer.

"How the devil did I come to be here?" Byron said to the air. "I never dreamed of marrying her. So why did I come here at all?"

And the awkwardness of the situation was not helped by the fact that he had had taken an instant dislike to Miss Milbanke's mother.

"Tomorrow, my dear Lord Byron," the gushing mother had said to him at the end of supper, "you and Annabella will be able to spend some time alone to converse more privately."

But what the deuce would he say to her? He had not anticipated that his proposal – even if he had actually written one – would have been accepted by Miss Milbanke. So *now* what was he to say to her?

And then, lying there thoughtfully, he remembered a piece of advice which Lady Melbourne had written to him before he had left London –

"At the beginning, you may start by speaking to her on the Prayer Book and its contents, and then after a while that subject should make way for other subjects without any effort."

The Prayer Book? He had smiled then, at such a ridiculous suggestion, but he was not smiling now.

He closed his eyes, thinking dreamily of the warm countries of the Mediterranean and the flower-lands of Greece and the Near East ... he and Hobhouse might have been there now, in Italy, or at least on their way ... yet he had ruined it all with a few rash strokes of his pen in a letter to Miss Milbanke.

Chapter Twenty-Four

~ ~ ~

In London, Lady Melbourne was anxious to know if all was going well up in Seaham. She had made Lord Byron promise to write to her daily, if only to allow her to help him understand some of the oddities of the Milbankes and their way of life.

"They are not like us," she had told him. "They are country people who live a very quiet way of life, so you must be very gentle with Annabella, and help her out of her very shy ways."

In his first letter Byron seemed to agree with her about Annabella's shyness.

"She is the most silent woman I have ever encountered, which perplexes me extremely – I like them to talk – talk more and think less. Much cogitation will not be in my favour.

I am studying her, but can't boast of my progress at getting at her disposition; and if the conversation is all to be on one side, I fear committing myself; and those who only listen, must have their thoughts so much about them as to be able to seize any weak point at once."

Lady Melbourne's uneasiness increased, knowing that Annabella could sit in a crowded room all night without saying a word – yet she could dissect the character of every single person in the room after they had all gone – highlighting their good points and bad points, as she saw them.

"Sir Ralph seems a good sort" she was pleased to read about her brother, *"but typical – loves all things*

English but a detester of the French."

Oh yes, that was her brother Ralph, whom long ago she had nicknamed "old twaddle". But then, after such a long war with them, why should Ralph *not* detest the French?

"Lady Milbanke I don't like at all. I can't tell why, for we don't differ, but so it is."

Lady Melbourne sat back frowning. She had never liked Judith Noel either, not from the day her brother had brought her home as his intended bride. A plain girl who had at first appeared quiet and timid, but on becoming *Lady Milbanke* she had become a dominating and devious woman with too much conceit for her own or anyone else's good.

Were it were not for the strong affection she had always felt for her dear brother, Lady Melbourne knew she would have nothing to do with Judith Noel – and it had not been to help *her,* that infernal sister-in-law – that she had agreed to assist in helping to find Annabella a suitable husband; it had been solely to help dear Ralph.

And yet, in her great fondness for Byron, Lady Melbourne worried for him, because she had her own misgivings about this match with her niece ... Annabella could be so *odd* at times.

But despite all that, Lady Melbourne did so dearly want Lord Byron to become a part of her family, to become her nephew-in-law, and so much so that she continually shoved her misgivings to the back of her mind.

After all, although ill-suited, Ralph and Judith had been happy enough. That marriage had worked out very well for both of them. So who could tell, or look into the future far enough, to be able to pass judgement about these things?

~~~

Lord Byron's next letter to Lady Melbourne was even

more worrying, for already he had picked up on Annabella's predisposition to hypochondria, which Lady Melbourne believed was based on nothing more than laziness and a need for attention. What else could you say about a girl who was rosy-cheeked with robust health, and yet was always taking to her bed with some imaginary or pretended illness? But to do it while Lord Byron was a guest in the house!

Lady Melbourne fumed, because she knew this self-centred behaviour was all due to Annabella's pampered upbringing. Of course it was. When an only child like Annabella has grown up in the cosseted atmosphere of the adoration of her middle-aged parents, what else could you expect but a fit of the sulks whenever things did not go her way. And Annabella *always* got her way.

And now, reading Lord Byron's letter, and the tone of it, Lady Melbourne could detect that he was becoming very irritated by it all.

She seems to take nothing I say at face value – the least word – or alteration of my tone – has some other inference drawn from it.

Oh, yes, that was Annabella, always suspicious and always ready to think the worst and take offence.

Her disposition is the very reverse of my imaginings – she is overrun with fine feelings – scruples about herself and <u>her</u> disposition (I suppose in fact she means mine) and to crown it all she is taken ill once every 3 days with I know not what – but the day before and the day after she seems well – looks & eats well – & is like any other person in good health.

In conversation however she has improved – but I don't like her agitations at the slightest thing on occasions – I don't know – but I think it by no means impossible that you will see me back in town again very soon – I can only interpret these things one way – & merely wait to be certain before I make my 'exit singly.'

Lady Melbourne had risen to her feet, *very* alarmed. She was not willing to forego this chance because of Annabella's ridiculous self-centredness. Especially as she considered it to be the best offer her niece would get, and possibly the only offer now. Most of the girls coming out in the Husband-Hunting Seasons were usually delectable creatures no older than seventeen or eighteen. Eighteen was the most usual and favoured age for a man choosing a wife, but Annabella was now *twenty-two* – another year or so and she would be regarded as an ageing spinster.

Lady Melbourne wasted no time. She immediately sent a letter by post-haste to her brother, warning him to tell Annabella to change her ways and swiftly, or Lord Byron would be gone.

~~~

In her room at Seaham, Annabella had constantly been in the sulks because Lord Byron's attitude to her was not quite as she had quite expected it to be. He was not ingratiating to her in any way, and did not seem to sufficiently rejoice in his good fortune of finally winning her favour.

Yet, as she sat in sombre silence staring out at the bleak grey weather, she knew the truth was that *she* was the one who had finally won *his* favour. And it was not something she had done lightly and without much thought, and once she had made up her mind, she had set to her task very carefully.

As gently as a hand moving soothingly over a stallion's back, she had been carefully grooming him for over a year, writing letters of sincere friendship to him, willing to advise and console him in any confusion or problem, because no one understood him as she did, and no one else could be as *willing* to understand him as she was, certainly not anyone in the artificial world of fashionable London. The people he met there were drawn solely to the limelight of his fame, and not the man behind it, and in her letters she had hinted this to him in various subtle ways.

Her rambling thoughts went on and on, until she was interrupted in mid-grievance by a knock on the door and her father entering the room.

"Bella, my dear," he said hesitantly, "there is something I need to discuss with you ... a problem of sorts ... I have received a letter from your Aunt Elizabeth."

Annabella frowned. There was nothing strange in her father receiving a letter from his sister Lady Melbourne. "So what is wrong? Is the king dead?"

"No, but Lord Byron's ardour might soon be, if you don't buck up and change your ways. He thinks you don't like him."

"What? I *adore* him," gasped Annabella.

"Then stop acting so pert and start entertaining him. You know how badly we *all* need this marriage, so cease thinking only of yourself, dearest, and endeavour to be more hospitable towards him, otherwise he might leave."

Annabella frowned again. "Did Aunt Elizabeth say that?"

"No, but she is somewhat concerned about him. Apparently he is a very unpredictable young man, and one never knows what he might think or do next."

Annabella rose to her feet in cold annoyance, thinking this was all very unfair. "How dare she attribute any problems to me? Lady Melbourne has always hated me, you know that, Dad, don't you?"

"Now, now, Bella, she has sponsored you through two seasons in London and has worked very hard on your behalf."

"And it has not been *easy* for me to entertain Lord Byron," Annabella protested, "not while I have been feeling so unwell, which you must surely grant is not my fault. "

"No, dearest, of course not."

"And nor have I been given much *chance* to entertain him when he seems to spend most of his mornings and afternoons out on the cliffs with his dog, or walking alone through the plantation in a surly mood."

Sir Ralph had to smile at Annabella's insistence upon referring to the grounds of Seaham Hall as "the plantation" in the American way.

"I expect he is reluctant to get down to business until his lawyer arrives, and the damned fellow is taking long enough, what? That could account for his lordship's surliness."

Annabella had not thought of that. "Yes, that could be so. It is traditionally out of the question for a suitor to arrive at the home of his intended and make any further proposals or advances until his attorney is at his side."

"Out of the question," Sir Ralph agreed. "Nothing can be settled until the finances have been agreed. But his attorney could arrive any time now – even later today or perhaps tomorrow. So buck up, dearest. Get some life into you and buck yourself up, there's a good girl."

~~~

Byron had spent a miserable week in Seaham, too cowardly to ask for a delay or mention the unsatisfactory state of his finances, not knowing quite how to even start the subject. And the Milbankes seemed to think he was incredibly rich, which made the truth very embarrassing.

He also sensed that much of Lady Milbanke's gushing good humour and flattery towards him was based on the false belief of his wealth, which only added to his increasing dislike of her

Nor did he like Seaham, a drab and desolate place, with no shops or trade, and very little else. A dismal backwoods, which had none of the beautiful green and serene country atmosphere of the lands around Newstead.

Sir Ralph had become a ponderous bore with his constant talk about the coal mines over dinner, and it was even worse *after* dinner when he sat down to play the cello – habitually, every night.

Every day Byron escaped for some very long walks along the windy cliffs, and standing there, gazing down at the choppy sea, he occasionally wondered how he could escape Seaham completely ... but in all decency how could he? His attorney would be arriving soon, and after the family crisis that poor Hanson had gone through, followed by his long journey up to Seaham – to arrive and find his client had suddenly and mysteriously gone, would be too much for Hanson to bear in his present state.

No, he would have to wait until John Hanson arrived to sort it out ... but sort out what? Hanson believed that the only reason he was coming up here to Seaham was to negotiate the legal aspects of a marriage contract.

And then, walking along the cliffs, Byron decided to sort it out himself; making the determination to do what he had intended to do, by simply being honest with the Milbankes and tell them the truth.

Returning to the Hall, he sought out Sir Ralph where he knew he would find him – in the library.

"Ah, Lord Byron ... been out on the cliffs again, have you?"

"Yes, sir."

"And Annabella is a lot more relaxed now I believe. Do you find her so?"

"I am told she is indisposed. I have not seen her since last evening."

"Oh, well, a delicate young female, you know.

Consideration must be given. They are not as strong as us men, what?"

"No, sir."

And still no sign of your lawyer. Is he coming by coach or a hand-cart?"

"I believe he is on his way, Sir Ralph, but before he arrives, I feel I must have a talk with you ... about the engagement."

"The engagement?"

"When you hear what I need to say, you may well agree that it might be better if the engagement was postponed."

"Postponed?"

Byron stared at the wall behind Sir Ralph's head, hating this kind of conversation where every last word he said was repeated back to him like an echo.

"I feel I should at least *offer* you and your daughter a postponement, for perhaps a year or two, in view of the circumstances."

"Circumstances?"

"The truth, Sir Ralph, is that I am immersed in heavy debts, and although I know Miss Milbanke is an heiress, it would be dishonourable of me not to be candid with you about my debts."

"Debts?"

Sir Ralph's face had turned quite pale. "But, Lord Byron, it is well known that you live your life like a prince and provide yourself with every luxury."

"Indeed. I know no other way to live. And that is why I now have so many debts."

"Debts," Sir Ralph repeated, and looked as if he was about to faint. "Debts are terrible things," he muttered, and slowly rose to his feet.

"I'm afraid I cannot continue this conversation with you, Lord Byron, not until I have conferred with Lady Milbanke. She will know what to say about it all."

~~~

Left on his own, with nothing else to do, and unwilling to stay cooped up in his bedroom where he went to get his writing case, Byron made his way down to a small conservatory overlooking the bleak garden. Yesterday he had noticed that the conservatory contained a long wooden table and a few chairs, and it was bright, so it would do.

He sat for some time at the table remembering and humming to himself the music Isaac Nathan had played to him, getting the metres right, and when the tune began to thump away very clearly inside his mind, he started to write ...

He was so engrossed in the images in his mind and the words to describe them, he did not hear Annabella entering the conservatory. She gave a little cough, and he slowly looked up, pen in hand.

"You are busy?" Annabella said, smiling.

"And you are feeling better," he observed.

"Oh yes, quite recovered, thank you. I'm sorry if I have neglected you."

She glanced down at the papers on the table. "Some new poetry?"

"In a way, old and yet new. It is based on a story in the Old Testament, in the Book of Kings."

Annabella drew in a quick breath of surprise. "The Bible? Yet you told me that you found no solace in religion."

She quickly sat herself down on a chair at the end of the table, asked a few more questions, in response to which he told her about Isaac Nathan and his Hebrew Melodies.

"So you are writing the words for his music?"

"Yes."

"May I see?"

Byron hesitated, thinking he should first explain to her, "It is based on the story of King Sennacherib's Assyrian army as they set out to destroy the holy city of Jerusalem."

"But before they do," said Annabella, "God sends the Angel of Death with a disease to wipe them all out before they reach Jerusalem."

"Exactly."

"You see," she said, her eyes glowing, "that story in the Bible shows that no matter how powerful a king or his army, the power of God is always mightier."

Byron was surprised to see the passion in her eyes; it changed her face completely.

"May I see?" she asked again.

Still he hesitated. "It's merely the first page and the first draft. I have not yet made a fair copy."

She smiled. "I would love to see it in its original form. Pray let me see it?"

"Well, as long as you promise not to take out a pencil from somewhere to start *correcting* it."

Annabella was still smiling. "I promise to do nothing more than read it.

He handed her the page, and sitting back in her chair, she began to read:

<u>The Destruction of King Sennarcherib</u>

The Assyrian came down like a wolf on the fold,
And his cohorts were gleaming in purple and gold;
And the sheen on their spears was like stars on the sea,
When the blue waves roll nightly on deep Galilee.

Like the leaves of the forest when Summer is green,
That host with their banners at sunset were seen;
Like the leaves of the forest when Autumn has blown,
That host on the morrow lay withered and strown.

For the Angel of Death spread his wings on the blast,
And breathed in the face of the foe as he passed,

*And the eyes of the sleepers waxed deadly and chill,
And their hearts at once heaved and forever grew still!*

*And there lay the steed with his nostrils all wide,
But through it there rolled not the breath of his pride;
And the foam of his gasping lay white on the turf,
As cold as the spray of the rock-beating surf.*

*And there lay the rider distorted and pale,
With the dew on his brow, and the rust on his mail;
And the tents were all silent, the banners alone,
The lances unlifted, the trumpets unblown.*

Annabella sat back, her heartbeat pounding with exhilaration. How could anyone say this man was an atheist?

"And did you write all this today?" she asked. "Here in Seaham Hall?"

"Yes. I tend to write very fast, and then read it later to see if it is needs burning or merely corrections."

"It needs *no* corrections, none at all." She snatched a few more breaths before saying, "Would you like me to write out the fair copy for you?"

"'It' is not finished. It needs another verse. It has to comply with the length of the music."

"But I can start by writing out the first page in a fair hand. That is, if it would be a help to you?"

Byron considered, and well, yes, it *would* be a help to him. The sooner it was done, the sooner he could send it to Nathan whose entire life seemed to be revolving around these poems at the moment.

"Thank you," he said. "I'm sure Isaac Nathan will be very grateful if you can speed up the process, because even I cannot write the poems fast enough for him."

She pushed back her chair. "I'll get a pen."

"Oh, I have plenty of pens," he said, reaching into his writing case. "I never go anywhere without them."

Annabella looked at his writing case. "Do all writers carry those cases with them wherever they go ... in case the creative muse suddenly strikes?"

"No, not all carry a case," Byron smiled, and then told her of the time he went to a ball where Madame de Staël arrived wearing a huge turban which contained a box of pens on top of it.

"I believe there was a small bottle of ink in the box too."

Annabella laughed, refusing to believe him, but it was true.

"Usually she arrives at balls or soirées looking more modestly decorous, with only a pencil stuck behind her ear."

"I thought her a very rude and dislikeable woman. Do you dislike her also?"

"No, I *pretend* to dislike her, but there is much about her I admire."

Annabella made no comment and took the new pen from his hand, waiting while he moved the ink bottle to stand between them on the table. "We can share it," he said.

He then lifted and handed her a few sheets of vellum. "Oh, before you start ... I think the title should be minus the word King and be simply *The Destruction of Sennacherib.*"

Annabella set to her task, but after writing only a few lines, she was interrupted by her maid, Ann Rood. "Miss Annabella ... Sir Ralph and Lady Milbanke wish to see you immediately."

Annabella stared. "Mam and Dad? Why, Rood, why do they wish to see me?"

"I've no idea, Miss, but they do say you are to come at once."

Annabella rose to her feet obediently. "Then I must go. Pray excuse me, Lord Byron."

When she had gone, Byron's mind lingered curiously on those two words "*Mam* and *Dad*". In the few words he had exchanged with her in London, he had not realised she spoke funny. It reminded him of how most of the people in Nottingham spoke – "*Oh tis grand, me duck! And me Mam sends you her best wishes an' all."*

He turned his attention back to the last verse needed for *Sennacherib*. If he could complete that, then his journey up here to Seaham would not have been entirely wasted. So ... the Assyrian army were now all dead of disease ...

And the widows of Ashur are loud in their wail,

As was Lady Milbanke's wail when Sir Ralph had told her of Lord Byron's heavy debts.

"Then he is not *fit* to marry Annabella!" she exclaimed. "How *dare* he propose to her when he is so burdened with debts. Did you not *say* that to him, Ralph, did you?"

"My dear ... I was too shocked. The first thing I did was pour myself a stiff brandy, but now I think we should both speak to Annabella."

And so they did, but Annabella could not be swayed from her determination. She *had* to marry Lord Byron. "If I agree to a postponement he will go off abroad, or fall in love with someone else. I could not bear that. I want him to be known as mine *exclusively,* and that can only be so if we are married."

"My dear," said her father, "the only reason we gave our sanction to the match was because we believed that Lord Byron was a man of ample and ready wealth. A man *good* enough for you in every way, but now ..."

Annabella remained silent in response to all their further reasoning, sitting stiffly on the edge of her chair, her hands folded in her lap, holding that steady and steely silence that showed her parents she was not about to give way.

Only when her mother appeared to be near collapse, rising from her chair in an attitude of agony and misery, murmuring that she must go and lay down, did Annabella finally come out of her statue-like stoniness and rise also, following her mother out of the room.

~~~

No one but Annabella appeared for dinner that evening, informing Lord Byron that both her parents were, sadly, feeling a little unwell.

"Perhaps its was the lamb they ate at luncheon," she said. "It is fortunate that you do not eat meat."

"And you?" he asked.

"Oh yes, I eat meat occasionally. I need the iron in meat. But today I had no appetite and hardly touched the lamb on my plate."

She was more amiable when she was more talkative, yet she was only talkative to the extent that she asked him a lot of questions, and then sat silent while he answered.

He attempted a little flattery to bring her out of herself ; not the teeth-breaking flattery of artificial compliments, but good-natured hints of admiration that encourage people to talk, to amuse and be amused.

As always with a woman, the wine was making him playful in his manner, and she relaxed back into her chair, no longer sitting stiffly on the edge of her seat. More and more she smiled, and even laughed; but occasionally she looked at him silently, and there was a worry in her eyes and a searching, too.

Gazing around at the panelled walls of the dining room, he asked curiously, "How old is this house?"

"Oh, quite old. I'm told it was a smaller house when Mam and Dad first moved in, but over the years they added a wing here and there. Mam was determined to make it as big as a Hall, and when all the work was done, she named it Seaham Hall."

Byron was amused. "Strange, isn't it, that in the country the gentry always refer to their homes as 'Halls'? Yet in London, all the grandest homes are simply called houses ... Melbourne House, Devonshire House ... even the Prince Regent lives in that huge barrack of a place named Carlton House."

"And Buckingham House," said Annabella. "They say that as soon as the king is dead, the Prince Regent intends to have Buckingham House renovated into a huge palace all for himself."

"And no doubt Prinny will have at least twenty wings added to that before he is finished. He's a man known for his love of ostentation and lack of subtlety. Have you seen the grandeur of his Royal Pavilion in Brighton?"

"No, I have never been to Brighton."

"Oh well, it's definitely worth a look, if only because the style of it's architecture is based on the opulent style of the palaces of the maharajas in India."

Annabella was more interested in matters more closer to home.

She asked him questions about his family, which consisted solely of Augusta, and in speaking of her Annabella could detect the great love Byron felt for his sister, and she felt a sharp pang of jealousy.

"She is the best hearted, kindest, and most inoffensive being in this world," Byron said, "and the *least* selfish person I know."

Annabella listened attentively, but her mind was weighing and calculating every word that he said. Always a quiet schemer, it was in her nature to think more than to speak, and to reflect carefully upon any situation before taking action.

"And your sister, Mrs Leigh, where in England does she live?"

"At the Paddocks, in Six Mile Bottom in Newmarket. Her husband stables and trains horses there."

That was all Annabella needed to know.

And later, in her bedroom, after careful reflection,

she wrote a long letter to Augusta Leigh, telling her how wonderfully her brother had spoken to her about his beloved sister, and how eager she now was to meet her – her future sister-in-law – whom she dearly hoped would be able to attend the wedding. *"The date, as yet, we have not arranged, but hopefully very soon."*

Chapter Twenty-Five

~~~

Neither Sir Ralph nor Lady Milbanke slept much that night, resulting in them both rising early and leaving their rooms to go downstairs and take breakfast at seven.

At the table they knew they could speak freely, as Annabella usually never came down to breakfast before ten, and Lord Byron never appeared for breakfast at all.

Nevertheless, they spoke quietly.

Lady Milbanke was still complaining about the thumping pain in her head, due to Annabella following her into bedroom yesterday afternoon and "*persecuting* me to allow her to marry him."

Sir Ralph nodded tiredly, knowing what Bella was like when she wanted her way.

"There are times," said Lady Milbanke, "when I think Bella's behaviour is like *proof spirits* – not for common use."

Sir Ralph agreed. "He's handsome enough, and dresses well, but she knows how dipped in funds we have been these last few years, so she must also know that we cannot afford to allow her to marry a man with heavy debts, even if he is a lord."

"She has always wanted to marry an aristocrat," said Lady Milbanke. "Even as a very young girl she used to say that when she grew up she wanted to marry a duke or a lord and have a townhouse in London."

Sir Ralph sighed. "All well and good if the duke or lord has wealth, but a title to her name and a tiara on her head won't pay the bally bills. One would have thought a man in Lord Byron's position would have learned to be more responsible with money."

"Oh, they are all the same," sniffed Lady Milbanke,

"those young gents of the *haute ton* in London. They swan around allowing themselves every luxury, every excess, and the traders encourage them to do so by refusing to take money and setting it all down to unlimited *credit*."

Her face sour and disapproving, she sipped her tea, then talked on – "And do you know why the shops and traders in London do that, Ralph?"

"Haven't a clue, dear."

"Because when they do finally send their bill, it is usually for double the amount it should be, but the dandies never notice, never remember what they bought or what they spent, and so merely pass the bill on to their accountant to pay it. And when their accountant no longer has enough funds to pay the bills, well, then the traders allow the debts to mount even higher, because they know their families have wealth and the bills will get paid eventually."

Sir Ralph frowned. "And that's exactly my point, you see? From what I know, Lord Byron does not have any family to speak of. He is completely self-reliant, so who else is there to cough up the money and pay off his debts if he cannot?"

"He still has the regular income from his estate, from the tenants and farmers ... but he is clearly a fool where money is concerned," said Lady Milbanke. "All that fuss in the newspapers about him not taking any money for his poetry! Why, in the name of God, why? When I read about it, I presumed it was because he did not need it – the income from his poetry – but now it seems he is not as wealthy as we thought he was."

"We cannot allow it," said Sir Ralph finally. "The marriage is off and Bella will have to accept it. A new prospect will be found for her, someone more suitable, and we will have to come up with some reasonable excuse for the cancellation of the engagement when we inform the rest of the world."

"Then *you* will have to be the one to tell her, Ralph,

because I cannot take another day of her badgering me about him. Really, it's too bad!"

By the time the clock chimed nine, they were both so depressed, and feeling so tired now, they decided to return to their rooms for a much-needed nap.

Leaving the dining room and heading for the stairs, they were halted in their steps by the arrival of Mr William Hoar, Sir Ralph's agent.

"Hoar!" declared Sir Ralph. "By God, you're up and out early, what?"

"I am, Sir Ralph, but I have to be in Sunderland by ten, so I thought I would get your business out of the way first."

"Out of the way? And what business of mine are you so anxious to get out of the way, pray?"

Hoar lowered his voice. "The information you wanted on Newstead Abbey in Nottinghamshire, sir."

"Oh, yes." Sir Ralph shrugged, no longer interested. "Well, we may as well go into the library."

He turned and led the way, followed by Mr Hoar and Lady Milbanke.

Once inside the library with the door firmly closed, Hoar took a paper from his pocket, perused it briefly, then gave Sir Ralph the following information:

"All I can tell you, Sir Ralph, is that very recently a gentleman named Claughton saw Newstead Abbey and wanted it so badly he offered Lord Byron the sum of £140,000 to buy it. The property is not sold, so it would appear that Lord Byron must have declined the offer."

"One hundred and forty thousand pounds ..." Sir Ralph gaped at such an astronomical sum. He had paid eight thousand for Seaham Hall.

"I'm told that the mansion itself is huge, you see, with over three hundred acres of land surrounding it, as well as two or three lakes. It also provides a regular quarterly income from the tenants and farmers and the nearby Mill."

"So, if sold, it would fetch one hundred and forty

thousand pounds," Sir Ralph said, and looked with amazement at his wife. "That much?"

Lady Milbanke was staring at Hoar, and she, too, asked the same amazed question – "That much?"

*

*£140,000 in 1814 = £8.5 million in 2016 = US $11.3 million

Chapter Twenty-Six

~~~

In his bedroom, Byron had taken his usual breakfast of tea and crackers. It was raining miserably outside, and he felt no desire to go downstairs and be the guest. His impatience at Hanson's delay was now beginning to fray his nerves. He had not expected to be stuck here in this bleak backwoods for so long.

"You do know," he said to Fletcher, "that I have an appointment to meet Hobhouse in Cambridge this week, so if Hanson does not arrive soon, I will be forced to leave in any event."

Fletcher's disappointment was visible. "Can it not be put off?"

"No, it cannot be put off. It is my duty as a Cambridge man to attend. It is also my *wish* to attend. Dr Clarke was always very good to me."

Fletcher had not a clue as to who Dr Clarke was, and his mind was too full of his own thoughts to ask or care.

"Have you noticed, my lord, how pretty Miss Milbanke's maid is?"

"No." Byron was opening his writing-case, determined to get a fair copy of *Sennacherib* off to Isaac Nathan in today's post.

"Her name is Ann."

Byron looked at him vaguely. "Whose name is Ann?"

"Miss Milbanke's maid, Ann Rood. She's from the town of Darlington, a few miles away, and I think the town must have been named after her – Darlington."

Byron had started to write, so Fletcher left him to it, eager to get back below stairs.

Some time later, Byron had finished writing out the fair copy of *Destruction of Sennacherib,* and was writing an accompanying note to Isaac Nathan when

Fletcher returned, holding out a letter for him. "It's from Mr Hanson, my lord. It has his seal on the back."

"Not another long delay!"

Byron broke open the seal and began to read Hanson's hurried note ... "He is still in London. He cannot leave there yet ..." He turned to Fletcher. "So now I am free to go to Cambridge and cast my vote."

Chapter Twenty-Seven

~ ~ ~

John Hobhouse stood outside the Great Courtyard of Cambridge University waiting for Byron to arrive, and yet not expecting him to turn up at all.

And so when Byron did arrive, his carriage pulling up at the gate, Hobhouse stared at him in delighted surprise as he stepped down from the carriage, already donned for the occasion, wearing his black Trinity gown over his clothes.

"Hobby, what in the world is happening?" Byron asked. "The place is thronged, and all for a vote!"

"Which we will miss if we don't hurry," Hobhouse said as they began their walk through the courtyard. "As for the excitement I can sense everywhere, I can only presume that it is due to the end of the Michaelmas term. Do you remember? How everyone used to get so excited at the prospect of returning home for the Christmas Hols?"

"Everyone – except you and I."

Hobhouse nodded. "I had forgotten that. You dreading going home to nobody but your mother, and I dreading going back to my asylum of noisy siblings."

Hobhouse looked at him. "So, what news of Miss Milbanke?"

Byron shrugged as he walked. "I have come to think her very agreeable, but she created a scene before I left – not altogether out of Caroline Lamb's style of scene – which not only surprised me, but did me no good at all."

"A scene? Good grief. What about?"

"Oh, it's too long and too trifling to repeat now. I will tell you some other time."

They had reached the Senate House where both intended to vote for Dr William Clarke, a candidate for the Professorship of Anatomy. "I do hope Clarke gets it," Byron muttered, "otherwise I will have suffered that scene for no good purpose."

As soon as they entered the Senate House, Hobhouse was amused to find himself ignored, while Dr Clarke himself and William Lort Mansel, Master of Trinity and Bishop of Bristol, were vying with each other for the honour of accompanying Lord Byron to the table.

'Well, this is indeed a fine thing,' thought Hobhouse with good-natured cynicism, 'to see a bishop eager to attend upon a poet who has the reputation of being an atheist.'

Yet he was glad to see that it was Dr Clarke who received the honour.

And then Hobhouse understood what had caused all the excitement when Byron, accompanied by Dr Clarke, walked to the podium to cast his vote.

The students in the packed upper gallery clapped him rapturously as soon as they saw him, and then after he had cast his vote, clapped rapturously again in a standing ovation which went on and on while the bishop told Hobhouse that it was completely "unprecedented" for a former son of Trinity to be applauded in this way.

The sensation was so great that Hobhouse felt as if drunk with the pleasure of seeing his friend so applauded, for only now was he seeing Byron in the full meridian of his fame – being lauded as one of the elite alumni of Trinity, his Alma Mater – yet when Hobhouse smiled proudly at his friend walking back towards him, he saw that Byron looked pale and deeply affected, his manner embarrassed, wanting only to be off and away.

Not until they were both inside the carriage did Hobhouse voice his thoughts, and only to say, "Apparently, not even Newton was known to have roused the students to – "

"Hobby, *don't* –" Byron said. "Just grant me a quiet moment, if you please."

"Yes, well, it was so very unexpected ..." Hobby

agreed, and then sat back to reflect upon the event, while Byron lapsed into one of his remote silences, his blue eyes fixed on the window as the carriage jogged off.

The silence continued until Hobhouse decided to talk of something else. "So what caused the scene with Miss Milbanke? Can you tell me now?"

"Oh, she became very upset when I told her I must leave to go to Cambridge. She had tears in her eyes, which totally disarmed me. She had come to the conclusion that I do not like her, and asked me if I was having second thoughts about the engagement."

"And what did you say?"

Byron hesitated. "I was taken aback, not only by her words, but her *emotion*. She is not as stiff and prim as I first thought, Hobby, not at all."

"So what did you do?"

"I consoled her. What else could I do? You know how I detest scenes – especially scenes caused by women. I never know what to do with them."

Hobhouse stared at him. "So is the engagement still on?"

"Yes, well, it *was* still on when I left Seaham ... but then, on my way here I detoured to spend a day with my sister at Newmarket, and while there I wrote a gentle and apologetic letter to Miss Milbanke, breaking off the engagement."

"So it's off?"

"No, because Augusta refused to let me send it, snatching the letter out of my hand and tearing it up, insisting it would be the depths of *cruelty* to send such a letter now, which I suppose it would be. And then I learned that Miss Milbanke had written to Augusta, a very sweet letter inviting her to the wedding, and although *she* would not be in a position to go all the way up to Seaham for the wedding, Augusta felt that *I* should go."

Hobhouse could not believe it. "You allowed your sister to decide your destiny?"

"No, of course not, but there are times when Augusta does talk a good deal of sense. And, unlike me, she can see the good in everyone, and Miss Milbanke is a very *good* young woman."

"Is she? You know her that well now?"

"I know her a great deal better than I did. We took some walks together, where we talked quite frankly, and from those discussions I now know that she is very trusting, very kind, and would simply be *incapable* of doing wrong or thinking ill of anyone."

"A paragon?"

"Not quite that, but she is a perfectly good person. And Augusta is right, she *would* make the perfect wife."

"And yet," said Hobhouse curiously, "as soon as you came away from her, you wrote her a letter breaking off the engagement."

Byron shifted uncomfortably on his seat. "Not because I don't like her, or that I think she is not good enough for me – on the contrary, she is *too* good, and I am so aware of my own faults and failings, that she leaves me wishing I was a better person than I am."

This was all getting very ridiculous and Hobhouse was losing his patience. "So is the marriage still on?"

Byron sighed. "This marriage business is all very complicated, Hobby. Settlements have to be drawn up and Hanson's delay is causing continuous irritation to the parents, especially the *mother*. And as I can't stand the mother, I was glad of the excuse to come down to Cambridge to vote, and then getting back to town."

Hobhouse was too confused, and left too speechless by it all to say a word in reply. All he knew for certain was that Byron was an absolute *fool* in his dealings with women. He had no way of managing them at all. Caroline Lamb and her continuing harassment of him was the proof of that.

Finally, after a long silence, Hobhouse said, "Getting back to town? I would have thought a true lover would have been eager to get back to the company of his beloved."

Byron smirked. "Don't be silly, Hobby. I have important appointments in town. Tom Moore is coming down next week to see me, and I cannot let *him* down, not Moore."

"No, of course not," Hobhouse agreed sarcastically.

"And anyway," Byron added, "a man with a London life and a London *mind*, cannot have his body stuck for too long in the dark quietness of the country, not without declining into a dull sleep of an existence ."

"Oh, silly me again!" Hobhouse mocked a face of sheer surprise. "And for so long I have mistakenly believed that you *loved* the quietness and solitude of the country?"

"I do," Byron said, "but only at Newstead, beautiful Newstead. The most serene and divine place on this earth."

Chapter Twenty-Eight

~~~

Arriving back at Albany, Fletcher set to unpacking the luggage while Hobhouse agreed to take the tea offered to him by Mrs Mule.

"I'll drink the tea and then I must go, because I've really had enough of you, Byron. Sometimes I think you are as confused and contradictory in your thoughts as your late mother always was."

Byron was looking at his post, and saw there was a letter from Miss Milbanke. He looked at the postmark. "She must have posted this shortly after I left Seaham."

Hobhouse was not surprised. He was now more convinced than ever that Miss Milbanke was a very clever young woman.

"Oh, bless her, she is utterly distressed because she fears she may have offended me before I left."

"Lord Byron, your lordship, begging your pardon, if you please ..." Mrs Mule came into the room.

"What is it?"

"Mr Fletcher, you see ..." she said in her slow way of talking, "well, he has taken some things from the trunk up to the spare bedroom on the top floor, else I would not have opened the door. And now the young lady is very insistent that I come and tell you she has called. I was not sure if I should admit her, so now she is waiting outside the front door."

"Not Miss D'Ussiéres again?"

"No, the other one."

"*Which* other one?"

"Miss Eliza Francis. So, my lord, if you please, what will I do?"

"Get rid of her," Byron said with some alarm. "Tell her I am not at home, not in town. Tell her whatever you like but do *not* let her in."

As soon as Mrs Mule had gone and closed the drawing-room door behind her, Hobhouse stared at Byron. "Now *who* is Miss Eliza Francis?"

"She *says* she is a poet, or hopes to be one, but she's as big a nuisance as Miss D'Ussiérres. No matter how many times I politely get rid of her, she still keeps on calling."

He sat down tiredly in his desk chair. "At least marriage would free me from all this. Give me some *domestic refuge* from it all."

Hobby had to agree. "A stern wife at the door would soon see off any uninvited callers in bonnets. Well, I'm off. When does Moore come to town?"

"Sometime next week. I'll let you know." Byron was reading Miss Milbanke's letter again, and minutes later he picked up his pen to answer her:

Pray don't scold yourself anymore – I told you before there was no occasion – you have not offended me –

More letters began to arrive every day from Miss Milbanke, or – *Annabella* – as he was now allowed to call her.

My own dearest Lord Byron, there is not a moment when I would not give my foolish head to see you. I knew it would be so, and think it a salutary chastisement for all my misdemeanours..."

Now that he was back in London in his usual routine of fun and parties, Byron was no longer feeling complaisant about a marriage to Miss Milbanke. But what to do? How to get out of it without causing any hurt feelings?

Fletcher entered the drawing-room to find Byron sitting morosely at his desk staring at the window. "My lord?"

"What?" Byron did not even turn his head to look at him.

"You are not forgetting that you have an appointment to attend a function at Lord Holland's tonight? I have your evening clothes all set out and ready."

Byron looked at him moodily. "I need ten minutes to answer a letter, and then I want you to get the letter onto the evening mail-coach."

His reply to Miss Milbanke was hesitant and tentative, carefully considering each sentence before he wrote it, knowing her tendency to misconstrue the true meaning of words.

So, very apologetically, he wrote telling her that his debts were even worse in their magnitude than he had originally calculated, and suggested, therefore, that it might be prudent to postpone the wedding until he could write another poetical epic when his financial prospects would brighten ...

"To marry or not, that is the question – or will you wait?"

~~~

She replied by return of post, unprepared to wait. She would marry him rich or poor, so her dearest was not to worry. Did he have an agreeable date yet for the ceremony? Her own choice was immediately after Christmas. Did he agree? The kitchen was busy baking the wedding cake.

He folded his arms onto his desk and dropped his face onto them, wondering what to do next? His mind kept changing from "I don't know" to "No," to "It could turn out to be the best thing I ever did."

~~~

John Hanson had received Byron's letter telling him of

the necessity of leaving Seaham and going to Cambridge to vote, so he knew his lordship would not be present at Seaham Hall when he arrived.

Still, it was a damned nuisance having to travel all the way up here to the North when his poor daughter at home was in such a terrible state at the realisation she had married a lunatic. A month or two, that's all the time it had taken for her to realise it. Yet the man had seemed quite sane on the one occasion Hanson had met Lord Portsmouth; and at the wedding he had also noticed nothing untoward.

Sitting in his window-seat of the coach, Hanson gloomed over it all. If only Lord Portsmouth himself had been allowed to personally negotiate the financial details of his marriage settlement, he would have gained a greater insight to his personality and state of mind. But no, with a fortune such as Portsmouth's, the lawyers were compelled to do it. It was a tradition that could not be changed. Besides, lay people had no knowledge of all the intricacies of the law. Nor did they need to know, not when they had lawyers to know it all on their behalf.

The coach stopped at Sunderland to allow passengers to disembark, leaving John Hanson alone inside and feeling very relieved. Only another few miles and he would be at Seaham Hall, where, he would be able to get out and stretch his legs, and then hopefully be greeted with the hospitality of a good dinner after such a long journey.

~~~

In her bedroom at Seaham Hall, Annabella was writing yet another long letter to Lord Byron, while feeling extremely frustrated and annoyed with him. It was so hard to get him to commit to a definite date for the ceremony, even though the wedding cake was now baked and iced and ready.

And being so, she wrote telling him of her very real

fear that the cake might go stale, or even mouldy, if a date was not settled upon soon.

Ann Rood knocked and entered the room. "Miss Annabella, a gentleman from London named Mr Hanson is down in the hall."

Annabella stared. "Lord Byron's lawyer?"

Seconds later she was up on her feet and rushing towards the door, but once out on the landing she changed her pace to a sedate walk as she descended the stairs to greet him, holding out her hand to him with a small smile.

Hanson was profuse with apologies for taking so long to arrive. "Family business, I'm afraid, and quite impossible to cut short.

"Where there is no offence intended," Annabella replied, "none can be taken."

Hanson was amazed by her perfect decorum. So very unlike his own daughter, who was about the same age.

~~~

Later, in his room and changing for dinner, now that he had time to think about matters other than his own family, John Hanson was very surprised by a number of things.

Firstly, that Lord Byron had proposed marriage to anyone – the last thing Hanson had expected – especially when only a few weeks ago, he had received a letter from his lordship informing him that Mr Hobhouse and himself would be going abroad to Italy within the month.

And secondly, Hanson was very surprised by his lordship's choice of bride. Lord Byron was a man of the world, a well-educated man of literature who had travelled abroad for two years. An aristocrat who was sophisticated and elegant. But Miss Milbanke, for all her decorum, was somewhat old-world and provincial, especially when compared to the fashionable young ladies of London.

Was the girl pregnant? Is that what had brought this all about? Her parents demanding he do the right thing by her? Surely not – that young lady looked far too prim for such behaviour before marriage.

And then, as he was tying his neckcloth, John Hanson suddenly remembered what Miss Milbanke from Seaham was famous for in the gossip of London – she was an heiress, reputed to be worth a fortune.

Is that why his lordship was marrying her? To eradicate his debts? Well, if it was, then he was merely following the example of his own father, who had married not one, but *two* heiresses.

He sat down on the side of his bed, feeling very tired, and rather sad about it all. He had been young Byron's guardian from the age of ten, and watching him growing up, he had done his best for him, caring for him fondly; but of course he had lost all control of him once he had reached the age of maturity at twenty-one.

And now, at the age of twenty-six, he was getting married – to an heiress.

It was hard to believe, but then they did say that the apple never fell very far from the tree ... Yet to think that Lord Byron might now be following in the mercenary ways of his father was a sad thing to contemplate, very sad indeed.

Chapter Twenty-Nine

~~~

Thomas Moore arrived in town and immediately called on Byron, ready to cheerfully toast the "*the happy groom-to-be!*" And found Byron rather gloomy.

"Dear me, this will not do! You cannot turn up at the altar looking so grim."

Byron excused his low mood due to tiredness, "Gadding up and down the country from here to there," but Moore was not fooled.

"There is something more, something you're not telling me, and as a married man myself with long experience, if there is any way I can advise you, pray let me do so."

Byron looked at Moore, a man he had a great affection for, and a man he *trusted*, almost as much as he trusted Hobhouse ... but Hobby was so very crabby at times, and what experience had he with women and marriage?

So he relaxed back on the sofa and told Tom all of it: Lady Melbourne extolling all the virtues of her niece – the letter of inquiry which had been accepted as a marriage proposal by return of post – *in duplicate* – the visit to Seaham. Sir Ralph and Lady Milbanke fractiously waiting for his lawyer, and all the rest.

"It's all happened so quickly, like a whirlwind," Byron said. "The day before Augusta persuaded me to write the letter to her at Newstead, I had no serious thought of marrying her. Now the bells are getting ready to ring for us, the cake is being baked, and my request to Sir Ralph at Seaham, and my recent letter to her suggesting a postponement, have been ignored or refused. Even Lady Melbourne is fussing me about a suitable wedding gift."

Tom sat thoughtful, but there was a glint of anger in his eyes, because he knew the instigator of all this was

Lady Melbourne. Even as far back as the summer of 1812, she had been pestering Byron about the perfection of her niece.

And now all this reminded him of the newspaper report of the Irishman who had been condemned to death, and was then asked by the judge of the court if he had anything to add. 'Oh, nothing," he replied, looking round at the lawyers, 'except that by Jasus you've settled it all very nicely amongst you!"

Of course, he could not say that to Byron.

"Do you want to be married?" he asked.

"It would give me the peace and respectability I sometimes crave," Byron said. "And I like Miss Milbanke, she has her ways, but she is a very intelligent and very *good* woman ... and I have had so many *bad* ones ..." he gave Moore a rakish smile.

"Well, you could always heed the advice of our old friend *Socrates,"* said Tommy – 'By all means, marry. If you get a good wife, you'll become happy; if you get a bad one, you'll become a philosopher."

Within a very short time, as always, Moore had Byron laughing, looking on the bright side, and even when they had taken themselves off for dinner, they were still swapping jokes about the ups and downs of matrimony.

"A man doesn't know what happiness is until he's married – but by then it's too late!" Moore laughed.

Byron had already arranged to have dinner with his boxing coach, Gentleman John Jackson, and took Moore along with him. "The more the merrier."

Tom Cribb, the ex-champion was also present at the dinner, and Moore saw Byron return to his old laughing self as they discussed the latest "fancy" for the championship.

His humour was just as bright the following night when they dined at the house of his banker, Douglas Kinnaird, who was also the director of the Drury Lane Theatre, which accounted for Edmund Kean the great actor, also being present, to the delight of Byron.

Dinner was followed by brandy and anecdotes and even a little singing now and then. Tommy was always ready to sing some of his *Irish Melodies* in company, renowned as he was for his beautiful voice. Byron called for one of his own favourites which Tom sang to a Portuguese air *"The song of war shall echo through our mountains ..."*

Kinnaird and the others clapped to the beat, all enjoying Moore's singing.

Yet when Tom later sang the beautiful love song, *"When I first met thee warm and young..."* he was surprised to see a tint of tears in Byron's eyes as he sat listening to the song with evident emotion.

Of all his loves, Tom wondered if Byron was thinking of her whom Byron had described as *"the love that lives unquenched through all"* ... Mary Chaworth.

Moore's time in London came to an end. His journey down could not have gone better. Thanks to the praise of Byron, the publisher John Murray had offered him the enormous sum of two thousand pounds to publish his Eastern epic *Lalla Rookh*, and hearing of that offer, Longmans were now prepared to offer him more than that. So what to do? Who to chose? He would have to discuss it with Bessy.

And business aside, he would have lots of news to tell Bessy. He had seen Byron every evening, usually attending supper-parties that had often gone on until dawn. They had also visited the theatre where he had witnessed the electrifying performance of Edmund Kean, one of the greatest actors he had ever seen. Oh, so much gossip, so much news to tell his dear Bessy, who would hang on to his every word.

Arriving at the coach station, Tommy was informed that the coach would not be leaving for at least an hour. Disappointed, and at a loss to do anything else, he decided to waste the hour by taking some coffee in Steven's Coffee Shop.

Stepping inside, he instantly recognised the familiar

face of William Harness, a young man who had attended Harrow with Lord Byron and had remained his friend ever since.

They sat at the same table to drink their coffee. Harness was a reserved yet friendly fellow, and within minutes their conversation, unsurprisingly, turned to their mutual friend, Lord Byron, a subject which seemed to sadden Harness.

"One of my favourite memories," said Harness, "is of two years ago, when I spent Christmas with Byron at Newstead Abbey, along with John Hobhouse and Francis Hodgson. Oh, it was wonderful; the early-morning shoots, the afternoons boating on the lake, and the late-night suppers. And being the perfect host, Byron made sure we had everything we could possibly want."

"Am I right in recalling," Moore asked, "that you were preparing to take Holy Orders then?"

Harness nodded. "And now I'm an ordained curate in Kilmeston. Although in a few months I shall be moving to another curacy in Dorking."

Moore sat thoughtful for a moment, and then said, "Tell me, why did your smile drop when I mentioned Lord Byron? I must confess it surprised me. You being such a long-time friend of his."

Harness sighed. "Oh, it's all these awful marriage rumours. I don't for one moment believe that Byron is marrying Miss Milbanke for her money, but at the same time I don't understand just *why* he is marrying her? I suppose that's because I knew her as a girl."

"Oh, did you?" Moore's attention became keen.

Harness nodded. "She is, or she was then, extremely self-willed and self-opinionated, and a person who never carried any cheerfulness with her."

"No?"

"No indeed. The majority of our acquaintances looked upon her as a reserved and frigid sort whom one would rather cross the room to avoid, rather than be brought into conversation with her unnecessarily."

Moore was very unhappy to hear this, especially about the "*no cheerfulness*". Everyone knew how Byron loved to laugh, and had always been attracted to women who could make him laugh. A good sense of humour and fun would win before beauty every time with him.

Later Tommy boarded his coach, beset with deep anxiety and grave forebodings about Byron's forthcoming marriage. Was the die truly cast? It would seem so, if Miss Milbanke had already declined his suggestion of a postponement.

Tommy sat back in his window-seat and watched the scenery passing by. Usually, in a situation like this, with any other friend or acquaintance, he would laugh it off with the words, "*Well, if he must marry, then how fortunate he is to be marrying an heiress.*"

But not now. His friendship and regard for Byron was too true to be dismissed so easily. Yet what could he do? He could not interfere on the basis of a conversation with William Harness; although he had no doubt that very serious and sincere young man ever spoke anything but the truth.

Yet Harness had spoken of a time when he and Miss Milbanke were in their *teens*, a troubled time, that most youth grew out of; and so it was unfair to judge people of that age too harshly.

Moore sighed and sighed as he watched the world passing by the coach window, finally deciding that all he could do now was to wait and wonder, and hope for the best.

Chapter Thirty

~~~

John Hanson returned to London feeling worn out and exhausted, and carrying with him the opinion that Sir Ralph and Lady Milbanke had to be the two most selfish people in this world.

"Royally selfish," as his wife would say.

And the sheer *arrogance* of both was astonishing. In truth, the impression they had given him was that no man on this earth could ever be good enough for their precious daughter, whom they clearly considered to be Perfection Incarnate.

All nonsense, silly nonsense. And now, after all the travelling, he longed to get home to his own family and to his own bed, but he chose to go directly to Albany in order to consult with Lord Byron immediately. Pray God he would find him at home.

Byron was at home, replying to a letter from his dear friend, Lady Melbourne:

You ask "am I sure of myself?" I answer – no – but you are sure for me –

"It's Mr Hanson, my lord, will you see him?"

"Of course I will see him." Byron immediately put down his pen and got to his feet. "Don't keep him in the hall, Fletcher, show him in, and make some tea for him."

As soon as Hanson entered the drawing-room, Byron saw his tiredness and sympathised. "They have tired you out – Miss Milbanke's parents?"

"No, no..." Hanson shrugged, "but I must confess, I am rather confused."

"Why so?"

"I was under the impression, probably due to town

gossip, that Miss Milbanke was an heiress."

"Well, that *is* the gossip, and stated regularly to me by Lady Melbourne, but I have never questioned it, one way another."

"Then either Lady Melbourne has been lying to you, or she has been kept in the dark; because Sir Ralph Milbanke is close to financial ruin, and has been in that perilous state of near poverty for the last few years."

"What?" Startled, Byron stared at him. "Why? How?"

"It seems this sorry state of affairs is all due to a series of badly-judged investments which Sir Ralph made some years ago, practically cleaning him out, and forcing him to take out a series of mortgages on his property, as well as a number of high-interest loans. Nor are his coal mines providing a reliable source of income, particularly as they have been failing over the last few years. That is why it became so imperative for their daughter to be matched with a man of wealth, and *only* a man of wealth."

Byron spent some moments thinking. "So how could they allow the dishonest rumour of their daughter being an heiress to continue and become so widespread?"

"Because, in principle, it *is* dishonest; but in legal technicalities it is not. Lady Milbanke, it seems, has every expectation of inheriting some wealth from her brother, Thomas Noel, and they are great expectations, but that is all they are ... expectations."

More out of amazement than anything else, Byron listen silently as John Hanson explained the reality of it.

"Thomas Noel, now Lord Wentworth, married a daughter of the Earl of Northington, but she died childless, although Wentworth had already fathered an illegitimate son. That illegitimate son has no legal claim in law – Lady Milbanke kept insisting that – although I respectfully made it very clear to her that I did not need to have the law explained to me."

Byron nodded, knowing only too well how domineering Lady Milbanke could be.

"So, at present, *she* is the heiress, Lady Milbanke, and ultimately her daughter will inherit from her, but who on earth can *rely* on that? There could be some sort of disagreement between brother and sister, and the will is changed in favour of another. Or Lord Wentworth could decide to marry again – who knows? I'm told he is older than her, so getting on in years, and men getting on in years have often been known to foolishly fall in love with their housekeeper or one of their maids. And if something like that were to happen, Wentworth's estate would rightfully go to his wife - and the Milbankes would receiving nothing at all, other than probably a few small bequests "

Byron was frowning. "Does Lady Melbourne know all this?"

"I have no idea, but there is a possibility that she does *not* know. Gentlemen such as Sir Ralph don't like the world to know they are financially dipped. And Sir Ralph was most insistent that anything said within the room must remain confidential. He knows, of course, that I must discuss it with you, but he muttered something about getting you to sign a Confidentiality Agreement."

Byron could not stop himself from laughing a little, because it was all so *absurd*. "It's a farce worthy of Grimaldi."

Hanson nodded. "And then there is the matter of the bride's dowry. When I queried that, Sir Ralph told me twenty thousand pounds was the figure he had considered as a suitable sum for his daughter's dowry."

Byron was surprised. "Oh, so he does have *some* money put by for his daughter's prospective marriage?"

"Well, no, not in fact. That was the sum he had *considered,* but all he can cough up at the moment is one thousand pounds a year, until the twenty thousand is paid off. And out of that one thousand pounds a year ..." Hanson sighed tiredly, "Lady Milbanke *insists* that three hundred pounds a year must be given to her daughter for pin money."

"Pin money?" Byron was laughing again. "Oh, I do wish Hobby was here to share the waggery of all this. The superiority and smugness of Lady Milbanke looking down her nose at *me* as if thinking I was a fortune-hunter, when all the time it has been herself and her husband who have been hunting for a fortune. Well, I don't have one, so that disqualifies me."

Hanson looked at him. "I believe Miss Milbanke thinks that you qualify extremely well."

"Even with all my debts?"

"Even with all your debts. Compared to most of your friends, you are still quite a rich man. You have the regular income from your tenants and farmers as well as the income from your poetry. And whether you realise it or not, you *do* possess a potential fortune, in Newstead Abbey."

"Indeed," Byron agreed, "but that is a fortune I intend to pass on to my son and heir, in the tradition of all the Byrons."

"Nevertheless," Hanson drank some tea, "for *your* portion of the marriage settlement ... in the event of your death or any other end to the marriage, her parents are insisting that you settle the sum of sixty thousand pounds on their daughter, to come into effect from the day she becomes your wife, and that sum is to be secured on the property of Newstead Abbey."

After a long silence, Byron asked, "Does Miss Milbanke know all this?"

"Yes. When Lady Milbanke inherits from her brother, Lord Wentworth, that money or property will remain Lady Milbanke's until her own death, when the property and income from it will then devolve to her daughter. So I don't think Miss Milbanke believes she is lying in any way when she claims to be an heiress ... she *will* eventually inherit from her mother ... although she must know that her own actual inheritance is still a long way off."

After another very long silence, Byron said, "And if I were to withdraw now, she would believe that my only interest in her was due to the belief that she was an heiress with plenty of ready money ... and then I would be labelled as being exactly like my father ... a man in search of a fortune."

"No, not at all, because nobody knows that she is *not* an actual heiress, and won't become one for some time; but you and I, Lord Byron, in our discretion, cannot allow anybody else to know that."

Byron frowned, losing himself in his thoughts.

"I think the sum of sixty thousand pounds is a damned impertinence," said Hanson. "*Sixty thousand!* Why, they'd be lucky to get even one tenth of that from anyone else."

Byron remained silent, still reflecting on it all.

"So?" said Hanson, after a few minutes. "What are your thoughts about all this?"

"My thoughts," Byron said, "are about Miss Milbanke. Now I think I finally understand her odd behaviour when I was in Seaham. Knowing all this, and knowing I would have to be told, no wonder she was so silent and stiff on occasions, and then strangely jittery and nervous at other times. Her father has placed her in a dreadful position."

He looked at Hanson. "You have not read her letters, but I have. She has a proud and high mind, so all this must be truly mortifying for her."

Hanson sighed despairingly, convinced that Miss Milbanke was incapable of feeling mortified about anything or anyone but her own superior self.

~

*£60,000 in 1814 = £3.3 million in 2016 = US $5.2. million.

PART FIVE

The Groomsman

~~~

'Miss Milbanke was to Lord Byron no heiress, and the financial advantage was all on the side of the Lady, and not of his Lordship. He married her because he thought he should marry her, but not for love, and certainly not for money.'

John Cam Hobhouse

Chapter Thirty-One

~~~

"Never was a lover less in haste," Hobhouse wrote in his diary.

Byron had finally arranged with Miss Milbanke to leave London *"next Saturday, the 18th,"* but Lord Holland's Christmas Ball had to be attended; and Lady Jersey's party; and another poem for Isaac Nathan had to be quickly written; until they finally managed to leave London on the 23rd December.

And even then, to the exasperation of Hobhouse, Byron's dawdling continued. First, a detour to see his sister at Newmarket; and then another detour to Newstead Abbey to see Joe Murray and the staff.

"You are not going to your death, Byron, you will see them all again quite soon."

"Yes, but it's *Christmas,* and it's traditional to see your friends and family at Christmas."

"It's also traditional," said Hobhouse, "that as your groomsman, it is my duty to get you to your wedding on time."

"There is no date or time, Hobby. The wedding will take place once we are safely arrived at Seaham. And no minister has to be sent for, because the officiating minister is already installed in Seaham Hall as he is every Christmas ... the Reverend Thomas Noel Junior."

Hobhouse frowned. "I thought Lord Wentworth had no children?"

"No *legitimate* children in the eyes of the Law and Lady Milbanke ... I really can't stand that woman. And don't you let her bully you when we are there, Hobby. She tried to bully me, but the look in my eyes seemed to quell her."

Hobhouse knew all about that *"look"* in Byron's eyes. When warm it would melt any woman of any age, but when cold it was chilling.

"And I would be willing to wager you, Hobby, that as soon as the wedding is over, she will start referring to me as Lord Annabella."

Byron sat forward to stare out of the window of the coach. The ground had been covered with snow from the time they had left Newark two days ago, and the frost so biting that the servants were having difficulty supporting themselves on the box of the carriage. Not a good time to be travelling anywhere.

"Your manservant and my Fletcher," Byron finally said, "I think we should allow them to sit inside with us, if only to prevent them from freezing to death. There's nothing we can do about the driver."

Hobhouse, normally, with his traditional upper-class ways, would have been extremely indignant at the suggestion of sharing a carriage with servants; but under these very cold circumstances ...

~~~

Numb with cold, they eventually arrived at Seaham Hall at 8 o'clock on the evening of 31st December.

Lady Milbanke was so furious at the lateness of the groom, she retired to her room and refused to go down and greet him; although she was very relieved to hear that he had arrived. They had all feared the wedding was off; that his lordship had changed his mind. Poor Bella had been in the most awful state of tension.

Annabella had no hesitation in rushing downstairs to greet his lordship. Even Hobhouse could see her tears of sheer relief as she put her arms around Byron and hugged him. "I knew you would come. Was it the weather?"

Byron was still shivering. "Yes, the weather. You should have chosen spring or summertime for your wedding. Most brides do."

"Well, it's too late to rearrange it now," Annabella

smiled. "Not after you have suffered so much to get here. And everything is ready. Oh, except the cake. I'm afraid the cake is no longer at its best."

Byron took that opportunity to introduce her to "Mr John Cam Hobhouse – my guide, my philosopher, and my very best friend."

Annabella took Hobhouse's hand and, with deep sincerity, welcomed him to Seaham.

Hobhouse responded with all the fine manners of a gentleman, but never having met or seen Miss Milbanke before, he was now quite taken aback by her. She was not at all like the beauties he usually saw with Byron, but "*rather dowdy-looking, wearing a long and high dress*".

Annabella escorted them into the library and the heat of a huge fire where they were glad to warm themselves before the flames.

A gentleman tottered in to the room, whom Hobhouse soon learned was Miss Milbanke's father. Sir Ralph was red-cheeked and portly, and was accompanied by a clergyman, the Reverend Thomas Noel.

Lady Milbanke finally made her appearance, pettish and tiresome as she kept demanding of Hobhouse the reason for their lateness, to which Hobhouse stuttered out some vague excuses. Their lack of speed was hard for the groomsman to explain; while Byron, completely unabashed, was open in his manner as he charmed the parson and Sir Ralph into laughter.

Lady Milbanke eventually turned away and ignored Hobhouse, allowing Hobby to gaze around the room and see something that puzzled him ... the same puzzlement he had experienced in the long hall. All over the walls were paintings of Miss Milbanke from the age of about sixteen years old until recently ... but they were not true to like, not at all.

In all the paintings she was depicted as slim and dainty, as if the artist had been instructed to paint her that way, much softer and slimmer than she actually was. But in reality she was of a heavier build, and her face was not quite so delicate.

Hobhouse looked at her again and saw that no, he was not imagining it ... in reality the lower part of Miss Milbanke's face was bad, and the upper part expressive but not handsome. Everything about her seemed to be old-fashioned and extremely ordinary. Yet, as the time and the conversation went on, he observed that she was modest and very sensible in her manner, and that alone pleased him.

Hobhouse finally consoled himself with the thought that at least Byron was not marrying a woman as silly and unstable as Lady Caroline Lamb.

~~~

In London, Caroline was absolutely furious while Lady Melbourne read from Byron's last letter to her, posted from Newark.

"As to you, Caroline, he says that now he is about to be married, he hopes you will be better disposed towards him, because he says that he and his wife intend to be very well-disposed towards you in future, especially once you are all related."

She held up the letter. "He writes, Caroline ... *'I can't see why there should not now be peace with her as well as with America.'*"

"Ha! Ha! Very funny. And he is a fool," Caroline snapped, "if he thinks that Annabella could ever be well-disposed towards *me*. I saw how jealous she was when Byron was spending his time with me at the balls and parties. I saw her sly eyes watching us all the time."

"Now, now, Caroline, you must control yourself, my dear. All this vexation does not become you."

"Control myself? My God, I would *kill* him – if I was not so certain that he will probably end up killing himself within a year – married to that dumpy and dull niece of yours."

"Caroline I will not listen – "

"And when he *does* finally shoot himself out of his misery, I hope you will have the honesty to take some responsibility for it, because this marriage, *if* it does actually take place, will all be of *your* making!"

After Caroline had stormed out of the drawing-room, she left Lady Melbourne feeling very disturbed, wondering if Caroline had been rummaging through her private letters in her bedroom?

She must have – the coincidence was too great – because those were the exact words which Byron had written to her upon his acceptance of the intended marriage ... *"I hope you are happy, my Machiavelli, because you know this match is all of YOUR making."*

~ ~ ~

At Seaham, during dinner, Byron had thawed and relaxed into a genial mood, his conversation light and friendly. So much so, Hobhouse noticed, that even the formidable Lady Milbanke had softened towards him, laughing along with the men, although there were times when she appeared puzzled and did not understand when Byron, in his usual way, said something with irony while keeping a straight face.

Yet the men laughed freely, especially the poor parson who seemed to have fallen under Byron's spell and was finding him fascinating. And Sir Ralph had now turned into a red-faced spirit of laughter and prosy, reeling off a string of anecdotes of his own.

Only once did a dark note overshadow the fair mood at the table – when Byron suddenly pushed back his chair as if in fright. "Take it back, sir, pray take it back."

Sir Ralph looked confused. "What the deuce is wrong with you? You were reaching for the salt, so I handed it to you."

"Yes but it is bad luck," Byron explained. "In Scotland

anyway, it's considered very bad luck for someone to hand you the salt ... an old superstition I have never been able to forget."

Hobhouse smiled, remembering Byron's mother, who would get up and flee from the table if anyone attempted to hand her the salt, certain it would bring her bad luck or some kind of harm.

"Scotland?" said Sir Ralph, taking the salt back. "I thought you were English, Lord Byron. Your barony is certainly English."

"On my father's side," Byron answered. "All my patriarchs were English, but not my mother, who was a direct descendent of King James of Scotland."

"Indeed?" the parson looked very impressed and started a long discussion with Byron on the beauty of Scotland; although Hobhouse observed that having Scottish blood appeared to be something of a black mark in Sir Ralph's eyes.

Hobhouse occasionally watched Miss Milbanke, whose face seemed to become more attractive the more he looked at her. She gained on appearance, but not at first sight.

She had not yet contributed a word to the conversation, Hobhouse noticed, remaining silent throughout, but her eyes were fixed constantly on Byron, gazing on his face. with pleasure. Yet her admiration was regulated by the most complete decorum and composure.

Amazingly though, at the end of the night when they were all preparing to retire to their rooms, Byron merely shook hands with Miss Milbanke, as he did with her mother and the men, which Hobhouse thought was an odd thing to do.

So odd in fact, that when he reached his room Hobhouse wrote worriedly in his diary – *Absit omen* – in the hope that his bad feeling, or premonition of disaster, would not become real.

Yet he could not sleep. He had known Byron too long

and too well not to worry. Byron liked his women sensual and soft and yielding, and never once had he been attracted to anyone so stiff and prim, unless she possessed amazing feminine beauty, which Miss Milbanke did not.

But then, according to Byron, she was a skilled mathematician and a high-minded metaphysician – and intelligence in a woman had also always held a great magnetism for him, a strong pull of interest.

So perhaps in Miss Milbanke he was hoping to find a feminine companion somewhat different and more refreshing than other female pursuers who flattered him on a daily basis?

But then ... another perplexing thing about her which was keeping sleep at bay ... throughout the evening when there had been so much jocularity and laughter, Miss Milbanke had not laughed once. Her eyes had rarely left Byron, but it was as if she was in her own world, her own thoughts, and any conversation taking place was of no interest to her.

A strange way to behave with guests, and surely she knew how to laugh? If not, she would have to learn and quickly, because intelligence or beauty aside, Byron loved nothing more than good company and good conversation, with plenty of humour and laughter.

Hobhouse shrugged away his worries, remembering all the times Byron had accused him of *"worrying like an old woman"* which was true, because Hobhouse knew he had as much propensity for worrying as Byron had for laughing.

He finally felt himself drifting off to sleep, but even as he did, he knew his lips were still muttering away at his fears *"absit omen, absit omen ..."*

~~~

In London, another friend, Scrope Davies, was also worrying about Byron, because this marriage business had all happened so quickly, and was so completely unexpected.

Usually when Byron believed he was in love with a girl he romanced about her quite openly, but Scrope had never heard of Miss Milbanke until a few weeks ago, and then only from Hobhouse who seemed to know as little about her as Scrope did.

And Scrope's perplexity was not alleviated in any way by the letter he had received from Byron that morning, posted from Newark, during his journey up north. His description of his intended bride was very brief, as if he didn't know her very well himself – but in true Byron style his letter had been light-hearted and flippant –

"She is a woman of Learning, which I have great hopes she means to keep to herself."

Chapter Thirty-Two

~~~

The following day Miss Milbanke was not to be seen, too busy preparing for her wedding; leaving Hobhouse to take her place in the wedding rehearsal.

Hobby stared at Reverend Noel in disbelief. "What ... *I* am to play the bride?"

The look of horror on his face reduced Byron to laughter, and from then on Reverend Noel could get no good from either of them. "Gentlemen, *please*, we must be serious!"

Both men attempted to be serious, but as soon as Hobhouse began to say the words, plighting his troth to Byron, the laughter disrupted everything again, and Reverend Noel finally gave up in despair.

They were both still laughing when they set off to take a walk along the beach with Leander. It was less cold, and remnants of snow were still visible here and there, but a glorious winter sunshine radiated over the land.

Hobhouse chose the privacy of their walk to finally become serious and question Byron about his feelings now for Miss Milbanke.

"You still hardly know her, so it would be ridiculous to pretend you love her."

"I know her well enough, through her letters ..." Byron shrugged and then confessed frankly that no, he was not in love with his intended bride, but he felt enough respect and regard for her as a person to believe that would be the surest guarantee of matrimonial contentment.

"You know how our system works, Hobby. A man sees a female he likes, and then has a quiet talk with her Papa, and after the two men shake hands, the pair are married, without really knowing each other at all. At least I *know* Miss Milbanke genuinely likes me for myself.."

"And you are sure your *fame* has nothing to do with it?"

It was on the tip of Byron's tongue to say that he did not feel sure about anything, but decided it was pointless.

"Does she appear the type that would be influenced by a man's fame, Hobby? I would say not. And women who are more interested in my fame are the type I have been trying to avoid for the past three years."

"Understandably," Hobhouse nodded. "But also, it's the *unequal* balance of affection that worries me. She seems rather more fond of you, than you do of her. Do you honestly think you should go through with this? Marriage is for life, and not something to be entered into lightly, as they say."

Byron stopped walking and stared at Hobhouse. "You say this to me *now* – at the eleventh hour – when it's too late to turn back. Do you think it helps? And what do you expect me to do? Do you expect me to jilt her the day before the wedding and make her a laughing-stock and a disgrace?"

"No, no, I was simply trying to ascertain..." Hobhouse was full of apologies, but Byron had turned back towards Seaham Hall, his mood changed and all the earlier laughter of the wedding rehearsal had vanished.

They continued walking for some time in silence, until Byron finally shrugged.

"Anyway, it is often the case that the feelings of two people are not mutual at first," he said, "but as time goes on, they eventually get into stride and become equally fond of each other. I've seen it many times. And I have also seen passionate love-matches where the couple very quickly end up detesting each other."

"True," Hobby agreed. "It's as risky as throwing a dice, so I shall never marry, not that I believe any woman will have me, not with my foolish ways with women. And I'm still trying to recover from what happened with Lady Jersey."

Byron turned to stare. "What happened with Lady Jersey?"

"Oh, it was silly and embarrassing. I went to her house in Berkeley Square carrying a letter for her husband from Lord Holland. I was led to the door of the drawing-room, and as the divine Lady Jersey advanced to welcome me in her stunningly beautiful way, I dropped my hat, bent to pick it up, and dropped it again. And then I became so tongue-tied, unable to stutter a word in response to her questions, I turned and quickly left the house, the letter still in my hand."

Byron thought of Lady Jersey, now in her mid-thirties, whose black hair and beautiful face had once left the Prince of Wales crying over his wine with love for her.

"She has never spoken to me since," said Hobhouse, "not unless I'm with you, and even then she mostly ignores me as if thinking I'm an idiot."

Byron smiled, but it was a sad smile. "Poor Hobby, as clever and intelligent as you are, I sometimes think you are as shy with women, as Leander is with everyone."

"Yet you will grant," Hobby added, "that it is *only* with women that I am lacking in suavity and confidence. In every other aspect of life I am known as a *force* to be reckoned with."

Byron did not disagree, because it was true. Hobhouse's main passion was to become a politician, and Byron had no doubt that not only would he become a great one, but also an honest one, and a real force for good, especially in his determination to one day bring about the legal abolition of child labour in factories.

"You're a good man, Hobby," he said quietly, and remained quiet and remote for the rest of the day, leaving Hobby to spend the afternoon alone reading the details of the Marriage Settlements which would be signed the following day after the wedding.

~~~

Hobhouse spent an hour reading every word carefully, and what he read shocked him, so much so that he went in search of Byron and found him wandering alone in the grounds.

"Have you *read* this?" he asked, holding up the Settlement document.

"No, but Hanson has read it for me. Why else do I employ a lawyer?"

"It's grossly unfair," Hobhouse pointed out. "It states that you will settle sixty thousand pounds on Miss Milbanke, to be secured on Newstead – yet when *she* inherits from her family there is no set-off from her inheritance to be settled on you."

Byron looked unconcerned. "When two people are married their finances are shared. Is that not so?"

"No, you don't understand," Hobhouse protested, "and I must say, I am very surprised at Hanson agreeing to any of this."

Hobhouse noticed a small wooden bench and urged, "Sit down, Byron, and allow me to explain it to you, because I do not believe that Hanson has fulfilled his fiduciary duty to you."

Byron sat down. "If it's the sixty thousand settlement, Hanson has explained that. And if it's Miss Milbanke's inheritance, Hanson has explained that also."

"Then how did he allow *this* to escape his attention?" Hobhouse sat down beside Byron and peered at the document in his hands.

"Now *this* particular condition clearly states that if you were to die, Miss Milbanke, as your widow, would not only receive sixty thousand pounds from your estate, but would also leave her in possession of an additional £3000 per annum if she has a male child, and £2000 per annum for any female child, and that would be besides the ownership of her own property upon her inheritance."

209

Byron was no mathematician. "I can't see the problem. Of course, herself and any children would have to be provided for upon my death."

"And that I agree," Hobhouse nodded. "But here is the unfairness ... if *she* was to die before you, not one penny of *her* inheritance from her mother would go to you. You would get nothing from the Milbanke estate, because that is how the articles are drawn up in this document. In the case of *her* death, you would receive no addition to your own income, nothing."

After a long silence, Byron said, "The truth is, Hobby, apart from her dowry, Miss Milbanke will not be inheriting anything at all for a very long time. Not until her own mother dies. And by the solid look of Lady Milbanke, she will probably live to be a thousand or more."

Hobhouse was shocked. "You mean ... Miss Milbanke is *not* an heiress?"

Byron shrugged. "She will be one day ... hopefully before the Second Coming of the Messiah, but in the meantime I believe my own income will be sufficient to keep myself and a wife in fair comfort. Although we will have to live modestly, but I don't think Miss Milbanke will object to that. Her tastes even now seem to be very modest."

Hobhouse was losing his patience. "Byron, you really are a *fool* when it comes to money. At the very least there should be a set-off for you against her future property as well as a settlement against yours for her."

Byron stood up, having heard enough. "Hobby, I am only twenty-six, young and healthy and strong. And Miss Milbanke is only twenty-two – so barring any accident, I doubt either of us will be dying anytime soon."

"But when she inherits – "

"Yes, *when*, that is the question with no answer. Anyway it's all academic and pointless, because with my luck we will probably find that Lord Wentworth turns out to be eternal, Sir Ralph immortal, and Lady Milbanke without end. She grows more healthy every day, so much so that I do verily believe that Lady Milbanke is, at this moment, probably cutting a fresh set of teeth in readiness for the next sixty years."

"But there are legal *rules* about these things that one must consider," Hobby insisted. "Contracts cannot be all one-sided to the benefit of one and the detriment of the other. And I still say Hanson has handled this very weakly."

"Probably because he has more important personal matters to deal with at present. Are you forgetting his poor daughter married a lunatic? And if *you* keep nagging me, Miss Milbanke might end up making the same complaint."

"Nevertheless, Hanson should have –"

"No! Not another word more from you about this, Hobby, because I have more important things to think about."

"Such as?"

"A new Jewish poem for Isaac Nathan. I have nothing else to do, so I may as well engage my thoughts in some poetry."

"Poetry?" Hobhouse stood up in a huff; all his warnings had been futile. "Well I'm off. I have some more *realistic* things to do than write poetry. I'll see you this evening at dinner."

Byron stood watching him go, and then continued wandering alone through the grounds, resuming his thoughts. Before Hobhouse had arrived, he had not been thinking of poetry, but of Mary Chaworth ... dear Mary ... if he had not loved Mary first ... still, that too was pointless now.

Yet, as with all his emotions, poetry invaded. He returned to his room and within an hour had written with passion ... *Herod's Lament for Mariamne.*

Chapter Thirty-Three

~ ~ ~

On the morning of 2nd January 1815, the Reverend Mr Wallace, Rector of Seaham, arrived at Seaham Hall to assist Reverend Noel with the Canonicals. The wedding was to take place in the drawing-room at eleven o'clock.

Hobhouse, in full dress and white gloves, went downstairs in readiness to do his duty as groomsman, until he was told the groom could not be found.

"Mr Hobhouse," whispered Fletcher, "I've searched everywhere for his lordship but he's vanished like the morning fog."

Hobhouse, so used to Byron's ways, headed outside and found him, wrapped in his cloak, wandering alone through the grounds.

"Byron?"

Byron slowly turned to him, his face so pale he looked ill.

"My dear fellow ... you look close to death!"

Byron shook his head, as if he did not understand it himself. "This morning, Hobby, I woke up, and the most melancholy feelings spread through me at seeing my wedding suit spread out before me ... and the realisation that I was actually about to be – *married*."

"I'm sure all grooms feel like that on the day. It's probably mere nerves."

"Mere nerves?" After a long silence, Byron nodded, and they began the walk back to the house.

Once inside, they ascended up to the drawing-room where Lady Milbanke, Sir Ralph and the two Reverends were waiting for them.

Hobhouse looked around the large room and saw that no guests had arrived yet, none at all. Strange. Perhaps they would be attending solely for the wedding breakfast or the reception afterwards.

Byron looked splendid, wearing a dark blue suit, white embroidered waistcoat and white frilled shirt; and now that he was in position, Miss Milbanke entered the room, followed by her governess who appeared tearfully affected.

Miss Milbanke was dressed in a plain muslin gown trimmed with lace at the bottom and a white muslin jacket. She wore no headdress, and in Hobhouse's opinion, she looked very plain indeed. Other brides he had seen were dressed to look like angels or floating princesses, but that was clearly not Miss Milbanke's style.

Hobhouse turned away, lowering his head, feeling unhappy with himself that he should be thinking such unflattering thoughts about Miss Milbanke. It was not his way to think meanly about people, not his normal code of decency; but he was still finding it difficult to forgive Miss Milbanke for the deceitful way she had seized upon Lord Byron's letter of inquiry and invented it into a definite marriage proposal.

Reverend Noel was now speaking.

Cushions had been arranged and the couple knelt before Reverend Noel who officiated, while Reverend Mr Wallace read the responses.

Hobhouse' eyes were still on Miss Milbanke who had turned her face to look steadfastly at Byron, remaining as firm as a rock throughout the ceremony, her voice clear and distinct; but Byron hitched at first, beginning very softly and hesitantly ... "I, George Gordon Lord Byron ..."

And then it was over, the register signed, and Miss Milbanke went off to change into her travelling dress.

In all his life Hobhouse had never attended such a paltry wedding. There was to be no wedding breakfast, no reception, and no guests except himself. This filled him with a strange outrage against Sir Ralph and Lady Milbanke as parents of the bride. Were they not sensitive or aware of the correct behaviour towards a man's rank? Their new son-in-law was a peer of the realm, and as such, Lord Byron deserved something more hospitable on his wedding day.

Yet Lady Milbanke seemed quite emotional as she kissed her daughter, and then Byron on the cheek, and Sir Ralph cheerfully shook Byron's hand and congratulated him.

Byron turned to Hobhouse, looking as if he had just awoken from a long sleep. Hobby was so filled with a mixture of troubling emotions, the only words he could utter were "My dear friend," and hugged him.

Miss Milbanke returned in a slate satin travelling dress. Hobhouse was given the duty of handing her downstairs to the carriage.

Hobhouse agreeably held out his arm to her, saying politely, "Miss Milbanke."

"She is *Baroness Byron* now," declared Lady Milbanke in a chuckling rebuke to Hobhouse. "So from now on you must address her as Lady Byron."

"Just so," said Hobhouse, and proceeded to escort Lady Byron down the stairs, followed by Lord Byron who was handing down Lady Milbanke, followed by Sir Ralph and the two Reverends.

At the open carriage door, Hobhouse stepped back a pace, and wished the bride "a happy life."

"If I am not happy," Annabella replied smiling, "it will be my own fault."

Now it was Byron's duty to hand her up into the carriage and he, too, called her "Miss Milbanke," and also received a rebuke from her mother. "She is now your *Lady Byron,* my lord. Pray remember it."

Fletcher climbed up onto the box with Leander, and it was time to go.

Of his dearest friend, Hobhouse took a melancholy leave. The two had come a long way together over the years, from the studious rooms of Cambridge University, to trekking through wild and dangerous parts of Albania and Turkey, and now Byron was travelling on with his bride into the unknown world of wedlock.

Through the carriage window, Byron suddenly grasped Hobby's hand in farewell again, and even when the carriage began to move, Byron seemed unwilling to let Hobby's hand go – as if desperately wishing to cling on to his life in the past – instead of the uncertain future.

All Hobhouse could do was to wish him happiness, and sincerely so; and Byron reluctantly released his hold as the carriage rolled off, and then was eventually lost to sight.

"Well now, didn't she behave well!" said Lady Milbanke, as if she was a mother speaking of her young child.

"Oh, perfect," Sir Ralph agreed.

Hobhouse took out his fob-watch ... it was not yet noon. Less than an hour since the wedding had begun, and already it was all over, the newlyweds packed off in a carriage to some place in Yorkshire owned by Lord Wentworth.

Hobhouse returned to his room, determined to leave Seaham straight away, yet he felt rather unwell, and had to sit down, close to tears.

His valet noticed and asked with concern, "Are you feeling all right, sir?"

"Yes ... just leave me alone for a few minutes, will you?" Hobby said quietly. "Then we must leave for London as soon as possible."

After his valet had left him alone, Hobhouse did shed a tear or two, and could not understand why, until he took out his private diary, the receptacle of all his true thoughts, and wrote: "*I feel as though I have just buried a friend.*"

PART SIX

Wedlock

~~~

"He was good then, not like he became after."

Lady Caroline Lamb

Chapter Thirty-Four

~ ~ ~

"Seriously, I will endeavour to make your niece happy."

When Lady Melbourne announced that Lord Byron had now married Annabella Milbanke, Caroline Lamb knew that her dream of an elopement with him had come to an end, and suffered a series of fainting fits.

A few days later, when Lady Melbourne read out a letter from Byron stating, *"Annabella and I go on extremely well,"* Caroline staggered from the room complaining of blurred vision, resulting in the doctor being called.

"I think her good resolutions seem to be ebbing," Lady Melbourne wrote back to Byron. *"Last night she injured herself upon Annabella's name being mentioned."*

Only one person consoled Lady Caroline, and that was Byron's publisher, John Murray, who genuinely felt sorry for her. He assured Caroline gently that her pain would pass.

"Oh, will it?" she snapped back. "Do you know my heart so well?"

"I know that *all* pain, any pain, even that of the heart, does pass eventually."

"Then you don't know my heart at all," Caroline whispered, wiping at the tears in her eyes. "You still don't understand and you never will..." she continued in a sad voice, "You see ... I loved him as no woman ever could love him because I am not like them, but more like an animal that sees no crime in loving and following its master ... he became such to me ... master of my soul more than anything else."

John Murray suspected that her soul had very little to do with it, but there was nothing more he could say to help her. All he knew with certainty was that Lady Caroline's adoration of Byron was simply not normal. It was a mania that fully ruled her, and, he feared, would ultimately ruin her.

~~~

After two weeks honeymoon at Halnaby Hall in Yorkshire, the newlyweds returned to Seaham to spend another few weeks with Annabella's parents.

Byron made the best of it, endeavouring to fit in and comply in every way; but due to the consequence of him being a man – and therefore being left alone every evening after dinner with Sir Ralph and his brandy – his boredom was almost suffocating. He explained why in a letter to Thomas Moore:

Upon this dreary coast, we have nothing but county meetings and shipwrecks. My new papa, Sir Ralpho, hath recently made a speech at a Durham tax-meeting; and not only at Durham, but here, several times, after dinner. He is now, I believe, speaking it to himself (I left him in the middle) over various decanters which can neither interrupt him nor make him fall asleep, – as might possibly have been the case with some of his audience.

So you want to know about milady and me? Well, I like Annabella –"

Annabella herself interrupted him, coming into the room. She had detected his boredom with Seaham, and had now decided on the only solution – moving down to London.

"I think you will find more entertainment down in London which would suit you better."

Well yes, it would – the entertainment of being near his friends again – but now that he was married with a wife to support, it was simply out of the question.

"The rooms at Albany are solely for gentlemen," he told her. "No married couples allowed. So we could not lodge there. Besides, we agreed that we would confine ourselves to a more modest living in the country."

Annabella had refused the suggestion of living at Newstead Abbey, insisting it was simply too big for two people – a former monastery which was reputed to contain a ghost – and upon learning of this refusal in a letter from Byron at Halnaby Hall, John Hanson had immediately replied to Byron offering the newlyweds his empty country house at Farleigh in Hampshire for as long as they wished.

"We may as well live here, as live in Hampshire," reasoned Annabella, never having seen Hampshire. "And, dearest, I don't believe the dullness of country life would content you for long."

Nevertheless, Byron was reluctant to consider the expense of a house in London; until a few days later when another letter arrived from John Hanson.

Hanson's letter was full of apologies and regrets, due to the increasing legal disputes surrounding his daughter's marriage to Lord Portsmouth, which now made the availability of the house in Hampshire uncertain as his daughter may need it for her own future residence.

Byron was disappointed, but Annabella was relieved. "Shall I write to my aunt asking her to find a little house for us in London?"

Byron was thoughtful. "No, if we must rent a house in London then I prefer to write to Hobhouse. He knows the kind of windows I like, bright rooms and all that. He also knows my budget."

Having written to Hobhouse, Byron was anxious to get down to London himself. He needed to sort out his financial affairs and attend to other business.

"If you are going to London," said Annabella, "then I must go with you."

Byron stared at her. "Why?"

She looked at him patiently. "Because, dearest, I am your wife."

"That does not mean you have to accompany me on *business*. Few wives do that. And besides, I can't simply leave it all to Hobhouse."

The truth was that he was not used to walking every step with a wife in tow.

"I will be back as soon as my business is done and all arrangements for a house are secured."

Annabella was having none of it, refusing to allow him to travel alone.

"Annabella, it is February," he protested, "the dead of winter and freezing, so you would be far more comfortable remaining here in the warmth with your parents instead of spending days on the road in a cold carriage."

But no matter what he said, Annabella remained inflexible in her stubborn determination to go with him.

"Could we not make a small detour on the way and call in to see your sister at Newmarket?" she asked. "It's about time I met *your* family."

"Augusta?" Byron was nonplussed. "No, no, there is no room. You don't understand, Augusta's house is a very *small* house and is filled with children and maids and noise all day long. And Augusta gets very flustered with strangers, especially strangers entering her home with the intention of staying overnight."

Annabella smiled at him with great patience. "But I am not a stranger, am I? Augusta and I are now *sisters*. And, you know, we have been writing quite frequently to each since the engagement, so I feel we already know each other very well."

In the end Byron yielded to her persuasion, but only on the condition that he be allowed to write to Augusta to ask permission first, which would mean a further delay of a week or so to send the letter and receive a reply.

In the interim he spent much of the time moping along the gritty beach, staring over the sea to the horizon, consoling himself with thoughts of poor Napoleon on the Isle of Elba – once an emperor, now a prisoner. Surely they allowed him out on his own occasionally? And if they did, was Napoleon also moping in a solitary walk along the bleak winter shores of Elba now?

~~~

Augusta's reply was as Byron expected – full of panic. Her house was too *small* for more than one visitor, only one spare room which was full of clutter, and at present she was short of money and could not afford the expenditure of entertaining anyone. Could they not rent somewhere in the neighbourhood where they would be more comfortable? No, probably not, as she now remembered that there was nowhere suitable nearby ...

Reading her hasty rambling words, Byron was not surprised when Augusta finally ended her letter with her usual good grace and agreement, saying she would try and rearrange her inadequate home in the hope of making their visit as comfortable as possible.

Despite all these problems, Annabella received the news with a smile, pleased to know that she was going to meet her husband's beloved sister at last; while Byron resented her lack of sensitivity to his sister's uncomfortable predicament.

Any other woman would have understood and put off the meeting until Augusta could visit them in London – and as Augusta spent two weeks out of every six weeks at St James's Palace in London, surely Annabella knew that meeting would come soon enough?

~~~

In London, Hobhouse's surprise upon receiving Byron's request had put him in a dither.

Firstly, because Byron and his lady living in London was the *last* thing he had expected – imagining himself making regular visits down to Hampshire or up to Newstead. And secondly – he had no idea what kind of a house to look for in London, or at what cost?

Knowing Byron's financial situation, Hobhouse did not believe he could afford to rent *any* house in London, especially as he was already paying a high rent for his rooms in Albany Court, which he had leased from Lord Althorp for seven years, with six years still to run.

And now, having dithered for almost three weeks, looking through the portfolios of one estate agent and the next, visiting one property and the next, and finding all of them either too expensive or unsuitable, Hobhouse finally took his problem to Lady Melbourne, seeking her help.

Lady Melbourne stared at him, astounded. "You should have come to me sooner, Mr Hobhouse, because if you had done so, I would have been able to save you a lot of trouble."

"How so, pray?"

"Annabella authorised me to find a suitable house for herself and Lord Byron weeks ago. I wrote and told her what was available, and she has made her choice. I completed the arrangements for the lease this morning."

Hobhouse stood there, feeling like a fool, and feeling even more furious with Byron for not letting him know that the matter had been put into the hands of Lady Melbourne.

"And the house, what is the address?"

"Number 13, Piccadilly Terrace."

Hobhouse dropped his hat, quickly picked it up again, and stared at Lady Melbourne. "I find it hard to believe that Lord Byron agreed to live in any house with the number thirteen on the door. You know how superstitious he is."

Lady Melbourne laughed. "Oh, Mr Hobhouse, you

know as well as I do that Lord Byron merely *plays* at being superstitious. It's all an amusing game to him."

"No, my lady, no, it is *not* a game – not since his mother died and her premonition came true. I can assure you, Lady Melbourne, that Lord Byron is truly *very* superstitious."

Lady Melbourne was still smiling. "Well, he knows the house and he has agreed to it. Here, let me show you the letter I received from him this morning, ..." She moved over to a spinet-desk near the window and took out a letter which she carried back to him. "This should put your mind at rest."

Hobhouse read the letter, which he could see from the address had been sent from Byron's sister's house at Newmarket, agreeing to whatever house Lady Melbourne thought best, on condition that it was available for occupation *immediately* ...

Hobhouse nodded, handed the letter back to Lady Melbourne, and apologised.

"Nonsense, no apology is needed. I only wish I could have saved you the worry and trouble," she replied, having already pulled the rope for the butler who appeared in an instant.

"Dunham, pray arrange for some tea and sweet pastries for myself and Mr Hobhouse. We are both in dire need."

Hobhouse was grateful for the tea, because he did not know what to think, and the tea served to calm him. "I am simply very surprised that Lord Byron agreed to rent such a house, particularly as it is right next door to his apartment in Albany Court."

"I should think that is the main attraction for him, returning to a location he knows so well and likes so much."

Hobhouse was too much of a gentleman to ask the cost of the yearly rent.

"Also ..." Lady Melbourne smiled, "I do believe it is his sincere intention to be a model husband and make

Annabella as happy as possible, and so he has acquiesced to her wishes on this."

Still, it was a damnably foolish thing to do, Hobhouse thought, but did not say so.

"And according to Annabella's letters to me, they are as happy with each other as two turtle-doves in a tree." Lady Melbourne sipped her tea, and frowned. "Although I must say, her account of their honeymoon at Halnaby Hall did not sound very romantic to me."

She looked at Hobhouse and watched his reaction to the curiousness of it. "She says that Lord Byron spent most of his days in the library at Halnaby Hall writing more poems for his Hebrew Melodies, while she sat at the same table copying them out for him in fair copy, and was happy to do so."

Hobhouse, who was not really listening or interested, merely shrugged. "That's Byron for you, a poet, even on his honeymoon. He can't help it."

"I'm sure not, but really, my goodness – *Hebrew* poems on one's honeymoon!" She gave a small amused laugh. "They'll be calling him a *Jew* next!"

"But *why* Devonshire House of all places?" Hobhouse could contain his anxious thoughts no longer. "Devonshire House is so ... *grandiose* ... and one of the largest houses in London."

"And Lord Byron is one of the most famous men in London," said Lady Melbourne, smiling at him reproachfully. "Do you not think he deserves to live in such a house?"

Hobhouse could only stare at her.

"And we were very lucky to get it, you know. If I had not known that the Duchess of Devonshire was preparing to leave London to spend a year or two in Paris, then Heaven knows where else we would have found a vacant house suitable for one of our aristocrats. Do you not approve?"

Hobhouse thought of Devonshire House which had hosted so many grand balls in its ballroom, as well as dinner and parties in it's salubrious salons ... "I think it is too large and too extravagant a house for only two persons."

"And the *staff,*" said Lady Melbourne. "Don't forget the staff, Mr Hobhouse, because *how* would we manage without them? The Duchess has agreed to leave most of her staff behind, although Lord Byron will be responsible for their pay. And do remember, also, that Lord and Lady Byron will have a lot of entertaining to do when they return to live in the metropolis. Everyone will want to congratulate them, not to mention the parties they will be required to host in celebration."

"But the *cost*, my lady?"

"The cost?" Lady Melbourne stared as if he had said something of the utmost impertinence.

"My *niece,* Mr Hobhouse, is an heiress to a considerable fortune, not only from my brother by way of a dowry, but in due time, upon his death, she will also inherit from her uncle, Lord Wentworth, and everyone knows that. So *cost* is not a consideration in our family, and nor, I presume, will it be a consideration for Lord Byron."

Only then did Hobhouse realise that Lady Melbourne knew nothing of Sir Ralph's true financial situation. Nor did it take him longer than a minute to suspect it was her sister-in-law Lady Milbanke, who had made sure that Lady Melbourne did *not* know ... During snippets of conversation at the dinner table in Seaham, he had detected that Lady Milbanke was rather jealous of her eminent sister-in-law in London.

"I sincerely beg your pardon, my lady," Hobhouse said contritely.

~~~

The visit to Augusta's home at Newmarket had lasted a full fortnight, and as soon as the carriage carrying her brother and Annabella on to London had disappeared from view, Augusta returned inside the house and went straight to her bed for a short rest, feeling exhausted.

Having visitors in one's home was physically tiring, but at least she had been relieved of any extra expense for food and wine by Byron's usual generosity – slipping her some money when Annabella was not in the room.

As tired as Augusta felt, she also felt happy – happy to know that her brother was married to a *good* woman, and she and Annabella had now become close friends.

A few days later she wrote a letter to her own and Byron's dear friend, Francis Hodgson, giving him an account of the visit.

My dear Mr Hodgson, – Byron and Lady B. left me on Tuesday for London. As for Lady B, the more I see of her the more I love and esteem her, and feel how grateful I am, and ought to be, for the blessing of such a wife for my dear darling Byron.

As to Byron himself, she regrettably confessed:

I am sorry to say his nerves and spirits are far from what I wish them. I think the uncomfortable state of his financial affairs is the cause, at least, I can discern no other. He now has every outward blessing this world can bestow.

Chapter Thirty-Five

~ ~ ~

Devonshire House stood at the Hyde Park corner end of Piccadilly, facing towards Green Park. A tall house surrounded by trees and a high gate and set back from the road.

As soon as Annabella walked through its doors she loved it. It was the perfect home for a Baroness. As soon as she had established herself within its rooms, she ordered new letter-paper topped with the Byron Crest and Coronet for her personal correspondence.

The only blot on the magnificence of the front hall of the house was the arrival of an old witch of a woman, bags in hand, and a stupid hat on her head, who announced in a cockney accent that she was "Mrs Mule."

"His lordship sent for me."

Annabella ordered a maid to fetch his lordship, who came on the scene with a smile, asking Mrs Mule if she was well.

"Well?" said Mrs Mule, looking around her. "Not if you expect me to clean this place, my lord." She stared at the grand staircase leading up to the main rooms. "Why, it would take me a month of Mondays just to do those stairs for a start."

Fletcher was also pleased to see the arrival of Mrs Mule, although he warned her gravely that her constant humming would get on his nerves again if she did it too often.

"I likes a good tune to hum," she countered, "helps me get on with my work. But if it gets on your nerves, Mr Fletcher, you just tell me, and I'll hum low."

Fletcher sighed and shrugged and then took her below stairs to meet the rest of the staff.

Annabella looked at Byron with some annoyance. "Why did you send for her to come here, an old crone like that? I implore you to discharge her at once."

Byron refused. "No, I'm keeping her on because in Bennet Street and then Albany the poor old dear was always kind to me. I'll use her solely for cleaning my study, since I trust her, and I don't want any of the maids going near my papers. Whereas Mrs Mule could pick up a letter or one of my poems and not be able to read a word of it."

"She is illiterate?"

"In a most agreeable way, as far as I'm concerned. And talking about my study reminds me ... we have received an invitation to attend a ball at Lord and Lady Jersey's tonight. Will we go?"

Annabella smiled. "If you wish. It has been a long time since I attended a ball in London."

At Lady Jersey's that night, when "*Lord and Lady Byron*" were announced ... everyone paused and turned to greet the newlyweds, and all were visibly surprised at the change in the dowdy Miss Milbanke.

Now, as Lady Byron, she walked majestically into the room on her husband's arm, her brown hair piled high on her head and wearing a delicate diamond tiara.

Most of the other ladies were also wearing tiaras as usual, but they had never expected to see Miss Milbanke wearing one, or looking so grand. She had acquired a poise they had never seen before. Her eyes were glowing and there was happiness in her face. Marriage had certainly brought out the very best in her.

And Annabella *was* happily married, apart from a few niggles of discontent here and there. During their honeymoon her husband had been charming and gallant, and often amusing, and during their nights she had realised he must have been a lover of many women because he had brought out in her a passion she never knew she possessed.

So much so, that when she sat with him in the library writing out his poems in fair copy, she would slyly gaze at him, wishing he would put down his pen and agree to take an afternoon rest with her in her bedroom, for she had very quickly developed a strange lust for what she called "a ruling passion for mischief in private."

At his sister's house in Newmarket though, he had unsettled her with a few occasional dark and gloomy moods, but Augusta had given her some sisterly advice on how to handle him on those occasions, insisting that Byron *"can always be laughed out of his dark moods. Humour is like medicine to him."*

Annabella had thought that suggestion rather silly, preferring instead to try and *analyse* and *understand* his moods, but the rest of his sister's advice had been more helpful.

She was brought out of her thoughts by people in the ballroom surrounding her, all eager to congratulate her and wish her years of happiness and hope she would attend their next soirée or join someone else's tea-party next Wednesday?

Now that she was Lady Byron, Annabella suddenly found she had a host of new friends. Ladies who had once carelessly ignored her were now fawning over her. It was all so very predictable, and she allowed herself a secret smile of triumph while remaining decorous and polite to all.

The night was a great success for Annabella and other invitations followed – although she refused to accept an invitation from Lady Holland, who was tainted by divorce. But to the rest, and to all who saw them, the Byrons appeared a fairly happy couple and everyone commented on it. Although, in a letter replying to Lady Melbourne, Byron's own comment was sardonically flippant –

"You know I am a very good-natured fellow, and the more easily governed because I am not ashamed of

being so. And so Annabella has her own way and no doubt means to keep it."

Lady Melbourne's uneasiness returned, for she knew Byron too well and recognised the subtle irony of his words. Did Annabella not know *anything* about how to treat a man? A domineering woman might get her own way in the beginning, but not much else in the long run. No, a wise woman knew to be more devious, more soothing and agreeable, using her femininity to persuade a man that every idea was his marvellous idea, to which she had amiably submitted.

Lady Melbourne knew she must act, and quickly. Instructions would have to be given to the girl. An arrangement made for a visit – a *family* visit laden with gifts – and then catching a few minutes alone with her, some private words must be said in that young wife's ear.

~~~

Lady Caroline refused, threatened, and was then forced to submit to her mother-in-law's persuasions. Lord Byron was now Caroline's cousin-in-law by marriage, so it was essential for her to now visit Devonshire House, if only for Caroline to show some good grace and save face by cheerfully offering Lord Byron and Annabella her good wishes.

Annabella's mother, Lady Milbanke, was present when Lady Melbourne and Caroline entered the drawing room at Devonshire House – Lady Milbanke immediately suffusing her sister-in-law in gushing conversation – while Annabella looked at Caroline as if she was some cat dragged in off the street.

Caroline was mortified by Annabella's icy coldness towards her, which really was unnecessary, especially as she had humbled herself to make the visit. She felt humiliated and beaten, and yet there was nothing she could do about it, not without making another scene, which Lady Milbanke would probably tell to all the world.

So Caroline sat down quietly with her hands clasped in her lap and her head bowed, and never uttered a word, and never once looked up.

Not until Lord Byron came in, and he seemed to Caroline to be agitated. He shook hands with her in a cold way, but then became kind to her, and even smiled as they talked briefly.

Caroline glanced towards Annabella and saw her staring at Byron with a look of outright condemnation, but fortunately he did not notice because his side was turned to her.

Annabella was indeed furious, and consumed with jealousy, for she still believed Byron had a weakness where Caroline was concerned. After all, he had once been in love with Caroline, and for that reason alone, Annabella would always detest her.

The meeting was cut short due to one of Annabella's headaches, much to the disappointment of Lady Melbourne who, due to the non-stop chattering of her insufferable sister-in-law, Lady Milbanke, had not managed to get even one word of advice into her niece's ear.

Chapter Thirty-Six

~~~

Even though she would never admit it, Annabella took great pleasure in having everyone's attention focused upon her. It was what she was accustomed to, having been brought up by worshipping parents and a household of indulgent staff.

Yet, although she now believed that her triumph in high society had been achieved, and her status as Lady Byron established; she very quickly began to realise that her provincial upbringing and sheltered life in Seaham had rendered her somewhat ill-adapted to the world of fashionable London.

Her manner, although polite, was as stiff and formal with everyone as it had been in the days when she had accompanied her aunt, Lady Melbourne, to balls and parties in earlier years, because that was how she believed she *should* hold herself in high society; and no matter how hard she tried, she could not unbend and lose the habit.

Not until now, due to her marriage raising her onto an equal level with them, did she notice that most of the young ladies of the *haut ton* were very *in*formal with each other – laughing and joking and completely at ease – and Byron was socialising amongst them in the same free and easy manner.

She stood gazing at the other people in the room, realising that her own idea of social etiquette was quite wrong and out of place in this London company – they were all so well-bred they knew that it was not the form to stand on ceremony in a social setting.

Her embarrassment made her feel bitter and resentful and all she wanted now was to leave these smugly-relaxed people who were probably slyly laughing at her.

She caught Byron's arm, complaining of the most "dreadful headache" and begged him take her home at once.

Thereafter she had no interest in attending parties or balls or any other functions, preferring to stay at home in Devonshire House and allow others to attend upon her instead.

The younger ladies of high station but of less rank than those of the *ton,* who had accepted her cards of invitation and visited her in the afternoons, now viewed her as an object of admiration, as Lady Byron, a woman of good heart and good *soul* who not only provided them with nice teas, but also reminded them of the importance of Christian virtues.

Byron, however, still wanted and needed a social life. In response to Annabella's complaint that she could no longer tolerate hot rooms or late hours, he resigned himself instead to hosting dinner parties at home. Companionable affairs of six or seven friends, sometimes more; but Annabella quickly grew tired of the dinner parties also.

She had always considered her own mind to be very intelligent and knowledgeable, whether it be on the science of mathematics or the intricacies of religion or the importance of good works to assist the lower classes. Yet the conversation of Byron and his London friends were not only about general everyday affairs, but the affairs of the country and the wider world, and most especially *politics,* for which she possessed little interest.

Her continued silence at the table embarrassed Byron. He kept looking at his wife, sitting there like a ghost at the banquet, and made several attempts to draw her into the conversation, as did others, but the only response they could get was a "Yes" or a "No" and the excuse that she was "feeling rather tired."

Gradually, Byron began to suspect that Annabella

had no liking for his male friends, noticing that she exerted no effort to make them feel welcome or comfortable. He did not challenge her on the subject, but it depressed him.

Scrope Davies was less silent. After calling in to Devonshire House one afternoon to see Byron and quickly leaving again, later that evening at Brooks's Club, Scrope told Beau Brummell and others – "Poor Byron does not have any authority in his own house. Her ladyship is mistress in everything."

Beau Brummell did not believe it, not of Byron, but when others attested it was true, Brummell, after a long moment of reflection, looked gravely at his friends and said, "Gentlemen, we must pray for him."

~~~

Douglas Kinnaird, a director of the Drury Lane Theatre was delighted to be invited and attend one of Lord Byron's "at home" dinner parties a week later.

The evening started off well. The conversation brilliant and witty and full of laughter as was usual with Byron, until Kinnaird observed Byron's wife, who had been sitting quietly throughout, was now deliberately and openly observing the air around her, as if she was extremely bored by it all.

Kinnaird said politely, "You are not interested in the anecdotes of the theatre world, my lady?"

After a silence, Annabella replied, "Sometimes, but not usually."

Conversation began to falter, descending into what Kinnaird called "one of the dullest evenings of my life."

Byron looked humiliated, and in the awkward silence that followed, the guests made their excuses and left, much earlier than was usual at dinner parties.

Once outside, while putting on his gloves, Douglas Kinnaird gave a wry look to Isaac Nathan saying, "I think I shocked her when I reached to help myself to a third potato. Did you see the look on her face when I did so?"

Isaac Nathan, who was very reluctant to criticise Lord Byron's lady, merely shook his head and hailed one of the many Hackney cabs circling around Piccadilly.

~

Inwardly fuming, as soon as his friends had left the house Byron rounded on Annabella, demanding to know why she thought he would accept her unfriendly behaviour towards his friends?

"Are you unaware of that facet of human vanity that allows us to forgive the people who bore us, but *never* the people *we* bore?"

"Dearest –"

"And tonight, Madam, you made my friends feel they were *boring* you beyond endurance."

"You are being very unfair," Annabella replied. "If I yawned it was because I felt tired."

"And what next? Another cold? Another headache? Another pain in your side?"

Leaving her in a fury he went straight to his bedroom and swore at Fletcher, yet Fletcher paid no heed because he knew he was not the cause; and of late Fletcher had seriously come to dislike Miss Milbanke, due to the insensitive way she often treated her maid, Ann Rood.

Returning below stairs, Fletcher found Ann anxiously waiting for him, and he shook his head. "I couldn't ask him, because he was in a devil of a mood."

Ann sighed her disappointment. "So how long must we wait?"

"Until I can catch him in a good mood. He'll say yes when I ask him, least I *think* he will. Then we can be married and live happily ever after."

Ann smiled, and moved to sit on a bench under a tree in the back yard, pulling the shawl she had wrapped around her even tighter against the chill of the night.

Fletcher sat down beside her and Ann said quietly, "Mind, I do think his lordship is a bit frightening at times. Sometimes, when he looks at me, it's like he knows what I'm thinking. As if he can see straight into my mind."

"Well, he always seems to know what *I'm* thinking," said Fletcher. "But he don't frighten me, no, not at all. I've been his lordship's valet for too long, and I've seen him in all his moods and during all his love affairs too."

"*All* his love affairs?"

"Aye," Fletcher nodded, "and I can tell you, hand on heart, that he's kind-hearted and easy-going most of the time, and almost any woman can manage him if she acts nicely and he has feelings for her. But Miss Milbanke is trying to manage him all the wrong way."

"*Lady Byron,*" hissed Ann and put her hand over her own mouth half-laughing. "You and me – we've got to *stop* calling her Miss Milbanke or she'll have us dismissed. And it's harder for me than for you, because I've been her maid for so long."

"What?" Fletcher squared his shoulders in umbrage. "She'd not be able to dismiss *me*. I'm his lordship's man."

Chapter Thirty-Seven

~ ~ ~

Augusta, who had once again returned to her post as a Lady-in-Waiting to the queen at St James's Palace, invited her friend, Lady Frances Shelley, to accompany her on a visit to see her brother in Piccadilly.

Lady Shelley agreed, for she had been away in the country and had not yet had the opportunity of congratulating Lord Byron on his marriage.

"His wife is unknown to me, although I have indeed heard her spoken of by Lady Melbourne."

"I liked her greatly when they came to visit us in Newmarket," said Augusta. "She is rather quiet in her manner, but I think you will find her to be one of the nicest beings in this world."

Lady Shelley had a very different opinion after the event of her visit to Devonshire House; an opinion which, during the following weeks, she told many of her friends at dinner parties. And knowing that she would never visit the Byrons home in Piccadilly again, she recorded the event in her private diary:

> "We arrived at Devonshire House and mounted the stairs, and were about to be ushered into the drawing room when the door suddenly opened, and Lord Byron stood before us. I was, for the moment, taken aback at his sudden appearance; but I contrived to utter a few words, by way of congratulation upon his marriage.
> Lord Byron did not seem to think the matter was adapted for good wishes; and looked as though he resented my intrusion into the house. At least I thought so, as he received my congratulations so coldly.

Lady Byron received us courteously, but I felt at once that she is not the sort of woman with whom I could ever be intimate with. I was not sorry when the visit was over. I felt like a person who had inadvertently dipped her finger into boiling water."

~~~

Hobhouse discovered the reason for Byron's fury later that day.

Slowly, it all came out, things that Hobhouse did not know. Life in Devonshire House was turning into a nightmare, due to the wide-spread rumour that Byron had married an heiress. Now creditors were besieging the house every day looking for immediate payment of their bills."

"Oh, good grief! That false *heiress* rumour! But did you not consider that when you agreed to rent such an expensive house?"

"Well I *did* think I would have some extra funds from Annabella's dowry , but despite the marriage at the beginning of January, here we are at the beginning of April, more than three months later, and Sir Ralph still has not coughed up a single penny of it."

"Nothing at all?"

"Nothing.""

Hobhouse was furious, half-blaming Sir Ralph for not yet honouring the marriage contract, and half-blaming John Hanson for being so negligent for not incorporating a clause specifying that it be paid within the first month after the ceremony.

"*Now* do you understand why I told you that some sort of set-off should have been secured against *his* property as well as yours?"

Byron nodded. "And now there is only one other solution. Newstead must be sold."

"Oh my dear fellow ..."

"It's the only way. Even with the income I presently receive from Newstead, it does not allow me to pay a high rent on two properties *and* live in the respectable manner to which her ladyship is entitled to expect."

"Two properties? Oh, do you mean your apartment in Albany Court?"

"Yes."

"Oh, well, I think I might be able to help you there," said Hobhouse, brightening. "You know that I have always admired that apartment of yours tremendously?"

Byron nodded. "I did suspect it, considering the amount of time you spent there, coming in every day and reading my post as if it was yours."

"So if you have no objections to transferring the lease to me, that would remove your liability for the rent of Albany at least. Would that not be of some help?"

Byron smiled. "You *know* it would be a great help. And it might save me from selling Newstead."

"Excellent!" said Hobhouse.

A few minutes later, as they turned and began the short walk back to Piccadilly Terrace, Hobhouse made Byron smile again when he imparted to him some incredible news.

"Oh, with all this business I nearly forgot what I called to tell you – Napoleon has escaped from Elba!"

Byron stared. "My little pagod – escaped?"

Hobby nodded quite definitely. "He escaped on a ship which set him down on the coast of France where some of his entourage were waiting, and as soon as the local Frenchmen saw him and recognised their exiled Emperor, they took up their guns to join him. They say he rode on all the way towards Paris without receiving one single shot from an opposing force, and he with thousands of Frenchmen marching behind him. And then, and then ..."

They were both grinning like two excited schoolboys. "And *then*?" asked Byron.

"And then when news reached Paris that Napoleon

was at the head of a marching army and had reached the outskirts of the city, the French soldiers threw off their allegiance to King Louis and rushed to join Bonaparte, calling him their 'true king' – *Notre vrai roi!* – and now King Louis and the rest of the Bourbons have fled Paris like frightened rabbits."

Byron smacked his hands jubilantly. "I told you I was sure Napoleon would play them some trick! Nothing ever disappointed me so much as his abdication, and nothing but *this* could have ever reconciled me to him again."

Annabella was surprised and pleased when Byron returned to the house looking in good spirits after such a short walk with his friend. It appeared that he had recovered from their quarrel and was now prepared to let it pass without any further discussion.

Chapter Thirty-Eight

~ ~ ~

Mr and Mrs Milward, the butler and housekeeper at Devonshire House, knew that the first year of marriage was the most difficult for two young people needing to learn and adjust to each other's ways and temperament. And in their opinion, Lord and Lady Byron still had a lot of adjustments ahead of them if they were to live easily together.

Lady Byron was governed by fixed rules and the exact time of the clock, and she became increasingly exasperated when Lord Byron showed no respect for the customary sitting-down to dinner at a certain time every evening.

Lord Byron endeavoured to mend his ways in that respect, but having always been a light eater, he began to dread the approach of the dinner hour due to Lady Byron's meticulous habit of not swallowing her food until she had chewed each mouthful for a set twenty times.

At first Byron found it funny, her ritual of chewing, but after a while it irritated him beyond measure as he found himself impatiently watching the fork of food going into her mouth and then mentally counting the chews, one two, three, four ...

He was energetic. She was lazy. Both were self-willed. He liked to laugh and joke. She had no sense of humour at all; always studying his every word with a searching intensity as if wondering if there was some hidden meaning behind it.

One day Mr Milward heard his lordship say to Lady Byron, "If you would not pay so much heed to my words, we could get on very well together."

He was impulsive and spoke easily. She had no spontaneity at all. Mr Milward felt certain that every word Lady Byron spoke had been well thought out before she uttered a sentence.

Mr and Mrs Milward shook their heads, certain that this first year of adjustment for the Byrons was going to be a tough one.

~~~

To Byron, Annabella's main idiosyncrasy was that she took everything too seriously, and almost everything literally, and as well as annoying him, it often amused him.

Instead of smiling or shaking her head at his superstitions, she showed her shock, causing him to laugh and make up some more superstitions just to see the alarm on her face.

He declined to join her for dinner one Friday evening, for the reason that Friday was the Mohammedan Sabbath, which he observed.

The following evening he declined dinner again, for the reason that Saturday until sunset was the Jewish Sabbath, which he also observed.

"If there was any sun today," she said, looking toward the window, "it has now set and the day is over."

"Yes, but I got up late, so *my* day is only halfway through."

And then all his teasing, all his jesting, came to an abrupt stop when Annabella told him that she was pregnant.

Byron's response was all and everything that Annabella had expected it to be.

They went out to a party at the Hollands and revealed their good news.

Lord Holland congratulated Byron on his prospective fatherhood. "I suppose you are hoping for a son and heir?"

"Indeed," Byron grinned. "All I need now is an heir for my fortune, and a fortune for my heir."

~~~

His potential fortune was being hotly discussed at Seaham Hall, and Lady Milbanke was furious.

Her brother, Lord Wentworth, had unexpectedly died of a stroke at the end of April and – once Lady Milbanke's sadness had quickly passed – the wording of her brother's Last Will and Testament was equally unexpected.

She could not believe it, nor could Sir Ralph, and so they called in their own attorney, who confirmed that yes, their understanding of Lord Wentworth's last Will and Testament was quite correct. The document had simply been updated and changed by Lord Wentworth after his niece's marriage.

For the most part, it was as expected. The bulk of Lord Wentworth's assets – consisting of two large houses and a fair amount of money – were left to Lady Milbanke and her only child. But Lord Wentworth's will was so worded that Annabella's husband, Lord Byron, would ultimately receive and control her portion of the estate when it eventually devolved to her.

"My lady," said the attorney, "it is perfectly normal and common for a husband to have control of his wife's property."

"It is *treachery* – on the part of my late brother," Lady Milbanke burst out. "Absolute treachery! The money should eventually go to Annabella, *not* Lord Byron"

"But in law, my lady, as you must know from your own marriage, a wife's property is deemed to be her husband's property also, for the benefit of both. As is the husband's property and fortune expected to be for the benefit of both. Those are the laws of marriage."

Sir Ralph leaned forward, asking earnestly, "So nothing can be done?"

"To change the will? No, sir. However, if you wish to contest it, you may do so, but I don't see on what grounds you would have any success. The court may request to know if you as a husband benefited from your own wife's dowry or property in any way."

And as he had, and now was about to do so again, Sir Ralph shrank back into his seat and said no more.

Chapter Thirty-Nine

~~~

George Ticknor, a young American on a visit to London, before journeying on to France, made his way to Piccadilly for the sole purpose of hopefully meeting his poetic idol, Lord Byron.

He eventually arrived at 13 Piccadilly Terrace and saw from the gate that the door was open, and a young woman preparing to leave. She stood with her back to the gate, was bonneted and dressed to go out, and talking to a young man whose manner was very friendly to her.

From his looks, Ticknor knew the young man could not be Lord Byron; he was too handsome, and too tall and too strong in his body. A relative perhaps? Or a friend residing at the house? And the woman – a favoured friend or sister of the man?

Ticknor thought she must be, when he walked her out to her carriage, and then shook hands with her as if he were not to see her again for a month.

Once the carriage moved off, and the young man turned to go back inside, George Ticknor followed him up the path. "Excuse me, sir, may I beg your pardon and ask if you know Lord Byron?"

The young man looked at him. "No

"I was told that this was his residence."

"Were you indeed? Told by whom?"

"By Mr Gifford, his lordship's editor at John Murray's publishing house.

"How extraordinary? Surely it is not the place of an editor to give the personal address of one of his authors to a stranger."

"I believe he did so because I am an American on my way to France, and because I carry a letter of recommendation from Thomas Jefferson."

A suspicious smile. "Thomas Jefferson – the former President of America?"

"Yes indeed. He instructed me to purchase some books in London and mail them straight over to him as soon as possible. He particularly wanted the books to carry the personal signature of Lord Byron."

"Oh, well, in that case, you had better come inside and we will see if we can find him."

Inside the drawing-room, Ticknor removed his hat and sat down, but after having been leisurely offered a glass of wine by the young man, he said, "Forgive my impertinence, but my time is short, so *are* you going to seek out Lord Byron for me?"

Byron placed the glass of wine down on the side-table by Ticknor's armchair, and held out his hand, "Your servant, sir."

"Ticknor stared. "*You* are he?"

Byron smiled. "It is not something I admit to every passing stranger."

George Ticknor half-laughed with embarrassment and jumped to his feet, taking the proffered hand in a enthusiastic handshake. "You are not as I expected, no, not at all! And you English have a strange way of jesting. I believed you when you said you did not know him."

"Which is true," Byron replied seriously. "Few men really know themselves, do they?"

Ticknor found himself at a loss for words. No one had warned him about Byron's eyes or that penetrating blue gaze.

"So," Byron said, sitting down, "You have told me about Thomas Jefferson and his need of some signed books."

"Yes ..." Ticknor reached into his coat and drew out a letter which he passed over to Byron.

It was a longish letter listing books and Byron's eyes merely looked at the address on the top – *Monticello, Charlottesville, Virginia* – and then fixed on the scrawled signature at the end. "Is this truly the hand of the great man himself?

"It is."

"And how do you know Thomas Jefferson?"

"I was recommended to him by President Madison."

"Indeed?" Byron looked impressed as he handed back the letter.

Ticknor said: "Like myself, Jefferson is a great admirer of your work, Lord Byron, and he particularly liked your *'Lines to A Lady Weeping"* criticising the Prince Regent. He still harbours his old loathing for all the British monopolistic royals."

Byron smiled. "Still a rebel at heart, eh?"

Ticknor continued to talk, telling Byron that Jefferson's first knowledge of the name Byron was due to Lord Byron's own grandfather, Admiral John Byron, owing to Jefferson having read every book written about the voyages of Captain James Cook.

"Yes, before he achieved the rank of an Admiral, my grandfather had been Cook's navigator on most of his expeditions around the globe."

Byron looked curiously at his visitor. "May we now go back to the beginning, pray, and start this conversation again, by you telling me something about yourself?"

"Me?" Ticknor could hardly think a clear thought, too over-awed at the realisation that he was actually sitting here in this beautiful drawing room in England with *Byron.*

"What do you wish to know?"

Byron smiled. "Well, your *name* would be a start."

~

Later that afternoon when Scrope Davies called in to Piccadilly Terrace, Byron told him about his American visitor.

"I suspect he was very disappointed with me, and will probably never read my poetry in the same way again."

"Why so?"

Byron explained the same problem he had experienced with other poetry lovers, and especially those who had read *Childe Harold's Pilgrimage* and *The Corsair.*

"I believe he expected to meet a reclusive and sulky type of gentleman, in wolf-skin breeches, and answering only in fierce monosyllables, instead of an ordinary man of the world."

Scrope grinned. "I would not say that you were an *ordinary* man of the world."

Byron sighed at the sheer nonsense of it. "I can never get people to understand that poetry is the expression of *excited passion,* which only lasts while writing it, and that there is no such thing as a *life* of passion – anymore than there is a continuous earthquake, or an eternal fever. Besides, what poet would ever be able to *shave* himself in such a state?"

~

Byron had been correct in thinking that George Ticknor, a graduate of Dartmouth College in Boston, had found him to be very different to his expectations; and as soon as Ticknor returned to his hotel, he sent an excited letter back to America about the meeting.

My anticipations were mistaken. Instead of being deformed, as I had heard, he is straight and well built. And instead of having a thin and rather sharp and anxious face, as he has in his pictures, it is open and smiling; his eyes are light, and not black, and his air is easy and careless, not forward, and I found his manner affable and gentle, the tones of his voice low and conciliating, his conversation pleasant and interesting to an uncommon degree.

I stayed with him about an hour and a half, during

which the conversation wandered over many subjects. He talked of course a great deal about America, wanted to know what was the state of our literature, and whether we looked upon Barlow as our Homer. He certainly feels a considerable interest in America, and says he intends to visit the United States one day. I answered all his questions about America as if I was speaking to one of my own countrymen ...

The letter went on and on, and George was feeling very pleased with his visit, especially as Byron had given him letters of recommendation to Madame de Staël, William Wordsworth, and Walter Scott, and all this he had done without any affectation.

George had also learned that the young lady who went in the carriage was Byron's wife, whom George thought "pretty, but not beautiful."

~ ~ ~

A few days later, George Ticknor could not resist calling on Lord Byron again, and finding him in, also found him as welcoming and easy-mannered as previously.

He showed me his library, and his collection of Romaic and Greek books, which is very rich and very curious. He offered me letters of introduction for when I go to Greece myself, and after I had made an appointment to visit him again, he took leave of me so cordially that I felt almost at home with him.

The following week, returning again to Piccadilly Terrace, George had just relaxed into an armchair in the drawing room with his glass of wine in hand, eager for more interesting conversation with Lord Byron, when another gentleman abruptly came rushing into the room, "My lord, my lord, I have news –"

Holding up his palm, and with that exquisite etiquette which George had noticed so often in the English, Byron halted any further conversation until he had introduced his visitor:

"Sir James Burgess, pray let me introduce you to Mr George Ticknor, who has come to us all the way from America."

Sir James had no time or humour for introductions to anyone. "The news has just come from Paris!"

"Paris? My friend Hobhouse is over there now, hoping to get another glimpse of Napoleon."

"My lord, he will not see him. A great battle has been fought in the Low Countries, at a place called Waterloo, and Bonaparte is entirely defeated!"

After a stare – "But is it true?" said Byron – "Is the news *true?"*

"Yes, my lord, it is certainly true. An aide-de-camp arrived in town last night. He was in Downing Street this morning, and I have just seen him as he was going to Lady Wellington's."

"Napoleon defeated?"

"Yes, my lord. He says most of the French Army are dead, and he thinks Bonaparte is in full retreat towards Paris."

After an instant's pause, Byron said, "Well I am damned sorry for it." And then, after another pause, he asked, "And Downing Street is gloating?"

"Understandably, especially the Foreign Secretary, Lord Castlereagh."

"Castlereagh," said Byron with displeasure. "After his destruction of Ireland and our own textile workers up north, I was hoping I might live to see Lord Castlereagh's head on a pole, but I suppose I shan't now."

George Ticknor looked from one man to the other, confused, not understanding their gloom. They were both English, so why were they not rejoicing at the news of Napoleon's defeat and the English victory?

George reluctantly made his excuses and left the two men to their conversation, and he was sorry to have to do so, because he was leaving England the following morning and would not be returning for years.

The following week Byron received a sad and angry letter from Hobhouse in France.

Hobby's younger brother, Benjamin, had been one of the many thousands of English soldiers killed in action at Waterloo, and Hobby wrote bitterly to Byron of – *'the mass of misery and deaths for the most wicked cause that brave young Englishmen have ever died for –* "

And Byron agreed – it was *a wicked cause*. Why should so many young Englishmen have to fight and die to defeat Napoleon in order to restore the repulsive Bourbon King Louis to the throne of France?

Because the Crowns of England and Europe had ordered it.

Byron was almost as devastated as Hobhouse at the death of Benjamin ... poor Benjamin ... and in his sadness Byron thought back to those words he had written in *Childe Harold's Pilgrimage,* at a time when young English soldiers were fighting and falling in a savage and bloody war to save the throne of the King of Spain –

And must they fall? the young, the proud, the brave,
To swell one bloated chief's unwholesome reign?

Chapter Forty

~~~

As June came to its end and England was still celebrating, Byron began to feel he was facing his own Waterloo.

Upon his marriage, creditors had been sending him their invoices for payment immediately. Most had been paid, but now Byron was running short of cash due to the cost of running such a large household.

The situation had become increasingly worse from the news of Lord Wentworth's death, and the consequent fortune that everyone believed Wentworth had left to his niece.

Creditors were now pressing even harder for payment, and Byron was astounded to discover that some establishments, which had sent him unwanted items as *gifts* as soon as his fame was established – were now sending him bills for the payment of those gifts sent to him three years ago – explaining that he had unfortunately *not* been billed for them at the time "due to an error."

Did they think he was a fool?

No, they truly thought he was *excessively* rich now, and all slow payments were credited to him as being *mean* and *miserly* with all his wealth.

He discussed the situation with Annabella, hoping for some help from the Milbankes, but she told him firmly that nothing could be done to alleviate his situation. Much of the money inherited from Lord Wentworth had gone to pay her father's debts. And her late uncle's fine property at Kirkby Mallory in Leicestershire had now been taken over by her parents, who intended to make it their main residence in future.

"They want to be as close to me as possible all year

round," Annabella explained, "and Kirkby Mallory is almost two hundred miles nearer to London."

"And Seaham? What are they going to do with that property?"

"Oh, keep it. But they say we can go there at any time. We could even live there if we wish."

"I don't want to live there. *Why* would I want to live in that bleak place on the edge of nowhere?"

Annabella, who could see no excuse for his derogatory tone about her childhood home, stood up and left the room.

There had been a change in her since Lord Wentworth's death, Byron noticed. Or had the change started with her pregnancy? He was not sure which, but there *was* a change in her.

~

Byron was not the only one who had noticed a change in Annabella.

Augusta, with the approval of the Prince Regent, had been elevated to the post of a *Lady of the Bedchamber* to his mother Queen Charlotte, and Augusta had now been allocated her own apartment within St James's Palace.

The rooms of the apartment were being redecorated and were not quite ready for Augusta, so she was mightily relieved when Annabella insisted that she really "*must*" stay with her at Devonshire House.

Augusta thought it "so nice" of Annabella to be so accommodating to her, until Annabella began to complain incessantly to her about Byron and his earlier frivolous ways with money.

Augusta, with her lifelong cowardice of vexing anyone, could not disagree with Annabella.

"He has always been carefree with money," she agreed. "He has never denied himself anything. Although I must say, he has never denied any friend or stranger who needed help either."

"Including you?"

Augusta's face flushed with embarrassment, but she pretended not to have heard the question. "Yes, I do agree, Byron *should* have been more careful with his money. For instance, why could he not have rented a *small* Townhouse in London, instead of this big place?"

As the days passed Annabella grew tired of Byron's sister constantly agreeing with her. She did not believe there was any real sincerity behind her words, and her timidity filled her with contempt. She also had a suspicion that it was the love of money that kept Augusta so attached to her brother.

Augusta in turn found her sister-in-law's attitude very perplexing, and ventured up to the library to ask Byron about it.

"Byron, does Annabella know that her father has not yet paid you her dowry?"

"Of course she does. She knows he has paid nothing. She even offered to ask her solicitor to try and arrange a loan for me, but I said not. Why, what has she said about it?"

"Oh, nothing. Nothing at all. That's why I asked you."

~ ~ ~

The next day, as the two women strolled around the garden, Annabella decided to say something that Augusta would find difficult to agree with.

"Do you know, dearest," she said in her quiet, confiding voice, "why Byron always now calls you 'Goose' instead of 'Guss'?"

Augusta stared. "I had noticed it, but I don't know why."

"He calls you Goose, as in 'silly Goose' because he says that you are very silly in so many ways."

August smiled slightly. "Well I *am* somewhat silly at times," she admitted. "Mostly when I feel nervous or frantic about anything."

"And Byron has often said to me – "Oh, the *way* Augusta flutters around like a silly goose! And when she writes one of her letters to me, I'm sure she just reaches over her shoulder and takes a quill from her wing."

Augusta laughed, "That is so typical of Byron's humour. I'm sure he has said many other things about me in that comic way, but he means no ill intent."

"Probably not," replied Annabella, but her expression clearly showed that she had reached a different conclusion.

Augusta was relieved when she received a note from St James's Palace informing her that the apartment was now ready. She was glad to be able to leave Devonshire House. Her time here had not been happy, due to Annabella's constant disparagement of Byron's love for her, as well as attacking and undermining Augusta's affection for her brother.

Augusta wondered if Annabella's pregnancy had slightly unbalanced her? She now seemed to disapprove of everything and everyone, and she appeared to feel no sympathy whatever about Byron being haunted by the duns demanding money – more annoyed at the situation *she* had been placed in with traders knocking at her door, and the dent it caused to her dignity and rank.

Yet she said none of these things in the presence of Byron, and at times even appeared to sympathise with him fondly, calling him "My dear duck" her pet name for him, and insisting he call her "Pippin" his pet name for her.

Augusta now realised that Annabella was a singular character, with a hardness of manner just below the surface that was only now beginning to show through.

Augusta was also taken aback by the revelation of Annabella's pristine hypocrisy in front of Byron, always behaving so *perfect* in front of him. It was all very strange, and extremely disappointing.

Sitting in the carriage on route to the palace, Augusta

fretfully began to realise that she would have to go very carefully with her brittle sister-in-law in future ... Was Annabella always like that? So critical behind people's back and nice to their face? Or was her uneven behaviour all due to her pregnancy?

Minutes later, as the carriage rolled inside the gates of St James's Palace, Augusta remembered one of Madame de Staël's philosophical sayings about marriage – *"When married, people do not change, they just take off the mask"*

Chapter Forty-One

~~~

In mid-July, having come back from France and then spending a week with his father and siblings in Richmond, John Hobhouse returned to London. He was still in deep mourning for his dead brother, but he was also a practical young man who knew that his own life must go on and forwards as usual.

On his first morning out, he headed straight for Byron's house. Byron would cheer him, and if Byron could not, then nobody could.

The first thing that made Hobhouse stop and stare in shock, was Byron's front door. It had a number of *Executions for Payment* nailed to it.

What on earth was going on? It was nothing less than a damned audacity to attempt to embarrass Lord Byron in such a way!

Hobby's first reaction was to tear the notices down, but then remembered that to do so would be against the law.

When the door was opened he was shown into the drawing-room by Mr Milward, the butler, who told him, "His lordship is in the library, sir, writing letters. I will inform him that you are here."

In the library Byron was dashing off a desperate note to his attorney.

Dear Mr Hanson,

Neither today nor yesterday have any advertisements respecting the sale of Newstead appeared in my two papers – Morning Chronicle or Morning Post. Do have this enquired into.

Yrs truly
B

In the drawing room, Hobhouse was sitting waiting when Lady Milbanke was shown in. She recognised him immediately as the groomsman at the wedding, and after a few flat pleasantries she demanded to know what he thought of the Executions on the front door.

"Well, I – "

"Disgraceful! Poor Annabella."

Then she demanded to know if he had any knowledge of Newstead Abbey being sold yet?

"It should have been sold before this," she said. "Lord Byron appears to have been very lackadaisical in putting the property up for sale. It should have been sold before this!"

For the second time that morning Hobhouse found himself staring in shock – shocked at Lady Milbanke's abominable cheek in pushing Lord Byron – after his having married a reputed heiress – to now part with a property that had been in his family since the reign of Henry the Eighth.

It was so indecent, and so impertinent, that Hobhouse decided not to let Byron know of her words and mercenary attitude towards him – not when his poor friend appeared to have more than enough problems to deal with.

Byron appeared at the door of the drawing room, dressed to leave, and after he had spoken a few curt words to Lady Milbanke, he gestured for Hobhouse to join him on his way out.

Hobhouse followed him out to his carriage where he instructed the driver to "Drive around for a while," and once they were both seated and the carriage was moving, Hobhouse finally spoke:

"How are you?"

"As you can see, I'm a very miserable dog, hounded by vultures. How are you? And your father?"

Hobhouse made it plain that he did not wish to speak about the loss of his brother Benjamin, now being too concerned about the awfulness of Byron's situation.

They eventually ended up taking lunch in a quiet corner of the dining room in Brooks's club where Hobby asked, "Can you not get help from the Milbankes? They must be quite flush with the Wentworth money now?"

"Apparently not. Lord Wentworth left all to Lady Milbanke and what money there was, has all gone to pay Sir Ralph's debts."

"And so you are now forced to sell Newstead?"

"I *have* to sell it, Hobby, and quickly. Otherwise I can see no way of meeting all the demands for payment. They all believe I entered into a marriage contract with a wealthy heiress and so can't understand the delay in payment. That's why they are nailing all those damned notices on my door."

Hobhouse fumed, seeing this as just another example of sheer *deceit* from the Milbanke family. "What of your portion of the marriage-settlement. Has Sir Ralph paid it?"

Byron shook his head. "Sir Ralph has still not coughed up a single penny of his portion. It seems he is now asserting that I am only entitled to the *interest* on her dowry of twenty thousand, which John Hanson reckons will amount to about *six* thousand. That alone would keep the hounds at bay; but no, Sir Ralph finds excuse after excuse not to pay any of it."

Hobhouse was disgusted; and again he found himself silently blaming the incompetence of Byron's attorney, John Hanson, for allowing such mischievous manoeuvrings on the part of Sir Ralph.

"Personally," said Byron, "I doubt that Sir Ralph will *ever* pay anything at all, and the only benefit of that to me is I will not be forced to thank him, for I have asked and received nothing from his hands."

"But surely Lady Byron could exert some influence on her father?"

"No, no, I cannot put any pressure on Annabella, not in her condition. The only solution is for Newstead to be sold as soon as possible."

When they parted some hours later, Hobhouse could not help feeling very sorry for Byron. To see him reduced in this way was appalling.

Back in his apartment, Hobby sat down with a glass of brandy and cogitated his thoughts on all that Byron had said ... It was clear that he attributed much of his situation to the folly of renting of Devonshire House and the large staff it needed, as well as the additional disgrace of Sir Ralph's meanness and lack of honour in meeting his obligations under the marriage-settlement.

It was also clear that Byron now detested Lady Milbanke; yet he had not once uttered a single word of disapproval against his wife.

~ ~ ~

On the morning of Friday, 28th July, the property of Newstead Abbey, was put up for sale by auction at Garroways in London.

In the aftermath of Waterloo, with the country so impoverished after the long war with France, and so many young officers from wealthy families now dead, it was a bad time to sell such a large estate, despite the glamour of it being the country home of Lord Byron.

At the back of the room, Hobhouse discreetly watched the bidding, dismayed to see the bids starting so low. Most of the bidders, he could see, were keenly interested, but all were hoping for a bargain.

Hobhouse fervently wished that he could buy Newstead himself, for it was almost as dear to him as it was to Byron. Newstead had become like his second home since their days at Cambridge.

Yet, as wealthy as Hobhouse's father was, and despite the fact that he, as the eldest son, would one day inherit that wealth, all he possessed at the moment was an annual allowance from his father – enough to live in the style of a gentleman, but not anywhere near enough to even *think* of buying an estate such as Newstead Abbey.

By Byron desperately needed this sale, and Hobhouse was determined to help him.

The bidding had reached forty thousand – a disgrace. The brochure's recommended price for a quick sale was £120,000, less than Newstead was worth.

Hobhouse raised his hand to bid, and the auctioneer called out – "Forty-five thousand! Do I have another bid?"

The bidding heated up, with Hobhouse raising his hand against every bid, pushing the price up and up until the price had reached eighty-five thousand and Hobby suddenly came back to his senses and got an attack of the jitters.

"Eighty-five thousand! Do I have another bid?"

In the silence that followed Hobhouse began to feel faint. If there were no further bids, Newstead would be sold to him – and that would not do at all.

He almost collapsed with relief when a bid was made for ninety thousand.

"Ninety thousand! Do I have another bid?" The auctioneer looked directly at Hobhouse, who quickly shook his head.

"The bidding has reached ninety thousand, gentlemen," said the auctioneer. "Do I have another bid?"

There were no further bids,

"Calling once at ninety thousand, calling twice ..." After a long silence the hammer came down, and the auctioneer announced that the estate and lands of Newstead Abbey had failed to reach the reserve price.

Deeply disappointed, and still in a nervous state from his experience, Hobhouse went straight to Steven's Coffee House and headed straight for a particular table, sitting down opposite Scrope Davies. He knew Scrope always took coffee in Steven's at this time of the morning and that was why he had come here. He was not yet feeling strong enough to face Byron with the bad news.

Scrope stared. "You look as pale as death. What's amiss?"

Hobhouse told him about the auction and the failure of Newstead to reach it's reserve price.

"I thought I would try and help Byron and kept bidding and bidding and pushing the price up, but when it reached eighty-five thousand, and I realised I was the highest bidder, I almost fainted ..."

Hobby took a quick gulp of coffee, "Because at that moment Scrope – oh, good grief – at that moment I realised that the only money I had in my pocket was the grand sum of nineteen shillings and sixpence – not even a full one pound."

Scrope's laughter cheered Hobby, who eventually saw the funny side of it. "I shall not tell Byron about my antics though."

Scrope smiled. "No, but *I* will. I'm sure he will appreciate it."

Later that evening the three friends met for dinner at Brooks's Club, with Scrope declaring that he would meet the bill.

"Unless, of course," Scrope looked at Hobhouse, "the bill comes to *less* than nineteen shilling and sixpence, and then *you* can pay it."

Even Byron laughed at that. "You did your best, Hobby, but for the sake of your heart and liver I should refrain from such tricks in future."

"By the way," Hobby asked, "what was the reserve price?"

"One hundred and twenty thousand."

"Drink up, gentlemen." Scrope had ordered his usual champagne. "Drink up and be merry."

The mood later changed when a messenger delivered an urgent letter to Scrope Davies, requiring an immediate answer.

Scrope opened and read the letter, frowned, and then handed it over to Byron.

My dear Scrope,

Lend me £500 for a few days; the funds are shut for the dividends, or I would not have made this request.

G Brummell

Byron's eyes widened. "Five hundred pounds? Do you carry such a fortune in your pocket?"

"Of course not. I came out tonight to dine with you, not to play at the gambling tables."

"And being Friday night," said Byron, "the banks are closed until Monday, so what will you do?"

Scrope waved the messenger away to wait; and then said in a low voice, "Whatever money I have in the bank, I will not lend it to Beau Brummell."

"No?" Byron was surprised. "I thought you and Brummell were friends and gambling partners."

"We are *still* friends," Scrope replied, "but we are no longer gambling partners."

"Why not?" asked Hobhouse.

"The truth is ..." Scrope hesitated, "Brummell thinks I don't know, so for God's sake neither of you must speak of it to anyone, not even to yourself in your sleep, but poor Brummell has had a terribly long run of bad luck, and now he is almost ruined."

"Ruined?"

Scrope looked at Byron. "You are not the only one who has creditors knocking on his door. A few have been knocking on Brummell's door."

Hobhouse was appalled. "Did I not warn you about gambling, Scrope? It's a fool's game."

"Oh shut up, Hobby," Scrope snapped. "Now is not the time for criticism." He looked at Byron. "How do I reply and refuse without causing offence or hurt to Brummell's pride? He must *not* know that I am aware of his situation."

Byron thought about it. "Well, you and Brummell have always said that gambling is your main business, so reply in the words of a businessman."

Scrope beckoned to a footman, requested pen and paper, and when it arrived he dipped the nib in the ink and then looked at Byron. "What?"

Byron leaned over and dictated the words which Scrope wrote down:

My dear Brummell,

Tis very unfortunate, but all my money is locked up in the three per cents.

Scrope Davies.

Byron felt very sorry for Brummell, whom he had always liked enormously, but Hobhouse felt no sympathy at all for any gambler – "Not even you, Scrope, not until you give the damned business up."

"I know one thing now for certain," Byron said. "Whenever Fortune comes to a man, whether it be good fortune or bad, it always comes with both hands full."

Hobhouse knew that Byron was referring to his own sudden and tremendous success and fame as a poet, where every word he wrote was considered to be gold, and all so different to the unlucky financial mess he was in now.

Returning to his apartment later that night, Hobhouse made a note in his diary as usual:

Dined with SD and B, all grumbling about life. B says he has the best of wives, but tells us – "don't marry."

PART SEVEN

Lies, lies, and more lies.

"My fortune, given by my father on my marriage was £20,000, which was entirely at Lord Byron's disposal."

Letter from Lady Byron to Madame Mojon.

Chapter Forty-Two

~~~

As Newstead had not sold at auction, Byron was forced to raise money by selling some of the furniture within the Abbey, much of it of great antique value to collectors. But again, due to the impoverished state of the country after the long war, most of the items were sold at sums well below their worth.

Byron was beginning to realise that the peace and stability which he had believed marriage would bring to him, was not turning out as he had hoped. Nor was his wife quite the sensible person with an independent mind, that he had once believed her to be.

He had thought, as in the style of other marriages in their society, he would go out and about occupying himself with his business; and his wife would go out and about entertaining herself with her friends at coffee mornings and afternoon teas. This is what he had seen others do – go about their own separate lives until dinner in the evening – and he had expected the same in his own marriage; yet Annabella seemed to need him to be in her sight at every moment of every day.

The prospect of his first child thrilled him, but in the confinement of her pregnancy, Annabella seemed to expect that he should be confined also, regularly becoming sulky when he ventured out with his friends for a few hours.

"Wedlock?" he often mused to himself. In his case the word should be "Padlock." At least that was how it felt at times.

And she too often frustrated him beyond words by her constant interruptions when he was trying to write, usually resulting in him losing the plot and giving up in despair.

He had written hardly anything at all since his marriage, much to the concern of John Murray who was constantly asking when he could expect "something new?"

Something new? But what?

Whatever it was, Murray was prepared to pay him a handsome fee for it – *"Anything at all, so long as it's written by your hand and has your name on it."*

Finally, Byron gritted his teeth and set his mind to the task of doing what someone in the Press had once falsely accused him of doing – writing for money.

~~~

In mid-August, William Fletcher and Ann Rood were married in a quiet ceremony, followed by a party with the rest of the staff below stairs. The bride and groom were glowing with happiness; and the two newlyweds appeared just as happy when they returned to their duties the following morning.

Lady Byron had spent the day of the wedding in bed, feeling too unwell to get up. Yet this morning, Ann noticed, she tucked into the food on her breakfast tray with the appetite of a ravenous horse.

"So, Rood, tell me about the wedding?"

"Oh, it was lovely, my lady, but very simple and quick. Mr Fletcher didn't want too much fuss, not with him being a widower and wanting to show respect to his dead wife."

"And are you happy now?"

"Oh, yes, my lady. Me and Mr Fletcher is as happy as can be. And his lordship gave us his blessing."

Annabella was quite certain that his lordship had given them a lot more than his blessing.

Annabella pushed the tray aside and lifted herself further up against the pillows. "Pass me my book."

Ann looked to where Lady Byron pointed, at the dresser, and moved to lift the book and bring it back to her mistress. It was a heavy book, bound in black leather, a book that Lady Byron read every morning and every night – her Bible.

"You know," said Annabella, opening the book, "after all this time I will find it very hard to start referring to you as Mrs Fletcher. Would you mind if I continued to call you Rood?"

"Oh no, my lady, I don't mind. It's hard when after a long time someone changes their name to something different, as I do know."

Annabella pressed her hands together as if she was about to pray, and rested them on the open Bible.

Ann rushed to lift up the tray and then carried it hurriedly out of the room, leaving her ladyship to talk to her God in private.

And now that she was outside the door, Ann turned up her eyes: she believed in the goodness of God as much as everyone else, but she didn't bother God every morning, noon and night, like her ladyship did.

~~~

Later that day, in his study, Byron was trying to write a new piece of poetry – *The Siege of Corinth* – a rhythmic and tragic poem based on the story of a young Venetian who had been falsely accused of a crime, forcing him to flee to the Morea, a Venetian peninsula of southern Greece ruled by the Turks. Once there, he enlisted in the Turkish army and quickly rose in the ranks, determined to execute his revenge on Venice with all the Turkish soldiers under his command.

Yet the battle between the Venetians and the Ottomans and the fate of that young man would only be the main body and conclusion of the poem.

But now, in its lighter opening, Byron could not help remembering and drawing upon his own time and experiences in the Morea, recalling the good humour and friendship that had existed between young men who still believed they could conquer the world.

> *In the year since Jesus died for men,*
> *Eighteen hundred years and ten,*
> *We were a gallant company,*
> *Riding o'er land, and sailing o'er Sea*
> *Oh ! but we went merrily !*
> *We forded the river, and climbed the high hill,*
> *Never our steeds for a day stood still;*
> *Whether we lay in the cave or the shed,*
> *Our sleep fell soft on the hardest bed:*
> *Whether we couched in our rough capote,*
> *Or the rougher plank of a gliding boat.*
> *Or stretched on the beach, or our saddles spread*
> *As a pillow beneath the resting head,*
> *For we woke upon the morrow:*
> *All our thoughts and words had scope,*
> *We had thoughts, and we had hope,*
> *Toil and travel, but no sorrow.*

He paused, a slight wavering of depression seeping through him as he looked back on his younger life. He was still only twenty-seven, yet was it all over now? The fun and the sun and the laughter?

Setting down his pen, he put his elbows on the desk and rested his chin on his clenched hands. How long could he stay in this house with the unlucky number 13 on the door, hemmed in by duns and creditors?

No creditor had ever harassed him in his bachelor days. All knew they would be paid eventually. and usually they were paid within a month or two. But in those bachelor days he did not have a palace of staff to maintain, just himself, Fletcher and Mrs Mule ... how simple and easy life had been then, even with the capricious Lady Caroline Lamb pursuing his every step.

He picked up his pen and got back to work, his pen fluid and rapid in every stroke.

"Dearest ..."

Annabella came into the room to ask him a question relating to the household. He looked up at her vaguely. "Whatever you wish, I leave it to you."

As soon as she had gone he returned to the world of the Morea.

We were of all tongues and creeds;
Some were those who counted beads,
Some of the mosque and some of the church,
And some ...

Annabella came back in to clarify her earlier question, and he responded in the same way, "Whatever you wish. I leave all the decisions of the household to you." When the door had closed behind her he finished the line, and started the next verse:

But some are dead, and some are gone
And some are scattered, and alone,
And some are rebels on the hills
That look along –

When Annabella came in yet again, he grabbed up the ink-bottle on his desk and flung it furiously through the open window. "There! Are you satisfied now?"

Annabella stared.

"Will you *never* respect a writer's need for solitude? I have explained it to you often enough."

She turned and left the room.

He picked up his pen, but his ink was gone, and his concentration had also flown.

He stood up in agitation and moved over to the fireplace, placing his hand on the marble ledge above it, his eyes fixed on the empty grate as he dwelt upon his frustration.

"Byron ..."

He could not believe she had come back into the room, and when she spoke, he did not turn round nor reply

He heard the swish of her gown as she walked over to him.

"Byron ... your manner is such that I am beginning to wonder if you are now beginning to feel that I am in your way."

She moved closer. "Byron ... am I in your way?"

"Damnably."

He heard her intake of breath as she took a step backwards. His eyes remained fixed on the empty grate as she walked out of the room.

He knew his response had been rude and reprehensible but he felt no inclination to follow her and apologise – not to a woman who disliked anyone to interrupt her when she was reading her Bible.

Chapter Forty-Three

~ ~ ~

Annabella was descending the main staircase when she saw Scrope Davis being shown into the hall.

Mr Milward, the butler, was about to show him up to the drawing-room when Annabella interrupted him.

"His lordship is not in the drawing-room, Milward. You will find him is his sulking room."

Milward hesitated, confused. "His *sulking* room, my lady?"

"His study."

She gave Scrope Davies the briefest of nods and walked on.

Scrope stared after her, surprised by her icy coldness as well as her sarcasm about Byron.

"Mr Davies?"

Milward showed him into the drawing-room where he sat down to wait.

Scrope sat back and sighed bleakly. His visits to Piccadilly Terrace were becoming less and less frequent due to the rigid formality of everything in this house, which he hated. It was all so very different to the easy and informal way one could drop in on Byron at any time in his bachelor past. Now Byron's social life had dwindled so much that one hardly ever saw him unless calling here, and most of his friends were complaining about it.

Milward entered the drawing-room. "If you please, sir, his lordship would be obliged if you would go on up to his study."

Scrope stood, and Milward moved to lead the way until Scrope said irritably, "There is really no need to escort me, Milward, I do *know* the way to the study."

Milward acquiesced without any sign of resentment. "Very good, sir."

Scrope entered the study to find Byron slowly pacing up and down the room.

Scrope sat down and even after they had started talking, Byron continued to pace up and down.

"Byron, for heaven's sake, either sit down or stand still but pray stop that damned walking while I am talking to you."

Byron stared at Scrope, utterly surprised, for he had not been aware that he was pacing. "There now, you see, Scrope, does that not prove to you what I have always said? That humans are not too dissimilar to animals."

Scrope frowned. "What do you mean?"

"That night we went to the indoor zoo at the exchange, it was the thing I most noticed, the way every animal kept pacing up and down inside its cage. There was a moment when I longed to unlock the cages and set them all free, but then I realised that might have led to a catastrophe for the humans."

"Byron, you are incorrigible," Scrope laughed, but it was a hollow laugh, for now he knew that Byron felt as restless as any caged animal.

~~~

On leaving Piccadilly Terrace, instead of heading back to his own apartment in Great Ryder Street, Scrope decided to call on John Hobhouse in Albany Court.

Hobby listened attentively to Scrope's concerns about Byron, and then sat back and sighed deeply. "I have my own theory, more a mere speculation, but it might have some truth in it."

"Which is?"

"Well, apart from his financial problems, I think his compliance to his wife's wishes, resulting in his withdrawal from society, is because he does not want to have a similar difficult relationship with her, as the one he endured throughout the earlier part of his life with his mother."

"His mother?"

"Oh yes. I know you have never heard Byron say a bad word about his mother, Scrope, but that was solely to protect his own pride and dignity."

"I never heard him say anything at all about his mother, good or bad, and I met her no more than once, and that was at his twenty-first celebration at Newstead."

"The night she was on her best behaviour, singing for us all so kindly? But I can tell you, Scrope, she was a vixen of the worst kind, and she made his life at home utter misery. I have been there at Newstead when she behaved appallingly towards him, yet he always did everything and anything to maintain some sort of peace with her."

Scrope frowned. "But his wife is nothing like that."

"No, quite the opposite. Whenever he did anything which his mother did not approve of, she responded by shouting and bawling and even throwing pokers and fire-tongs in his direction; but now, conversely, whenever he does anything to discommode Lady Byron, her response is always a freezing silence of disapproval."

Did he tell you that?"

"No, I have seen it with my own eyes, and on too many occasions for my liking. Or maybe she simply disapproves of *me*?"

"She certainly disapproves of me," said Scrope, "if her manner towards me today is anything to judge by."

"And the main problem seems to be," Hobby went on, "that most of the time when she takes offence, Byron is usually amusing himself with some sundry playful paradoxes, but she has a total incomprehension of *irony* or *humour*. Every word he says is examined with the most earnest rigour and questions."

"Poor Byron. I once had a schoolmaster like that."

"But whatever is going on, or whatever we may think or feel – " Hobby held up his two palms – "we must *not* interfere in any measure by word or deed. To interfere in any man's marriage is very bad form."

~~~

At the same time that Hobby and Scrope were discussing his marriage in Albany, Byron had slipped out of his house to pay a visit to Lady Melbourne.

He had seen very little of his old friend of late, due to the fact that once they had married, Annabella had decided she no longer approved of her aunt, and begged Byron to have as little as possible to do with her.

"For a *single* man to befriend her is one thing, but Lady Melbourne really does not have a suitable character for communion with a married man," Annabella had advised, and then had launched into one of her quietly-spoken sermons about her aunt's deplorable past ... her five-year affair with the Prince of Wales, and even before that, her affair with Lord Egremont, and all that had been carried on *after* her marriage.

Byron had said little and swiftly excused himself, knowing he did not pull well in conversations with those who stood in moral judgement of others, nor was he in a position to do so, not when his own past was littered with affairs.

Arriving in Whitehall, Lady Melbourne was all love and heartiness on greeting him, full of solicitude and declaring herself to be "So happy to finally *see* you again."

Yet she quickly detected his restless mood and although she did not pry too deeply as to the cause, or say a word against her niece, she urged him to take a few days away from London on his own.

"Why not visit a friend or two? No man needs to be tied to his wife's side all the time. And no – *no* – I do *not* agree! The fact that your wife is pregnant does not mean she has to have a constant bodyguard in attendance. Why, it's preposterous! And you must not allow Annabella to bully you with feminine persuasions. She has her maid, and there are enough men and women in the staff who can take care of her every need."

Byron's mood rapidly improved. "It would be a real pleasure for me to see Francis Hodgson again in Cambridge. Or perhaps Tom Moore in Derbyshire?"

"Then go!" urged Lady Melbourne.

And taking her advice, and despite Annabella's protestations, Byron left London the following morning for Cambridge.

PART EIGHT

Friends Near and Far

"Everywhere was too narrow for him, for Byron. He felt himself confined; the world seemed to him a prison.

But when he can create, he always succeeds, and then everything that comes from the man, especially from his heart, is excellent.

GOETHE

Chapter Forty-Four

~~~

As the carriage rolled up the drive towards Newstead Abbey, Byron breathed in the smell of clean grass and mature trees and the fragrant scent of wild honeysuckle.

The Great Lake finally came into view, cool and serene, and to Byron it was all a refreshment to the eyes and a lift to the spirit.

Before the carriage had even reached the front courtyard the main door opened and old Joe Murray stood on the step peering curiously.

"Ho! Joe!" Fletcher called from the box up top, and Joe quickly stepped out, a smile moving on his face as he rushed towards the slowing carriage and peered inside the open window.

"You didn't write saying you were coming, my lord. Well now, this *is* a confounding surprise!"

"I took the notion on impulse, after leaving Cambridge."

"Well, you are a sight for sore eyes! Aye, indeed. We thought you had abandoned us."

"Why so?"

"Newstead – it's up for sale! Is it true it failed to get a buyer at an auction?"

"Yes."

"So what's going to happen to us when it does sell? Where will we go?"

Byron looked steadily at the old man. "Joe, are you intent on having this complex conversation with me here and now, or are you going to step back and allow me to get out of the carriage?"

Joe, who had been leaning in through the window, his body holding the door shut, jumped back with a hail of apologies. "It's because we are all concerned about our futures and our fate, my lord, as you must surely understand."

"I do," Byron said, stepping out, "but you and I can discuss it later. At this moment all I want to do is drink a large glass of water."

"Why, do you have a headache?"

"No, a hangover."

"Then you must have been drinking port."

"No, I drank nothing but claret. Port makes men ferocious, claret makes them civil. At least, that's what Francis Hodgson says."

"Port goes straight down to the legs and gives men the gout in their ankles."

Byron looked at Joe. "So why do you always say port leaves a terrible headache, if it goes straight down to the legs?"

"I don't know, but it does."

They had entered the hall where Nanny Smith was attempting to dip into her usual quick curtsy while at the same time dabbing a handkerchief to her teary eyes. "Oh, my lord, say it's not true."

"It's not true," Byron said. "Newstead is still here, still standing, still mine. And even if and when it does sell, Nanny, I won't be leaving you without a roof over your head."

"No?"

"No, but allow me to discuss the matter first with Joe, *after* you have brought me a large glass of water."

~

Joe thought they might sit in the library to have their conversation, until Byron reminded him that he had been sitting for hours in a carriage on the journey here, so they wandered around the side of the lake down to the great waterfall.

"If and when Newstead sells, I intend to do my utmost to persuade the new owners to keep you and Nanny Smith on the staff. I can give no assurance for the others, but you never know."

"And if the new owners say no to me and Nanny? Where do we go then?"

"There are two cottages that have recently become empty on the estate, are there not?"

"*Three* cottages," Joe said. "Mr Hanson's agent was here and ordered Owen Mealey out of his house and off this property or he would be dragged off to jail by the police. So Mealey collected all his belongings and went, mighty quick."

"Would you mind taking me to see those cottages tomorrow?"

"Aye, my lord."

Next morning, Nanny Smith was surprised when Joe told her, "His lordship says you are to come with us. He says we can all go in the carriage."

"The carriage – for a ride?" Nanny looked as excited as a girl as she whipped off her apron. "I've never been for a ride in a carriage before."

"I don't know why we have to go in the carriage," Joe said. "It's no more than a smart walk of ten or fifteen minutes."

"Aye, but you and me can march faster than his lordship with his limp."

"Oh, aye, I forgot that. He can walk far, but not as fast as us."

At the entrance to Willowtree Lane, a leafy and peaceful spot on the estate, beside a small stream, the carriage stopped outside the gate of the first cottage and all three walked up the path and Joe opened the door with his keys.

"The agent got all the keys back from Mealey," Joe said, turning the lock, "and I have them all now."

Nanny Smith walked through the parlour and headed straight for the kitchen, all of which was spotlessly clean. "Well, she kept it nice enough, Mrs Turner," said Nanny, looking around her, and then peeked into the small bedroom.

"What happened to her, Mrs Turner?" Byron asked.

"Oh, when her son died at Waterloo, her heart was broke and she gave up living, and died not long after. See..." Nanny was looking through the window onto the back garden, "she even stopped tending her garden, poor heartbroken soul."

Byron turned to Joe. "According to the map, there are four cottages on this lane, so which is the other empty cottage?"

"Oh, that belonged to old Bill Hensham who emigrated to Yorkshire to live with his daughter. His cottage is exactly the same as this one, but at the far end of the lane, by the bend in the stream, but his place has a bigger garden with more trees in it."

"Very well," Byron said. "I shall get Mr Hanson to arrange two new leases for a period of fifty years each, rent free. Would that be long enough?"

"For what?" asked Nanny.

"For you to live in when Newstead is sold. Is that acceptable to you?"

"My own cottage?" Nanny had to sit down. "I've always wanted my own cottage."

"But if the new owner objects?" Joe said. "We could be turned out."

"No," Byron replied quite definitely. "I have discussed the matter with Hanson, and no matter who the new owner will be, a lease is a lease, and in law the tenure must stand for the duration of the lease and cannot be set aside."

"Well, Mrs Smith seems to like this cottage, so old Bensham's will be mine and I prefer it." Joe was pleased to have his own cottage, although he was still not happy: "And you will remember that you did *promise,* my lord, that we might be able to stay working at the Abbey."

"Joe I promise that I will plead and beg and even try to *bribe* any new owner to keep you both at the Abbey, but if that fails, then this is the best I can do for you."

"Aye, aye," Joe nodded, "and mighty grateful to you

we are too, my lord. I suppose I could always walk up to the Abbey every day and take a look at it. After fifty years it would be hard for me to not see it every day, if only from afar."

"And in the meantime," said Nanny Smith, "we could spend our days off looking after our own cottages. Won't that be fine, Joe?"

"Days off?" Joe replied indignantly. "When have *I* ever taken a day off?"

He turned to Byron. "Now Mealey's house, what do you intend to do with that place? It's a lot bigger than these houses on Willowtree."

"Yes, and that's why I intend to instruct John Hanson to draw up a new ninety-nine-year lease on it for Fletcher and his wife. If I do it now, as the owner, before Newstead is sold, then the lease cannot be broken by the new purchaser. Owen Mealey did not have a lease, just a peppercorn rent on the house while he was employed here."

"Oh my, Fletcher *will* be pleased," said Nanny, and then tears suddenly sprang from her eyes. "But Newstead won't be the same without a Byron in charge ... and especially without *you*, my lord ... No, this place won't be the same without you at all."

Chapter Forty-Five

~~~

After eight enjoyable days away from London, Byron returned to find a new lodger in his house.

Mrs Clermont, his wife's former governess, had been sent down to London by Lady Milbanke to perform the role of "companion" to her daughter during the last four months of her confinement.

Byron had not even noticed Mrs Clermont at the wedding, but he looked at her now – a middle-aged woman, short and thin, in a black taffeta dress buttoned tightly up to the neck beneath a white lace collar. Her hair was a dull brown streaked heavily with iron-grey, but it was the eyes in her thin face that fixed his attention the most – large staring eyes that held a look of defiance in them – but who or what was she defying? Surely not himself, for he had no objection whatsoever to his wife having another servant; although she would be yet another mouth to feed.

However, he *did* object later that evening at dinner when Mrs Clermont walked into the dining room and impudently sat herself down at the table, bold as brass, causing him to stare at Annabella who simply lowered her eyes and got on with her chewing.

He excused himself quickly, for no man could indulge in a private conversation with his wife in front of a listening servant.

Annabella found him later, sparring in one of the garden rooms with Fletcher wiping the sweat off their brows with their boxing gloves.

"Dearest?" She walked over to Byron. "Dearest, about Mrs Clermont – "

"The impudence of the woman!" Byron said. "Has Fletcher ever walked into the dining room and sat himself down to dine with us?"

"Fletcher is merely a servant, a valet. Mrs Clermont is no longer a servant, no longer my governess, her status is now that of a 'lady's companion'. A very humble one, I admit, but she is still entitled to join us at table."

"Your humble companion did not look very humble to me."

"She is very amiable and genial, as you will find when you get to know her."

Byron looked in disbelief at Fletcher, and then at his wife. "Does this mean she will be sitting there every time we dine, listening to every word we say?"

"Oh, really, Byron, it is hardly a problem. You know I dislike to talk when eating, not until dinner is over. At least, you *should* know that by now."

Fletcher, standing aside but listening, and knowing well all the rules and etiquette of the upper class, was quite miffed by it all.

"If you ask me," he said to Ann later that night, "it's her ladyship who has all the impudence. She *will* insist on always having her own way with his lordship, always commanding and over-ruling him in *his* roost. Did she do that with her father in Seaham?"

"No, she wouldn't dare, but Miss Annabella was always a spoiled child. And she always knew how to get her way in the end, no matter how sly or mean she had to be to get it."

Fletcher stared. "Sly or mean?"

Ann nodded. "If you don't believe me, ask Mrs Milward. She knows all about her tricks, and it was she who *warned* me how to behave with her. She told me – 'always be meek and agreeable with her and never cross her, otherwise she'll have you out on your ear with no character and no mercy'."

Fletcher frowned. "How can she do that? Not give you a reference or character, if you've done nothing wrong?"

Ann lowered her voice. "When I first went there, to Seaham Hall, there was a rumour that one maid who crossed Miss Annabella in some way, was accused of stealing a ring, which Mrs Milward is certain she never did, but the poor thing was sent packing by Lady Milbanke with no reference or character to help her get another job."

After a silence, Fletcher said, "Then you'd better watch your step, Ann, and make sure not to cross Lady Byron in any way, d'you hear?"

"I never do. It's not my way to be disagreeable."

"Because if you were to be sent packing, I would have to leave his lordship's house and service too, and I would not be happy about that, Ann, not happy at all."

"Don't worry. Mrs Milward always keeps a close watch on me, always advising and protecting me, so's I never get into trouble or accused of anything."

Fletcher smiled. "She must like you fondly then, must Mrs Milward."

Ann nodded. "Oh she does like me ... but Mrs Milward is not very happy at the moment. No, not happy at all. When I saw her earlier, her face looked like a loaf of dough in the oven, swelling up and up in the heat of her anger."

~

Mrs Milward, who had been the housekeeper at Seaham Hall before being sent down to London in service to Miss Annabella, was sitting in her office-cum-parlour with Mrs Henderson the cook, glooming over it all.

"And we was all doing so nicely down here, nice and peaceful, until that Clermont woman comes along to ruin it all."

Mrs Henderson, a Londoner, couldn't quite understand her friend's alarm.

"What's so wrong with her? She don't look that fearsome to me. When I seen her, coming along the corridor down here to gawk in all the rooms, she was creeping along like a mouse looking for a bit of cheese."

Mrs Milward nodded. "Aye, that's what she does,

creeps around the place, always creeping and looking and watching. Whereas me now, I walk heavily on my heels and everyone hears me coming before they see me."

Mrs Henderson chuckled. "You do *march* along, you do. I would say they can hear you coming in Berkeley Square."

"All honest and above board, that's me," smiled Mrs Milward, but a moment later she was glooming again.

"I tell you, Mrs H, that Mary Clermont is here to cause trouble, and no mistake. And whatever she sees or hears, she'll be reporting it straight back to Lady Milbanke. And if she finds nowt worth reporting, she'll make something up. Anything to keep her ladyship's ear flapping."

~

It was only a matter of weeks before Byron began to think along the same lines as Mrs Milward, although he didn't know of her warnings to others.

He was still not sure what it was, in word or deed, that had given him the suspicion that Mrs Clermont had been sent to Piccadilly Terrace to act as Lady Milbanke's spy. But who was she sent to spy on? Annabella? The staff? Himself? Or perhaps he was simply imagining it?

Either way, he found the woman and her watchful eyes repellent, avoiding her at every turn; but she was not to be blocked. Somehow she always managed to be there, at Annabella's side, or standing nearby, like a shadow.

Chapter Forty-Six

~~~

Now that his wife had a regular companion, Byron accepted an invitation signed by George Lamb and Douglas Kinnaird to become a joint director on the committee of the Drury Lane Theatre. He had always loved the theatre, and now he was to play a part in it.

George Lamb, he had always got on with; and surprisingly, although he was William Lamb's younger brother, George Lamb had always taken Byron's side against Lady Caroline.

Douglas Kinnaird he had also known for a long time, as well as his long-time mistress, Maria Keppel, who was a singer by profession, and who had once given Byron sixty bottles of brandy because she did not know what else to do with them. Why and where she had got them, he still had not a clue.

Annabella did not approve of "theatre people" considering them vain and immoral, and making her disapproval very clear to Byron, but this time her sermon had no effect; it was too exciting an opportunity to reject.

As the weeks went by he spent less and less time at home, regularly going to John Murray's establishment in Albermarle Street for morning coffee and conversation with other authors, one of them being the famous Walter Scott, whom Byron greatly admired

The Drury Lane Committee sat most afternoons in lively discussions, and then attended the performances in the evenings where Byron had his own box, although he preferred to spend most of his time backstage, enjoying the banter of the actors in the Green Room.

Yet it was not all fun – he took his duties as a director very seriously; reading and judging the scripts sent in from playwrights, and upon his arrival he found a backlog of over five hundred scripts waiting to be read.

Taking many of the scripts home with him and reading late into the night, he was dismayed to find himself rejecting almost all of them, due to the poor quality of the writing. Only one script – *Bertram* – a tragedy from an author named Robert Charles Maturin, he immediately recommended for production at Drury Lane, and the committee, trusting his judgement, agreed.

When Annabella again voiced her increasing disapproval of his role at the theatre, he half-earnestly, half-jestingly begged her for sympathy.

"The *scenes* I have to go through as a committee director! It is not only the scripts, most of which should never have been put to paper – but the amount of *people* I am forced to deal with every day – the authors – and the authoresses – the milliners – the wild Irishmen – the people from Brighton – from Chatham – from Dublin – from Dundee – all of whom come demanding an audience with *me* – and to all I must give a civil answer – and a hearing – and a *reading!*"

"And most of what is portrayed in theatres is childish playacting and nonsense," Annabella replied coldly, causing Byron's playful good humour to instantly vanish.

"Are the plays of Shakespeare childish nonsense? Hamlet? Othello? Macbeth?"

"Well, no, but –"

"Why do you insist on continually *belittling* actors and the people of the theatre? And why, in God's name, do you believe that your opinions are always so infallibly *right*?"

Annabella remained cool and composed, refusing to lose her temper "I merely wish to know why, in the evenings, instead of staying at home with your wife, you prefer to keep going out to the theatre?"

"I go out to the theatre instead of staying at home for

the same reason most people do – to be amused, not lectured."

He left her and went up to his library, tired of her carping and demeaning *everything* he did. His two most lauded poems, *Childe Harold* and *The Corsair,* she now considered to be nothing more than "naughty versifying," preferring instead the more religious words of the *Hebrew Melodies.*

He had suffered himself to tolerate it all under the pretence of humour, due to her pregnancy. He had been warned that women could become very thorny during their confinement, so understanding and consideration *must* be given at all times.

But pregnant or not, who was *she* – who had spent all her life in the backwoods of Seaham – to consider herself so knowledgeable that she could speak so condescendingly about the work of actors? She had no idea what went on backstage. No idea how hard actors worked to improve and perfect their art.

He turned and ran his hand along the library shelves until he found his own "*Hints From Horace"*. Opening it, he flicked through the book until he came to the page he was looking to find, and read –

And Nature formed at first the inward man,
And actors copy Nature – when they can.

He had written that six years ago, when he was twenty-one. His love of Shakespeare and serious theatre and the work of great actors was a part of him long before he joined the Committee at Drury Lane – yet she primly mocked his admiration and talked about the actors as if they were no better than hapless burlesque players of parody and caricatures.

Of course, there were some trivial performers like that in the world, but not one of them ever got onto the stage of the renowned Drury Lane Theatre.

~

In the drawing-room he had left Annabella standing in grim condemnation and anger.

Mrs Clermont, who had been listening by the drawing-room door, had scurried away when his lordship had walked out, and then crept back to the drawing-room to give Annabella consolation.

"What has you looking so white, pet? Did his lordship upset you?"

Annabella shrugged slightly. "We had a disagreement about the theatre, that is all."

"Oh, the theatre ... " Mrs Clermont sucked in her lips for a thoughtful moment ... "And all those actresses ... most are shameless strumpets not fit to be in the same room as his lordship ... mind, he *does* have a reputation for being led on by women."

"He *did* have a reputation," Annabella snapped, "but that is all in the past, and most of it was false."

But the embers of Annabella's jealousy had been stoked, and Mrs Clermont knew it, hiding her delight when Annabella refused to speak to Byron for four days, communicating with him solely by written notes, to which he just as tersely sent back a brief written reply.

Chapter Forty-Seven

~~~

A few mornings later, having taken a short nap after breakfast, Mrs Clermont yawned and then got up off her bed to move over to her mirror and re-pin her brown and grey ropy hair into a knot at the back of her neck.

Smoothing down her dress in preparation for returning downstairs, she walked towards the door but – passing by the window – she stopped abruptly and stared down into the garden.

Annabella and Lord Byron were strolling slowly together, their manner normal and they seemed to be talking to each other in a friendly way.

Mrs Clermont bit her lip so hard it turned white. She had known hatred in the past for Lord Byron, but now her hatred was powerful and consuming because she had never forgiven him for stealing away her precious girl. He was the one at fault. *He* was the one to blame, because before she had met him, Bella had never shown any real interest in a man.

And during these past days she had been beginning to persuade herself that she *could* get Annabella back, if only because she so desperately needed to be needed by her. Otherwise what was she to do? Where was she to go?

Through her habit of listening and eavesdropping on her master and mistress's conversations in their new residence at Kirkby Mallory, she had learned that Sir Ralph wanted to pension her off; and no doubt he would try and lodge her in some miserable hut of a cottage on the outskirts of the Seaham estate. How could she live all on her own, with no one to talk to? At forty-three she was not yet ready to live the life of a lonely hermit.

So far though, Lady Milbanke had sounded reluctant,

always answering, "Not yet, Ralph, not yet. Annabella may need her in the future."

She knew that Lady Milbanke had been referring to the coming child, and the help that might be needed in his care. But now she knew for certain that *he* would never allow it. Lord Byron would never agree to her being a part of his child's nursery care. He hated her and she knew it and the feeling was mutual.

If only Annabella had married someone less aristocratic and above himself, someone more meek and malleable, although it would have been better if Annabella had not married at all.

On her own, Annabella would always need someone to look after her, tortured as she was with her tendency to bouts of hypochondria and imaginary illnesses, and all due to that damned Medical Encyclopaedia she was always reading.

Mrs Clermont was sure that the only reason Bella sat reading that medical book was to search for a suitable illness she could suffer from for a week or two.

But Bella wouldn't be suffering today. Not now that his lordship had stepped down from his high and mighty pedestal to be friendly with her again.

Too annoyed to go downstairs, Mrs Clermont walked over to her armchair and sat down, closing her eyes to think, while constantly biting her lower lip.

How long she had been sitting in her chair she did not know – coming back to reality when someone knocked on her door.

"Enter," she called, in the same tone used by Lady Milbanke.

Rood popped her head inside the door. "Lady Byron wants to know if you wish to join her and her Christian ladies for morning coffee?"

"Are that lot here again?" She shrugged her annoyance; ever since Annabella had joined that Evangelical Sect those women were always coming here.

"Oh, well, I'll bring down my knitting and sit to the

side by the window," she said, "but I'll not be doing any Bible reading, not with that sanctimonious lot and their toffee-nosed way of speaking."

"As you wish," said Rood, and her face disappeared as she turned and hurried away.

~

Rushing along the landing to the drawing-room, Mrs Clermont almost tripped up when she saw his lordship standing in the room, surrounded by the group of ladies, all surprised and delighted that he had graced their presence and flitting round him like moths to a flame.

"C," Annabella declared, "Lord Byron has agreed to join us, but only for coffee. Come and sit down."

"I'll sit by the window and do some knitting, if you don't mind."

"No, not at all." Annabella turned to the group. "Ladies, shall we begin?"

Two trays of coffee and china were brought in by servants who placed them on a long low table standing between two sofas where the ladies seated themselves. Lady Byron sat in a high-backed armchair at the top end of the table, directing the servants who were pouring the coffee and then another who carried in a tray of pastries.

Byron sat down in a matching high-backed armchair at the far end of the two sofas, nearest to the door, feeling completely out of place; but he had decided that the impasse between himself and Annabella could not continue, and some great gesture had to be made to her if he was to obtain her forgiveness.

So here he was, sitting with a group of holy Christian ladies whom, to his surprise, were all quite nice and not as stuffed-up as he had imagined.

He had expected the religious conversations not to begin until after they had drank their coffee and ate their pastries; but no, it started straight away, nothing but talk of the Christian way of life, probably because they all lived it, and good luck to them.

He sat silent, attempting to be as unobtrusive as possible, for he had nothing to offer to the conversation except his own doubts, which would not be helpful at all.

Unconsciously, as he often did when he was thinking, he took out his fob-watch from the pocket of his waistcoat, his eyes lowered while his fingers played with the links of the chain as his mind wandered and drifted. He was thinking of Douglas Kinnaird, who had now dispensed with his mistress of seven years, Maria Keppel, which was all rather sad in his opinion. He had always liked Maria, a pretty and likable woman whom everyone referred to as "Mrs K" for the sake of respectability, and as the surname of both began with that letter.

"She was no more than his whore," George Lamb had said when telling him the news. "Why else would she live with a man for so long without insisting on marriage?"

It was then Byron understood why Maria did not like George Lamb, who was otherwise an agreeable man, but too much under the influence of his stiff bitch of a wife who doubtlessly had given Maria the name of "whore".

Annabella was watching Byron and knew he was not listening to the conversation at all. She could tell from the way he was fiddling with his watch-chain that his mind was far away. She had hoped he would listen and learn and even participate, if only for her sake, in front of her friends.

She also noticed that Mrs Sheppard, a round-faced jolly lady in her forties, whom Annabella did not really like, could not take her eyes off Byron, continually trying to catch his attention, but no doubt his mind was off in some medieval poetic dream.

Mrs Sheppard's mind had also taken a poetic turn,

referring to those elegant lines, commencing with " If that High World ..." which led to a speculative discussion amongst the ladies on what Heaven would be like, and the probable nature of happiness in that future world, until Mrs Sheppard was suddenly inspired by a desire to know Lord Byron's opinion on the subject.

"Lord Byron," she said loudly, "pray may I ask to know what might constitute, in *your* mind, if you were to arrive in Heaven and look around, what would be the one thing you saw there, that would give you the greatest happiness?"

"The pleasure, Madam, of seeing *you* there."

Mrs Sheppard was so surprised, she almost choked with delight, her hand going to her breast in a paroxysm of girlish giggles – "Oh Lordy Lord – wait till I tell that to Alfred!"

Annabella was glaring at Byron, annoyed by his complimentary effusion to Mrs Sheppard instead of giving her, and everyone else, a serious answer.

Byron saw the lecture in his wife's glaring eyes and quickly excused himself, bowing gallantly to the ladies before leaving the room and heading to his study.

Today, being Sunday, there was no Committee meeting or performance at Drury Lane, so he would write a letter to Douglas Kinnaird and get Fletcher to deliver it.

Dear Douglas,

Poor Maria! I do not understand the particulars – nor wish to hear them – all I know is that she made your house very pleasant to your friends, and therefore whatever has or may happen – she has my good will, go where she will ...

He paused, for it suddenly struck him that in comparison to Maria, his own wedded wife had rarely ever attempted to make his house pleasant to his friends

... and for some unknown reason, the two friends she most disliked were John Hobhouse and Scrope Davies ... two of the most honourable and finest men in the world.

Chapter Forty-Eight

~~~

In the opinion of the ladies of London's *beau monde*, Lord Byron's marriage appeared to have tamed him; although many were still wondering why Lady Byron's fortune was not put to some good use towards their entertainment. After all, had they not always entertained Lord Byron well during his bachelor days?

Some said it was because Lady Byron was not inclined to High Society; while others responded – "Then why the damnation did she marry the most celebrated man in it?"

It really was too bad. The Byrons had given no dinner parties, no soirées, and that beautiful ballroom in Devonshire House must be covered in dust.

Some blamed Lady Byron for forcing his lordship to live so economically. What was she thinking? This was London – the Great Metropolis of the Country – not the parish of Seaham.

The men, of course, viewed it differently, for being just a short walk away, Byron still dropped into Brook's Club occasionally. They were all so used to Byron's laughter and playful wit in the past, but now they could not help noticing that his manner and mood had become increasingly quiet and gloomy.

Deputising as "Acting Manager" for a few weeks, various people from the theatre occasionally called in to see him at his home in Piccadilly Terrace, sometimes seeking instructions, sometimes carrying notes, and sometimes actresses came to the house, pleading with him to get the author to take out a speech in the play, or to add a few more speeches to make their part bigger – and Byron loved it all; the hustle and the bustle and the drama of theatre life – until his wife sought to spoil it all.

Whenever an actress called at the house, Annabella made sure she was present throughout the interview, casting very cold eyes over the visitor; and when the actress had left, she enjoyed making condescending remarks about the colourful flamboyance of her clothes or the cheapness of her jewellery.

"She has a habit," Byron furiously told Hobhouse, "of deciding on a person's character after she has seen them only once."

Hobhouse also noticed, when visiting the house, that Byron and his wife no longer dined together – a matter which had become a new ground for grievance to Lady Byron.

"I'll not eat with that impudent Clermont woman in the room," Byron told Hobhouse. "Annabella knows it, and yet she insists upon it, because her *mother* ordered it."

The situation went from bad to worse when Byron came home one night from the theatre, and knew instantly that someone had broken into his private writing bureau and his desk.

Annabella was outraged when he accused her, insisting it must have been one of the servants.

Fletcher was instructed to find out; and returned shaking his head, certain that not one of the servants had been near his lordship's bureau or desk.

"And why would they? All you keep in there is papers. If they were going to pilfer anything, why not some of the shillings and sixpences you leave thrown on your dressing-table?"

Fletcher was completely convinced of the innocence of all the servants he had questioned.

Byron let the matter drop, but he had his own suspicion that it *was* Annabella. Her ridiculous jealousy about the actresses at the theatre was getting worse by the day.

He was wrong. Annabella would never lower herself

to do such a thing – but she had instructed Mrs Clermont to do it.

The search was fruitless, for all C had found was a passionate love-letter from a married woman, which had been written to Byron before his own marriage.

Annabella did not know the woman, but after reading her declarations of undying love, she looked at the name, and looked at the address, and then forwarded the letter anonymously to the woman's husband.

A few nights later, partly out of defiance, and partly for his own pleasure, Byron submitted to temptation and began a secret affair with an actress at the Drury Lane theatre – not one of the leading actresses who had called at the house – but a girl from the chorus, the pretty Susan Boyce.

~ ~ ~

In early November, a month before Annabella was due to give birth, Augusta complied with Byron's request and came to stay at Devonshire House in order to help Annabella during the last month of her confinement.

"*Dearest Augusta...*" Annabella welcomed her sister-in-law with the most tender and appreciative words, and gave her the warmest of embraces. She was even more delighted when Augusta confided that she too was pregnant – again – and this time George was demanding that it *must* be a son.

"And what number will this child be ... your fifth? How wonderful," said Annabella, touching her lips to Augusta's cheek.

So Augusta was warmly welcomed into her brother's house by a sister-in-law who truly despised her.

"Why did Byron send for her – that dunce?" Annabella complained to Mrs Clermont. "What help can *she* give to me?"

Byron's reaction to the news of Augusta's fifth

pregnancy was typically flippant:

"Well, your lord and president may be very bad at breeding horses, but he is evidently a master at breeding humans. And you, my dear, seem to have a true *vocation* for it."

Augusta laughed, taking no offence, knowing he did not say it maliciously.

That laughter of Augusta's soon got on Annabella's nerves, knowing that Byron had caused it. Always so humorous and merry in his sister's company, yet now always so remote or lukewarm towards her.

Retiring to bed early, as she always did, she lay awake until she heard Byron and his sister finally climbing the stairs, still talking merrily together, and her jealousy rose to such a pitch of burning rage, she got out of bed and wrote furiously in her journal:

I thought of his silver dagger, lying in the library, and I longed to get it and plunge it into her heart.

Chapter Forty-Nine

~~~

All the servants in Devonshire House liked Lord Byron's sister, Mrs Leigh. She had a simplicity of character and a softness in her manner which truly endeared her to them. She also had an unwillingness to put them to too much trouble on her behalf, and when she decided to do a particular job herself, she did it very efficiently.

But today Augusta was in one of her flaps, pinning on her hat, grabbing up her purse, and rushing out of her room and along the landing and almost bumping into Annabella.

"Good gracious, Goose, where are you flying to now?"

"Back to the palace. I left something there which I need to collect, but I'll be straight back."

"And your brother? Where is he?"

"In the drawing-room with his friend Mr Hobhouse."

"Friend?" Annabella smirked. "Remove the 'r' from that word, dearest, and what do you get?"

Augusta wrinkled her brow. "Fiend."

"Exactly. Fiend. An evil genius who I believe to be a very bad influence on Byron."

"Mr Hobhouse?"

"And that other blackguard with the ridiculous name, *Scrope* Davies. Why can't they accept that Byron is a married man now and leave him alone."

Augusta fidgeted with her hat. "I really must dash now, take care, dear sis, I won't be long."

Annabella watched her go, wondering how she could get that over-humble and yet *presumptuous* creature out of her house? She was indeed presumptuous to come here and stay, for she had not invited her, nor did she need her help. She had her own dear Clermont to look after her, and there would be enough midwives and a doctor to attend upon her at the time of the birth.

Yet it would be quite difficult to remove the silly goose and send her on her way, due to Byron's high regard for her – his precious older sister. The way he openly spoke of his affection for her was quite juvenile.

"Annabella!" Mrs Clermont came rushing up to her. "Annabella, there's another actress in the drawing-room with his lordship. She was shown in there just a minute ago. You told me to tell you when any of the sluts called here."

Annabella drew in a breath. "And that's just the most disgusting thing about it, my dear C, the fact that those women dare to call her here, to see *my* husband, in *my* house."

"Will I come along with you?"

"No, that would not be appropriate. His lordship would be furious if you were to venture into the drawing-room while he had company."

"Furious?" Mrs Clermont clasped her hands vehemently against her breast. "I know it's not my place to express my opinion on his lordship, but I have my feelings, I have my thoughts, and it would distress me sorely if his lordship in his furiousness should seek to bully you."

"Don't be silly, C, he would never do that. Besides, I can always quell him with my eye."

"But if –"

Annabella now quelled Mrs Clermont with her eye, before making her solitary way to the drawing-room, where she silently stood by the open door and saw Byron and Hobhouse and the woman looking over a colourful costume in bright colours of amber and red and gold.

The woman was young, no more than mid-twenties, with auburn hair under an exquisite hat of cream velvet, below which she wore a matching cream velvet costume in the style of a riding habit.

Her choice of clothes was very good, quite elegant, so it would be hard to mock or point out any faults in them afterwards. Nevertheless ... she walked into the room and pretended to be astounded at what was going on.

"Surely the theatre's costume room is where this should be taking place?"

All three turned to stare at her. Annabella's glare was fixed on the female. She was handsome, and had fine grey eyes and she was attractive. Nor was she shy, for she came straight up to Annabella and smiled. She was also tall, which Annabella disliked, because she herself was small.

The impudent trollop held out her hand in greeting and said in a plush upper-class voice which she had obviously studied to perfection at the theatre. "Good morning, Lady Byron. Pray excuse my calling in without an invitation."

Annabella looked down at the proffered hand, and then up at Byron who had rushed forward.

"Annabella, this is Miss Margaret Mercer Elphinstone. I think I may have told you about her – a friend of Princess Charlotte?"

Annabella stared. "Princess Charlotte – the heir to the throne?"

"Oh, not for a long time yet," said Miss Elphinstone smiling, " not until her father has sat on it first."

"How do you do," said Annabella stiffly, and might then have turned and rushed out of the room in humiliation, had not Byron taken her by the arm and escorted her solicitously to an armchair, where she sat down, her face still blushing, while the others sat down around her.

"Miss Elphinstone," said Byron, "was the very person who told me what happened between the Prince Regent and his daughter which led to my poem, "*Lines To A Lady Weeping?*"

"Was it, by Jove!" said Hobhouse, gazing at Miss Elphinstone as if in love with her. "You were there when it happened? Oh pray tell?"

She looked at Lord Byron, who smiled, and so encouraged, Miss Elphinstone agreeably told Hobhouse and Annabella of the incident.

"The princess was so upset at hearing her father abusing his former friends in the Whig Party, she burst into tears at the table. The Prince was fairly drunk. And when Princess Charlotte began to sob, the Prince said to her, 'You had better retire,' to which all the ladies rose. But as we were leaving, the Prince Regent followed and laid hold of my arm and dragged me into an inner drawing-room where he sat for half an hour bitterly haranguing me."

"But why – and why *you?*" asked Hobhouse.

Miss Elphinstone shrugged. "Because he knew I was a Whig, as is my father and all my family, so he had ridiculously decided that *I* must have been the one responsible for turning Princess Charlotte into a Whig."

"Who *is* your father?" Annabella asked.

"Viscount Keith."

"What happened then?" asked Hobhouse impatiently. "With the Prince in the inner room?"

"Oh, as I say, he was quite drunk, and I was wishing he would cease his haranguing and lecturing and shut up, which he eventually did, and seemed to relent. He said, 'Well, my dear, I know you are a good girl, and a good friend to the princess, so my punishment will be lenient."

"Punishment? Good grief!" Hobhouse looked appalled. "What punishment?"

"I was to be barred from entering the house or speaking to the princess for a period of six months." Miss Elphinstone smiled in amusement. "However, after only two weeks, when the princess sent for me, I suffered no obstruction on entering the house, and the Prince Regent appeared to have not a jot of memory of his decree against me."

Annabella's mind was reeling; to think she had

mistaken this lady, an intimate of the royal family, for a common actress.

Her eyes moved to the costume draped over one of the chairs. "But what is that ... " she pointed, "that colourful costume?"

"That is my *Albanian* costume," Byron told her. "The one I wore in the painting by Thomas Phillips. I loaned it to Miss Elphinstone for her to wear to a masquerade ball."

"And now, over a year later, I have brought it back to its rightful owner," said Miss Elphinstone, looking at Byron. "Did I tell you I was a great success in it, the envy of all?"

"Then you must keep it," Byron said. "I certainly have no further use for it."

Miss Elphinstone clasped her hands in delight, but demurred. "No, you are so kind, but no, I could not keep it, it's too magnificent."

"Say no more – it's yours."

Byron stood and walked over to the chair and began to fold the various pieces of the costume to return them to her box.

Miss Elphinstone tripped lightly over to join him on her dainty heels. "Are you sure? If you are, then you really are an angel, because now you have saved me a great deal of embarrassment."

"Why so?"

"I had to turn up the skirt, it was too long, and the seamstress made such a good job of it, that now I can't unpick her tiny stitching."

Byron smiled. "And now you won't need to."

Annabella watched the two of them, seething with jealousy, and wanting to know more about the relationship between Miss Elphinstone and Lord Byron.

But she waited, rising to her feet and saying her goodbye graciously, until Byron had left the room to escort Miss Elphinstone and the dress-box down to her carriage.

Then she turned to Hobhouse and asked: "Was Byron very friendly with Miss Elphinstone in the past?"

"Not *very* friendly, but they were friends, and they might have become even closer if she had not moved down to Tunbridge Wells for the summer. I know they do write to each other occasionally, but Miss Elphinstone has so many men wishing for her hand. She is a great heiress, you see. Truly, a great heiress, and one day she will become one of the richest women in England. Although she is wealthy enough in her own right even now."

Annabella did not miss the words – "Truly, a great heiress" – but she went on inquisitively: "Just friends? Is that all?"

Hobhouse nodded. "That's all. Although at one time Byron did think of proposing to her, but was deterred by his fear of being called a fortune-hunter."

"Indeed," said Annabella, and walked out of the room without uttering another word, leaving Hobhouse to stand and wonder what he had said to offend her.

~

Augusta returned from the palace, and found Annabella in the small sitting room in a bad mood.

"What is wrong, dear? Are you feeling unwell?"

Annabella looked at her curiously. "Do you know Miss Mercer Elphinstone?"

"Margaret? Oh yes, I know her very well. She is often at the palace, a true darling of a girl."

"Really? I found her quite incomprehensible. I suppose she thinks it becoming to her situation to be assuming, and obviously the encouragement she obviously meets with everywhere has increased this disagreeable habit of hers."

Augusta was baffled. "Have *you* ever met her?"

Annabella nodded. "She came here today, all eyes for Byron, although she was very roughly agreeable to me."

After her dash to the palace and back, Augusta felt too tired to ask what "very roughly agreeable" actually meant, rising to her feet and saying instead, "I'll ask Milward to tell the kitchen to send us up some tea."

Chapter Fifty

~ ~ ~

Annabella could not stop thinking about Miss Margaret Mercer Elphinstone, especially now that she had called at the house. And no doubt Byron, with his usual gallantry, would have invited her to call again "anytime".

She tossed and moved about in her bed. Sleep would not come. She looked at the clock and saw it was not yet ten. Usually, when she could not sleep, she got up and sought out her husband to talk for a while, but tonight he had gone to the theatre, and of late he often did not return from Drury Lane until long after midnight.

She lay musing ... the fiend had said that Byron and Miss Elphinstone wrote to each another occasionally .... Had he been writing letters to Miss Elphinstone at the same time he had been writing to herself ... during their courtship? She knew he had a habit of keeping letters, especially those from 'friends' he valued.

Her jealousy and curiosity were tormenting her, spurring her to get out of bed, to put on a robe, pick up a few hairpins from her dressing table, and then make her way slowly to Byron's bedroom and his writing bureau.

Usually Fletcher slept in the room adjoining Byron's dressing-room, but not since he had married. Now he and Rood had their own room at the back of the house, and Fletcher only appeared when his lordship pulled the rope that connected to a bell in Fletcher's room.

It was very easy to pick the lock with a hairpin, just a few twists here and there, before she heard the click, then she carefully put the hairpin into the pocket of her robe, and began investigating. She was wise enough to look for any letters pushed to the back of the bureau, and there she pulled out two which aroused her curiosity for the very reason they had been hidden at the very back of the compartment.

She opened the first one, and straight away she saw it had been written by a female hand – men wrote more neatly, more business-like, but the writing on this letter flowered all over the page.

Lord Byron – I lost my brooch in the carriage last night. If you receive this before anything is said about it you will then be on your guard and can say what you think proper – not for any particular value I put on the thing itself, but I fear it may lead to something unpleasant for you. Don't consider the loss but our general good in whatever steps you take in consequence of this information. Pray pray – be at the theatre on Friday night – S.

Annabella's face was white and her hands trembling as she unfolded the second letter.

Why have I not heard from you? Since last Thursday I have thought of nothing but you. For some women to say and do as I have would be the extreme of wrong, but I have all my life spoke and acted from my heart. I hope my Lord our acquaintance will not end here. I know not what to think. I am confounded – S.

PS. I must know what your intentions are as to our future. I entreat you to send an answer to this, or let me see you this evening, what time you please even if it is late. I fear you are ill. You certainly was not very well on Friday as you did not come.. I was all alone from six o'clock till twelve, then I got completely in the doldrums, and went to bed alone.

Annabella read the letters again, no address, no actual name, but the second letter had a date: *November 15th* ... only a few days ago.

She folded each letter and carefully returned them to their place at the back of the bureau, then returned to her room and got back into bed, lying on her back and staring at the ceiling, dry-eyed.

Just the thought of her husband being affectionate to any other woman made her bite her lip almost to bleeding, a habit she had picked up in childhood from her governess.

She lay thinking, brooding, until the objective and mathematical part of her mind began to view the situation in a different light as she carefully recalled every detail of the two letters ...

It was clear that whatever had happened, he had quickly changed his mind about the liaison and was now keeping out of the slut's way and ignoring her letters. And what else could a female like that expect? Strumpets rarely held the affection of a gentleman for long.

~ ~ ~

Although Annabella was unaware of it, during those autumn and early winter months, Byron had not in fact been spending his nights at the Drury Lane Theatre, apart from a few evenings now and again, but had instead been out enjoying himself with his male friends at the clubs, or just having dinner in affable company.

Like many husbands, he found that domestic life and social life were not a good mix; unless, like Lord and Lady Holland and the Jerseys and others, a compromise was made by jointly hosting regular soirées and parties in their home.

Annabella did not like parties or any type of social gathering, apart from the visits of her Christian ladies who came regularly for morning coffee or afternoon tea.

His affair with Susan Boyce had quickly waned. The girl, it turned out, had a six-year-old son, and after only two nights of seeing her, she had wanted him to leave his wife and marry her. It had been a foolish fling, and one that he had quickly and guiltily ended.

With his male friends though, he could be seriously intellectual or brilliantly sociable and throw off all that tedium.

When Thomas Moore came to town Byron dined out with him every night, but he had never once invited Tom back to his home.

Tonight he was dining at Long's restaurant with the poet, Walter Scott , and Scott had never seen Byron so full of fun and frolic and wit and whim, "as playful as a kitten".

Yet when he returned to the house in Piccadilly Terrace, usually close on midnight, Byron's dark moods of depression returned.

Occasionally he wandered alone through the empty rooms and occasionally he thought of his mother, remembering her loud voice and fiery temper – yet she had always filled the house with the sound of life and on occasions she had even filled it with laughter – but his wife ...

Oh, his wife was the complete opposite; a woman who never raised her voice, nor lost her self-command or cool composure ... yet her stubborn silences now inwardly infuriated or depressed him more than his mothers bawling voice had ever done.

Some women use their tongues – she looked a lecture,
Each eye a sermon, and her brow a homily.

Usually though, on coming home late, he locked himself away in his study to sit alone, the window open, allowing him to hear the trickling waters of the fountain in the garden below, while writing fragments of wistful poetry.

> *It is the hour when from the boughs,*
> *The nightingale's high note is heard:*
> *It is the hour when lover's vows*
> *Seem sweet in every whispered word;*
> *And gentle winds, and waters near*
> *Make music to the lonely ear.*

Chapter Fifty-One

~~~

On the morning of 3rd December two new visitors arrived at Devonshire House requesting to speak to Lord Byron.

Milward eyed them charily as he showed them into the drawing-room – two men, dressed fairly neatly, but not of the style or class of gentlemen that normally called on his lordship.

Sitting with hats in hand, the two men immediately rose to their feet when Lord Byron entered the room, but only one man spoke, introducing himself as a bailiff, and holding up a court document.

"An order from the court, my lord," he said somewhat apologetically. "There are still four executions for payment of bills which remain outstanding. So I'm afraid, until they are paid in full, we must remain in your house."

"Remain in my house? For what purpose?"

"In case you abscond without payment."

"*What?*"

Byron called Milward. "Escort these men out of my house ."

Milward, who had some experience of this kind of thing in the past as butler to Sir Ralph Milbanke, suggested quietly, "They have a court order, my lord, so perhaps I should escort them down to the servants' floor."

"Why?"

"To lodge, my lord. They are ordered to stay until payment is made." Milward turned to the bailiff. "For how long are you ordered to stay?"

"Six months, longer than usual, due to your rank, my lord."

"And if I don't or can't pay?"

"The we will have to remove your furniture and all

possessions to be sold in payment."

Byron was mentally reeling from the shock of it, unable to know what to do or say next. He gestured vaguely to Milward to take them down below, and then, as if in a dream, he took himself upstairs to speak to Fletcher.

Fletcher calmed him by advising him to leave the bailiffs where they were, down in the servant's floor, and not to provoke them.

"If you leave them alone and just ignore them," Fletcher said, "lodged down there in the basement all warm and well-fed and living on free board, they'll likely be happy to stay down there for the full six months, without causing you any trouble."

"My wife must *not* be told!" Byron warned. "Not in her condition. Now is not the time to overburden her with worries about finances or bailiffs."

"No, my lord."

"Will you go down and instruct all the servants on that? Lady Byron must *not* be told. At least not until *after* the birth and her lying-in period."

"I'll go down now," said Fletcher, and scooted off, leaving Byron to stand in despair and see now so clearly just what this marriage had done to his life. It was the worst thing he had ever done.

They had been married for only a few months when he had realised that he had made a colossal and irrevocable mistake, but he had done the honourable thing and made the best of it, even though he had soon learned that he and Annabella had nothing in common.

They were incompatible in their tastes, their temperaments and their sympathies. She had *no* sympathy for anyone but herself; and her attitude to the servants, to Augusta, to the ordinary man and woman in the street, was never anything but condescending.

Oh, yes, in their early days in London she had occasionally stepped out to do some charity work, but it was a frigid kind of charity, giving some of his old clothes to the poor, but never standing too close too them, giving the items to Ann Rood to hand over instead.

But her worst behaviour in those early days was the way she had disrespected his friends. The Hollands, who had hosted a dinner in her honour, Lady Jersey, also, had gone to great trouble a few nights later – but although she gave both hostesses her compliments on their "delicious" food when leaving – he had been shocked a few days later to come across a half-written letter to her mother on her desk, full of condescending criticism – *"the salmon not quite fresh, the sheep's wool still on the mutton fat, and all their amiability masking 'the varnish of vice'.*

He had said nothing because the letter in her bedroom was personal and private and he had no right to question her private correspondence, but even now it rankled him just to think of it, because it was all so unfair and untrue.

In the kitchen, Mrs Clermont was sitting at the back of the room drinking a cup of tea when Fletcher came in with his lordship's instructions. "Lady Byron must *not* be let know about the bailiffs."

Mrs Clermont waited until Fletcher had gone, and then could not get up on her feet fast enough, creeping out, and then rushing upstairs to inform Annabella.

"There's bailiffs in the house! Two of them! His lordship says they can lodge in the basement at night, but you know what bailiffs do in the day – they spend all the day long sitting in the hall! And anyone who calls will see them! Oh, the *disgrace!* What will your dear mother say?"

"Nothing, because you will *not* tell her," Annabella commanded. "And if you do, C, you will be very sorry that you did."

Annabella left the room and went to find Byron, and when she found him, she kept the calm in her voice as she castigated him for allowing this to happen.

"Bailiffs in my house? How could you, Byron? How

could you bring this misfortune on me now?"

He rounded on her, furious. "You brought this misfortune on yourself! I told you of my debts in Seaham. I then wrote and asked you to wait, but you would not be put off! If you had been less selfish, less self-centred and not always insisting on having your own way, *none* of this would be happening."

Annabella was astounded. "You are blaming *me?*"

He walked over to one of the library shelves, took down the Bible and brought it back to her. "I want you to swear on this Bible – *swear* that you and Lady Melbourne were not co-conspirators in the plot to get me to marry you –her by praise and persuasion and you by deliberate deceit."

Annabella looked at the Bible, horrified. "I will do no such thing. Do you think I *lied* to you?"

"Well you have lied about everything else – being an heiress, having a dowry, living only for the happiness of others – *none* of it was true."

She smiled unpleasantly. "So now you think *I* married *you* for your fortune?"

"No, you married me for the glamour of my fame, and because you are vain, and because you thought you could convert me. And yes – probably also for a share of the fortune I own in Newstead Abbey. Or perhaps it was only your parents who wanted *their* share of that?"

"You are mad!" Annabella declared, turning and leaving the room – her usual recourse to everything – leaving the room.

But he was not deceived by her now – for now he knew what she was really like – the *true* Annabella Milbanke. Underneath that pious and calm exterior, she was a sullen little nucleus of concentrated savageness.

Chapter Fifty-Two

~~~

After the defeat of Napoleon at Waterloo, many from England's High Society had flocked over to Paris to finally see the famous city – crowded as it was with officers from the English regiments – and to join in the post-war celebrations.

The Lambs had gone, and so had Caroline's mother, Lady Bessborough, and a whole host of others, and the gossip they wrote or brought home kept everyone occupied for weeks.

Caroline was happy to be back home, although in Paris she had added to her fame and shame by seducing the Duke of Wellington, but Caroline was not impressed, because he was not Byron, nothing like, never could be, and the duke was a disgraceful philanderer in any event.

Lady Melbourne had gone nowhere, and Caroline's absence and Byron's marriage had removed a lot of their past animosity. And so Caroline listened avidly as Lady Melbourne imparted to her all the home news.

On 10th December Annabella had given birth to Byron's daughter – "The most adorable little girl!" The child had been named "Ada Augusta". It seems Ada is a very antique name from the Byron ancestry and has not been used since the reign of King John, but Byron also says that "Ada" is a Biblical name from Genesis – 'Adah, wife of Lamech'."

"He wanted a son," Caroline said. "So I expect he was terribly disappointed?"

"On the contrary ..." Lady Melbourne's smile was tender, "I have never seen a man so proud and fond of his child as Lord Byron. And during my visit yesterday, I heard Annabella say to him that he was fonder of the infant than she was."

Caroline frowned. "That's a strange thing for a mother to say."

Lady Melbourne nodded; she too had thought it odd, but she did not divulge to Caroline what Annabella had said sulkily to Byron after that – "and fonder of it than you are of me."

"And I suppose they are gloriously happy now?" Caroline asked bitterly "All lovey-dovey and cooing over their child?"

Lady Melbourne hesitated. "Well, there *is* some tension there, understandably, because now there are two bailiffs in the house waiting for payment of some executions, which must be very hard to endure. I know Lord Byron is extremely embarrassed by it all."

Caroline was confounded. "But how so? I thought the main attraction was due to her being an heiress! So where is her ton of loot? Could they not use some of that to pay off the bailiffs?"

"It seems they cannot. According to Annabella the inheritance from Lord Wentworth to her mother and herself is still tied up in probate."

"Eight months later? Did he not leave a will?"

Lady Melbourne became agitated. "Oh, Caroline, do not *test* me with all these questions. You have not asked me once about the rheumatism in my knee. All I can say is that I offered Lord Byron a loan, but he refused, and seems determined to resolve the matter by selling off the last of his library."

~ ~ ~

Hearing of Byron's intention to sell his books due to financial difficulties, his publisher John Murray was extremely upset.

"His precious Romaic and Greek books? *Everything* in his library?"

William Gifford nodded. "I'm told he has already spoken to a bookseller to arrange the sale of his library by auction."

"Oh, then he must have reached that decision in a state of *agony,"* Murray said. *"*Byron's relationship with his books is very personal ..." He looked at Gifford. "This is actually heartbreaking for me to hear this."

Gifford made no comment, knowing that Murray loved and favoured Byron above all his authors.

Murray shook his head. "No, this *cannot* be allowed. If I had known he was in such financial difficulties I would have sought to help him immediately."

Byron was occupying himself with the wrapping and packing of each precious book, when the letter from John Murray arrived by messenger. It contained a cheque for £1,500, and note from Murray assuring him that he would receive another cheque for the same amount in a few weeks – *"I will also now seek to sell the copyrights of all your work, on your behalf."*

Byron could not help feeling emotionally affected by such kind generosity. John Murray had already bought and paid him for the ownership of the copyrights to most of his work, and yet now he was ready to sell them on and pass all money earned over to him, losing all profit for himself.

It took him an hour or two before he felt ready to send a reply:

I return your cheque – not accepted – but certainly not unhonoured. Your offer is a favour which I would accept from you, if I was to accept such from any man. Had such been my intention, I would have asked you fairly, and as freely as I know you would give. I cannot say more.

The circumstances which induce me to part with my books – are not immediately pressing – but I have made up my mind to sell them – & there's an end to it.

Believe me very truly

your obliged and humble Servant.
BYRON

"He is extremely proud and sensitive," Murray said to Gifford. "I should have taken that into consideration."

~~~

Having spent Christmas with his father and siblings down at Whitton Park, Hobhouse returned to London to find Byron looking pale and his mood extremely low – all due to the bailiffs and his financial embarrassments.

"It has all been enough to drive me *half mad*," Byron told him. "No one can know what I have gone through. No man should marry. It has doubled all my misfortunes and diminished all my comforts ... The best of it though, is my little girl. Have you seen her?"

"I saw her before I left London."

"Oh, did you? Oh yes, of course you did. You should see her now though – she's fattening nicely and even more beautiful. Will I take you up to the nursery?"

"Not yet, Byron. First, some sort of solution has to be found for all this. Have you decided anything?"

Byron paused. "Yes, and all I can conclude is that it *must* come to a separation."

Mrs Clermont, who had been listening near the drawing-door which was slightly ajar, had now heard all she needed to hear, and crept away. Now she had a nugget of information which she would nurse to herself until the time came to use it.

"A separation?" Hobby was shocked. "Oh, my dear friend, that is somewhat drastic, surely? You have a child now."

"A *temporary* separation," Byron explained. "Just while I close this house and bring an end to the enormous expense of it all. Our only choice now is to get away from London and live more cheaply in the country."

"That's sensible," Hobby nodded. "Does Lady Byron agree?"

Byron sighed dubiously. "I have not yet discussed it with her ... but I'm sure she *will* agree. There is no alternative."

Later that day when Byron visited Annabella in her room, she was sitting at her escritoire looking highly amused.

"I have just received a letter from *ma chére cousine,* Lady Caroline. She is returned from France and has brought me a gift – a silk scarf which she imported back from Paris."

Annabella held up the scarf. "As you can see, it is slightly torn, for which she sends the explanation that she had worn it herself to avoid paying duty on it or having it impounded by the customs men."

Annabella was almost laughing. "So with this torn French scarf and Lady Holland's necklace, my servant's costume for a night out at the opera will be quite complete."

Her mockery of Caroline's gift was understandable, but Lady Holland – "What is wrong with the necklace from Lady Holland?"

Annabella looked at him. "Have you seen it? *Garish* is not the word."

"The rubies in the necklace are beautiful."

"But the setting – so gaudy."

Her mood was too viperish today for him to discuss anything serious with her, so he took himself off to the nursery and spent an hour with his sleeping daughter. Occasionally she opened her eyes to stare at him, and he smiled, because her eyes were almost as light and blue as his own.

Later, another gift arrived from Caroline, this time for Byron.

Knowing how much Caroline now hated him, he opened her gift with some trepidation ... catching his breath when he saw it ... a book which had belonged to Napoleon, stamped with the Imperial Eagle ... he examined it minutely, and knew it was indisputably genuine ... Oh, good God, how had Caroline managed to get her hands on something like this? What trick or game had she played to secure it for him?

He locked the book away, deciding not to show it to Annabella, who would undoubtedly compare it to her torn scarf and respond with acidulated fury.

~~~

A few mornings later Fletcher handed Byron a letter. "It's urgent, my lord, delivered by messenger."

Byron opened the letter to find enclosed yet another bill with a demand for immediate payment.

"Damnation! How *dare* they?"

He handed the bill to Fletcher who saw that it was a bill for something bought by Mrs Byron, his lordship's mother, in 1809.

"Seven years ago!" Byron exclaimed. "How am I to know if my mother purchased that item at all?"

Fletcher tore up the bill, threw the pieces on the fire, and then turned and looked at his lordship with a heart full of pity ... all these damned tricks and troubles that life was throwing at his lord ... and he had also noticed that during these past few days his lordship's limp seemed worse.

"I will have to speak to her ladyship," Byron said. "It can't be put off any longer."

On entering Annabella's bedroom, she turned from the window and greeted him with that rigid and aloof expression he had come to know and fear – someone or something had upset her again.

"I need to talk to you," he said. "Sit down."

Annabella sat down. She was indeed very upset. Mrs Clermont had now revealed to her how she had overheard Byron speaking with Hobhouse, saying "It *must* come to a separation."

She listened silently, and with increasing relief, as her husband very calmly explained his anguish at having his wife and child living in a house stalked by bailiffs threatening to sell their possessions from under them.

"It must distress you."

Annabella nodded.

"So here is my solution. Your mother has invited you to go to Kirkby and stay in her home for a while, in order for you to recover from the birth with rest and peace, and I suggest that you do go – away from this house and all the embarrassment of bailiffs and creditors."

"That would indeed be pleasant."

"And while you are at Kirkby, it will allow me the time to pack up everything that belongs to us in this house, and also to hound and harass John Hanson to get Newstead sold as soon as possible, and then we can pay off all debts, perhaps purchase a smaller property, and put an end to all this ... what do you say?"

He gazed at his wife, and she gazed back at him, saying, "So our separation is to be only transitory?"

"Of course. No more than a few months. And in the meantime I will visit you and Ada every few weeks at Kirkby."

Annabella's suspicious mind was now working at full speed again. Was his proposition truly so honourable and based solely on his consideration for her? Or was it based on his hope that while the cat is away, the rat will play?

She said quietly: "Will you pray allow me to think about it?"

Chapter Fifty-Three

~~~

Annabella eventually agreed with Byron that there really was no alternative to giving up this expensive house in Piccadilly, although she suspected he blamed her for all the extra expenses.

Naturally she was pleased to know they would be living with her dear parents for a while ... yet she knew she would never be truly happy again until she had got Byron away from his entourage of friends and all the temptations of London.

But then where would they go? Surely not Newstead Abbey until it was sold? No, that place *had* to be sold and soon. The reserve price of £120,000 was too high, so perhaps it should be dropped to £100,000 for a quicker sale.

Annabella's mind was engrossed in all the calculations of the amount owed, and the net amount that would be received from the Newstead sale, when Rood brought her in a letter from his lordship.

She opened the letter, and what she read chilled her.

A – when you are disposed to leave London – it would be convenient that a day should be fixed – & (if possible) not a very remote one. When you are in the country I will write to you more fully – as your mother has asked you to Kirkby – there you can be for the present – unless you prefer Seaham?

As the urgent dismissal of the present establishment is important to me – the sooner you can fix the day the better – though of course your convenience & inclination shall be the first consideration. There is a more easier and safer carriage than the chariot –

(unless you prefer it) – on that you can choose as you please. – B.

The letter dropped from her hand, as if she had lost all strength in her fingers. It was so formal, so cold, and not one word of sorrow at their being separated for weeks. She had forgiven him his last outburst against her, forgiven him everything, so why such formality now?

She replied to his letter with a note written in the same formal manner,: *'I will obey your wishes and fix the earliest day that circumstances will admit for leaving London.'*

She then sought out Augusta to show her Byron's letter, and was mollified to a point when Augusta gave her humble opinion that –"He probably wrote you a letter instead of speaking to you in order to avoid a scene. You have no idea, Annabella, the personal shame he now feels at finding himself unable to support his family. It is quite a disgrace to him."

Annabella stood thoughtful for a moment, and then patted Augusta's arm. "We will say no more about it."

~~~

Annabella delayed as long as she could, but finally left Devonshire House on the 15th of January, very early in the morning, while Byron was still asleep.

Augusta, who was still under the fond delusion that she was truly beloved by her "dearest sis" was already up and about, as she always was at the crack of dawn.

"You will stay until the house is closed, dearest, and keep your eyes on everything for me?" Annabella said, giving her a light kiss on the cheek.

Augusta nodded. "I will stay for as long as my husband allows me to stay."

"But he knows your brother is suffering under great difficulties. Surely he must take that into consideration, and your children will do well enough in the care of himself and their nursemaids until whenever you return."

Augusta meekly nodded, aware that Annabella did not know George Leigh as well as she did.

"Now you *will* write to me every day and tell me everything that goes on." Annabella pulled on her gloves and then lowered her voice. "I want you to keep your eye on that fiend Hobhouse. I have a suspicion he might take advantage of my absence and haul Byron off on a trip to the Continent – for his health."

Augusta, who had been thoroughly turned against Hobhouse by Annabella, agreed. "I will certainly keep my eyes on that one."

"And Davies."

There Augusta faltered. "I really do believe you are quite wrong about Scrope Davies. I know him so well. Over the years he has often called into my house at Newmarket when travelling up and down to London from Cambridge, and he is truly an absolute gentleman."

"Believe me, dearest, they are *all* blackguards under their fine clothes and gentlemanly ways. So you take care, and write to me every single day – promise?"

Augusta nodded, "I promise."

Fletcher, who had been standing by the open door of the carriage speaking to Ann, quickly stepped back when Lady Byron approached, and then helped her into the carriage. Apart from Ann there were two other females travelling with Lady Byron – a nursemaid holding the baby, and Mrs Clermont.

Moving back to stand beside Mrs Leigh while both watched the carriage roll off, Fletcher smiled. "Well, I for one, am very glad to see the back of that Clermont woman."

Augusta gave no response, for she had become as fond and almost as attached to Mrs Clermont as Annabella was. Mrs Clermont was a very *genial* woman most of the time, always finding time to sit and talk with

Augusta, always so kindly interested in her worries and problems, until Augusta found herself confiding all her fears about the children and their occasional illnesses, George's gambling, and how kind and considerate her brother Byron had always been to her, and how much she loved him.

~ ~ ~

On the road to Woburn, having spent half a day inside the rocking carriage, Annabella discovered that she was already missing Byron, and even wondered if she should turn back?

Their old controversies seemed no longer important to her now. He was a man she had never really understood, because of his complex temperament, and she had often found him exasperating with all his caprices, but Byron was Byron and the weeks ahead would be very dull without him.

Stopping at the inn at Woburn, the first thing she did was to request the innkeeper to supply her with pen and paper, and when it was brought she hastily wrote to her husband.

Dearest B.

The child is quite well and the best of travellers. I hope you are being 'good' and remember my medical prayers and injunctions to you. Don't give yourself up to the abominable trade of versifying – nor to brandy – nor to anything or anybody that is not 'lawful' and' right'.

Though I disobey in writing to you, let me hear of your own obedience, addressed to Kirkby. Love to the good goose, and Ada's love to you with mine – Pip.

Byron had to smile when he read her letter, showing it

to Augusta – "Does she not write like an anxious mother to her son?"

Augusta was still reading, perplexed. "What does she mean by "nor to anything or anybody that is not *lawful* and *right?*"

"I've no idea," Byron shrugged, knowing full well that Annabella was referring to his short fling with an actress, although how she had found out was still a mystery. "Someone had come to the house and *told* her," she had said, and he was still wondering if that "someone" was Susan Boyce, the chit.

Still, it was over and forgotten, and now he felt a great sense of relief at not having Annabella stalking and watching his every move, if only for a while. And now he could walk around the drawing-room without her eyes always following him. Now he could go anywhere he wanted and be his own man again, starting from *today*.

His publisher, John Murray, had sent him a note informing him that a special guest would be attending his coffee morning gathering today; an American writer whom he had now agreed to publish in England.

"He says he particularly chose my establishment to publish the British edition of his work solely because I publish you, Lord Byron. He is a great admirer of your poetry, but has an even greater desire to meet you in person. His name is Washington Irving, and as a favour to me, my lord, do come today if you can.

Why not? It would be like a breath of fresh air to be amongst male writers again and hear all their literary gossip.

~~~

In John Murray's drawing room there were eleven male writers in the room, all sitting and drinking their coffee while listening to Mr Murray telling them his latest literary news.

"Gentlemen, pray forgive the interruption of my high spirits, but apart from the pleasure of having Mr Irving with us, I must tell you ... this morning when I entered my office I found a thin packet on my desk. As soon as I saw the red seal and insignia on the postal frank, I knew from whom it came. I tore open the packet and within it I found a *pearl* ... pathetic, beautiful ... so now, before the billows of passion which it has excited in me have subsided, pray allow me to read it to you ... it is, of course, from Lord Byron.

A hush fell over the group as Murray held up the pages and read from *The Siege of Corinth* –

> *In the year since Jesus died for men,*
> *Eighteen hundred years and ten,*
> *We were a gallant company,*
> *Riding o'er land, and sailing o'er Sea*
> *Oh ! but we went merrily !*

Washington Irving was leaning forward, listening very attentively, and when the poem unfolded from its lighter opening and gradually became more dark, more tragic, he was utterly enthralled, for no poet had ever written like Byron, at times humorous and yet so dark, so masculine, every line, every image ... masculine.

Although he was disappointed, because the very fact that Mr Murray had stood by the fireplace and read the poem aloud to the gathering, was surely because Murray did not expect Lord Byron himself to make an appearance today.

The group eventually broke up into pairs of men talking together, all speaking quietly and somewhat jealously about the success of Byron, speculating in soft voices about the huge sum they suspected Murray would pay Byron for his new piece.

And all of *them* were personally rather dull in Washington Irving's opinion – all except Samuel Taylor Coleridge who hogged his attention by the window, asking many questions about America.

In his late forties, Coleridge was much older than Irving who had just passed thirty, but he admired Coleridge's work.

"I won't ask you about American *literature*," Coleridge said, "because I believe as yet it does not exist over there."

"Oh, it does exist in plenty," Irving assured him, "It just hasn't reached as far as Europe yet, but it will one day, in all of its American splendour, it will."

Coleridge looked unconvinced and Irving changed the subject. "I did hope to meet Lord Byron today. Have you met him, sir?"

Coleridge stared. "Met him? Lord Byron recently did me the courtesy of saving my life!"

"Indeed?" Now it was Irving who stared. "How so?"

Coleridge took something out of his pocket and put it in his mouth to chew on it, before telling Irving of how difficult his literary life had been of late. He'd had another spat with Wordsworth, more marital difficulties with a wife he had left long ago, serious money problems – oh, a bad time to be alive – until he had the sudden idea of contacting Lord Byron.

"His lordship, you see, had attended two of my lectures here in London, on Shakespeare, in the winter of 1811. So he knew me, and I knew him, so I wrote to him, enclosing a portion of my unfinished epic *Kubla Khan* for him to read and give his opinion – and how did that scandalous Lord Byron respond to me?"

Irving waited while Coleridge chewed some more of whatever was in his mouth.

"Why, he wrote back saying that in his opinion *Kubla* was even better than my *'Rime of the Ancient Mariner'* and encouraged me to strive on and finish it. And to help me finish it, he sent me a cheque for three hundred pounds to keep me going, and then persuaded John Murray to take on the job of publishing it."

Irving smiled. "I suspect Mr Murray needed very little persuasion to publish *you*, Mr Coleridge."

"Oh, he certainly *did* need to be persuaded, due to my letting him down last year. You see, Murray had hired me to translate Goethe's *Faust* from the German, and – well by God!"

Irving felt a hand on his shoulder and turned to John Murray who had his other hand laid on the arm of a dark-haired young man who was extremely handsome, and was saying something quietly to Coleridge.

"Lord Byron, pray allow me the pleasure of introducing you to Mr Washington Irving, my new American author."

"Well indeed, the pleasure is all mine," said Irving with a huge smile on his face and holding out his hand to shake. "Lord Byron, it is indeed a pleasure to meet you."

Byron shook his hand. "Your servant, sir."

"Now Mr Irving here," said John Murray, "has supplied us with a delightful sketchbook of stories with the title *Geoffrey Crayon, Gent*. It is not fully completed, not yet ready for publication, but I have here, especially for you, Lord Byron, a handwritten copy of my favourite story in the collection, 'The Legend of Sleepy Hollow'. Mr Irving has agreed that I may give this copy to you."

Byron took the thin manuscript, and read the title again. *The Legend of Sleepy Hollow?* He smiled inquisitively at the author. "Is it a sleepy story? Bedtime reading?"

"No, exactly the opposite. It is a story of ghosts and hauntings and a headless horseman."

"A headless horseman?" Byron said archly. "Does it take place in Albania or Turkey? I've seen a few headless horsemen there."

"No, it is set right here at home, in Tarrytown, New

York."

Byron smiled. "Do you mean right *there* at home, in Tarrytown New York."

Irving blinked. "Goodness, I forget myself, and where I am ... Lord Byron, it is *such* a pleasure to meet you at last, and if I may say so, an honour."

"Gentlemen, pray come and sit down and. I will send for fresh coffee, although ..." Murray took out his fob-watch ... "it is now past the hour of noon, so some wine perhaps?"

~~~

A few evenings later a second letter arrived from Annabella, from Kirkby Mallory.

Dearest Duck,

We got here quite well last night and were ushered into the kitchen instead of the drawing-room, by a mistake that might have been agreeable to hungry people. Of this and other incidents Dad wants to write you a jocose account and Mam longs to have the family party completed. Such a W.C! And such a sitting-room or 'sulking-room' that you could have all to yourself.

If I were not always looking about for B, I should be a great deal better already for the country air.

<div style="text-align:right">

Ever thy most loving
Pippin ... Pip – Pip

</div>

Byron had thoroughly enjoyed his long conversation at Murray's with Washington Irving, and had even take him to Brooks's Club afterwards where they had continued their conversation over wine throughout the afternoon, and then had met for lunch the following day.

And now, this evening, he was rushing out to escort

Irving to a soirée at Holland House where he intended to introduce his new American friend to the French novelist, Madame de Staël, and to the Italian poet, also now in London, Ugo Foscolo.

He read Annabella's letter very quickly and then passed it over to Augusta, asking her to convey his reply. "Tell her that all is well here, etc., etc,. Oh, and tell her I have an appointment with Hanson tomorrow and I will write more fully myself in a day or two."

Not for a minute did he consider that it was wrong to ask Augusta to convey his response to Annabella's letter, due to the very close friendship that now existed between his sister and his wife; and besides, Augusta was now writing to Annabella every day, so why not include in her letter a message from him?

It was a hurried request made with little thought, but the effect on Annabella, of not receiving a reply from Byron himself, when her letter to him had been so loving, was devastating. It engulfed her in a cold fury that was almost demonic.

PART NINE

Retribution

~

"Annabella Milbanke should have married Wordsworth, so he could learn how awful goodness can be."

William E. Henley

"And Hell hath no fury like a woman scorned."

Congreve.

Chapter Fifty-Four

~ ~ ~

Augusta, motherly and kind-hearted but weak and timid, had become somewhat fond, but also frightened of her more self-commanding sister-in-law, and did indeed obey her instructions to write every day; always including the latest message from Byron. By doing so, she believed she was doing good and being helpful to both her brother and his wife.

Seven days after Annabella's departure, Augusta dutifully reported to her sister-in-law that Byron had celebrated his 28th birthday by going with Hobhouse to the Royal Society and then to see a Play at the theatre.

Although pregnant and feeling tired, Augusta had stayed up awaiting Byron's return like a doting mother, but ended up wishing she had gone to bed instead – feeling so very angry with her brother that she dashed off another letter to Annabella – irate in the extreme.

Dearest A – B returned between 12 and 1 this Morning with Hobhouse – both drunk – sent me to bed, & called for Brandy! Hobhouse drank none, but B drank two glasses – would not take his Calomel, & in short so far so bad! One comfort is Hobhouse looked really dying – God forgive me, but I hope God will soon take him to a better world.

However B frowned to such a degree at me to go away, that his dear friend (I mean fiend) either was or pretended to be quite shocked – and when B pursued me out of the room to apologise for his frowns (when by the bye he tumbled flat on his face up the staircase) Hobhouse then came out and said up all sorts of tendresses to me – I was 'All the Angels in the world and it was fortunate for him I was married!'

Fletcher has just told me that Hobhouse left the house door open at 3 o'clock in the morning and said it was lucky we had not all our throats cut.

PS: B has ordered horses to go and see you and his daughter at Kirkby next Sunday.

Byron was given no opportunity to go to Kirkby Mallory the following Sunday to see his wife and daughter, due to a letter being delivered to him by messenger from R. A Noel.

At first, upon opening the letter, Byron had to stare at the name, until he remembered that on the death of Lord Wentworth and by contractual condition of their inheritance, Sir Ralph and Lady Milbanke had now changed their surname to Noel – although for Lady Milbanke that was simply a reversion back to her maiden name.

So this letter from rambling Ralph must be about Annabella and her entourage being ushered into the wrong rooms upon arriving at Kirkby for which "*Dad wants to write you a jocose account ...*"

Mivart's Hotel, Lower Brook Street.
February 2, 1816.

My Lord,

I find myself compelled by every feeling as a parent, to address your Lordship on a subject which I hardly suppose will be any surprise to you.

Very recently, circumstances have come to my knowledge which convince me that, with your opinions, it cannot tend to your happiness to continue to live with Lady Byron, and I am yet more forcibly convinced of this after her dismissal from your house, and the treatment she experienced whilst in it, is not consistent with her Comfort, or, I regret to add, her personal safety. And those on whose protection she has the strongest natural claims, could not feel themselves justified in permitting her to return.

I therefore propose that a professional friend should be fixed by you to confer with a person of the same description appointed by me, that they may discuss and settle such terms of a separation as may be mutually approved. Therefore I hope to have as immediate answer as possible directed to me at Mivart's Hotel.

I remain, my Lord
Your obedient servt.,
*R*A: *Noel.*

Contrary to Sir Ralph's belief that the letter would not be of any surprise to Byron, he was utterly shocked.

He read the letter twice, in absolute puzzlement. Annabella had given not the slightest intimation of any of this to him – quite the opposite – the night before she had left for Kirkby she had come into his room to sleep with him, very lovingly, before returning to her own room ... so either she was capable of incredible artifice, or this was the work of her odious parents.

When Hobby and Scrope called to collect him for lunch at Brooks's, Byron was convinced that Annabella knew nothing about Sir Ralph's letter.

He showed his two friends her letter of the 16th January, only two weeks previous, ending with the words – *If I were not always looking about for B, I should be a great deal better already for the country air.*

"Surely," said Hobby, "any man who had been

addressed by his wife as her 'dearest duck' only two weeks previously, and never having it in his power to commit any fault against her in the interval, would have to question on whose *authority* Sir Ralph wrote such a proposition?"

Scrope Davies had Annabella's letter still in his hand. "And signed *'ever lovingly thine ...'* It *is* strange. Do you have any clue what could have prompted her father to write to you in such a manner?"

"I cannot even *guess* why! Nor do I understand his comment about her 'personal safety'. I have never laid a hand or lifted up a finger against Lady Byron, nor any female, in my life."

"I should think not," said Hobhouse, revolted at the very idea. And after a close friendship of eleven years, he knew that Byron would be just as disgusted to hear of any man placing a menacing hand on a woman.

Hobhouse was reading Sir Ralph's letter again. "So why does he claim she was *dismissed* from your house?"

"She was *not* dismissed from my house. All I can think ... about a week previous to her leaving for Kirkby, I told her my wish of breaking up this establishment, and suggested she retired into the country to live with her parents while I was about it. A day or so later I sent her down a note – she *knows* it is not so easy for me to hop up and down stairs as it is for others – but when Augusta told me Annabella seemed offended by the tone of my note, I went down to her, and after a short conversation she declared herself satisfied with my explanation."

Hobhouse was still scrutinising Sir Ralph's letter. "And this here ..."*with your opinions*" ... what can he mean by that?"

Byron shrugged. "Unless it's due to my refusal to attend the services at Annabella's sect every Sunday or have anything to do with it."

"Quite right too," said Scrope. "Those people see the devil around every corner."

After a silence, Byron said, "I would not be surprised if this is all due to that Clermont woman. God knows what lies she may have told to the Milbankes."

After another silence, he looked at his friends: "You two go on without me. I need time to reply to Sir Ralph."

And as soon as his friends left, he did reply, quite moderately.

Feb. 2nd 1816.

Sir,

I have received your letter. To the vague and general charges contained in it, I must be at a loss how to answer. Lady Byron received no dismissal from my house in the sense you have attached to the word. She parted from me in apparent – and on my part – real harmony.

It is true that previous to this period I had suggested to her the expedience of a temporary residence with her parents. My reason for this was quite simple, viz., the embarrassment of my circumstances, and my inability to maintain our present establishment. The truth of what is thus stated may be easily ascertained by reference to Lady Byron herself.

During the past year I have had to contend with distress without and within, which may have made me less agreeable to others. I am, however, ignorant of any particular ill-treatment which your daughter has encountered. She may have seen me gloomy, and at times irritable and occasionally angry, but she knows the causes too well to attribute such inequalities of disposition to herself, or even to me, if all things be fairly considered.

And now, Sir, not for your satisfaction, for I owe you none, I come to the point – on which subject I must for a few days decline giving you a decided answer, as it is a step which cannot be recalled once taken.

Also there are parts of your letter which, I must be permitted to say, arrogate a right which you do not now possess. For the present at least, your daughter is my wife; she is the mother of my child; and until I have her express sanctions of your proceedings, I shall take leave to doubt the propriety of your interference.

This will soon be ascertained, and when it is, I will submit to you my determination, which will depend very materially on hers.

BYRON

Byron could not believe that Sir Ralph had acted on the voluntary direction and approval of his daughter. All he could conclude was that someone at Kirkby Mallory had been misrepresenting and abusing him to the Milbankes. He was quite sure it was not Fletcher's wife, Roody; and he was certain it was not Annabella.

He would have been doubly-shocked if he had known that on that very day, in Kirkby Mallory, Annabella was reading a letter from her friend in London, Selina Doyle:

"We have both (you & me) at times talked of his treatment of you as an experiment, but would he love you if he were to conquer your strong sense of virtue?"

Annabella immediately wrote back to Selena Doyle, explaining her "reason" and her *unreasoned* attachment to Byron, and even in these past days, despite all the pain he had caused her –

"There were moments when sorrow and resignation yielded to frenzy – and I would have forgotten myself, my child, my principles, to devote myself to that man who has now cast me off."

She spent all her time writing letters in the same tone to other friends, despairing of the man she still loved and even idolised; writing of *"his eyes which gleamed as in flashes from Heaven, whose glances from angels and demons seemed given ..."*

Her true reason was that for too long she had known Byron did not love her, and his negligence in not personally replying to her letter was the last straw. His restlessness and gloomy moods were all indicative of his wish to leave her, and if and when he did – as he seemed to be doing so now under the pretence of dismantling their household – she would be reduced, and traduced, and become the absolute laughing-stock of fashionable London – but not so – if she left him first.

She had made her plans, plotting with herself, and disagreeing with Mrs Bennet in *Pride & Prejudice* that the only security for a young lady with no money was to find a husband and marry to achieve financially security.

Well now she had his child, and now she was ready to become not only financially secure, but financially *independent* in her own right. But in the tempest looming ahead, she was determined not to allow the smallest portion of blame to be attached to her.

So now she must reveal to the world what she had gone through, what she had suffered, the abused and abandoned wife.

~~~

Lady Milbanke-Noel, who had determinedly accompanied her husband down to London, was now sitting in the office of her lawyer's chambers in Lincoln's Inn, accompanied by Mrs Clermont.

"Sir, with respect, all I can tell you is the truth of what I saw while I was there," said Mrs Clermont. "And what I saw was as plain as day – his lordship's hatred of my lady. My fear was that he was likely to put her to death at any moment, if he could do it privately."

Lady Noel was beside herself with rage. "Such a man is not fit to live!"

The lawyer, Dr Stephen Lushington, found it all quite hard to believe. "And would you," he asked Mrs Clermont, "be prepared to swear an affidavit under oath to this?"

Mrs Clermont nodded emphatically. "I would, to that and more. I told his sister Mrs Leigh what I feared, that I feared he might put my lady to death at any moment, and she replied – 'I will never leave him alone with her until she is brought to bed with the child, and then *you* must always stay with her'."

"So," said Lushington, "do you believe that his lordship's sister would also swear to your statement to her?"

"No, I think not, because she also is terrified of him."

Stephen Lushington, who knew Lord Byron, although not very well, but enough to harbour grave doubts as to the veracity of all these claims, finally concluded the consultation by advising Lady Noel:

"As to a Judicial Separation, and the legal grounds therefore, it would be impossible for me to give you my considered legal opinion, without a detailed statement of those grounds, written by Lady Byron herself."

~~~

Augusta had never been frightened of her brother, not in the slightest; she thought him one of the most gentlest and kindest men on this earth.

The only person Augusta was now truly terrified of was her unpredictable sister-in-law, due to all the tittle-tattle she had obediently been writing to Annabella in her daily bulletins – Byron at the theatre, Byron coming home with Hobhouse and both drunk; Byron at a party at Holland House; at Lady Jersey's house ... oh, what had she *not* said?

And now it seemed that she had not only betrayed her brother by tittle-tattling to his wife behind his back, but was undoubtedly the cause of all this trouble.

Augusta was dreadfully upset at her own foolishness; but even worse was the distress caused to her poor dear brother by the shock of Sir Ralph's letter. As if Byron had not suffered enough trials and troubles this past year – and all that on top of his worry about the hazards of his wife giving birth to his child and everything else – and now this!

Byron was still certain that Annabella had been kept ignorant of her father's actions – yet she had still not responded to his letter.

When he questioned Augusta, she told him near enough the truth. She had written to Annabella every day, always including his messages; and in her replies Annabella had given no hint – except ... she had occasionally sounded despondent and sometimes even critical of him, but Augusta had attributed that to the weakness of health and jittery nerves that often affect women after a birth – "The slightest thing can upset terribly."

Byron, in his own perplexed state, asked Augusta, "So will you write to her now and ask her if she sanctioned her father's actions? And if so, will she explain? She may reply to you, because she has not yet replied to me."

Augusta wrote the letter, and two days later she was flowing in tears when she showed Annabella's reply to

Byron, confirming that she had given her full agreement to her father's proposal for a separation, and ... "*I would ask you to recall to Lord Byron's mind his avowed and insurmountable aversion to the married state.*"

Byron was shaking his head in bewilderment. "All men complain now and then in a trivial way about the bondage of marriage. She did not take it seriously then, so why is she levelling it as a serious charge against me now?"

Augusta was too upset to answer.

"Why, if I were to harbour all my grievances in the same way," Byron said in protest, "I would mention her more grievous fault of marrying a poet – and then grumbling about his trade of 'abominable versifying'. That is like marrying a Reverend of the Church, and then complaining whenever he wrote a sermon or read his Bible."

Augusta nodded, still unable to speak because all her past conversations with Annabella were coming back to choke her. She had listened to all of Annabella's complaints and grumbles about Byron and, due to her own stupidity and cowardice, she had always agreed with her.

Her face was very pale; she moved to touch Byron's arm timidly.

"I'm sorry," she whispered.

Chapter Fifty-Five

~~~

Hobhouse had decided, in his own very correct way, that as he had been the groomsman at the marriage, it was now his duty to try and help the situation. And in order to do so, he asked Byron – "Would you object to my writing personally to Lady Byron?"

"You?" Byron frowned. "Why?"

"It may help. And I would like to remind her of what she said to me when I handed her down to the carriage on the morning of the marriage – I wished her happiness and she replied, 'If I am not happy, it will be my own fault."

If Byron had not been already late for an appointment with Isaac Nathan, he might have given Hobby's suggestion more consideration than merely a shrug; and minutes later he was rushing through the hall where he stopped dead at the sight of Mrs Clermont coming in.

"What are you doing here?"

"I was sent down to collect some more of the baby's clothes, the ones sent as presents." She looked at him in blank innocence. "Why, is something wrong, my lord?"

Byron, having no knowledge of any meetings with a lawyer or this woman's lies against him, was now only aware once again of his intense dislike of her.

He gave a brief wave of his hand to indicate to her to carry on, and then headed out.

"I'll be staying for a day or two to rest, before making the journey back," she called after him, but he was gone, and she was glad, because now she could find and ferret out any information that might be useful to her cause.

In the library, Hobhouse was preparing to write his letter to Lady Byron. He did not like her, but now that he had put his youthful period of atheism behind him, and had become more considerate of Christianity, he believed it was his duty to at least *try* to support the sanctity of marriage, and also to ensure that any disputes in the marriage should be conducted reasonably and fairly.

He could not rid himself of his suspicion that Lady Byron was simply playing one of her deceitful games, for she had taken Lord Byron's carriage and several receipts for large sums belonging to his lordship to be scrutinised and computed by her own mathematical brain, and why would she do that of she was intending to decamp for ever?

So, with the best of intentions, and for the good of all, Hobhouse wrote his letter, and succeeded in making matters a whole lot worse.

Perhaps, Lady Byron, my long friendship and love for the man whom you have honoured by consenting to bear his name, may account to you for my interfering in a point so connected with his happiness.

The word "treatment" in Sir Ralph's letter is so vague as to have no meaning except to a person conscious of some great offence, and your own letter of 16th January would be sufficient proof to any unprejudiced person that you did not leave his house under the grudge of any great offence.

Were I on my oath, I would say that in every conversation I have had with Lord Byron respecting your Ladyship, he has always used words to the following effect and no other : – "I cannot be supposed to be happy under my present financial embarrassments, which are very much increased by the circumstances of my being a married man."

What is expected of a husband, I cannot pretend to say; but if unvaried esteem, admiration, and a regard the most tender always expressed to his friends, is that not presumptuous of the sort of conduct which constitutes kindness in a husband?

Had you all the cause for complaint which is assumed by others, is it possible that you could wish to come at once to that step, which is generally the last instead of the first resource, and to irrevocably injure the character of Lord Byron – of him against whom your sole charge has always been that you love him more than he loves you –

Annabella read no more, throwing the letter down, her temper furious, for *there* it was – in black ink – all the proof she needed! Even his *friends* knew that Byron did not love her in the way he *should* love her – his wife.

Her mood and temper was not improved when later that evening, on the nine o'clock delivery, she received two letters. The first she opened was from Byron:

I am really ignorant of what Sir Ralph's letter alludes? – Will you explain? – To conclude – I shall eventually abide by your decision – but I request you most earnestly to weigh all the probable consequences – and to pause before you pronounce.

She opened the second letter, which came from Mrs Clermont down in London.

I find he has wrote to you. For the sake of your feelings I wish he had not, but trust you will not send any unguarded answer, as you know he is very capable of taking advantage of them – your feelings.

Meanwhile he goes out and about as usual with his

friends, and tonight he has gone to the theatre – C.

Annabella's jealousy and rage knew no bounds. She had visualised him moping around in grief and mourning for her, desperately wishing he had paid more attention and been more loving to her, desperate to get her back – but no, he was out and about as usual – everyone's favourite man!

How swiftly he had recovered from his shock? And now he was even calmly prepared to abide by her decision to leave him. And, no doubt, within a year of any separation she would be completely forgotten by him, no more than an occasional memory ...

Well, it would not be so, for now there were two things more that she was determined upon. Firstly – that he would not get possession of their child, or be allowed anywhere near her. And secondly – she would leave her mark on Byron, so deep, that he would remember her for as long as he lived.

PART TEN

~

In short, she was a walking calculation,
Miss Edgeworth's novels stepping from their covers
Morality's prim personification,
In which not Envy's self a flaw discovers.

BYRON – *Don Juan*

Chapter Fifty-Six

~~~

Lady Melbourne was pleased to admit that her relationship with Caroline was much easier these days, mostly due to her daughter-in-law's quiet behaviour.

Caroline may have been quiet, but beneath her good behaviour she was far from calm, resenting how she had been *planted* back in her place by Byron, while he went off to marry that insufferable prig, Annabella Milbanke.

Caroline had been waiting patiently for the marriage to fail – as she was certain it would, and now it had – for what man on earth would be able to endure that sanctimonious impostor for long?

Oh, how amused she been in those first few months of their marriage to see the vain way Annabella had tried to behave in a manner equal to her new title of Lady Byron. Oh, so much *fine-ladyism* had never before been seen outside of the salons of St James's Palace.

And then poor old Lady Melbourne, after all her scheming on behalf of the little bitch, had been discarded and ignored once the marriage had taken place.

Although Lady Melbourne had persevered, refusing to be cut off from her beloved Byron, bravely going round there in her carriage when the child was born – and suffering with her rheumatic swollen knee every minute that she was there, poor thing – but Annabella, apparently, had welcomed her aunt with nothing more than a few glacial glances and hardly any words, leaving all the conversation to his lordship.

Of course, Lady Melbourne had not confided that to Caroline until the night she had foolishly imbibed one too many glasses of gin, a rare thing for her to do, but she was still upset about it all – and now Annabella had upset her again.

"What is it, dear?" asked Caroline, rushing across the drawing-room to pour out some gin from a crystal decanter. "Here, take this for your knee."

Lady Melbourne did not even notice what she was drinking, so upset was she with Annabella's horrendous mother. And why her brother Ralph had ever married that woman was still a mystery.

"It is my belief," she said, "that Judith Noel and that Clermont woman have been plotting Lord Byron's ruin and going around London whispering and gossiping in an attempt to turn everyone against him."

"But *why?*" asked Caroline. "They went everywhere trumpeting loudly enough about the engagement when Annabella bagged him – even advertised it in the newspapers."

"I don't know ..." Lady Melbourne was frowning in bewilderment. "But Judith Noel's first love has always been money. Perhaps they hope to get a big settlement out of him."

She knocked back her gin. "In any event, they have failed to get their legal separation, and quite right too. Annabella herself has come down to London with a list of all her complaints, but Mr Lushington has informed her that she has not enough grounds to obtain one."

Caroline's heart almost stopped. "Why not?"

Lady Melbourne looked steadily at her daughter-in-law. "Caroline," she said, "if a bad temper, irritable behaviour, throwing an ink-bottle out of a window, and one single act of infidelity were enough to achieve a legal separation, then William would long ago have been able to secure a full *divorce* from you."

"I know, I am so very fortunate," Caroline said with irony. "Although I can't recall ever throwing an ink-bottle out of the window."

"A spouse cannot just walk into a lawyer and say their husband did this and that and expect the law to convict him. The law states a couple must have severe and serious grounds. Of course this is usually achieved in the meantime by a private civil agreement between both parties through their lawyers."

"So why does Annabella and her hideous mother not accept that and get on with it? I'm sure Lord Byron would not hesitate to financially support her and the child. I know he receives a fair income from the Newstead estate every quarter, and isn't Newstead now up for sale. If Newstead sold he would be very, very rich."

"Oh, this intolerable knee of mine! You have really no idea how I suffer with it." Lady Melbourne handed her glass to Caroline for a refill. "I think I prefer to take a few small glasses of gin than laudanum for the pain. Laudanum makes me very slow and drowsy."

Caroline hid her smile, because she knew it was not laudanum that Lady Melbourne took for the pain, but opium pellets, which she occasionally took out of her pocket to chew on.

"They say the London cockneys refer to gin as 'mother's ruin', Caroline said.

"I am already ruined, physically anyway," Lady Melbourne replied. "There are days when I simply cannot walk at all."

"So why do they not make a private agreement to separate and get on with it?" Caroline persisted.

"Well, according to Judith Noel, in one of his letters Lord Byron made some reference to his child, saying her welfare was his first concern; and as the father is usually given full custody of any children, being the breadwinner, Annabella is frightened she will lose control of the child. And because she does not have sufficient grounds against Lord Byron to have him declared as an unfit father, Judith Noel is so distressed that the silly woman has now stopped wearing her wig – declaring it too tight for her to suffer with her constant aggravations – and now she is wearing only her cap!"

Lady Melbourne sipped her gin. "My own view is that Annabella still loves Byron, and may well in the end go back to him after this marital spat."

Caroline stared. "Do you honestly think so?"

Lady Melbourne nodded. "It's a possibility. Who knows with Annabella, she is so odd, and so unpredictable, as recent events have proved."

Caroline's mind was ticking away furiously. Somehow she had to get Annabella *away* from Byron – and no going back.

"Is Annabella also lodged at Mivart's Hotel with her mother?"

"Yes, at Mivart's ... of course, there is one other thing that could be driving Annabella and her intolerable mother to break this marriage against the rocks ... the late Lord Wentworth's will ... I must confess, it *has* crossed my mind."

"The will that is supposed to be still in probate?"

"According to Ralph, by the terms of Lord Wentworth's will, the sum of Annabella's inheritance would be under the full control of her husband, Lord Byron ... "

Lady Melbourne's eyes were narrowed in thought ... "And that of course would apply to any property or money which would be passed on to Annabella at a later date by her mother and father ... all would go to Lord Byron ... but if he was *not* her husband, or if he was considered unfit ..."

Caroline yawned, always bored when a conversation descended to being solely about money; something she had always possessed more than enough of. "Would you mind, Lady M, if I left you now. I need to go up and see Augustus before he is put to bed."

Lady Melbourne came out of her thoughts. "Oh, yes, you go on up, and pray send my maid down to me. And give my precious grandson a kiss from his grandmamma. Tell him Grammy's poor knee is too sore to climb the stairs."

Caroline headed up quickly to the nursery and looked in on Augustus. "My angel ..."

357

Augustus was already in bed asleep, so Caroline sat by his bed in the dim light and reached for his hand, holding it tenderly in hers.

Poor Augustus, her most treasured possession, her sweet boy, had been diagnosed some time ago as "backward" and yet she had never known that he was anything but beautiful. And now, at seven, years old, he was bigger and fatter but had only the mental understanding of a child of two or three. Even William had been shocked when two eminent doctors had given their diagnosis of his son's condition.

Yet three years ago, Byron had known it as soon as he had seen the boy, although he had not said it to her, had never said it to her; but looking back at the way he had behaved when he had first met Augustus, she now realised that Byron had known straight away that her son was mentally feeble.

On that first day here at Melbourne House, Byron had been brought along to see her by Samuel Rogers and Thomas Moore. Eager to get him away and have him all to herself, she had taken him along to the nursery to meet her son. Augustus had been aged four then, and like a puppy he had immediately taken to Byron, holding his arms up to be lifted by his new friend.

Byron had sat cradling the sleeping boy in his arms while they talked softly in the nursery. Poor Augustus had always been prone to sleepiness, nodding off in an instant as soon as he knew he was being held by someone who made him feel safe. And Byron, not moving for hours for fear of wakening him, had eventually edged out of the chair very slowly before laying the boy down on his bed.

That was the day she had truly fallen in love with Byron. His tender kindness to children was one of his most endearing traits. So Annabella was right to believe that he would not give up his own child so easily.

Caroline slipped out of the nursery and went to her

own room and to her escritoire where she sat down and wrote a letter to Byron at Piccadilly Terrace.

I scarcely dare hope that I shall not offend you, however I care not – I must write one line, I must indeed, though I cannot hope to presume that anything I can say will have any effect, yet do hear those who may advise you, and whatever may have happened to occasion a quarrel between you and your wife, let no pride on your part prevent an immediate reconciliation. Go to her – whatever the cause, it must be made up.

Lord Byron, you will no doubt be angry at my interfering, but I have witnessed some scenes that I cannot forget, and the agony I suffer at this moment from suspense and alarm is not affected.

If you knew what reports people circulate about men who leave their wives, you would act in this instant prudently – you should not try to irritate Lady Noel or speak with harshness to Lady Byron, who loves you, would you but conciliate with her. I know you – and fear that you will be too proud to listen to those who would advise you.

I have disbelieved all the reports till now, but could you know what some are saying about you, you would be on your guard. Believe me,
 With regret and obediently, your friend and Cousin
  CAROLINE

When the letter was sealed, she then wrote a letter to Annabella at Mivart's Hotel.

Lady Byron,

It is not for me to write to you in any way or to appear in this most melancholy scene – God protect you and preserve you through it – I too have suffered many griefs through his barbarity, but I can assure that not till this hour did I feel disgust and indifference for one who deserves no other sentiments – so different is the feeling which arises from the blow given to ourselves.

There may come a time when I can prove in more than words how I esteem you – but for God's sake have no communication with him. I will not suffer another hour without telling you that I will stand by you and not by him, even were the whole world and everything in it in his favour – & if he has the cruelty to tear the child from you, I will tell you something that should you menace him with it, it shall make him tremble.

Believe me,
Your friend and Cousin
CAROLINE

The letter was delivered the following day to Mivart's Hotel.

Annabella was out – taking her mother's frantic advice and making a last-ditch effort to try and persuade John Hanson to become an ally in her cause.

In his chambers at Lincoln's Inn, John Hanson received Lady Byron somewhat reluctantly. He knew that she and her family had consulted Lushington against Lord Byron, and so it really was inappropriate for her to consult him also.

"Lady Byron, you must know that I represent his lordship."

"Yes, but I have come to consult you more as a friend of the family, on which I would hope to receive your advice."

"As long as it is not legal advice."

"No, medical."

Hanson stared at her. "Medical? I am a lawyer, not a doctor."

"No, but I believe you have had some experience ... " From her bag Annabella lifted out her Medical Encyclopaedia and opened it at a marked page.

"Do you see this illness here ... ?" She turned the book around on the desk for him to see. "I believe Lord Byron has all the symptoms of this illness."

Hanson looked at the word – *Encephalitis,* and then looked in astonishment at Lady Byron. "I know his lordship recently suffered for a short time with a disorder of the liver, but not a disorder of the *brain*."

"I believe he may have been wrongly diagnosed," Annabella replied with gravity. "If you look at all the symptoms here, one of the early symptoms is temporary nausea and vomiting."

"As it is with problems of the liver."

"Also, changes in personality and uncharacteristic behaviour."

"And has his lordship displayed any signs of changes in his personality and uncharacteristic behaviour?"

"Yes, he has been bad-tempered, incredibly restless and irritable, and has been cruel to me in the extreme."

"Cruel? In what way?"

"He dismissed me from his house by manner of a written letter; and against all his solemn marriage vows, he has admitted to infidelity with a common actress."

Hanson was unsure if her main complaint was against the infidelity or the fact that she considered the actress common.

"I believe his lordship is quite mad," Annabella continued. "Even Lady Caroline Lamb said he was mad. And now I discover that he has always had a reputation of being 'mad and bad and dangerous to know'."

Hanson had to hold on to his patience, because the

whole of London knew that Lady Caroline Lamb was the one who was truly mad and bad and dangerous to know – something she had proved time and time again due to her shocking antics in public and her obsessive persecution of Lord Byron.

"Madam, what is your objective for all these questions?"

"As stated, I do believe Lord Byron is mad," Annabella replied. "And if he is, surely that would make him an unfit father for his child, as well as being grounds for a judicial separation."

Hanson had to put a hand over his brow, trying to decide if this woman was mad herself, or just ready to use any vindictive claims in order to obtain her objective.

"Lady Byron, throughout your marriage to date with Lord Byron, have you every had any personal fear for your own safety due to any actions or words from Lord Byron?"

"Oh no, not in the least; my eye can always put down his."

John Hanson had heard enough, and he was not prepared to allow this interview to go on any longer.

"Lady Byron, I have known his lordship since his age of ten, and I can tell you now that if you have some devious intention of endeavouring to have Lord Byron declared mad, you will be sorely disappointed. Now pray leave."

Annabella's face flushed crimson at his sharp tone. "I can assure you, my only objective is to help him."

"By seeking to assert he is mad, and possibly having him restrained from going anywhere near his child? Madam, please leave my office, and pray do not venture here again."

She stood and abruptly left the room, leaving Hanson thinking her a devious and horrible little being, unfit for the title of "Lady" – and just in case she did endeavour to try and bring a case of madness against his lordship, he immediately took the lawyer's precaution of writing down official minutes of the meeting, and in particular his question:

"Throughout your marriage to date, have you every had any personal fear for your own safety due to any actions or words from Lord Byron?

"Oh no, not in the least; my eye can always put down his."

After such a statement, Lushington would have a hard task proving any kind of cruelty against Lord Byron, let alone madness.

He called his clerk to confirm assurance that a record of Lady Byron's visit to his chambers had been logged; date, time and length of visit; and then asked him to write up his minutes in fair copy and securely file them with Lord Byron's personal papers.

~~~

Returning to Mivart's Hotel, Annabella read Lady Caroline Lamb's letter with some surprise and much distaste.

She decided to ignore the letter, knowing how deceptive Caroline could be, and certain that her only reason for pretending to stand by her now was for the sole purpose of gaining information to pass on to Byron.

Instead she spent the afternoon writing letters to her stalwart friends, Mrs George Lamb, the wife of Caroline's brother-in-law; Mrs Elizabeth Hervey, a friend of her mother, and Selina Doyle.

Her reason for writing to these good ladies was imperative. During the past days she had been happy to allow them to spread as many disparaging and damaging rumours against Byron – in particular that it was *he* who had dismissed and dispensed of her, and not she who had left him.

But now her meeting with John Hanson had unnerved her, inspiring her to write anxiously to her friends with the instruction – "Nothing of any sort should be mentioned to people *as coming from me.*"

~~~

Within days letters were flying all over England about Lord Byron and what his poor wife had suffered in her year of marriage to him:

"The poor lady had never a comfortable meal since their marriage. Her husband had no fixed hour for breakfast and was always too late for dinner."

"Poor Lady Byron was afraid for her life! Her husband slept with loaded pistols by his bedside."

"Her governess believed he hated her so much that he was ready to put her to death if he could do it secretly and not be found out!"

Annabella heard all the rumours with the modest face of a martyr.

Yet behind closed doors she kept writing and confiding to every person she could muster to her side; and telling Mrs Clermont – "Lady Caroline Lamb says she will take my part, although Lady Melbourne must not know of it. And William Lamb, apparently, is maintaining his silence on the matter, but George Lamb is declaiming angrily against me. However, I *do* have the secret support of his wife."

Annabella's mood was somewhat deflated a few days later when she was told that everyone in Melbourne House was now against her, including Lord and Lady Melbourne, who were all now so staunchly on Byron's side, that Lady Melbourne had declared that she would never allow Annabella or her mother inside her house again.

Annabella was visibly shocked. What on earth had she done to warrant such odium against her? Was she not the injured party in all this?

~

"Lies! Disgusting lies! All this evil-speaking against her husband!" Lady Melbourne was furious. "Why, she is every bit as bad as her mother!"

And so many others of the upper class agreed with the sentiments of Lady Melbourne. Most of Annabella's supporters were of minor society or from the middle class, such as Selena Doyle, but the upper class and the *haut ton* were disgusted by Lady Byron's lack of discretion and, well, *common,* behaviour.

"The woman has no dignity," sniffed Lady Holland. "These matters should be settled in private, not by spreading rumours all over London like a pack of yelping hounds intent on tearing a fox to shreds."

Lady Jersey agreed. "I feel such pity for Lord Byron, though God knows why he married her. But he did, and now it's over, so do you think I should hold a party and invite him as the guest of honour, by way of showing him our love and support?"

Lady Holland considered. "Yes, a good idea, but not until *after* we know the separation has been agreed by the lawyers on both sides. We don't want to be taken by surprise and have him arriving with Little Miss Muffet by his side, do we?"

"Oh, gracious, no." Lady Jersey sighed sadly. "It would have been so much better if he had married Margaret Mercer Elphinstone. She has always been so in love with him ... but I suppose that is all water gone under the bridge now."

Lady Holland looked at her. "Oh, I don't know ... Miss Muffet may be seeking a mere separation, but if Lord Byron was to demand a full *divorce,* then he would be free to marry again." Lady Holland smiled. "Second time lucky, eh? Well, it certainly was lucky for *me.*"

Chapter Fifty-Seven

~ ~ ~

Byron continued to go out and about and continued living his life as if nothing very serious had happened.

He had heard some of the rumours floating around about the breakdown of his marriage, in particular that his wife considered him to be mad.

At first he was stunned by the things people were saying, and then amused, and then indifferent.

From as far back as his childhood in Aberdeen, when he had been jeered daily by the ruffians because of his limping walk, he had suffered enough in his life without paying attention to the opinions of strangers now.

He was fortunate in having many friends, and he was welcomed wherever he went – although friends afar, such as Francis Hodgson and Thomas Moore, were constantly writing to him, expressing their anxiety about his welfare.

Moore, he knew, was very concerned, and he had written back briefly, assuring him there was no need – *"If my heart could have been broken, it would have been so years ago, and by events more afflicting than these."*

Hobhouse was curiously puzzled by Byron's appearance of detachment to it all, wondering if it was delayed shock. He finally sought an explanation from Byron.

"What do you want me to do, Hobby? Debase myself by imploring for the restoration of a reluctant wife?"

"No, but you are now displaying all the appearance of a disinterested husband."

"So what *more* do you want me to do that I have not already done? I have invited her to return, it was refused. I have requested to know with what I am charged, it is refused."

Hobhouse had to agree. There were too many things that did not make sense. From Byron's side there had been appeals for reconciliation, for explanations, for personal meetings. In response, from his wife's side, came only refusals to give specific reasons or even to discuss the matter. All that came were continual threats from Sir Ralph of "legal measures" to ensure that a Judicial Separation was effected.

Scrope Davies, more objective than Hobhouse, was not at all puzzled by Byron's appearance of detachment.

"He is a proud man, Hobby, and if he is proud it is because he is sensitive. Do you think he is not hurt every day by the rumours that are being spread about him? And now they are saying that he used *physical* cruelty on his wife. That alone would hurt him the most. But he won't give in or bow his head under any of it. What would you have him do instead – snivel and grovel and make explanations in defence of himself – that is not Byron's way, and you should know that by now."

Hobby nodded, sat back and sighed heavily. "And yet, would it not be better for him to end all this now by agreeing to a judicial separation?"

"To do that would lead people to believe all the accusations were true."

"Of course," Hobhouse realised. "They would believe that."

"Whether he wants his wife back or not," Scrope said, "I don't know. But all this has gone so far; I believe that for Byron, this is no longer solely about her, but his own reputation. And why should he allow her to stamp it into the ground?"

"Why, indeed? But I am still baffled as to why she is doing it. For what reason, what cause?"

"Unless it be that he has run out of money," Scrope said. "Very few women would be happy to live in a house with bailiffs under the bed."

"Oh, that reminds me –" said Hobby, sitting up. "Byron has now struck up a great friendship with one of the bailiffs – the one that his wife always referred to as 'a sad brute' of a man. Now Byron has him sitting in the library with him, drinking wine, and talking together for hours."

Scrope half-smiled. "I don't believe you."

"It's true, and do you know why? Because the bailiff told Byron that he had once sat in the kitchen of Richard Brinsley Sheridan for a full year waiting for payment."

"A full *year*?"

"Yes, and you know how much Byron admires Sheridan and thinks him to be such a great playwright, but I –"

"He *is* great playwright," Scrope was grinning with enthusiasm, "*School for Scandal? The Rivals?* Two great comedies. Although my favourite has always been, *A Trip to Scarborough.*"

Hobhouse could not understand why anyone got so excited about fictional plays in a theatre, when the true comedy and drama of real life was played out every day in the real world of politics and Parliament.

And yet he had to admit – "Sheridan was a great *politician*, fought like a demon for the Whigs. He could knock the blocks off the other side with just a few sentences of perfect satire ... In his kitchen for a full year? I wonder what that sad brute of a bailiff told Byron about Sheridan?"

Scrope Davies and Hobhouse now practically lived at the house in Piccadilly, merely to support Byron and not allow him to be alone without friends nearby.

When Byron came in from his coffee morning at John Murray's, the first thing Hobby and Scrope asked him, was to tell *them*, all that the bailiff had told *him*, about his year in the kitchen of Richard Brinsley Sheridan.

Byron smiled. "Ah, dear Sherry. I'm meeting him tonight, so I shall probably come home drunk, because the old boy does like to drink a lot."

"Well he *is* Irish," said Hobhouse.

"*Anglo*-Irish. So although he drinks a lot, he *sips* every drop."

Scrope was curious. "Was Sheridan really so very much in debt?"

"Absolutely. He still is."

Hobhouse and Scrope stared. "Then why was the sad brute bailiff removed from his house?"

"He was merely *replaced*," Byron said, "probably for a less lethargic one."

The following few hours were spent in hoots of laughter as Byron told his friends all of the bailiff's anecdotes about the comings and goings and all the in-betweens that had taken place at Sheridan's house during that year of his sitting.

The fun and laughter of it was like old times again, until Hobhouse inadvertently spoiled it all by asking Byron if he had heard any more rumours about himself.

Byron shrugged. "Let's stick with Sheridan, who once wisely said that 'tale-bearers are as bad as tale-makers,' and the activity of gossips is nothing more than the business of – 'swapping lies'."

~ ~ ~

Annabella finally agreed to a meeting with Lady Caroline Lamb, mostly due to feminine curiosity, and to find out what this woman knew about her husband, that she, Annabella, did not already know. How dare she pretend to know more than she did, Byron's wife.

The meeting took place after dark, at the house of Mrs George Lamb. It was the safest time to meet, when George Lamb would be out at the Drury Lane Theatre and so would not have any knowledge, or be able to inform Byron about it.

Mrs George delicately withdrew, leaving her sister-in-law Lady Caroline and Lady Byron in the privacy of the study to speak together in strict confidence.

Annabella was feeling rather drained by it all. She

had not expected the society ladies of the *monde* to turn against her, as if she was in any way at fault. And she was even more surprised now when Caroline revealed that she hard overheard *Lord* Holland referring to her as being nothing more than "*a grievance-monger.*"

And it was not a lie, for Caroline truly had heard Lord Holland making that statement about Lady Byron.

Annabella was so offended by such an insult from such a respected man, the leader of the Whig Party, it brought back her energy and steeled her nerve to listen carefully to whatever Caroline had to say.

"Think of my own situation," Caroline said plaintively, "when I also saw *you*, Annabella, an innocent and unsuspicious sacrifice to his selfish and cruel vanity – but still I reproach myself for not flying to you and telling you all I know – all I had sworn never to reveal. But I did not because I still loved Byron even then. But now, if he has behaved so cruelly to you as you say, then I hate and despise him, and I will help you all I can."

Annabella did not believe her, but allowed her to carry on talking.

"Trust no one. All will tell you they have taken your part, but do not believe them – keep all at a distance, Be cold to his friends and relatives, they are more *his* friends than yours, especially Mrs Leigh, his sister. I'm sure she also pretends to support your part – but don't trust her. And above all ..." Caroline warned, "don't trust those who tell you he is ill and unhappy. I will let you know if he really is so."

"And how would *you* know if Byron is ill or unhappy?" asked Annabella. "Have you had any contact with him?"

"No, but I hear all through Lady Melbourne. She talks of Byron and no one else, and she will *not* hear a word against him. She blames *you* for everything."

"Indeed?" Annabella said dryly, but this she *did* believe, because a few days earlier, when Lady

Melbourne had made it very clear to her mother that she and Annabella were no longer welcome at Melbourne House, she had insisted it was because she had her own suspicions and reasons, but would not state them.

"It seems everyone at Melbourne House is against me now," said Annabella. "Even *Lord* Melbourne?"

Lord Melbourne had always disliked Annabella, but Caroline did not say so. "Everyone except I," she said.

"And your husband, William?"

"Yes, William now agrees with his mother. But I myself *cannot* openly disagree with her, even though I do, but I must pretend otherwise, because when it comes to me, Lady Melbourne does have the *law* on her side."

Annabella blinked. "The law? In what respect?"

"In respect of her being my mother-in-law."

Caroline smiled, but Annabella was not amused. She had heard enough of Caroline's warnings, and now she wanted to know what it was that Caroline wished to tell her – *the secret* – that she had claimed she had promised never to reveal.

Caroline became agitated, as if she had changed her mind, but then she seemed to remember her purpose.

"Three years ago, in 1813," Caroline said slowly, "I went to see Lord Byron in his rooms in Bennet Street. I was so in love with him at the time, but he was very cold to me. He told me it was useless to keep pursuing him, because he was very much in love with a married woman and nothing could change it."

Annabella sat more alert. "Did he tell you her name?"

"No, but he said she was expecting his child ... and if it was a girl, she would be named ... Medora."

"Medora? Like the girl in his poem of *The Corsair?*"

"Yes, and when I heard of a child with that name, although only a second name, I knew that married woman was his sister, Mrs Leigh."

Annabella's glacial stare unnerved Caroline, forcing

her to add, "They have always been like that, those two. A servant once told me that when they were both children, Lady Holderness had to keep separating the two of them, because they were always kissing."

"When they were children?"

"Yes, the servant said Lady Holderness had a terrible task keeping the two of them apart."

Annabella knew that could not possibly be true, because both Byron and Augusta had told her at differing times that they had met each other until Byron was sixteen, when Augusta had been told about him by Lord Carlisle, and she had then gone to see Byron in his school at Harrow. They had led completely separate lives until then; and *even* then, due to Augusta's marriage up in Yorkshire, before the move years later down to Newmarket, the half-brother and sister had not met again until Augusta came to perform her role as a lady-in-waiting at St James's Palace in London, when Byron was twenty-five."

Caroline could not read Annabella's expression, unsure if she believed her or not,.

"I later asked Byron if the married woman was Mrs Leigh, and he confirmed it was. If you have any doubts about what I say, you only have to ask Madame de Staël, because a few times at parties she has commented upon Byron's unusual affection for his timid plain-faced sister."

Caroline thought she saw a fleeting expression of pain in Annabella's eyes, and she was glad to see it. Had Annabella not cruelly mocked her in the past? Mocked her love for Byron and telling Lady Melbourne *"Caroline makes me sick."*

"Incest, with his own sister," Caroline said. "But that is not his only crime. When he was a boy at Harrow, he had romances with other boys, but the one he loved most was Lord Clare. *He* says there were *'pure passions'* the sort all boys have in boarding schools, *'infatuations'* and *'calf-love'* he called them, but nothing truly physical. Although I *do* believe he had more serious relations of that kind when he was in Greece, especially with a young monk named Nicolo Giraud, his Italian teacher."

"A monk?"

Caroline nodded. "Byron said Nicolo was only seventeen, but fluent in Latin and Italian and so was designated as his Italian master, and they were very close. And when Byron was leaving Athens, he told me he took Nicolo with him as far as Malta, where he paid an enormous sum of money for Nicolo to study at a much better monastery in Valetta. He told me he often thought of Nicolo, studying in his monastery, high up on the hills overlooking the harbour at Valetta."

Annabella, in her innocence, could not quite grasp what Caroline was saying to her, for she too had a history of romantic attachments to other girls, *religious* girls, but there was nothing wrong with it. Everyone, in his or her youth, liked having a special friend.

Seeing the confusion on her face, Caroline said, "I believe, in his past, Lord Byron has had *homo*-sexual relationships."

Annabella immediately got to her feet.

"But you must not tell anyone," Caroline said. "No, not anyone."

Annabella stared her icy stare. "Then why did you tell me? If not for me to use?"

"No, no, you have *completely* misunderstood my intention," Caroline said in alarm, also now up on her feet. "My *intention* was that you could menace him by saying that you know something terrible about him, something *'too horrid to reveal'* but that you *will* reveal it, if he does not agree to grant you a legal separation."

Returning to Mivart's Hotel, Annabella went straight to bed, laying for hours thinking about it all – not about Harrow or Greece, for that she dismissed – but about Augusta and Byron ... and now it all made sense, for she had always suspected there was something special between them, but she had not realised that it was something *wicked*.

Her mind went back to a month after her wedding when Byron had taken her to Newmarket to meet Augusta for the first time ... even then he had behaved as if he possessed the most adorable sister in the world ... but it was when their stay at Newmarket had ended and they were leaving, and the carriage was drawing away ... she remembered how Byron had leaned out of the window and kept on waving and waving to Augusta until all sight of her was gone.

Annabella got out of bed and began to write a detailed account of it all ... "*And it was then, as he kept on waving back to her, that I thought he seemed fonder of her than he was of me, his bride.*"

And although she did not write it down, it had also been then, when she had felt her first thrill of hatred for Augusta Leigh.

Chapter Fifty-Eight

~~~

In his office, in preparation for an interview with his client, Stephen Lushington was again reading the detailed account, written by Lady Byron, of all the wrongs she had suffered throughout her year of marriage to Lord Byron; and what Lushington read was truly extraordinary.

"He married me with the deepest determination of Revenge, which he avowed to me on the day of our marriage ... "

And, according to her account, even in the carriage on the way to their honeymoon in Yorkshire, Byron had shown his hatred by saying to her –

"If you had not rejected my proposal two years ago, you would have spared me from something that now I can never get over. I will make you pay for it." And he executed that revenge upon me ever since with systematic and increasing cruelty, which no affection on my part could change ..."

"Extraordinary, quite extraordinary..." and all very hard to believe.

Lushington immediately rose to his feet when Lady Byron was shown into his office. "Your ladyship."

He moved round the desk and pulled back a chair for her to be seated, and then returned to his own seat, and looked down at the document on his desk.

"The statement made by Lord Byron in the carriage on the day of your marriage," he said, "about something that *'now I can never get over'* ... do you know what that 'something' is?"

"I do now," Annabella said. "He was referring to his incestuous relationship with his half-sister, Augusta Leigh."

Lushington's head shot up, his eyes staring at her.

Lady Byron went on to give him a great deal more information about Lord Byron and his sister, and then she appeared utterly shocked when Lushington told her:

"Although repulsive, I'm afraid that, at present at least, incest is not against the law."

"Not against the law?"

"Well, perhaps if we took the case to be heard in the Ecclesiastic Court."

"Even so, would there be a risk that the Ecclesiastic Court would still give him custody of the child?"

"There is always a risk, my lady, and without a sworn statement of confession by both Lord Byron and his sister, none of this can be proven. Do you have any proof?"

"No, no proof, only my long-held suspicions, and the words of my cousin-in-law, Lady Caroline Lamb."

"Lady Caroline Lamb ..." Lushington knew all about that particular lady and her disgraceful persecution of Lord Byron in the past. Why, her obsessive behaviour had even been articled in all the newspapers.

"This is the lady who took a knife to herself in order to get his lordship's attention?"

Annabella nodded bleakly, realising now that any testimony from Caroline would be useless, not that she had ever expected Caroline to come out in public against Byron, but her aim now was to influence Lushington and get him truly on her side.

"I cannot tell you how I know, or who it was who told me, but I now believe that in his past, Lord Byron allowed himself to indulge in ... unnatural vice."

Lushington frowned. "With Lady Caroline Lamb?"

"No ... homo ..." Annabella lowered her head, unable to sully her mouth with the word.

"Homosexuality? Are you sure?" Stephen Lushington

was so shocked, his face and voice hardened. "Madam, are you aware that you are speaking of a *crime*, and if convicted, leads to the Capital sentence of death by hanging?"

Annabella had not known, and now in terror pulled back on her words. "No, I am not sure, in fact I don't believe it ... but I thought –" and then she repeated Caroline's advice, "I thought we could *menace* his lordship with the threat of it, to get him to agree to the judicial separation."

Lushington sat back in his chair, his face full of loathing; he *detested* all men who indulged in unnatural vice.

"No," he said finally, "without proof we cannot proceed on that issue, not even to threaten; but we *can* threaten his lordship with revelation in the Ecclesiastic Court about his incestuous relationship with his sister."

"I *did* tell you," Annabella said with pristine rectitude, "that on that matter I have only the words of Lady Caroline Lamb and my own long-held suspicions."

"We will threaten him with it in any event," Lushington replied tersely. "And I would advise you, Lady Byron, to have no more contact or correspondence with his lordship. We have no proof of anything, but yes, we can *menace* him into submission."

Annabella nodded, hugely gratified, for now she knew she truly did have Mr Lushington on her side, and most determinedly at that. So cousin Caroline had been of some use after all.

~~~

Hobhouse was of the opinion that Lady Byron had never truly been able to perceive Byron's true character, due to her habit of seeing everything in accordance to her own preconceptions, and always looking for hidden meanings behind his words; certain of his intent to deceive her in some way.

But he had never thought of Lady Byron as being *evil*, not until now.

When the letter from his wife's lawyers arrived, Byron has expected to be charged with one single act of infidelity, along with the more minor offence of occasional drunkenness and other misdemeanours of who knew what.

So he was utterly astonished when Lushington's letter mentioned two other very serious but unspecified accusations against him.

It was made clear that Lady Byron had every intention of going into the Ecclesiastic Court and bringing these charges of an extremely abominable nature against him, if he did not agree to sign a private and confidential Deed of Separation.

Not one person in the house in Piccadilly, including Byron, had a clue as to what these "unspecified" charges could be.

"Poor fellow," Hobhouse said to Scrope Davies, "the plot is thickening against him."

Augusta finally wrote to Annabella on behalf of Byron, asking her about the two "mysterious and unspecified accusations", because *"he knows NOT what they are."*

Annabella wrote back to Augusta in her usual tone of stern rectitude –

"He does know – too well – what he affects to inquire. The circumstances, which are too convincing of a nature, shall not be generally known whilst Lord Byron allows me to spare him."

Yet even that she did not do; for she spared no time in telling Mrs George Lamb, Selena Doyle, and many others about the sinful incestuous relationship between Byron and his sister, which she had suspected from the very first – but all must be in the strictest confidence, and – *"not coming from me."*

Within a week the rumours were spreading all over London, from door to door, street to street, and some ladies were so shocked, one even collapsed into a dead faint from the horror of it all.

"On his wedding night he left his poor wife to sleep alone while he slept with his sister."

"He often made his poor wife sit and watch while he and his sister had sex."

"His sister had a child by him, named Medora."

When the rumours had reached even as far as Newmarket, George Leigh immediately came up to London to stand by his wife and show his faith in her. He had no doubts that Elizabeth Medora was his child, otherwise, based on the dates, she would have had to sleep with Byron within half an hour of meeting him in 1813, and that was not the way or behaviour of his Augusta.

George Leigh's rage was fierce. Who had made these accusations against his wife and child? Let them come to him and say it! If a man – he would kill him stone dead! If a woman – he would have her up in Court quicker than she could say it was all a mistake!

Byron knew exactly who the woman was, his vindictive wife.

For the sake of Augusta, he threw in the towel. "Let her have her separation," he told Hobhouse. "The mistake was all mine. I should never have married her."

Hobhouse prepared himself. From the start he had designated to himself the role of Byron's "professional friend" in the matter, and he was now determined not to allow John Hanson to be as pre-occupied with his own family problems in this, as he had been at time of the arrangement of the marriage settlement. No, he would not leave it all up to Hanson, not this time. Every move

Hanson made would be watched by Hobhouse at his shoulder.

Scrope Davies objected very strongly to Byron throwing in the towel.

"Rumour is already busy," said Scrope. "Charges of a monstrous and malignant nature are being made against you, Byron, and if you give in now and let her have her way, the voice of gossip will believe that you must have pleaded guilty to those charges."

"I don't even know what the charges are," Byron replied. "All I know is that I have been guilty of infidelity with one female, but I have *never* committed an act that would put me under the law."

After a pause, he said, "And yes, you are right, Scrope, why should I allow my name or Augusta's name to be trampled into the dirt?"

He wrote to Annabella, informing her that he was ready for legal measures and would meet her in court to answer to any and all charges, "specified or unspecified".

Annabella fired back: *"Know this – I am not to be intimidated by legal measures."*

He just as swiftly replied:

The words 'legal measures' were first used by your father in a letter to me, and all that has been said or done since then, amounts to my determination not to resist to such proceedings as truth and justice permit to the accused as well as the accuser.

These measures have not been of my seeking, and whatever the results may be – I shall defend myself from attacks which strike at the root of every tie – every connection – and hope – of my child's welfare.

Annabella knew Byron too well to know he meant it and would do it. His tone had changed; he was ready to fight her all the way for the sake of his own and his precious sister's reputation.

And what did she have to fight back with? Her own foolish complaints to her parents in Kirkby, based on her own hurt and fury because he had not personally answered her letter, and left it to Augusta ... Her suspicions that he did not love her ... And gossip from Caroline Lamb, possibly invented, possibly not, but who could ever know for sure with that crack-brained cousin of hers.

She felt ill, and went to bed, wishing none of this had ever happened, wishing she could turn the clock back to the day *before* she had left the house in Piccadilly Terrace, but it was all too late, She should have been happy with the fact that Byron had *liked* her, in the way that most husbands liked their wives, instead of being so determined upon insisting that Byron should *love* her.

And now he hated her.

She had no one else to blame but herself, and she was incapable of doing that, so she blamed it all on her reading of that ridiculous romantic novel, *Pride and Prejudice,* wishing someone would find the unnamed "Lady" who had written it, and strangle her.

Chapter Fifty-Nine

~~~

John Hanson was not surprised.

From the moment Lord Byron had determined on making preparations for the public defence of his conduct, and Drs Robinson, Adams and Jenner were retained for him as Counsellors in the Commons – the tables were turned and all hints and menaces from Lady Byron's side were dropped.

A "private arrangement" was begged.

Hanson noted that the tone of Lushington's letters had now changed completely. Instead of being full of threats of a trial in court, they now contained appeals for pity and reason, and objected to "*the cruelty of dragging Lady Byron into a public Court.*"

A second letter stated, "*Lady Byron is quite willing to declare that the rumours indicated had not emanated from her or from her family.*"

That did not satisfy Hobhouse. He instructed Hanson to insist that Lady Byron should state in a signed document – "not only that the rumours did not originate with her or her family, *but that the charges which they involved made no part of her charges against Lord Byron.*"

A statement to that effect was drawn up for her to sign, and she signed it.

Then Byron received the following letter from John Hanson.

Mr Dear Lord,

I have had a long interview with Sir James Bland Burgess this morning; it has served to convince me that I was right in the advice I gave you, and your

Lordship may with confidence look to a very early period when the results of all this mysterious trick will develop itself to the chagrin of the contrivers, and will turn the tide of any invective which may prevail – if it does prevail at all, which I rather doubt.

> *Believe me, my dear Lord*
> *Yours ever devotedly*
> *JOHN HANSON*

At the outset of all this strange behaviour from Lady Byron, John Hanson was convinced that she had left him for the sole reason of escaping his scattered fortunes; and now he was learning that the whole terrible event had been a scheme based more on money than morals.

It had been a scheme contrived by Lady Byron's family to legally obtain from the sale of Newstead Abbey, a certain financial provision for Lady Byron's father, in the case of the death of her mother – when all her mother's money and property would go to Lord Byron on behalf of his wife.

So, upon her arrival at Kirby, aided by Annabella's annoyance at her husband for not answering her letter, it had been schemed that Lord Byron should be shamed or blamed into losing all authority over Annabella's future inheritance, as well as securing for her a half-share of the sale of Newstead Abbey.

And for that purpose, they had all been prepared to sacrifice not only the reputation of Lord Byron, but also the reputation of his sister, Augusta Leigh.

Byron was so disgusted; he could not restrain himself from writing to Annabella:

"So it was all a matter of pounds, shillings, and pence! No allusion to my child; and all on hard, dry, attorney's paper."

But still Annabella would not allow the smallest portion of blame to be attached to her.

"Certainly I am guiltless of any intentional misstatements, and still more strongly do I disclaim all design of insult and offence to you."

~~~

John Cam Hobhouse – "Cam of the Cornish" as Byron and Scrope Davies often affectionately called him, was standing in a store in Piccadilly waiting to make a purchase, when he heard two women, standing by the door, talking about Lord Byron.

"Tis said, that while she was in the bed in labour, he walked into the room and asked her, 'Is the child dead?'"

The other woman responded, "What I heard, was that while she was in labour, poor thing, he was in the room below throwing soda bottles hard against the ceiling to annoy her. They say half the ceiling came down on the floor.

Hobhouse was so shaken by the absurdity and vitriol of such lies, he turned and left the store and walked straight back to Devonshire House where he inspected the ceiling of the room directly below Lady Byron's bedroom – it was in perfect condition and not a mark on it – yet if such a horrible thing had been done, the plaster at least would have been marked and dented.

Determined not to hurt his friend by informing him of such vile gossip, Hobby instead sat down and in great wrath wrote a letter to the cause of it all, Lady Byron.

Dear Madam,

As this affair is about to be brought to termination, I can assure you that – except as far as Mrs Leigh is concerned – Lord Byron has expressed a perfect indifference to rumours which concern him personally, as they relate only to some imaginary monster created by the envy and malice of others.

His friends however, look to your Ladyship's justice and candour for some efficacious means of giving a flat denial to scandals, which, however absurd and unfounded, should not be left to the tardy progress of time and truth to contradict.

A reluctance to make the character and honour of my friend the apparent price of any bargain with you, prevented me from touching upon this subject during the progress of the negotiations, but I am sure your Ladyship will not refuse now to bring these unfounded rumours to an end.

John Cam Hobhouse

Her reply, as usual, was about her own good self.

"I beg to assure you, in regard to the subject of your letter, that I have every wish to consider the feelings and interests of others, as far as may be in my power, consistently with the most candid considerations.

A. I. BYRON

Hobhouse then spoke to Mrs Milward, the housekeeper, to try and ascertain if any of the rumours had come from a member of the household staff.

"Oh, yes," said Mrs Milward, "it was that demon Mrs Clermont! She was always down here spreading the most awful gossip about Lord and Lady Byron, but none of us believed her, because until that woman arrived here, not one of us had ever seen anything but harmony between his lordship and his lady. And now look what she's done – broken up a marriage and poured heaps of sulphur on his lordship's name."

Hobhouse repeated Mrs Milward's words to Byron who merely shrugged, eager to get back to normal and on with his life.

His hope was to move back into Albany, to which Hobhouse did not object, because he had recently learned that from the end of April, Apartment 6A would be vacant, so he now decided that he would put his name down immediately to secure the lease on that apartment, and Byron could return to Apartment 2A.

"And then," said Hobby, "how convenient it will be for us both to have apartments in the same building? Scrope will be flitting from one to the other and driving us both mad."

Byron smiled and agreed, because now he truly appreciated his two closest friends who had proved their loyalty to him beyond all measure.

The Siege of Corinth and *Parisina,* in one volume, had been published a few day's earlier by John Murray, and he had dedicated the poems to both – *Corinth* to John Cam Hobhouse, and *Parisina* to Scrope Berdmore Davies.

"What date in April?" Byron asked

"Apartment 6A?" Hobhouse shrugged. "All I know is that it will free from the end of April. I don't know the exact date."

But the end of April would prove too late for Byron, for when he left his house to go out that night, he found a small crowd gathered, and as soon as they saw him they began to yell all sorts of abuse.

He pushed through them and got into his carriage as if they did not exist, but when he stepped out of it again at Drury Lane, he had only walked a few steps when a man spat at his feet, *"Sodomite."*

Inside the theatre when he entered his box, the audience in the pits sent up a loud seething hiss and a few voices yelled *"Wife beater ... adulterer ... sister-*

fucker!"

He was so taken aback and shaken, he stood up and left the theatre; but the abuse went on and on, day after day; week after week. As soon as he stepped outside his door or walked down a street, he was either spat at, or hissed, or called the foulest names.

Walter Scott, during his visit to London, was deeply upset and truly horrified by it all. Byron, who had been so famous, had now become *infamous*. Every rumour that his wife's friends had spread about him had been added to or changed or more lies invented, until Lord Byron was now the most maligned man in the country.

Scott described Byron as "*like a bull in a bullring,*" being attacked with lances of abuse from all directions, and the crowd baying for blood.

It all became too much for any soul to endure, and Hobhouse and Scrope Davies were very sad, although not surprised, when Byron made his decision to leave England.

"If all they say of me is true, I am not fit for England. If false, England is not fit for me."

PART ELEVEN

Exile

~

"It would have been better that I had never been born, than to have met you and known you."

Lord Byron to Lady Byron.

Chapter Sixty

~ ~ ~

Although his departure the following morning would have to be kept a secret, the house in Piccadilly Terrace was filled with his friends who had come to say their sad farewells to him on his last night in London.

Due to the lameness of his right foot, and the pain it often caused to his lower leg, a young doctor named John Polidori had been hired to accompany Byron abroad as his private physician. Fletcher too, and his wife Ann, were also preparing to leave with him.

Douglas Kinnaird arrived, carrying two bottles of champagne, and Byron was very happy to see Kinnaird back in the company of Maria, who had baked him a cake.

John Murray was there also, very sad in his manner, and speaking quietly with the young doctor, John Polidori.

Byron's friend, Isaac Nathan had sent him some Passover Cakes to take with him on his journey:

7 Poland Street, Tue Morning.

My Lord,

I cannot deny myself the pleasure of sending you some holy biscuits, commonly called unleavened bread, denominated by the Nazarenes as 'Motsas", better known in this enlightened age by the name of Passover Cakes; when a certain Angel, at a certain hour, by his presence, ensured the safety of a whole nation. May the same guardian spirit pass with your lordship to that land where the fates may have decreed for you to sojourn for a while.

My Lord, I have the honour to remain,

Your Very Devoted Servant,
Isaac Nathan

The rumours had forced Augusta to return to her apartment in St James's Palace, but she was here tonight, holding onto Byron's arm throughout.

When the time came for her to leave, Hobhouse saw Byron standing with Augusta by the front door; both were tearful.

"I will never again in my life have anything to do with Annabella," Augusta was saying.

"But you must," Byron said. "If only so that you can keep me informed about my daughter. You *must* write to me regularly, Augusta, and tell me about the child. How she looks, if she is fat or thin..."

More tears seeped from his eyes, but he collected himself and said, "Miss Milbanke doesn't know, but I have made a new will. And apart from the bulk of what I possess, which I have left to my daughter, Miss Byron, I have left the rest to you, Augusta."

"Byron don't talk like that ... as if we will never see you again. And your will ... what about Annabella?"

Byron's expression darkened, his voice bitter. "Her future has been well taken care of. She made sure of that. It was all about money, Augusta ... all about the Milbanke's greed for money."

He escorted his sister outside and handed into her carriage, with one last desperate plea, "You must write to her regularly, Augusta, asking her about the child and her welfare, and then write and tell *me* about her, my daughter."

Augusta nodded mutely; and then sobbed in heartbreak all the way back to St James's Palace.

Meanwhile, at a soirée at Lady Jersey's house, Madame de Staël was having her last night out in London before she returned to her home in Geneva, and was extremely disappointed to find her favourite sleepy-eyed poet absent from the gathering. She had been confined to bed for almost two weeks, suffering with such severe migraines, her only relief had been to lie in a darkened room and sleep her head off with the help of doses of laudanum. Consequently she had no idea of what had been going on in society in her absence.

She listened without any sympathy to all the petty complaints that had been made by Lady Byron against her husband. "She claims to have been unhappy," said Lady Jersey.

Madame de Staël appeared dumbfounded for a moment, and then threw her hands out wide with an amused laugh. "Unhappy? Oh! I think I speak now for so many women in England when I say – I would *love* the chance to live unhappily with Byron!"

Margaret Mercer Elphinstone laughed along with the rest of the ladies. "Byron should have married me," she said. "I would have managed him much better and we *both* would have been very happy."

~~~

Now that everyone had left and the house was silent, Byron sat alone in his study and wrote a final letter to his wife.

"More last words – not many – an answer I do not expect, nor less does it import; but you will at least hear me – I have just parted from Augusta, almost the last person whom you have left me to part with.

Wherever I may go – and I am going far – you and I can never again meet in this world, nor in the next. Let this content or atone – If any accident occurs to me, be kind to Augusta."

When the letter had been sealed, he wrote a last note to Augusta.

My own Sweet Sis,

All I have now to beg is that you never mention nor allude to Lady Byron's name to me again in any shape – or on any occasion – except indispensable business – Of my child you will inform me and write about poor little Ada – and see her whenever you can – I will write to you from Dover – my own kindest, best Sis.

B.

~~~

The following morning Hobhouse got up at six and hurried downstairs to make sure the bailiffs were not yet about. And as soon as they were all ready, they all set off.

Hobhouse left first with John Polidori in Scrope Davies's chaise. Byron and Scrope followed in his lordship's much bigger carriage.

It was fortunate that Hobhouse had roused them all so early and in good time, for only ten minutes after they had left, the bailiffs were about, and shortly after that, more bailiffs came to seize all of the property within the house marked as belonging to Lord Byron. Some items were not marked, because in the rush Byron had forgotten them, and some Hobhouse had forced him to leave behind.

Only the servants remained, for not one would leave his lordship, including Mrs Milward, who had vowed to look after him until the moment of his departure.

A crowd had formed outside the house, all amazed at the sight of some of the things the bailiffs brought out, all belonging to the man who was now reputed to have been cruel to his wife ... a tame squirrel in a cage; various birds, a small red fox with a white bandage on one of his legs ...

~~~

A Runaway Star

The cavalcade of carriages reached Dover at eight o'clock.

Hobhouse, fearing the bailiffs might be in hot pursuit, arranged for Byron's carriage to be put aboard the ship straight away so they could not seize it. The ship would not set sail for Ostend until the morning, and Byron would have great need of his carriage on the other side, so Hobhouse was making sure they suffered no surprises during the night.

The following morning they all awoke late; and followed by some agitated hurry and bustle running to and fro down to the harbour to make sure the ship waited. A crowd of sightseers had now gathered outside the inn, all eager to get a glimpse of the famous poet.

Byron emerged from the inn, and they saw him ... and to them he looked dignified and aloof, but so handsome, so beautiful in the face, a real Adonis but for his limp.

Byron finally accepted the aid of Hobhouse's arm as he limped hurriedly over the cobbles down to the ferry.

As he was about to board the boat, Byron turned and looked at his two friends wistfully and said, "I feel I will be gone for a very long time."

"If that turns out to be true," Scrope said, "then wherever you go, Byron, we will go there to visit you. For certain we will."

Hobhouse was unable to speak, watching every step Byron took as he boarded the boat, and then he saw that Byron looked extremely sad when the ropes were loosened and the packet began to sail out towards the deeper waters of the open channel.

Hobhouse suddenly sprang into a sprint and ran down to the end of the wooden pier and waved and waved, until he saw Byron appear at the rail, pull off his hat, and wave it high to him.

Hobby stood on the pier waving for a long time, and then slowly he made his way back to join Scrope, where both stood staring out to sea, watching the ship.

"That woman has destroyed him," Scrope said.

Hobhouse nodded. "And yet it has all been the making of her. It has set her up for life. She now walks away with the fame of his name, his child, and half the proceeds of the sale of Newstead whenever it is sold, a fortune. And on top of that, she receives two thousand a year in support of herself and the child."

"What I find so bewildering, so shocking," said Scrope, "is that someone like her could not only set out to destroy him, but to destroy him so *publicly* in order to get the world and every matron and servant in it on her side."

Hobby agreed. "Right from the start she was an unconscionable little liar, and always will be. And now her father must be very satisfied with her half-share of the Newstead estate."

Scrope was frowning. "How will Byron live over there when he has little money?"

"Oh, he does have money. He rarely took any money from his publisher for his poetry, you know? But John Murray kept putting all monies due to him safely away in an account. And now he has given it all to him in one lump sum, and a thousand guineas on top for the *Siege of Corinth*."

Scrope was pleased to hear it. "Although Byron will always be able to make plenty of money with his poetry. The whole world loves his poetry."

Hobhouse agreed. "And his poetry is the man himself, heart and soul."

They stood staring out to sea until they could no longer see the ship carrying Byron away from them, taking him on now to a new life in a strange world.

Hobby's eyes filled with tears. "God bless him for always being a gallant spirit, and a kind one."

Chapter Sixty-One

~~~

In Melbourne House in Whitehall a high-pitched screaming shattered through the house, bringing servants running to Lady Caroline' bedroom.

By the time Lady Melbourne arrived in the room, Caroline was rolling and rocking on the floor in anguish and grief, her eyes staring out of her head as she screamed like a mad woman.

"What on earth...?"

Caroline's maid, Dotty, was sobbing woefully. "I shouldn't have told her. I heard it on the street, and it's in all the newspapers, but I shouldn't have told her."

"Told her what?" demanded Lady Melbourne.

"Lord Byron has gone away from England."

"Caroline!" Lady Melbourne bent over Caroline and tried to control her. "Caroline, stop this screaming."

Caroline pulled herself to her knees, clutching Lady Melbourne's hands with tears gushing down her face. "I did it! I ruined him! I wanted to get him away from that bitch of a wife!"

"What did you do?"

"I thought..." Caroline struggled with more sobs. "I thought if everyone turned against him ... if everyone in the world hated him, he would know that he had no one else to love him but me, only me, his faithful Caroline, and we could at last go away together, far away ... but now he has gone without me, my beloved Byron has gone from England without me – *and may never come back!*"

"You wicked, *wicked* woman!"cried Lady Melbourne. "You and Annabella are as bad as each other! You have both deliberately and wilfully destroyed him for your own ends, and I will have neither of you in my house from now on! I want you out, Caroline! I want you out of my house at first light first in the morning. You can go to our country house in Hertfordshire and stay there. I never want to look on your face again, because for *this*, Caroline, I can *never* forgive you!"

~~~

In London, in his drawing-room in Albermarle Street, John Murray was also feeling extremely sad at the departure of Lord Byron. Neither London nor his publishing business would ever be quite the same without him.

But it was not the end, for he had enjoyed a very good conversation the previous evening with the young doctor, John Polidori, who had confessed to having some literary talent himself. In the past, he claimed, he had written some very fine prose, which many of his associates had admired.

Now what could a business-minded publisher do when he was told something like that?

He had done what any other business-minded publisher would have done. He had made an agreement to pay Polidori the munificent sum of five hundred guineas for the copyright of the book if he would write a secret journal detailing all the sweets and sours of Lord Byron's life abroad.

John Polidori had been delighted to agree, considering it an opportunity and a blessing for him to be commissioned to do such a secret and wonderful thing as to write about Lord Byron, and to be paid such a large amount of money for it too.

"Mr Murray, you are very generous," Polidori had whispered in a secret hush.

John Murray sighed now, knowing he had not been generous at all. He loved Byron, and wanted no one else to publish Byron, and he would have paid a lot more for such a treasure of a book to be written, because Byron was still a young man, just turned twenty-eight, and knowing Byron as well as he did, he knew Byron's success and Byron's story was far from over.

Thank You

Thank you for taking the time to read *'A **Runaway Star'*** the fourth book in the *The LORD BYRON* series. I hope you enjoyed it.
Please be nice and leave a review.

*

I occasionally send out newsletters with details of new releases, or discount offers, or any other news I may have, although not so regularly to be intrusive, so if you wish to sign up to for my newsletters – go to my Website and click on the "Subscribe" Tab.

*

If you would like to follow me on **BookBub** go to:-
www.bookbub.com/profile/gretta-curran-browne
and click on the "*Follow*" button.

Many thanks,

Gretta

www.grettacurranbrowne.com

Also by Gretta Curran Browne

LORD BYRON SERIES

A STRANGE BEGINNING
A STRANGE WORLD
MAD, BAD, AND DELIGHTFUL TO KNOW
A RUNAWAY STAR
A MAN OF NO COUNTRY
ANOTHER KIND OF LIGHT
NO MOON AT MIDNIGHT

***

LIBERTY TRILOGY

TREAD SOFTLY ON MY DREAMS
FIRE ON THE HILL
A WORLD APART

***

MACQUARIE SERIES

BY EASTERN WINDOWS
THE FAR HORIZON
JARVISFIELD
THE WAYWARD SON

***

ALL BECAUSE OF HER
A Novel
(Originally published as GHOSTS IN SUNLIGHT)

RELATIVE STRANGERS
(Tie-in Novel to TV series)

ORDINARY DECENT CRIMINAL
(Novel of Film starring Oscar-winner, Kevin Spacey)